Praise for Scott
and his electrifying thrillers

"Scott Mariani is an author to watch."
—International bestselling author M. J. Rose

"Mariani certainly knows how to rack up the tension."
***—Lancashire Evening News* (UK)**

THE MOZART CONSPIRACY

"A fast, exciting read in *The Da Vinci Code* tradition."
—*Publishers Weekly*

"Mariani channels Dan Brown on steroids in this exciting (and violent) historical puzzle thriller. . . . Racing along at breakneck speed and promising more in a series, this action read will excite fans of Brown, James Rollins, and Robert Ludlum."
—*Booklist*

"*The Mozart Conspiracy* hits thrilling, suspenseful notes. . . . It's a rollickingly good way to pass some time in an easy chair."
—*USA Today*

"An action-packed thriller that introduces a fine, new hero, retired British commando Benedict Hope, a former soldier who's tormented by regret. . . . Fast-paced and fun, and Hope is a hero you can't help but root for."
—Mark Alpert, international bestselling author of *The Omega Theory*

"A breathtaking ride through England and Europe."
—*Suspense Magazine*

***The Mozart Conspiracy* is also available as an eBook and in eAudio**

"Music to the minds of thriller fans. Now readers on both sides of the Atlantic can enjoy Scott Mariani's gift for international menace with a Continental flair."

—Thomas Greanias, *New York Times* bestselling author of *The 34th Degree*

"James Bond meets Jason Bourne meets *The Da Vinci Code* in a tale as driven as a dark Mozart symphony—but Scott Mariani writes with a steely lightness that is all his own."

—*New York Times* bestselling author Jennifer Lee Carrell

"Fans of Dan Brown will love this thrilling adventure."

—*Closer* magazine (UK)

"Ingenious construction. . . . Scott Mariani certainly knows how to write a thriller. . . . Hollywood would love the blood, the gore, the car chases and the intrigue."

—*The Western Mail* (UK)

"Goes straight for the jugular . . . action-packed, not empty-headed." —*Redhanded* magazine (UK)

"Mariani is tipped for the top." —*The Bookseller* (UK)

THE HOPE VENDETTA

(Previously published as *The Doomsday Prophecy*)
A *Closer* magazine "Book of the Month"

"Scott Mariani's latest page-turning roller coaster of a thriller takes the sort of conspiracy theory that made Dan Brown's *The Da Vinci Code* an international hit and gave it an injection of steroids. . . . Mariani is a master of edge-of-the-seat suspense. A genuinely gripping thriller that holds the attention of its readers from the first page to the last and establishes Hope and Mariani as major new figures within the genre." —Shots Crime & Thriller eZine

"Head and shoulders over other novels of the same ilk. . . . The ending is a showstopper and 100% satisfying. . . . Awesome thrilling stuff."
—My Favorite Books

"Simply thrilling. . . . If you like Dan Brown you will like all of Scott Mariani's work—but you will like it better. This guy knows exactly how to bait his hook, cast his line and reel you in, nice and slow."
—The Bookbag (5 stars)

. . . And all Scott Mariani's thrillers

"A fast-paced thriller that rockets off the first page and never slows down. *The Alchemist's Secret* is packed with dark intrigue, danger around every corner, bullets flying, sexual tension, and an endless assault of nasty villains. . . . Everything a thriller should be, and more."
—Joe Moore, international bestselling coauthor of *The Grail Conspiracy*

"With twists and turns at every corner and a brutal and terrifying showdown, be prepared for the long haul. . . . A book you won't want to put down!"
—*Lancashire Evening Post* on *The Heretic's Treasure*

"*The Shadow Project* is an absolute delight to read. . . . You really won't want to put it down."
—*News of the World* (UK)

"*The Lost Relic* is a first-rate thriller with just the right blend of adventure and historical background to make it stick. . . . A brilliant piece of pure escapism grounded in fact."
—Books Monthly (UK)

SCOTT MARIANI

THE MOZART CONSPIRACY

A BEN HOPE THRILLER

POCKET BOOKS
New York London Toronto Sydney New Delhi

Pocket Books
A Division of Simon & Schuster, Inc.
1230 Avenue of the Americas
New York, NY 10020

This book is a work of fiction. Names, characters, places, and incidents either are products of the author's imagination or are used fictitiously. Any resemblance to actual events or locales or persons, living or dead, is entirely coincidental.

Originally published in Great Britain in 2008 by Avon, a division of HarperCollins Publishers Ltd.

First Pocket Books paperback edition January 2012

POCKET and colophon are registered trademarks of Simon & Schuster, Inc.

For information about special discounts for bulk purchases,
please contact Simon & Schuster Special Sales at 1-866-506-1949
or business@simonandschuster.com.

The Simon & Schuster Speakers Bureau can bring authors to your live event. For more information or to book an event, contact the Simon & Schuster Speakers Bureau at 1-866-248-3049
or visit our website at www.simonspeakers.com.

Cover design by Jae Song
Images (except flames) matt latos/stock.xchng, patita_rd/stock.xchng

Manufactured in the United States of America

10 9 8 7 6 5 4 3 2 1

ISBN 978-1-4391-9337-2
ISBN 978-1-4391-9338-9 (ebook)

To Mary, Lana, and Richard

I know I must die.
Someone has given me *aqua toffana* and has calculated the precise time of my death—for which they have ordered a Requiem.
It is for myself that I am writing this.

Wolfgang Amadeus Mozart, 1791

THE MOZART CONSPIRACY

1.

AUSTRIA
9 JANUARY

Breathless with shock and terror, Oliver Llewellyn stumbled away from the scene he had just witnessed. He paused to lean against a bare stone wall. Nausea washed over him. His mouth was dry.

He hadn't known exactly what he would find when he'd slipped away to explore the house. But what he'd seen—what they'd done to the man in that strange vaulted room—was more horrible than anything he could have imagined.

He ran on. Up a winding flight of stone steps and through the connecting bridgeway, then back into the main part of the house with its classical architecture and decor. He could hear the chatter and laughter of the party guests. The string quartet in the ballroom had started up a Strauss waltz.

The Sony Ericsson phone was still switched on and in video mode. He turned it off and slipped it in his tuxedo pocket, then glanced at the old wind-up watch on his wrist. It was almost nine thirty—his recital was due to resume in fifteen minutes. Oliver straightened his tux and took a deep breath. He walked down the sweeping double staircase to rejoin the party, attempting to conceal the panic in his step. Chandeliers glittered. Waiters attended to the guests, carrying silver trays laden with champagne flutes. As he reached the bottom of the stairs, he snatched a glass from a tray and gulped it down. Across the room, near a tall marble fireplace, he could see the gleaming Bechstein grand piano he'd been playing just a few minutes earlier. It seemed like hours ago.

A hand landed on his shoulder. He tensed and spun around. An elderly gentleman with wire-framed glasses and a trim beard was smiling at him.

"May I congratulate you on a fine recital, Herr Meyer," the man said in German. "The Debussy was magnificent. I eagerly await the second half of your program."

"D-danke schön," Oliver stammered. He looked around him nervously. Could they have spotted him? He had to get away from this place.

"But you look very pale, Herr Meyer," the old man said, frowning at him. "Are you unwell? Shall I fetch you a glass of water?"

Oliver searched for the words. *"Krank,"* he muttered. "I'm feeling sick." He broke away from the old man and reeled through the crowd. He stumbled into a pretty woman in a sequined gown, spilling her drink. People stared at him. He blurted out an apology and pushed on.

He knew he was drawing attention to himself. Over his shoulder he spotted security guards with radios. They were coming down the stairs, mingling with the crowd, pointing in his direction. Someone must have seen him slip under the cordon. What else did they know?

The phone was in his pocket. If they found it, it would give him away and they'd kill him.

He made it to the main doorway. The cold, crisp air hit him, and his breath billowed. The sweat on his forehead suddenly felt clammy.

The grounds of the mansion were deep in snow. A flash of lightning cut across the night sky, and for a moment the eighteenth-century facade of the house was lit up like daylight. His classic racing-green MG Midget was parked between a glistening Bentley and a Lamborghini, and he headed towards it. A voice behind him called out "Halt!"

Oliver ignored the security guard and climbed into his car. The engine fired up, he put his foot down, and the MG's wheels spun on the icy cobbles. He headed up the long driveway towards the main gates. By the gatehouse, another security guard was standing talking on a radio.

The tall gilded wrought-iron gates were gliding shut.

Oliver aimed the MG at the closing gap and rammed them. He was thrown forward in his seat and the car's front wings buckled, but he made it through and kept going. The guard yelled at him to stop. He accelerated hard down the icy road.

Within less than a minute he saw the lights of a car behind him, dazzling in his rear-view mirror as it gained in speed. Snow-laden conifers flashed by in the yellow glow of his headlights.

He saw the sheet ice up ahead, but it was too late to do anything. He felt the car go into a skid as he hit it and grappled with the wheel, just managing to regain control. The car traveling behind him hit the glassy surface in his wake and spun into the trees at the side of the road.

Twenty minutes later he was back at the guesthouse. He parked the dented MG out of sight around the back and ran up to his room. The storm was gathering, and wispy snow was giving way to torrential rain that drummed on the roof. The lamp on his desk flickered as he turned on the laptop.

It seemed to take forever to load up. He didn't know

how much time he had. "Come on. Come on," he implored.

Logging on to his e-mail account, he scrolled urgently through the in-box to a message titled *The Mozart Letter.* It was from the professor. He hit Reply, his fingers jittery on the keys as he typed.

> *Professor—*
>
> *Must talk to you again about the letter. Urgent. Will call you. Have discovered something. Danger.*

He hit Send and fumbled for his phone, attaching it to the laptop with a USB cable. *Calm. Stay calm.* Working fast, he downloaded the video-clip file from the Sony Ericsson onto the hard drive.

He didn't want to look at the video, but knew he mustn't be caught with it. There was only one place he could send it safely. He would e-mail it to her. Then she'd definitely receive it, wherever she was.

The lights went out halfway through typing the e-mail. In the darkened room, the screen was telling him his Internet connection was broken. He swore, picked up the phone. Dead. The storm had taken out the phone lines, too.

Oliver bit his lip, thinking hard. The laptop was still running on its own power. He dug in his briefcase and found the CD-ROM he'd been using to store his research photographs. He slammed it into the laptop's disc drive and hurriedly copied the video file onto it.

Fumbling in the dark, he found the box set of Mozart's opera *The Magic Flute.* He'd been meaning to post it back to her anyway and had already stamped and addressed the padded envelope. He nodded to himself. It was the only way. He pulled out one of the Mozart discs and put the

CD he'd just copied in its place. Grabbing a marker pen, he scribbled a few quick words on the disc's shiny surface before he placed the music CD on top of it and shut the box. He prayed that if she saw it before he got there, she'd take his warning seriously.

He knew there was a post box not far from the guesthouse, off the square at the end of Fischer Strasse, and he ran downstairs and out into the street. The power was still down, the houses in darkness. The lashing rain had turned to sleet, and his tuxedo was quickly soaked as he jogged down the slushy pavements. Dirty snow lay piled against the sleeping buildings. The streets were deserted.

Oliver shoved his package into the post box, his fingers shaking with cold and fear, and turned back to the guesthouse. Now to pack his things and get the hell out of here—fast.

He was fifty yards from the darkened guesthouse when the powerful headlamps came around the street corner and washed over him. The big car bore down on him. He turned to run back the other way but slipped and grazed a knee on the pavement. The Mercedes pulled up next to him. There were four men inside. The back doors opened, and two of them stepped out and seized his arms. Their faces were grim. They bundled him into the backseat, and the car powered away up through the quiet village.

Nobody spoke. Oliver sat staring at his feet in the darkness. The Mercedes came to a halt, and the men pulled him roughly out of the car.

They were at the side of a lake. The sleet had stopped, and pale moonlight shone down across the water's frozen surface. The village lights were back on now and glimmering in the distance.

The men slammed him against the side of the car. One arm was twisted up painfully behind his back. Someone kicked his feet apart. He felt expert hands frisking him.

He remembered the phone just a second before they found it in his jacket pocket. Fear rose within him as he realized that in his haste he hadn't deleted the video clip.

The men hauled Oliver off the cold metal of the car, and he saw the pistol glint in the moonlight. The man holding it was tall, about six four, and heavily built. His eyes were impassive, and below the line of his sandy crew cut one of his earlobes was twisted and mangled.

Oliver stared at him. "I've seen you before."

"Walk." The man with the gun motioned towards the lake.

Oliver stepped through the rushes and placed one foot on the ice. He walked out across the lake. Ten yards, fifteen. The ice was thick and solid underneath him. Every nerve in his body was screaming, his heart thudding in the base of his throat. There had to be a way out of this.

But there wasn't, and he knew it. He walked on, slipping on the hard, smooth ice. His tuxedo was soaked with sweat.

He'd walked about thirty yards from the lakeside when he heard the gunshot. He flinched—but there was no impact, no pain. He felt the strike of the bullet resonate through the ice under his feet.

That was when he realized they weren't going to shoot him.

He watched helplessly as the blue fissure spread from the bullet hole in the ice and ran past his feet with a slow, ripping crackle. He glanced back at the lakeside. Saw another man reach inside the car, come out with a stubby submachine gun, and hand it to the tall man.

Oliver closed his eyes.

The tall man had a wide grin on his face as he held the weapon tightly at the hip and squeezed off a short fully automatic blast at Oliver's feet.

The ice was churned into flying splinters. A spider's web of cracks appeared all around him. There was nowhere to run. The frozen surface beneath his feet groaned, and then gave way.

The stunning shock of the icy water drove the breath out of him. He clawed at the ragged edge of the hole but lost his grip. The water closed over his head, filled his nose and mouth, pressure roaring in his ears as he kicked and struggled. In the blackness, he knew he'd slipped under the ice sheet. His fingers slithered helplessly against its underside as he drifted away from the hole. Bubbles streamed from his lips. There was no way up, no way back.

He held his breath and fought and kicked against the ice until he couldn't hold it any longer. His body convulsed as the freezing water poured into his lungs.

And as he died, he thought he could hear the killers laughing.

2.

SOUTHERN TURKEY
ELEVEN MONTHS LATER

The two men playing cards at the kitchen table heard the sudden roar of an engine and looked up just in time to see the pickup truck looming in the patio windows.

Then it hit. Glass shards, splinters of timber, and shattered brickwork exploded into the room. The truck lurched to a halt with its front wheels and its rust-pitted, plaster-covered hood protruding through the ragged hole in the wall.

The men dived for cover, scattering beer bottles, but they were too slow. The truck door flew open. The man who stepped out from behind the dusty windscreen was dressed all in black. Black combat jacket, black ski mask, black gloves. He watched for a moment as the card players backed away across the room. Then he drew the silenced 9 mm Browning from its holster and shot them both twice in the chest, rapid fire. The bodies slumped to the floor. A spent case tinkled across the tiles. He walked over to the nearest body and put a bullet in its head. Then the other.

The man in black had been observing the secluded house for three days, taking his time, well concealed in the trees beyond the fence. He knew the routine. He knew that round the back of the house was a garage block that housed a rusted Ford pickup with the keys left in it, and that he could slip over the wall and reach it without being seen from the rear windows where the guys usually sat, playing cards and drinking beer.

He also knew where the girl was.

The dust was beginning to settle in the wrecked kitchen. When he'd made sure the two men were permanently down, the intruder replaced the warm Browning in its holster and made his way through the house. He looked at his watch. Less than two minutes since he'd come over the wall. Things were going according to plan.

The girl's door was flimsy and buckled off its hinges at the third kick. By then, he could hear her screaming inside the room. He burst in. She was curled up at the far end of the bed, sheets drawn over her, terror in her eyes. He knew that she had just turned thirteen.

The man walked over to her and paused at the edge of the bed. She screamed harder. He wondered whether he would have to give her one of the tranquilizers he always carried with him. He took off the ski mask, revealing his lean, tanned face and thick blond hair. He put out his hand to her. "Come with me," he said softly.

She stopped screaming and looked up at him hesitantly. The other men had hard eyes. This man was different.

He reached into his jacket and showed her the photo of him together with her parents. She hadn't seen them for a long time. "It's okay," he said. "My name's Ben, and I'm here to help you. Your family sent me, Catherine. They're waiting. I'll take you to them."

Her cheeks were moist with tears. "Are you a policeman?" she asked in a low voice.

"No," he said. "Just a friend."

He reached his hand out farther, gently, and she let him take her arm to guide her to her feet. Her arm felt wasted under the grubby blouse she was wearing. She didn't protest as he led her out of the room, and she didn't react at the sight of the two dead men lying on the kitchen floor.

Back outside, she blinked at the sunlight. It had been a while since she'd last left the confines of the house. She was unsteady on her feet, and Ben carried her to the Land Rover he'd left parked fifty yards from the house, hidden in a clump of bushes. He opened the passenger's door and put the girl onto the seat. She was shivering. There was a blanket in the back, and he covered her with it.

He checked his watch again. Five minutes before the other three men would be back, if they kept to their routine. "Let's go," he muttered, and walked round to the driver's side.

The girl said something in reply, but her voice was weak.

"What?" he said.

"What about Maria?" she repeated, looking up at him.

His eyes narrowed. "Maria?"

Catherine pointed back at the house. "She's still in there."

"Is Maria a girl like you? They're holding her?"

Catherine nodded solemnly.

He made a decision. "Okay, I need you to stay put for a minute. Can I trust you?"

She nodded again.

"Where is she?"

In three minutes he'd found where they were keeping Maria. To get there he had to walk through a dingy room where some cameras were set up on tripods around a rumpled single bed, with cheap lighting equipment dumped in a corner and a TV and video sitting on a squat table. The VCR had been left running, the sound off. He paused and looked at the images, then realized what he was seeing. He recognized one of the men he'd shot earlier. The naked, writhing girl in the crudely shot film was no more than eleven or twelve.

Rage flashed through him, and he kicked the TV off the table. It hit the floor and imploded in a shower of sparks.

Maria's door wasn't locked, and when he went into the squalid room his first thought was that she was dead.

She was the girl in the video. She was still breathing but heavily doped. A grimy T-shirt and underwear were all that covered her thin body. He lifted her carefully from the bed and carried her back through the house and out to the Land Rover. He gently laid her on the backseat, took off his jacket, and placed it over her. Catherine reached out for her hand and looked up at Ben with questioning eyes.

"She'll be all right," he said softly.

The sound of an approaching vehicle made him tense. They were back. The Land Rover was well hidden from their view. So was the pickup truck, which was still sitting half buried in the hole in the kitchen wall at the back of the house, but they'd find that soon enough.

Ben climbed into the driver's seat and listened. He heard voices as one of the three men got out. The creak of the iron gates. The roll and crunch of the Suzuki's tires on the gravel. The engine burbling through a shot muffler as it pulled up in front of the house. Car doors opening and slamming. Footsteps and laughter.

He pulled his door quietly shut and went to twist the key. They'd be out of here before anyone could react. Then Catherine would be back with her family, and he'd hand Maria over to the authorities he could still trust.

His hand stopped halfway to the ignition. He leaned back in his seat and closed his eyes. He saw them again.

The images on the TV. Big hands pawing at young flesh. Bad teeth flashing in wide grins. The imploring eyes of the girl on the bed.

He looked over his shoulder at Maria's slight body lying slumped in the back. Catherine was frowning at him from the passenger's seat.

Fuck it. He reached down under his seat and drew out his backup weapon. The shotgun was an Ithaca 12 gauge, black and brutal, less than two feet long from its pistol grip to its sawn-off muzzle. Its tube magazine was loaded up with 00 Buck rounds, the type that would let you into a barricaded room without needing to open the door.

He swung his legs out of the Land Rover. "I'll be right back," he told Catherine.

The three men were just at the front porch by the time he walked up behind them. Two of them, the fat one and the long-haired one, were joking about something in Turkish. The third guy looked serious, tattoos, slicked-back hair, jangling a bunch of keys. He had a Chinese Colt 1911-A1 copy tucked in his belt, behind the hip, hammer down in amateur fashion.

When the metallic *clack-clunk* of the Ithaca slide action cut the air, all three of them wheeled around with wide eyes. Nobody had time to reach for a gun. A cigarette dropped from an open mouth.

He stared at them coldly for half a second before he emptied the Ithaca's magazine into their bodies at point-blank range.

3.

SOMEWHERE OVER FRANCE
TWO DAYS LATER

Benedict Hope gazed out of the window of the 747 and took another long sip of whiskey as he watched the white ocean of cloud drift by below. Ice clinked in his glass. The whiskey traced a burning path across his tongue. Airline Scotch, some nameless blended thing, but better than nothing. It was his fourth. Or maybe his fifth. He couldn't remember anymore.

The seat next to him was empty, as was much of the business-class section of the plane. He turned away from the window, stretched out, and closed his eyes.

Three jobs this year. He'd been busy, and he was tired. It had taken two months in Turkey to track down the men who were holding Catherine Petersen. Two long months of dirt and sweat, following false trails, chasing up dud information, overturning every stone. The girl's parents had despaired many times of ever seeing her alive again. He never made promises to people. He knew there was always a chance of sending the subject home in a body bag.

That had happened to him only once. Mexico City, one of the big kidnap-and-ransom hot spots of the world. It hadn't been his fault. The kidnappers had slaughtered the child even before the ransom demands. Ben had been the one who found the body. A young boy, just short of his eleventh birthday, stuffed in a barrel. He had no ears and no fingers. Sometimes the kidnappers weren't even doing it for the money. He still didn't like to think of it, but the half-repressed memory drove him on.

He'd persisted in Turkey, just as he always persisted. He'd never given up on anyone, even though there were plenty of times when it had seemed hopeless. Like with a lot of these jobs, there had been nothing, no leads, just a lot of people too frightened to talk. Then a chance piece of information unlocked the whole thing and led him right to the house. People had died for it. But now Catherine Petersen was back with her parents, and little Maria was being looked after until her family could be traced.

Now all Ben wanted to do was go home, back to the sanctuary of the old house on the remote west coast of Ireland. He thought about his private, lonely stretch of beach, the rocky cove where he liked to spend time alone with the waves, the gulls, and his thoughts. His plan after the Turkish job had been to rest there quietly for as long as he could. Until the next call. That was one thing he could be sure of. There'd always be another call.

And it had come sooner than he'd expected. Around midnight the night before, and he'd been sitting in the hotel bar with nothing more to occupy him than a row of drinks, counting the hours before he could get out of Istanbul. He'd checked his phone for the first time in a week. There had been a message waiting for him, and the voice was one he knew well.

It was Leigh Llewellyn. She was about the last person he'd expected to hear from. He'd listened to the message several times. She sounded tense, nervous, a little breathless.

"Ben, I don't know where you are or when you might get

this message. But I need to see you. I don't know who else to call. I'm staying in London, at the Dorchester. Come and find me. I'll wait here as long as I can for you." A pause. Then, in a tight voice: *"Ben, I'm scared. Please, come quick if you can."*

The message was five days old, dated the fourth of December. On hearing it, he'd canceled the Dublin flight. He'd be at Heathrow in less than an hour.

What could she want from him? They hadn't spoken for fifteen years.

The last time he'd seen Leigh Llewellyn was at Oliver's funeral back in January, back on that terrible day, watching his old friend's coffin go into the ground as the icy Welsh rain lashed over the desolate cemetery. With her long black hair streaming in the wind, she'd stood at the edge of the grave. She'd already lost her parents, a long time ago. Now her brother was gone, too, tragically drowned in an accident. Someone held an umbrella over her. She didn't seem to notice. Her beautiful features were pale and drawn. Those jade-green eyes, whose glitter Ben remembered so well from years before, gazed dully into the void. She was oblivious of the photographers, hovering like vultures to get a snap of the opera star who had cut short her European tour to bring her brother's coffin back from Vienna by private jet to her native Wales.

He'd wanted to talk to her that day, but there was too much pain between them. She hadn't seen him, and he'd kept away from her. On his way out of the cemetery he'd pressed a business card into her PA's hand. It was all he could do. Then he'd slipped away unseen.

After the funeral, Leigh had disappeared from public view and retreated to her home in Monte Carlo. He thought about her often, but he couldn't call her.

Not after what he'd done to her fifteen years ago.

4.

BALLYKELLY, NORTHERN IRELAND
FIFTEEN YEARS EARLIER

On a washed-out Tuesday night, Lance Corporal Benedict Hope turned in off the street and walked down the puddled alley past the bins and the fresh graffiti that said FUCK THE POPE. The sign for the little wine bar creaked in the wind.

He went in through the stone entrance and shook the rain from his clothes, glad to be out of uniform. A rusty iron stairway led up to the double doors of the bar. As he got nearer he could hear the sound of the piano drifting down. He pushed through the doors and walked across the peeling linoleum floor. The place was almost empty.

Ben pulled up a stool at the bar. The barman was polishing a pint glass with a cloth.

"How're you doing, Joe?"

Joe smiled through his heavy beard. "Doin' rightly, thanks. Same as usual?"

"Why not?" Ben said.

Joe grabbed a spirit glass and filled it from the bottle of Black Bush that hung behind the bar. "You'll be through that one soon," he said, gazing at the level in the bottle.

The pianist started up again. The battered old upright was missing most of its finish and badly in need of a tuning, but it sounded good under his fingers. He was doing a pretty good rendition of Jerry Lee Lewis boogie-woogie, keeping up a thumping stride rhythm with his left hand as his right churned out lightning blues scales.

"Not bad, is he?" said Joe. "One of your lot, from the look of him."

Ben turned round on the barstool. "Yeah, as a matter of fact, he is."

"Pity. I was thinking of hiring him. Might bring in a bit o' trade."

Ben knew his name, too. Private Oliver Llewellyn. He was tall and slender, and his black hair was cropped short in a severe buzz cut. He was too busy at the keyboard to notice Ben sitting watching him.

A pretty young blonde of about twenty was leaning against the side of the piano, gazing admiringly as Oliver's fingers shot up and down the keys. He suddenly played a fast downward run that terminated in a series of shimmering jazzy chords as Jerry Lee Lewis gave way to Oscar Peterson.

"You're fantastic, so you are," the girl breathed. "You're not really a soldier, are you?"

"Sure I am." Oliver smiled up at her, still playing. "SAS."

"You're kidding," she said.

"Nope," he replied. "I never kid. SAS. Sexy . . . Attractive . . . Sophisticated. That's me."

She giggled and thumped him playfully on the shoulder, and he kept playing with his right hand while he slipped his left arm around her waist and tugged her towards him. "There's plenty of room on this piano stool for two of us," he said. "Come on, I'll teach you a duet."

She sat up close next to him, her thigh pressing against his. "What's your name?" he asked.

"Bernie."

Ben grinned and turned back to his drink, exchanging a knowing look with Joe. Private Llewellyn didn't waste time.

The doors swung open, and four guys walked in and took a table in the middle of the room. They were in their mid-twenties, surly, overconfident. One of them went to the bar for pints of lager, ignoring Ben's friendly nod. One of his friends, the big overweight one with the pasty face, twisted heavily in his seat and called over to the girl as Oliver was showing her a simple duet. "Bernie! Get over here!" His narrowed eyes shot a long glance at Oliver's back.

Bernie broke away from the piano and got nervously to her feet. "Got to go," she whispered to Oliver. Oliver shrugged sadly and launched into a Chopin Nocturne.

Bernie sat down with the four lads. "Fuck were you doing with *him?*" the fat one demanded, staring at her hard. "Can't you see what he is?"

"Just having a giggle," she said quietly. "Leave him alone, Gary."

Oliver stopped playing. He grabbed the half-finished pint from the top of the piano and drained it, glanced at his watch, and walked out of the bar. Bernie craned her head and gave him a wistful smile as he went by.

The four guys exchanged looks. Gary raised his eyebrows and jerked his chin at the door. "You wait here," he growled at Bernie. He pushed his chair back from the table. The four of them slurped down the last of their beer and stood up. They headed for the door. Bernie looked worried. "Gary . . ." she started.

"You . . . shut . . . your . . . hole." Gary pointed a stubby warning finger in her face. "This is your fault, you slag. I told you not to hang around with them fuckin' soldiers."

The four of them filed out purposefully.

Ben had been watching. He sighed. He set his glass on the bar and slid down from his stool.

Outside in the alleyway, the four guys had already caught up with Oliver. They had him shoved up against the wall. Two of them had lock knives. Gary aimed a punch at Oliver's stomach that doubled him up. Oliver straightened suddenly and head-butted him between the eyes. The fat guy let out a scream and reeled backwards, blood pouring from a broken nose. The other three started on Oliver, two holding him with knives to his throat as the third kicked him in the belly. They had his wallet, ripping notes out of it.

Ben had come up silently behind them. Gary was too busy with his broken nose, so Ben focused on the others. A fistful of hair and a sharp kick to the back of the knee, and one of the knifemen was writhing on his back. Ben could easily have killed him then. Instead, he stamped hard on his genitals. The guy let out an animal scream. The other two let go of Oliver and ran.

Gary raised his fists. His face was slicked with blood. Ben knew exactly what to expect from him. He was the typical sloppy brawler, no brains and no discipline. Rage and strength and luck would be the only things going for him. He'd come roaring in like a big dumb bull. His punches would be slow and fly in a curved arc that a trained fighter could take his time blocking. Once you blocked it and got inside the arc, you could hit him hard.

Gary came on just the way Ben had thought. The only problem was thinking of the best way to stop him without causing major injury. He caught the fist that swung at him, locked it, and broke the wrist. He followed that up with a jab that pulverized Gary's lips and sent him crashing headlong into a row of bins. Gary flopped down on the wet concrete and lay still next to his friend, who was still squirming on his back, screaming in agony and clutching his crushed balls.

Ben helped Oliver to his feet. He was fighting for air after the heavy kick in the stomach. "Come on, let's go," Ben said, supporting him. Something hard and brittle crunched underfoot. He looked down at the splintered pieces of Gary's teeth on the ground.

"Good thing you turned up when you did," Oliver wheezed. "I might have killed them." He frowned at Ben, recognition showing on his face. "Sir," he added.

"Oh, I noticed that. SAS, huh?" Oliver's wallet was lying on the wet ground. Ben knelt down and picked up the papers that had fallen out of it. Driving license, money, a photo. Ben folded it into the wallet and was about to hand it back to Oliver.

Then he stopped. He opened the wallet again. Took out the photo. Unfolded it and looked at it again. He took a good long look at it.

It was a shot of Oliver with a girl, taken at a party. He had his arm round her, fooling about, pulling a stupid face.

But Ben wasn't looking at Oliver.

She was wearing a green evening dress that brought out the color of her eyes, and her lustrous black hair cascaded over her bare shoulders.

For a moment he couldn't take his eyes off the photo. It took an effort to tear his gaze away. He waved it at Oliver before he finally folded it up again and replaced it in the wallet. "If I had a girlfriend like that," he said sternly, "I wouldn't be getting myself into trouble chasing after the likes of Bernie up there."

Oliver took the wallet and dropped it in his pocket. He wiped blood from his upper lip. "Sound advice, sir," he said. "But that's not my girlfriend. She's my little sister."

5.

LONDON

THE PRESENT DAY

Ben walked through the opulent foyer of the Dorchester Hotel and approached the reception desk. "Is Miss Llewellyn still in room 1221?" he asked.

Three minutes later he was walking fast over the soft carpet of the corridor approaching her door. He was thinking of what she wanted and what he could say to her after all this time.

He rounded a corner. There was a guy standing just up ahead. He didn't look like he was waiting for anyone, and he didn't look like a guest. He was just standing there with his back to one of the doors. Ben checked the number on it: 1221.

He looked the guy up and down. He was a very big man. He was five inches taller than Ben, about six four. And he was broad. Probably about twice his weight, maybe four hundred pounds. He was wearing a dark polyester suit that stretched too tight over his chest and shoulders. His arms looked as though they were ready to pop the jacket sleeves apart at the seams. A decade or more of heavy steroid use had left his face cratered with acne scars. His tiny head was shaved to a polish and sat on his massive shoulders like a pea on a ruler.

Ben walked up to him without breaking stride. "I'm here to see Leigh Llewellyn."

The big man folded his arms across his chest and shook his head. A flicker of amusement passed over his face. "Nobody sees her," he said in a bass rumble. "She's not to be disturbed."

"I'm a friend. She's expecting me."

The wide-set eyes bored hard into his. "Not that I've been told."

"Can you tell her I'm here?" Ben said. "The name's Hope."

A short shake of the head. "Uh-uh. No way."

"You'd better let me through."

"Piss off, dwarf."

Ben reached across to knock on the door. The man's square hand shot out, and the stubby fingers closed around his wrist.

"You shouldn't have done that," Ben said.

The big man was about to answer when Ben twisted his hand into a lock that was a fraction away from breaking the wrist joint. He bent the arm up behind the guy's back and forced him down on his knees. Pain was like that. It didn't matter how big they were.

"Maybe we should start again," Ben said softly. "I came here to see Leigh Llewellyn. I don't want to hurt you unless you make me. All I want is to be let inside. Do you think you can manage that?"

"Okay, okay. Let go." The big man's voice was high-pitched and panicky, and he was beginning to shake.

The door opened. Two more men appeared in the doorway. They were both wearing the same cheap suits, but neither was as big as the first guy.

Ben threw them a warning look. "You men had better let me in," he said. "Or I'll break his arm off."

A familiar face appeared behind them. They moved aside for her. "It's all right," she said to them. "I know him."

"Hello, Leigh," he said.

She stared at him. "What are you doing with my bodyguard?"

He couldn't help but smile at the sound of her voice. There was still that melodic Welsh lilt in her accent, only slightly tempered by the years of traveling around the world and living abroad.

Ben let the guy go, and he slumped heavily to the floor. "Is that what you call this sack of shit?" he asked.

The other two bodyguards were hovering around the doorway, exchanging nervous looks. The big one picked himself slowly up off the floor, sheepish, rubbing his hand and groaning.

"You'd better come inside," she said to Ben.

He shouldered past the two men and stepped into the room.

Room 1221 was a vast suite filled with the scent of flowers. Pale sunlight filtered in through three tall windows, flanked with heavy drapes. Leigh led him inside and closed the door quietly, shutting the bodyguards out in the corridor.

They faced each other uncertainly.

"Fifteen years," he said. She was still the same Leigh he remembered, still beautiful. The same willowy figure, the same perfect skin. Those green eyes. She was wearing faded jeans and a navy sweater. No makeup. She didn't need it. The only piece of jewelry she had on was a gold locket on a thin chain around her neck. Her hair hung down loose over her shoulders, black and glossy, just as he'd remembered it.

"Ben Hope," she said frostily, looking up at him. "I promised myself that the next time I saw you I was going to slap your face."

"Is that what you called me for?" he said. "Now I'm here, feel free."

"It didn't look like you were going to turn up."

"I just got your message last night. I came straight here."

"I left it days ago."

"I was busy," he said.

"Right," she snorted.

"I got the impression you needed my help," he said. "Now it seems as though I'm not exactly welcome."

She looked at him defiantly. "I don't need you anymore. I panicked, that's all. I shouldn't have called you. I've got things under control now."

"Your reception committee? I noticed."

"If you've gone out of your way to get here, I'll make it worth your while." Her handbag was lying on an armchair. She walked over to it, took out her purse, and started counting banknotes.

"I don't want your money, Leigh. I want to know what's going on." He jerked his thumb over his shoulder. "You're putting on a circus?"

She put the purse down. "I don't understand."

"Why else would you hire a bunch of clowns?"

"They're for protection."

"They couldn't protect you from a gang of Quakers."

"I had to hire someone. You weren't there. Just like the other time."

"I'm here now," he said. "I've come all this way—at least tell me what's going on."

She sighed, relenting. "All right. I'm sorry. I'm tired and I'm scared. I need a drink. Want one?"

Ben laid his brown leather jacket on the back of a settee. "That sounds like a good start," he said. "I could do with a decent Scotch, after that crap they gave me on the flight."

"You still like your whiskey." Leigh opened an Oriental drinks cabinet and took out a green bottle. He thought he could see a slight tremor in her hand. "Single malt?" she asked. She filled her own glass as full as his. He couldn't recall that she drank. But then, she'd been a girl of nineteen in those days. So much time had passed. He realized he hardly knew her anymore.

She took an agitated sip of the whiskey, pulled a disgusted face, and gave a little splutter. "I'm in trouble. Something happened to me."

"Sit down and tell me everything," he said.

They sat facing each other in comfortable armchairs on either side of a coffee table with an ornate etched glass top. His glass was already empty. He reached for the bottle and poured another double measure.

Leigh brushed a strand of hair away from her face. She swiveled her whiskey glass on the tabletop as she spoke. "I've been in London for six weeks for work," she said. "Doing *Tosca* at the Royal Opera. I rent a little flat not far from the opera house. It was the morning after the last show. I was planning to hang around for a while. I'd been doing some shopping in Covent Garden. I was walking back towards the flat. It's on a quiet street where there's often nobody about. I could sense that someone was watching me. You know, that feeling that you're not alone?"

"Go on."

"They were in a car, a big dark-colored car. I don't remember what type. Just following me along at walking pace. At first I thought it was photographers, or some kind of curb crawler. I was trying to ignore them, walking faster. Then the car swerved up onto the pavement in front of me, cut me off. I tried to go round the other way, but they got out and blocked me."

"Can you describe them?"

She nodded. "There were three, the driver plus two

more. Well dressed, dark suits. They looked like businessmen. One of them told me to get into the car. When I tried to run, he grabbed me."

"How did you manage to get away?"

She smiled darkly. "One thing about living in Monte Carlo—some people say it's a bit of a police state, but at least it's safe for women to walk the streets. Anywhere else I go, Europe or the United States, I always carry a can of Mace."

He blinked. "You had Mace?"

She shook her head. "In free Britain? You must be kidding. I carry a little can of hairspray. While he was hanging on to my arm, I sprayed him in the eyes with it."

"Crude, but effective."

She sighed, leaning her head on her hands, the thick black hair hiding her face. "I never thought I'd have to use it," she said quietly. "It was terrible. I keep seeing it, over and over in my mind. He let go, screaming and rubbing his eyes. He reached into his jacket and pulled out a gun. I ran like crazy. They came after me. I'm a fast runner, but they would have caught me if it hadn't been for the cab that just happened to come by. I told the cabbie *Drive, just drive.* I haven't been back to the flat since." She looked at him with worry in her eyes. "So what do you think?"

"I think that your friends outside aren't going to help you with this."

"It *was* a kidnap attempt, wasn't it?"

"Sounds like it," he agreed. "People in your position are a target. You're high profile, you're wealthy. Unless, of course, someone is out to do you some harm. Do you have any particular enemies?"

Leigh pursed her lips. "Not that I can think of. Why would I? I'm just a singer."

"A pretty well-known singer, though. Have you ever thought anyone was stalking you, ever received any strange phone calls, e-mails, letters?"

She shrugged. "I get fans trying to contact me through Pam, my PA. People sometimes recognize me and want an autograph for a CD cover, things like that. But never anything you'd call strange or threatening."

"When you got away from your attackers and took the cab, did you come straight here?"

"I'm not that stupid. I thought they might get the number of the cab and trace me."

He nodded. "So nobody knows you're here apart from the hotel staff?"

"Just the police."

"They're never much use in these cases."

"Well, they took a statement from me and said they'd look into it."

"I don't suppose you got the number of the car?"

"Ben, it happened so fast—"

"That's all right. It was probably either a false plate or a stolen car anyway." He paused, measuring his words for what he wanted to say next. "Leigh, I have to ask . . . it's been a long time since . . ."

"Since you ditched me and vanished?"

He ignored that. "I meant, we haven't been in touch for a long time. Did you ever marry?"

"Strange question, Ben. I'm not sure I—"

"It might be important."

She hesitated before replying. "It was a long time after you," she said.

"Who is he?"

"He's a composer, writes film scores. His name's Chris. Chris Anderson."

"You're still together?"

"It only lasted about two years," she said. "It just didn't work out. We still meet occasionally, as friends." She frowned. "What are you getting at?"

"Kidnapping is just a business like any other, Leigh. It's not personal. It's all about money, and if there's no family or spouse to pay for your safe return, there's no motive. It's the ultimate emotional blackmail. It only works if there's a third party who's scared enough of losing someone they love." He took a swig of Scotch, draining the glass almost to the bottom. "There's only one exception to that rule, and that's if the victim has K and R insurance."

"K and R?"

"Kidnap and ransom."

"I didn't even know you could take out insurance against that."

"So I take it you haven't got any?"

She shook her head.

"That means we can largely rule out a financial motive," he said. "Unless it was an amateur job. Snatch the person first and worry about the details later. But these guys sound more professional than that. And I don't think it was a case of mistaken identity, either. They knew where you were living. Someone had done his homework." He paused to take another long drink of whiskey. He put the empty glass down with a clunk on the table. "What are you planning to do now?" he asked.

"I want to get out of London, for a start. I can't stand it here anymore, trapped like an animal in this hotel. I've got to be in Venice in mid-January for *The Magic Flute*. But first I'm heading for West Oxfordshire, in the country. Dave and his team are escorting me there."

"Why there?"

"It's a place I bought a while ago. I've been thinking of setting up an opera school."

"Who knows about it?"

"Nobody yet, apart from myself, my PA, and my business manager," she said. "At the moment it's still just a big old empty house with nothing but a few boxes of stuff sent over from Monte Carlo. I haven't got around to furnishing it. But it's livable. I'll stay there for a few days until I decide what to do next."

"I'll tell you what you need to do," Ben said. He jerked his thumb over his shoulder in the direction of the door. "First thing, you need to ditch those idiots outside. They're a liability. I could have been anybody walking in here. They didn't even slow me down."

She nodded. "You've put things into perspective a little. So, say I agree to ditch them right away. What next?"

"You want me to step in?"

"That's what I was hoping," she said.

"I'm not a bodyguard, Leigh. It isn't what I do. But I know people. We'll get you some proper protection."

She looked unhappy. "Why should I exchange one bunch of heavies for another?"

He smiled and shook his head. "The people I have in mind are professionals. The real thing. You would barely even know they were there, but you'd be safe. I know, I trained them."

"I'd feel safer with you," she said.

"Even after what I did to you?"

"You won't let me down again?" she asked. "Not this time?"

He sighed. "No," he said. "I won't let you down again."

6.

BERNE, SWITZERLAND

Heini Müller huddled closer to the fire and warmed his hands. Snowflakes were spiraling down from the heavy sky, sizzling against the metal sides of the brazier.

It had been a long afternoon, and some of the protesters were getting restless waiting for something to happen. He ran his eye over the crowd. They weren't as vociferous as they'd been this morning. People were standing around smoking herbal cigarettes, sipping black currant tea and decaf from their flasks, talking in groups, kicking their feet, looking tired and cold. Some people had given up and gone home, but there were still about four hundred of them.

They'd tried earlier to get inside the hotel grounds, but when these bastards had their conferences the security was tight. The place was locked up solid, and they'd had to content themselves with waving banners outside the tall gates. The police were keeping their distance, vans and motorcycles parked some way up the road, and more inside the grounds. The cops were nervous. They knew they were seriously outnumbered.

The big hotel stood a few hundred yards away, across snowy lawns. There were thirteen limos parked outside the conference building, black, identical. A few minutes ago,

Heini's girlfriend Franka had spotted a bunch of drivers emerge from a side entrance to wipe snow off the cars. It looked like something was beginning to happen at last.

"Here they come," someone yelled. The protesters picked up their banners like weapons. STOP CLIMATE CHAOS. ARAGON FOR EUROPE.

Heini watched through Franka's binoculars as the conference building opened and the attendees filed out under the snow. The youngest of the men were middle-aged. They were all smartly dressed, and some of the older ones wore hats. The hotel forecourt had been salted and swept for the Important Men, and the drivers and hotel staff were in attendance with umbrellas. Motorcycle police mounted their white Honda Pan Europeans, and plainclothes security men stood around talking on radios.

Thirteen drivers simultaneously opened thirteen limo rear doors, and the passengers got in. The doors slammed, and the hotel staff gathered respectfully under the snow as the cars pulled away. The procession purred softly down the private road towards the tall gates where the protesters were waiting. Flanking motorcycles led the way, and four security cars brought up the rear.

In the back of the lead limousine a slightly built, smartly dressed man in his late sixties reclined on the leather seat. His name was Werner Kroll, and he was the committee president. He folded his hands delicately on his lap and waited patiently as the limo approached the thronging, raging crowd.

Kroll's assistant sat opposite him. He was a younger man, in his early forties. He was muscular and still wore his hair the way he had in his military days. He turned to watch the waving banners with a scowl of derision. "Idiots," he said, pointing a gloved finger. "Look at them. What do they think they're achieving?"

"Democracy gives them the illusion of freedom," Kroll replied softly, gazing at them.

The gates swung open automatically to let the limousines through. The protesters immediately swarmed around the cars, yelling slogans and shaking their banners angrily. There were a lot more of them than usual, Kroll observed. Two years ago the demonstrators outside these meetings were little more than a disordered band of hippies, sixty or seventy at the most and easily within the police's power to subdue. Things were different now.

The crowd swarmed around the car. The police were mingling with the demonstrators now, grabbing people and dragging them away to the waiting vans. The pitch was rising fast. Three officers grabbed hold of a young man carrying an ARAGON FOR EUROPE banner who was blocking the car's path. The banner clattered against the windscreen, the rough painted words large against the glass.

Kroll knew the name Aragon very well. Aragon was the man who was giving these people their power. In a few short years the charismatic young Europolitician had risen from obscurity to being able to command massive popular support for his Green and antinuclear policies. It wasn't just a group of hippies, radicals, and committed lefties protesting any longer. Aragon was appealing to the middle classes. And that was dangerous.

Heini Müller reached into his bag and took out a box of eggs. He was a vegan and didn't normally buy them, but for this he'd made an exception. The eggs were months old. Heini stood grinning as the lead limo approached, its headlights blazing. He grabbed an egg out of the box and raised his arm to hurl it against the window of the limo. Someone else was shaking up a spray can of red paint.

As Heini was about to smash the egg against the first car, it stopped. The opaque window whirred down.

Heini froze. Suddenly the roar of the crowd was silent in his ears. The old man in the back of the limo was staring at him. His gaze was like ice. It seemed to drain the blood out of Heini, who stood transfixed with the egg in his hand. His arm fell limp, and something cracked. The window whirred up again and the gleaming black limo moved silently on.

Heini Müller looked down at his hand. The rotten yolk dripped from his fingers. The cars went by him and he just stood there. Then the yelling filled his ears again. A policeman grabbed his hair, and he was on the ground, kicking and squirming.

Kroll eased back in his seat as the car swept away between the flanking police outriders. His phone rang, and he picked it up slowly.

"Llewellyn left before we could get to her," said the voice on the line. He sounded apologetic and frightened. "We were half an hour late."

Kroll listened impassively, looking at the snowy hills rolling past.

The voice went on, sounding more hopeful. "But we have found her again. I have an address for you."

Kroll reached for a notepad and wrote as he listened. He ended the call without a word, then pressed a button on his console. A small flat-screen TV flashed into life, and he pressed Play on the DVD control. Kroll looked intently at the screen. He'd seen this before. He enjoyed watching her.

She was reclining in a large armchair in a television studio in London. Her face was animated as she spoke to her interviewer. She wore a creamy cashmere dress and a string of glittering pearls that contrasted strikingly with her jet-black hair.

"She's something, isn't she?" asked Kroll's assistant.

Kroll didn't look away from the screen. "She certainly is," he replied softly. He stopped the video playback. The screen went dark. He fixed the other man with cold eyes for a second before glancing down to the notepad on the seat next to him. He tore off the top sheet and handed it to the younger man. "Make the necessary arrangements, Jack," he said.

7.

THE VILLAGE OF ASTON
WEST OXFORDSHIRE

It was dark by the time they reached the sleepy village. Ben had the taxi drop them in the square. They bought a few provisions from the village shop and called a local taxi service to take them the two miles to Langton Hall.

The country house lay secluded in its own land, among wintry oaks and willows at the end of a long, twisty driveway. Its gables and chimney stacks stood silhouetted against the dark blue sky, and moonlit frost glittered on the roof. The windows were in darkness. An owl hooted from a nearby tree.

Leigh unlocked the heavy oak front door and quickly punched a number into a wall panel to disable the alarm system. She turned on the lights.

"Nice place." Ben's voice echoed in the empty entrance hall. He looked around him, admiring the ornate wood paneling and the sweep of the wide staircase.

"It will be when it's all done up," she said. She shivered. "Cold, though. The boiler's almost as old as the rest of the place, and the heating doesn't work."

"No problem," he said. "I'll get the fires going. We'll soon warm the place up."

"Thanks, Ben. There's a pile of logs in the woodshed."

He followed her into a large stone-floored country

kitchen and laid the plastic bags of shopping on a long pine table. He checked that the old-fashioned lock on the kitchen door worked, then quietly slid open a drawer and found what he was looking for. He discreetly slipped the carving knife inside his jacket.

"Leigh, I'm going to fetch some logs and take a look around the place. Lock the door after me."

"What—"

"Don't worry, just being cautious."

Leigh did what he said. The big iron key turned smoothly in the lock, and she heard his footsteps moving away up the corridor.

She opened a bottle of village-shop wine. There were some glasses and basic cooking equipment stored in the walk-in pantry. She took a heavy cast-iron skillet down from a hook and put it on the gas range.

She smiled to herself as she took a box of eggs out of one of the shopping bags. It was strange, having Ben Hope around her again after all these years. She'd loved him once, loved him madly enough to have thought about giving up her career for him even before it had begun.

"You'll like him," Oliver had said that day. And he'd been right. Her brother's new army friend wasn't like the others she'd met. She'd just turned nineteen, and Benedict—as he'd been introduced—was four years older. He had an easy smile and a quick mind. He'd talked to her like no other boy had ever done before. Until then she'd thought love at first sight was a fairy tale, but it had happened to her with him. It hadn't happened to her since, and she could still remember every day of those five months they'd been together.

Had he changed a lot since those days? Physically he didn't seem that different. His face was a little leaner, perhaps. A little more careworn, with more frown lines than laugh lines. He was still toned and in perfect physical shape. But he *had* changed. The Ben she'd known back then had been softer and gentler. He could even seem vulnerable at times.

Not anymore. Through Oliver she'd heard enough about Ben's life during the intervening fifteen years to know that he'd seen, and perhaps done, some terrible things. Experiences like that had to leave a mark on a person. There were moments when she could see a cold kind of light in his blue eyes, a glacial hardness that hadn't been there before.

They ate sitting on the hearth rug in the unfurnished study. It was the smallest room in the cavernous house, and Ben's crackling log blaze had quickly chased the chill from the air. Firelight danced on the oak panels. In the shadowy corners of the room, packing cases and tape-sealed cardboard boxes were still piled up unopened from the move.

"Fried egg sandwiches and cheap wine," he said. "You should have been a soldier."

"When you work the hours I do, you learn to appreciate the quick and simple things in life," she said with a smile. The bottle between them was half empty now, and she was feeling more relaxed than she had for days. They sat in silence for a while, and she let her gaze be drawn by the hypnotic rhythm of the flames.

Ben watched her face in the firelight. He had a clear image in his mind of the last time they'd sat alone together like this, a decade and a half earlier. He and Oliver had been on leave from the army and had traveled up to mid-Wales together to the Llewellyn family home in Builth Wells. The old merchant town house, once grand, had by then grown tatty and neglected with the decline of Richard Llewellyn's antique-piano-restoration business. Ben had only briefly met Leigh and Oliver's father, a kindly, heavy man in his mid-sixties, with a graying beard, a face reddened by a little too much port, and the sad eyes of a man widowed for six years.

It had been evening, the rain lashing down outside, wind howling through the chimney. Oliver was taking advantage of his week's freedom to go *in search of pulchritude,* as he had put it. Richard Llewellyn was up in his private study, as he always seemed to be, poring over old books and papers.

Alone downstairs, Ben had built a roaring log fire, and Leigh had sat by him. They'd talked quietly for hours. That had been the night of their first kiss. There hadn't been many.

He smiled to himself, returning to the present—watching her now, the flickering glow on her cheek. Neither time nor fame had changed her.

"What are you thinking about?" he asked.

She turned away from the fire to look at him. "Thinking about you," she said.

"What about me?"

"Did you ever marry, find someone?"

He was silent for a moment. "It's hard for me, with the life I lead. I don't think I'm the settling kind."

"You haven't changed, then."

He felt the sting of her words, but said nothing.

"I hated you for a long time," she said quietly, looking into the flames. "After what you did to me."

He said nothing.

"Why didn't you turn up that night?" she asked, looking round at him.

He sighed and paused a long time before replying. "I don't know," he said. He'd thought about it so often.

"I loved you," she said.

"I loved you," he answered.

"Did you, really?"

"Yes, I did."

"But you loved the regiment more."

"I was young, Leigh. I thought I knew what I wanted."

She looked back into the fire. "I waited for you that night after the show. I was so excited. It was my debut. I thought you were in the audience. I sang my heart out for you. You said you'd meet me backstage and we'd go to the party together. But you never came. You just disappeared."

He didn't know what to say to her.

"You really broke my heart," she said. "Maybe you don't realize that."

He reached out and touched her shoulder. "I've always felt bad about what I did. I've never forgotten it, and I've often thought about you."

"I'm sorry," she said. "I shouldn't drag out the past. It was a long time ago."

They sat in silence for a while. He tossed another log on the fire, gazing at the orange sparks flying up the chimney. He didn't know what more to say to her.

"I miss Oliver," she said suddenly.

"I miss him, too," he said. "I wish I'd seen more of him in the last few years."

"He talked about you a lot."

Ben shook his head. "What the hell was he doing on that lake?"

"Nobody really knows," she said. "The only witness to the accident was his lady companion for the evening."

"Who was she?"

"Madeleine Laurent. Wife of some diplomat. It caused a bit of a scandal. There were people behind the scenes trying to keep the investigation under wraps. Some of the details were pretty hazy."

"Tell me what happened," he said.

"All I know is that apparently they'd been at a party, some black-tie affair with a bunch of important people. I don't know where it was or who else was there. If there were other witnesses, maybe they didn't want to get involved."

"Black ties and VIPs," Ben said. "It doesn't sound like Oliver's kind of party."

"He went along with her. She said he'd been chasing her around. The husband was away somewhere. And there was champagne. He drank a lot of it."

"That does sound like him," Ben admitted.

"They were dancing and drinking. She'd had quite a bit, too, but not as much as him. One thing started leading to another. He wanted to get her away somewhere private. She said he kept insisting he wanted to drive her to a hotel, get a room together."

"They couldn't have sneaked into a bedroom?"

"Apparently not."

"That doesn't sound like him. Drinking and driving wasn't his style."

"I didn't think so, either," Leigh said. "But he crashed the car on the way to the hotel. That's true. I saw the damage."

"That old MG of his?"

"He smashed it up pretty badly. The front was all dented in. Looked like he'd hit a wall or something."

"If he turned up drunk at the hotel with a damaged car, there must have been other witnesses," Ben said.

She shook her head. "They never made it to the hotel. Apparently they couldn't wait. They stopped off somewhere quiet on the way."

"At the lakeside?"

She nodded. Her face tightened. "That's when it

happened. According to the woman, he thought it'd be a laugh to have a skate on the ice."

"That *really* doesn't sound like him."

"I know," she said. "But it looks like that's what happened. He got this crazy idea in his head, and he went out on the ice. She thought it was funny at first. Then she got bored and went back to the car. She fell asleep on the seat."

"Drunk enough to pass out," he said. "But she remembered a lot of detail afterwards."

"I'm only telling you what she claimed happened. There's no evidence that it didn't happen the way she said it did."

"He went out on the ice before or after the sex?"

"She said it never went that far."

"So he was too horny to wait to get to the hotel, but then he decides to go skating first?"

"I know," she said. "I thought about that, too. It doesn't make a lot of sense. But I guess if he'd been drinking—"

He sighed. "Okay. Tell me the rest."

"She woke up shivering with the cold. She reckoned she'd been out of it for about half an hour." Leigh paused, sighed, closed her eyes, sipped a little more wine. "And that was it. She was alone. He hadn't come back from the ice. There was no sign of him. Just a hole where he'd gone through."

Ben flipped the burning log in the fire. He said nothing, turning it over in his mind. *Dammit, Oliver, you were* trained *not to do things like that. Bloody fool, dying so stupidly.* "What was he doing in Austria?" he asked.

"He was there researching his book."

Ben laid down the poker and turned to look at her. "A book? What was it, a novel?"

"No, it was about Mozart."

"A biography or something?"

"It wasn't the story of Mozart's life," she said. "That's been written about a million times. This was the story of Mozart's death."

"Strange subject. Not that I'd know anything much about it."

"Olly was devoted to it. He was always sending me his notes, keeping me up-to-date on his research. I was funding him, so I think he felt obliged. I never had much time to read the stuff, and then when . . . when he had the accident, I couldn't bring myself to look at it anymore. He even posted me something on the day he died. I've never opened it." She hung her head, sipped her wine, and went on. "But in the last couple of months I've started getting the idea of carrying on where he left off."

"You mean finish his book for him?"

"Yeah. I think I'd like to do that in his memory." She pointed over her shoulder with her thumb. "I had all his notes sent over from Monte Carlo. They're still packed up in one of those boxes over there." She smiled. "You think it's a crazy idea?"

"Finishing his book? No, I think it's a great idea. You reckon you can do it?"

"I'm a singer, not a writer," she replied. "But it's an interesting subject, and yes, I reckon I can do it. Maybe it'll be good for me, too. You know, help me come to terms with death, and loss."

Ben nodded thoughtfully. He refilled their glasses. The bottle was empty now, and he thought about fetching another. "Mozart's death," he said. "I thought people already knew what happened to Mozart."

"That a jealous rival composer poisoned him?" She chuckled. "*That* old theory. It's just one of those myths that got blown up."

Ben held up his glass so that he could watch the dancing flames filtered redly through the wine. "What was Oliver's angle?" he asked.

"He said his research uncovered a whole new take on the Mozart murder theory. That's what made his book so important."

"So who did it?"

"I think he believed it might have been the Freemasons," she said.

"A bunch of guys in sashes with one trouser leg rolled up."

She looked at him hard. "Oliver took it seriously enough."

"Why would the Masons have gone and done something like that?"

"Because of *The Magic Flute*."

"The opera you mentioned. Is there more to that, or am I supposed to guess?"

"*The Magic Flute* is full of Masonic symbolism," she explained patiently. "Secrets that Masons are sworn to protect."

"So how did Mozart know all these secrets?"

"Because he was a Freemason himself."

"I didn't know that. So . . . what? He blabbed, and they knocked him on the head?"

"That's the idea. I don't know much, though."

"Should make for an interesting read." Ben smiled. "And where was Oliver getting all this stuff from?"

"From Dad's discovery," she said. "Remember?"

He did. "The letter."

Leigh nodded. "It was the center of his research. The book's named after it. *The Mozart Letter*."

He was about to reply when Leigh's phone rang. She fished it out of her pocket. "Leigh Llewellyn."

Ben could hear a man's voice on the other end. Leigh listened, frowning. "I'm not at the Dorchester anymore," she said. A pause. "I'm at my country house, Langton Hall . . . What's this about?"

Ben couldn't make out what the caller was saying. He watched Leigh closely.

Her eyes opened wide. "Oh my God . . . The whole place?" Pause. She looked agitated. "They weren't touched? No . . . Okay . . ." Another pause. She put her head in her hand, ruffling her hair. "All right," she said quietly. "I will . . . thanks for letting me know."

She ended the call with a deep sigh. "Jesus," she muttered.

"What is it?"

"That was the police. My flat in London . . . it's been torn apart."

8.

VIENNA

Detective Sergeant Markus Kinski never forgot a face. And when he'd spotted the woman across the crowded square, he'd instinctively followed her.

It was a cold afternoon in Vienna, and snow threatened from a heavy sky. She filtered through the crowds of tourists and shoppers. She was wearing a navy-blue cape and matching beret, casual but expensive. Kinski was hanging back thirty yards, locked onto his target, his old greatcoat flapping in the December chill, when he saw her go inside the tearoom.

He paused at the entrance and watched her through the glass. It was one of those frilly kinds of joints, like an overdecorated wedding cake, which Vienna was full of and which Kinski, still an East Berliner in his heart, hated.

She took a table in the far corner. Laying her blue cape beside her, she took a paperback from her handbag and began to read. Kinski went inside and sat himself down where he could observe her over the top of his newspaper. He was too bulky for the little round marble-topped table, and the slender chair felt creaky and rickety under him. Everything was so fucking *dainty*.

Kinski had been the officer in charge and was in the interview room when they'd brought Madeleine Laurent in for questioning, almost a year ago, after the Llewellyn drowning case. She'd been blond, with long hair. The woman sitting opposite him now was a brunette, her hair cut in a bob that disguised the contours of her face. But the features were the same. The gray-blue eyes that were scanning the menu and then flashing up as the waiter came to her table—those were the same, too. She ordered Sacher torte and a hot cocoa with cream and a dash of green Chartreuse.

Greedy bitch, he thought. *And your German suddenly got a whole lot better.* But it had to be her. It *was* her.

Kinski ordered an espresso. Straight, black, no sugar. He leaned back in his creaking chair and pretended to read the paper. He cast his mind back to the Llewellyn case.

Madeleine Laurent. Twenty-six years of age. Nationality French. Married to Pierre Laurent, a French diplomat posted in Vienna. The scandal had been neatly covered up. Laurent's people had leaned hard on the cops to keep quiet about Madeleine's indiscretion with the foreigner Oliver Llewellyn. Her tearful statement had been recorded and filed—and then suddenly nobody could find it anymore. It seemed just to vanish from the records. By then the coroner's report was already in, so nobody had made much of the clerical snafu.

Nobody except Kinski. But when he'd asked questions, he'd been formally instructed to leave off. It was a sensitive matter. The case was closed. A few days later they'd heard that the diplomat was being pulled out of Austria and given a new three-year posting, somewhere conveniently far away. Venezuela, Kinski remembered. He'd smarted over it for weeks afterwards.

If it was the same woman, what was she doing back

here? Visiting friends for Christmas? Maybe he should just give her the benefit of the doubt. Perhaps he was wasting his time.

But his gut told him differently, and twenty-six years as a cop—the first nine of those served in the hard streets of Communist East Berlin—had taught Markus Kinski not to ignore a hunch.

He went to the gents and shut himself in a cubicle, then dialed the number he'd memorized from the tearoom menu.

Kinski was back finishing his coffee when the manageress called out across the counter. "Excuse me, ladies and gentlemen—is there a Madeleine Laurent here? I have an urgent message for her. No?" The manageress scanned around the room, shrugged, and went back to what she was doing.

The woman had frozen when the name was called. Her cup stopped an inch from her mouth, then she collected herself and set it down without drinking. She looked around her nervously. Kinski smiled behind his paper. *Got you.*

The woman gathered her cape and bag, abandoned the half-eaten Sacher torte. She hurried to the counter, paid, and left the tearoom.

Kinski tossed money down on the table and followed her. She slipped between the bustling shoppers and hailed a taxi. Kinski's path was blocked by bodies. He pushed through angrily. He was twenty feet from her when she hopped into the car. A slim leg disappeared inside, the door slammed, and the taxi melted into the traffic.

"Scheisse!"

Back at the tearoom, he asked for the manageress. When

she appeared, he flashed his badge. "*Polizei.* A woman left here two minutes ago. She paid by card. I want her name."

The manager went coolly over to the stack of credit card slips on the counter. She handed him the topmost one. Kinski glanced at it.

The name and signature on the credit card slip wasn't Madeleine Laurent. It was Erika Mann.

9.

LANGTON HALL, OXFORDSHIRE

Ben spent a restless night in the drafty passageway outside Leigh's bedroom door. She'd tried to persuade him to sleep in one of Langton Hall's eight empty bedrooms, but he'd wanted to stay close to her, and this was the closest he could be without sleeping in her room.

As he sat there leaning uncomfortably against the wall, his mind was full of thoughts of Leigh. It was strange to think that she was just on the other side of the wall. They'd been so close once, and it saddened him to be near to her now, yet so far away.

He managed to stay awake until sometime before six, chain-smoking his way through most of a pack of Turkish cigarettes. As the dawn light began to creep across the hallway through the dusty window, he was thinking about the phone call from the police the night before. He went back over and over the details in his mind. Leigh's flat in Covent Garden could have been ransacked any time in the last five days. The neighbors had returned from a holiday to find her door ajar and had called the police when they saw the damage.

It had been no ordinary burglary. They'd lifted carpets and floorboards, ripped through every piece of furniture, even slashed pillows and cushions. But nothing had been stolen. The police had found her string of pearls, gold watch, and diamond earrings on her bedside table, just where she'd left them. He couldn't make sense of it.

He got up and stretched, folded away his sleeping bag, and went downstairs. He was making coffee when Leigh came in shivering, her hair tousled. They drank mugs of hot coffee and spoke little as they watched the sunrise from the kitchen window. Leigh was clutching her mug with both hands to warm her fingers. Ben could see from the pallor of her face that she felt almost as tired as he did.

"What are you going to do?" she asked. "Are you sticking around, or making that call?"

"I'd feel better if you had the right kind of protection," he said. "I can't be with you twenty-four/seven, going everywhere you go, watching your back every moment." He paused. "But I want to know what's happening here."

"So you're staying?"

He nodded. "For a while, at least."

She laid down her cup. "Okay. And if I'm going to be stuck here for a while, I might as well get started on unpacking some of the stuff in those boxes. I've got some sweaters in there, and it's freezing in this house."

Ben fetched more logs and kindling from the woodshed and carried them into the study. Leigh watched as he quickly cleaned out the cold grate and piled up the sticks of kindling. He lit the fire, and the orange flames began to roar up the chimney. He sensed a movement behind him. "What on earth are you doing?" he asked, looking up at her.

She stopped jumping up and down. "This reminds me of years ago in the old house in Builth Wells," she said, laughing. "We were so strapped for cash, Dad would have us jumping and running around so he could save on the heating. He'd take us on long walks, and when we'd come home all rosy-cheeked, that freezing old place seemed nice and warm again."

Ben piled on a couple of logs. "Sounds like the army," he said. "I think they call it *character building*."

Leigh gazed out of the window. "I wouldn't mind a walk, you know. I've been cooped up for days. D'you feel like some air?"

"Sure, you can show me around your estate."

She shut the heavy back door and put the key in the pocket of her tan suede coat. She raised her face to the sun, closed her eyes, and smiled sadly.

They walked in silence for a while. The grounds of the house sloped gently away over lawns and an ornamental lake into a rambling stretch of woodland. They followed a path that was strewn with fallen twigs and dead leaves softened by the winter rains, and passed through an evergreen tunnel of arching cherry laurels. Cold bright sunlight sparkled through the gaps in the canopy overhead.

"This is my favorite part," she said with a smile, pointing ahead. As they turned a corner the lush green tunnel opened up to a clear view across the meadows and a glittering river beyond. Some horses were grazing by the riverbank in the distance.

"Come the summer, I'm going to have some benches put here," Leigh said. "It's such a lovely spot." Her smile faded as she gazed across the valley.

Ben could see her troubled thoughts clouding her eyes. "I know you don't want to go over all this again," he said. "But we need to know what's happening."

She looked down at her feet. "I can't understand it."

"Are you positive they couldn't have been after something in your flat?"

Leigh sighed. "I told you, I only used the place as a base

for the Opera House. I hardly had anything there, I didn't spend much time there."

"And you're absolutely sure that the place was empty when you moved in? There's nothing that could have been left behind by the previous occupants?"

She shook her head. "Like I said, it was all cleaned out when I rented it. No, it's me they're after. Something to do with me, but what it is I . . ."

Ben didn't reply. He reached out his arm and gently squeezed her shoulder, feeling the tension in her muscles. She took a step away from him, breaking the contact.

He looked up at the sky. It was threatening to rain. They'd been walking for almost an hour. "Let's go back," he said.

Gunmetal clouds had passed over the sun's face by the time they had walked the path back through the woods and up the gently sloping lawns to the manor. A thin, steady drizzle was drifting on the rising wind. Leigh opened the back door, and Ben led the way up the passage to the kitchen, where he'd left his backpack. He was reaching for his phone when he froze. His eyes narrowed.

Leigh saw his expression. "What's up?"

He looked at her hard and pressed a finger to his lips. She made a gesture to say, I don't understand.

He said nothing. He reached out, grasped her by the upper arm, and jerked her roughly across the room. He tore open the door of the walk-in pantry and pushed her inside.

"Ben . . ." Leigh's eyes were wide with fear and confusion.

"Don't move. Don't make a sound," he whispered, and shut her in.

He looked around him and quietly grabbed the heavy cast-iron skillet from the range. He slipped through the gap in the kitchen door and moved fast and silently up the paneled hallway.

He found them in the study. There were two of them, their backs to him. They were masked and armed. Identical combat jackets and semiautomatic pistols in Cordura rigs.

They'd been busy. Packing cases were overturned, their contents spilled across the bare floorboards. Music manuscripts were scattered everywhere. Letters, business documents. The guy on the left was rifling through a trunk, tossing clothes in a rough pile on the floor. The guy on the right was kneeling near the fireplace and using a double-edged killing knife to slice open a large cardboard box that was wrapped up in brown packing tape.

Neither one heard Ben step into the room.

The cardboard box fell open, and the contents tumbled out—papers, books, folders. The man reached inside and pulled out a slim box file. He studied it for a moment and waved it at his companion.

The guy on the left was half turned round when Ben buried the edge of the iron skillet in his skull. It went in like an ax, and he dropped to the floor with his legs kicking.

The other threw aside the box file and went for his pistol. Ben was faster. He hit him a blow to the throat that was meant to disorientate rather than kill. He kept a pincer grip on the man's windpipe as he went down. "Who are you working for?" he asked quietly. As he spoke he took the gun from the man's trembling fingers with his free hand. It was a big, heavy pistol. A Para-Ordnance .45, high-capacity magazine, stainless steel, cocked and locked. It was shiny and smelled of fresh gun oil.

Ben was a believer in simple, straightforward interrogation. He flicked off the safety, then pressed the muzzle of the .45 against the intruder's temple. "Tell me quick, or you're dead," he said.

The man's eyes rolled in the oval slits in his mask. Ben let some pressure off his windpipe. He looked down at the slim box file. It was lying on the floor, faceup. Written across its front in neat marker pen were the words *The Mozart Letter*.

Ben pressed the gun harder into the man's head. "What's this about?" he asked.

The door crashed open. A third intruder burst inside the room shooting. The room was filled with gunfire. Ben had nowhere to take cover. He felt the shock wave of a heavy bullet passing close by his head.

He grasped his prisoner by the collar and swung his body up and round in front of him, using him as a shield. The man screamed and jerked as bullets thudded into him. His thrashing foot caught the box file. It burst open and papers flew into the fireplace.

Ben aimed the Para-Ordnance over the man's shoulder. The pistol kicked and boomed twice in his hand. The attacker twisted, slammed against the wall, slumped to the floor.

Ben let the dead body of his human shield fall. The contents of the file were strewn across the hearth. Paper curled and blackened as the flames spread hungrily. The corner of the rug was burning. He stamped out the flames and kicked the blackened fragments of paper away from the fireplace.

He strode across the study and squatted down to examine the third man. His mask, weapon, and clothing were identical to the others'. The first bullet had caught him in the chest. The second, rising on recoil, had taken the top off his head. Ben sighed. None of the three would be doing much talking to him.

He tensed. A door had slammed somewhere in the house. Leigh? He sprang to his feet and ran out across the wide hallway. He could hear shouts and the noise of a diesel engine revving hard outside. Rapid footsteps across the gravel at the front of the house. He ran up the passage into the front entrance hall, slipping on the polished parquet. He ripped the front door open just in time to see a fourth intruder jump into the Transit van. It took off down the drive with its wheels spinning.

Ben raised the .45 and punched a line of six holes across the back doors of the van. The rear windows shattered.

The van slewed and kept going. Ben fired three more rounds at the tires, the target diminishing now. A plastic hubcap spun across the gravel. The van disappeared down the drive. Then it was gone.

Ben swore and ran back into the house. He hurried to the kitchen and opened the pantry door.

Leigh flew at him with a scream and swung the long steel Maglite torch at his head with all her strength. If it had landed, it would have put him into a coma. He dodged it and caught her wrist. She was panting. Her eyes were wild. She didn't seem to recognize him.

He shook her. "Leigh—it's me. It's Ben."

She came to her senses and looked up at him. Her face was white.

"We've had some unexpected visitors," he said. "You're safe now. But we need to leave quickly. More of them will be coming back here." He turned to head out of the room.

She was shaking. "Where are you going?"

"Get your things together," he said. He picked up his bag and carried it to the study. Closing the door behind him, he knelt and gathered the fire-damaged papers. He sighed as some of them crumbled in his hands.

Among the documents was a small padded envelope, about four inches square, light and slim. One of its corners was singed from the fire, but otherwise it was undamaged. It hadn't been opened. It was addressed to Leigh in Monte Carlo. The postmark was Vienna—stamped just the day after Oliver's death.

Ben tossed everything together into the box file. Across THE MOZART LETTER label, a spatter of blood was still wet and glistening. He unbuckled the straps of his bag and put the file inside.

He collected the two identical .45 pistols from the dead men and took the spare magazines from the pouches on their tactical rigs. Clearly, these men had been professionals. He searched them. No papers, no ID of any kind.

He looked up to see the door handle turning. Before he could stop her, Leigh had stepped into the study.

She froze as she took it all in. The three dead men lying there with their eyes glazed and staring through the holes in their ski masks, arms and legs outflung. The pool of blood on the floor. The long smear of it on the far wall. The handle of the skillet still protruding from the head of one of the corpses. She reeled, swaying a little on her feet.

"I didn't mean for you to see this," he said, steadying her. He took her by the elbow and guided her out of the room.

"Did you do this?" Her voice was barely audible.

"Look, we haven't got time to discuss it now. Are you ready to leave?" She nodded weakly. He checked his watch. Ten minutes had gone by since the attackers had fled. "We'll have to cut across the meadow and see where we can get some transport."

"I have a car here," Leigh said. "It's in the garage out back."

10.

AUSTRIA

Eve locked the bedroom door behind her and leaned against it for a few moments with her eyes tightly shut. How long had the big cop been tailing her? What was his name? She remembered. Kinski. Detective Markus Kinski.

Two big screwups. They wouldn't be happy with her. First, she should have left the café the moment she recognized him. She should have acted casual, walked away. Taken a cab and got out of there before she left any traces.

The traces were the second big mistake. She'd failed to carry enough cash on her, the way they'd always told her to. She'd panicked in her rush to get out of there and had had to use the Erika Mann credit card. That cover would be blown now. Kinski was bound to chase up the false name, and when it led him down a blind alley, he'd become even more suspicious. She'd been lucky this time and managed to lose him—but if he was on to her, he'd be back.

Eve's neck and shoulders felt rigid, and her mouth was dry. What was he doing following her? Was he sniffing around the Llewellyn case again? *Why would he?* It had been closed months ago, and as far as the police were concerned it had stayed closed. Only a small number of people knew differently.

She reached inside her handbag and brought out the tiny Black Widow .22 Magnum revolver. She turned the miniature stainless-steel pistol over in her hands. It was only six inches long and weighed just eight ounces, but the five slim cartridges in its cylinder would drill straight through a man's skull. She'd never shot anyone with it, but she knew how to use it.

She wondered what it would feel like to point the gun at a living person and pull the trigger. She'd do it if she had to. She was in too precarious a position to risk exposure.

Maybe it would have been better to let Kinski follow her, she thought. She could have lured him somewhere. Used her charms. That was something she *had* done before. Then killing him would have been easy.

She thought of Oliver Llewellyn and wondered how long it would be before they caught up with the sister. There was no escape from these people. Eve knew that.

She walked to the bed, still holding the little pistol. There was something lying on her pillow, red velvet against the white silk. It was a jewel case. She opened it. It was the Lalique Art Nouveau brooch she'd admired in the antiques shop window in Vienna the week before. It was exquisite. Gold, inlaid with diamonds and sapphires. There was a note inside, neatly folded. She opened it.

It was from him. *Wear this tonight,* it read.

Eve closed the jewel case and tossed it away across the bed. She lay down as the darkness closed over her.

Slowly, she brought the Black Widow revolver up until she could feel the coldness of its muzzle against her temple. She closed her eyes and listened to the *snick-snack* of its oiled action as she thumbed back the little hammer. Just a flick of a finger and she could be free of the whole thing.

Her fingers relaxed around the gun, and she let out a long breath.

She couldn't do it.

No escape.

11.

OXFORDSHIRE

The TVR Tuscan skidded out of the drive, and Ben accelerated hard away from Langton Hall. He didn't know where he was going. Traffic was thin on the country roads, and he drove fast for six miles, keeping the revs high and the gears low, constantly checking the mirrors. He saw nothing.

He pulled up in a lay-by and turned off the engine. Leigh was sitting quietly beside him, ashen-faced. "Are you all right?" he asked. He twisted round and grabbed his backpack from behind the seat. There was still some whiskey in his flask. "I know you don't like this stuff very much," he said, trying to smile, "but it'll take the edge off."

Leigh took a sip of the whiskey and winced at the burn on her lips. She coughed. "Thanks." She screwed the cap of the flask back on and handed it back to him.

He finished what was left. "What are you doing?" he asked as she took out her phone.

"Calling the police."

He grabbed the phone from her before she could finish dialing 999. "I don't think that's a good idea," he said.

"Why?"

"Until last night nobody knew where we were. Then you told the police where to find us, and the next thing we have company."

"What are you saying?"

"I'm saying I don't like coincidences," he replied. "And there's also the slight problem of three dead men lying in your house, Leigh. I killed them, and you're an accomplice. I'm not sticking around to be arrested." He took the file out of the bag and showed her. "This is what they were looking for," he said. The spots of blood on the label were turning russety brown.

"*The Mozart Letter*? Oliver's work? But . . ." She looked at him helplessly. "Why would anyone want—"

"I think it's time we had a look at this stuff," he said. He pushed the backpack to his feet with a dull metallic clunk from the guns inside, and rested the box file on his lap against the steering wheel. He popped the catch and opened the lid of the file.

"What happened?" Leigh gasped. "They're all burned."

The small padded envelope fell out and landed in the footwell. Ben ignored it and sifted carefully through the rest of the file's contents, trying not to damage the brittle papers any further.

Some of the documents had been handwritten, some computer printed. Many were barely legible any longer, just singed fragments showing names, dates, and scraps of what looked like historical information. Here and there he could make out the name Mozart.

Leigh reached across and lifted out a badly singed sheet. It crumbled into pieces as she lifted it. "This was Oliver's writing," she said, biting her lip. "One of the notes he sent me during his travels."

"They're ruined," Ben muttered. He laid the fragments back inside the file and closed the lid. He turned to her. "So what's this about, Leigh? What did they want with Oliver's stuff?"

"How should I know?"

"I don't understand," he said. "You told me last night you'd had the notes for months. Now all of a sudden someone's very interested in them. Why? What was in here? And how would they know you even had them?"

She looked blank.

"Who else knows about this book project?"

There was sudden realization in her eyes. "Oh *shit*."

"What?"

She turned to look at him. "About two million people know about it."

"What the hell are you on about?"

"The TV interview. I was on a BBC music program talking about next year's European tour. I told them about my plan to carry on with the book. How Oliver had been sending me his research material, right up until the day he died, and that I'd always been too upset to look at any of it."

"And when was this program on?"

She made a face. "Two days before they tried to snatch me in London."

Ben felt something resting against his foot and remembered the fallen package. He leaned down and picked it up.

"God. I recognize this," Leigh whispered, taking it from him. "It's the package I told you about. The last one he ever sent me." She turned it over in her hands. "It was there waiting for me after the funeral. I had Pam put it in the box with the rest of the stuff."

"It's got to be opened now," he told her.

"I know."

Ben tore open the singed envelope. Inside the thin layer of bubble wrap, undamaged by the heat of the fire, was a CD case. He took it out. "It's *music*," he said, showing her the cover. "Mozart's opera *The Magic Flute*. Why did he send you this?"

She sighed. "It's mine. He'd borrowed it from me. He must have been returning it."

"So that's all it was."

She slumped in her seat. "What's happening, Ben?"

He opened the CD case. The yellow-and-silver Deutsche Grammophon disc had come loose from its fastening. It dropped in his lap. Behind it was another disc. Printed on its surface was the legend CD-RECORDABLE.

Underneath it, in marker pen, was an urgent scrawl:

Leigh—Do NOT run this disc under ANY circumstances.
Keep it hidden, I'm coming home.
Olly.

"What the . . ." Leigh reached out and pressed a button on the dashboard. The car's CD player lit up. "Let's play it."

"It's not an audio disc," Ben said. "We'll need a computer."

An hour later they were checked into a small nearby hotel as Mr. and Mrs. Connors. On the way there, Ben had made a quick shopping detour. He ripped the protective wrapping off the new laptop and laid it down on the hotel room table. In a few minutes he had the machine set up and ready to play the disc. He took the CD-ROM out of the *Magic Flute* case and inserted it into the computer's disc drive. The machine whirred into action, and after a few seconds a window opened on the flat screen.

As he waited for the disc to load, Ben went to the minibar and found two miniatures of Bell's Scotch. He cracked them open and poured them both into a single glass.

Leigh sat at the desk and peered at the screen. "These all

seem to be photo files taken in different parts of Europe," she said. "It's like a photo diary of Olly's research trip."

Ben frowned. "Why would he put a CD of travel snapshots into your Mozart box?"

"I've no idea." She clicked, and the face of an old man appeared on the screen. He was in his late seventies. His face was gray and deeply scoured with wrinkles, but there was an inquisitive twinkle to the eyes. Behind him was a tall open-fronted bookcase, and Ben could make out titles of volumes bearing the names of famous composers—Chopin, Beethoven, Elgar.

"Who's that?" Ben asked.

"I don't know him," she said. She clicked again. The old man disappeared, and a new picture filled the screen. It was of a white stone building that looked to Ben like a small temple or some kind of monument. It had a domed top and a classical frontage. "This I recognize," she said. "Ravenna, Italy. That's Dante's tomb. I've been there."

"Why would Oliver go to Italy if his research was in Vienna?"

"I don't know."

"Did Mozart spend a lot of time in Italy?"

She thought for a moment. "If I remember rightly from music school, I think he spent some time in Bologna in his teens," she said. "But apart from that, I don't think he did more than travel there occasionally."

"This isn't helping us," Ben said. "Move on to the next one."

Click. The next picture showed Oliver at a party with two pretty girls, one on each arm. They were kissing him on the cheeks as he happily toasted the camera with a cocktail.

Leigh clicked again. It was another shot from the same party. This time Oliver was sitting at a piano. On the double stool next to him sat a younger man, mid-twenties or so, and the two were playing a duet together. They seemed to be having a good time, Oliver's face caught in mid-laugh as he hammered the keys. Around the piano there were women in party dresses, leaning on it, watching him play, smiling at him, smiling at one another, drinks in their hands. Faces were glowing. It was a very natural shot of happy-looking people enjoying themselves.

Leigh couldn't look at it for long. She clicked and moved on.

A shot of a snowy village flashed up. There were trees and mountains in the background, laced with white. Leigh frowned. "Switzerland?"

Ben studied it. "Could be. Or it could be Austria." He reached across, clicked, and scrolled down to reveal the properties of the picture. It had been taken three days before Oliver's death.

Leigh sighed. "Still doesn't tell us anything."

Ben walked away from the desk and left her to browse through the rest of the photographs. He went over to the bed, sat down, and drained his glass in one swallow. Beside him, spread out on sheets of newspaper laid across the bed, were the charred remnants of the box file's contents. Sifting through them gingerly, he turned over one of the papers and winced as its edges crumbled away.

Underneath it he saw the burned, tattered remains of a document that looked different from the others. The fire had eaten away most of the text in black-edged bites that looked like missing pieces from a jigsaw puzzle. Nearly all the rest was so charred that the German handwriting was barely readable. All that was left were a few disjointed phrases that meant nothing to him.

For an instant Ben thought he was holding the original, and he caught his breath. No. It was just a photocopy.

It was the Mozart letter. Richard Llewellyn's discovery. Oliver had told the story so often that Ben still remembered it clearly.

Many years ago, the Llewellyn antique-piano-restoration workshop and showroom had been situated on a busy street in the center of Builth Wells. After the death of his wife, Margaret, in 1987, when Leigh had been thirteen and Oliver seventeen, Richard Llewellyn had gone into decline and taken his business with him. He was drinking too much to do his work well. Custom had tailed off dramatically. Then one day a chance find in the attic of an old house promised to change Richard Llewellyn's fortunes forever.

The decaying pianoforte had been made in the early nineteenth century by the celebrated Viennese craftsman Josef Bohm. It had traveled to Britain sometime in the 1930s and fallen out of use a long time ago. It hadn't been stored very carefully. Woodworm had infected much of the casework, and it needed a major overhaul to get it back into prime condition. But even in that poor state it was one of the most beautiful instruments that Richard Llewellyn had ever come across, and he was excited by the price it might fetch at auction once it was restored—maybe ten thousand pounds, maybe even more. He put away the port and sherry bottles and got to work.

He'd never finished the job. It was while restoring one of the instrument's legs that Llewellyn had made his discovery. The leg was hollow, and inside it he found a rolled-up document, old and yellowed and bound with a ribbon. It was a letter written in German, dated November 1791.

When Richard Llewellyn had seen the signature at the bottom, his heart had almost given out.

The last surviving letter written by Wolfgang Amadeus

Mozart before his death just weeks later. How it had found its way into the hollow piano leg was a mystery, and would remain that way forever. All Llewellyn knew was that he'd found a historic treasure that was going to change his life.

At the time, the discovery had been all Oliver could talk about. His father had taken his prize to London for the scrutiny of expert musicologists and antiquarians. But his vision of the fortune the Mozart letter was going to earn him crumbled away when the experts declared it a fake.

"Maybe it wasn't, though," Ben said out loud.

Leigh turned with a quizzical look. "Maybe what?"

"Your dad's letter. Is it possible it wasn't a fake after all, and that's why these people are after you? What would it be worth?"

She shook her head. "Dad sold it, remember? Maybe you don't. Years ago, about the time we stopped seeing each other."

"Someone bought it, even though nobody believed it was genuine?"

"Yeah." She smiled. "Just when Dad was becoming completely despondent about the whole thing, this crazy collector got in touch with him. An Italian music scholar. He made an offer for the letter. It wasn't the kind of money Dad had dreamed of, but he accepted it right away. Then the Italian said he wanted to buy the old piano, too. It was only half restored, but the Italian paid top dollar for it anyway. I remember it being crated up and taken away in a big van. Then Dad was solvent again. He was still hurting over the response from the experts, but at least he had some money in his pocket. That was how I was able to go to New York, to study at the music academy."

"What was the Italian's name?" Ben asked.

"I don't remember," she said after a moment's thought.

"It was a long time ago, and I never met him. Oliver did. He said he was ancient. I suppose he'd be dead by now."

Ben put down the fragment of the photocopied letter and sifted through some of the other documents. Something caught his eye, and he looked more closely.

The fire had eaten away the right margin of the lined notepaper. The scribbled writing on the page was Oliver's. Ben's eye followed a line that was written in large bold capitals, triple-underlined as though out of frustration. The end of the sentence was burned away where the paper had darkened from yellow to brown to crumbled ash. "'What is the Order of R—?'" he read aloud. "Do you know what that might be?"

"I haven't a clue."

He chucked the sheet down with the rest of the papers. "Shit. What a mess."

Leigh had finished going through the photographs. There was just one file left on the disc. He leaned on the back of her chair as she opened it up.

"It's not a photo file," he said. "It's a video clip."

12.

NEAR VIENNA

It was a murky, foggy midafternoon, and getting cold. The lake was beginning to freeze over, and light powdery snow was settling on its surface. Four hundred yards out across the thin ice, the pine forest was a black jagged silhouette against the gray sky.

Markus Kinski clapped his hands together and pulled up his jacket collar. He leaned back against the side of the four-wheel drive, remembering the last time he'd been here. The day the foreigner had been brought out from under the ice.

The year was coming full circle, winter closing in again. So what was he doing back here? Maybe Monika had been right when she'd said he was obsessive by nature.

For a moment he thought about his wife. She'd been gone nearly three years now. Too young to die. Misdiagnosed twice. He missed her.

He sighed, and his mind drifted back to the Llewellyn case. It had been shut months ago, but the damn thing haunted him. There was something not right about it. It had been closed too neatly, dealt with too efficiently, even by perfectionist Austrian standards. Things just didn't *happen* like that. It had taken him months to get it out of his head, and then just when he was beginning to forget about the whole damn thing, who should pop up out of nowhere but Madeleine Laurent. *Or whoever she was.*

So far, the search for Laurent was going nowhere. The Erika Mann credit card had been real enough, but who was she? The address from the credit company had led him to a deserted warehouse in an industrial zone of the city. No big surprise.

So now there was more to add to the bunch of unanswered, nagging questions that already clustered around the Llewellyn case.

Madeleine Laurent wasn't the only mystery connected to the drowned man. There was the matter of Fred Meyer, too. Meyer had a lot in common with Llewellyn. Too much. Both musicians, both pianists, both dead. Just a few kilometers apart, and both on the same night. Llewellyn's watch, an old clockwork relic, had stopped when the water hit it, and they pretty much knew the exact time of death. When they'd found Fred Meyer hanging in his student digs, he'd been dead about twelve hours. Which meant the two pianists had met their end within a short time of each other. Meyer first, probably, then Llewellyn soon after.

There'd been no suicide note in the Meyer case, no apparent motive. Interviews with family had thrown up no history of depression. As with most students, money was tight, but he'd been careful and there was no significant debt hanging over him. No emotional problems, either, and from all accounts he was getting on well with his steady girlfriend. He'd recently landed a job teaching music at a school in Salzburg and was looking forward to starting after the summer, when his studies at the Vienna Conservatoire were over. Life had been pretty good for Fred Meyer. *Until he'd found himself on the end of a rope.*

Okay, coincidences happened, and maybe there wasn't anything to connect one musician's foolish accident to another's pointless suicide. At least, that was what Kinski had been trying to make himself believe over the last few months. Just one other detail stuck in his craw, like a bread crumb that wouldn't go down. It was the matter of the opera tickets found in Meyer's room.

Kinski sighed and looked out across the misty lake. The ice was still too thin to walk on, but in a few weeks it would have thickened enough to take the weight of a man. He'd seen people out here skating on the lake sometimes.

He tried to imagine what it would be like to fall through ice. The shock of the freezing water, enough to stop a man's heart. The current carrying you away under the solid ice sheet, so hard it would take a sledgehammer to fight your way back to the air just a couple of inches away.

He thought about all the different types of death he'd seen, and the looks on the faces of all the dead people his work had brought him into contact with. The look on Oliver Llewellyn's blue, half-frozen face had been one of the worst things he'd ever seen. For months afterwards he only had to close his eyes and it was there staring at him. No shutting it out. Standing here by the lakeside was bringing that image back sharp in his mind.

He glanced at his watch. He'd been here too long. His misgivings about the case seemed to hold him here, when he should be getting back. He'd told Helga, Clara's sitter, that he'd pick the kid up from school himself today for a change. She was growing up fast, coming on nine and a half now, and he was missing a lot of it. It would be a nice surprise for her. He was determined to spend the evening doing something fun, like taking her skating, or going to a movie. He threw everything at his child—the private bilingual school that would give her the best education, the violin lessons, the expensive toys. Clara had everything, except time with her father.

He heard footsteps coming up behind him in the frosty grass. He turned. "Hey, Max, where were you?"

The dog sat on his haunches and looked up expectantly with his big black head slightly cocked to one side, the rubber ball clenched in his powerful jaws. The gentle Rottweiler was old for his breed, but Kinski kept him in shape.

"Give it, then," Kinski said gently. "One throw, and then we're out of here. Should never have come here in the first place," he added.

The dog dropped the ball delicately in his hand. It was slimy with saliva and mud. "You don't know how lucky you are," Kinski said to him. "Chasing balls all day would suit me just fine. Better than the shit I have to deal with, believe me, my friend." He tossed the ball away into the long grass and watched as the dog thundered after it, sending up a spray of frosty mud.

Max hunted around for the ball, snuffling in the reeds. He looked hesitant, pawing the ground and turning his big head this way and that.

"Don't tell me you've lost it again," Kinski called out in exasperation. He walked over and searched among the reeds for a glimpse of blue rubber among the frosty grass and mud. The dog had flattened a lot of the rushes searching for the ball. "Nice going, Max," he muttered. "You know, those fucking things cost eight euros each, and how many is that you've lost now? *Du Arschloch.*"

There were cigarette butts in the mud. Kinski drew his hand away, thinking of hypodermics. Fucking junkies shitting the place up.

But then he looked more closely. He picked one up and examined it. It wasn't a cigarette butt. It was a spent cartridge case. The brass was tarnished and dull, green in places. The rusted primer was indented in the middle, where the firing pin had hit. Around the bottom of the case's rim were stamped in tiny letters the words 9 MM PARABELLUM—CBC.

Who's been firing 9 mm out here? Kinski thought. He rummaged in the grass. Max stood over him, watching fixedly. Kinski bent back a frosty clump and found another. It was just the same. Then another, and then two more, lying half buried in the yellowed roots. He pulled the grass back in fistfuls and kept finding more. After three minutes of searching he'd gathered up twenty-one of them, using the end of a ballpoint to pick them up and lay them in a little pile.

Twenty-one was a lot of brass. All lying in one spot. That meant a single shooter, firing all the shots from a fixed position. Too many rounds for a standard pistol, unless he was using an extended magazine. It was more likely a burst from a fully automatic weapon, about a second and a half from a typical submachine gun. Serious. Disconcerting.

He examined each cartridge case carefully in turn on the end of his pen, careful not to handle them. They all had the same scrape marks where they'd been slotted into a tight-fitting magazine, and the same slight dent on the lip where they'd been violently spat through the ejector port. The scent of cordite was long gone. He dropped the cases one by one in a small plastic bag and stored it in his jacket pocket. He straightened up. He'd forgotten the ball. He estimated the throw from the ejector and tried to figure out where the shooter might have been standing.

A thought began to form in his mind. There was nobody about. He reached down and brushed the dog's head pensively with his fingers. "Come, boy." They walked back to the car. He opened the hatch, and Max bounded inside, tongue lolling. The spare wheel was strapped to the inside wheel arch, and he unfastened it. He rolled it back down to the lakeside.

The fog was thickening all the time, and when Kinski sent the spare wheel trundling out across the frozen lake all he could see was a fuzzy patch of blackness against the gray ice. The wheel rolled to a halt, then fell over and lay still. The ice held its weight.

He reached inside his jacket and popped open the thumb strap of his holster. He flipped off the safety on his service SIG Sauer P226, looked around him, then fired at the ice where the wheel lay. The flat report of the 9 mm pistol jabbed painfully at his eardrums and echoed far across the lake. He fired again, and again, then waited.

The ice cracked. Fifteen yards from the shore, the spare wheel slipped into the water with a gurgle.

Kinski wasn't thinking about the cost of replacing an expensive Mercedes wheel. He was thinking about the weight of a man. Thicker ice would take more cracking. How much more? Would twenty-one rounds of 9 mm do it? He felt in his pocket and heard the dull jangle of the spent cases that his gut was now telling him had been lying here since last January.

13.

OXFORDSHIRE

The video clip was shaky, and the picture quality was poor and grainy. The camera panned slowly around a big stone-walled room that was lit orange-gold by hundreds of candles. Long shadows lay across the black-and-white-tiled floor. Three thick stone pillars stood in a wide-spaced triangle around the edges of the room, reaching to the vaulted ceiling. Against the far wall stood a raised platform, looking like a small stage. Above it, a golden sculpture of a ram's head with long, curled horns glittered in the flickering light.

Leigh frowned. "What the hell is this place?"

"I can hear something," Ben muttered. He turned up the volume on the laptop. The sound was the heavy breathing of whoever had been filming. Suddenly, the camera whipped sideways and the picture became confused. "*Oh, fuck,*" said a frightened voice, close into the microphone.

"That's Oliver's voice," Leigh whispered. She was gripping the edge of the table with white fingers.

They watched. The camera righted itself. A dark, craggy edge obscured a third of the picture. "He's hiding behind a pillar," Ben said.

Some people were coming into the room. Blurred at first, the picture jerky, then sharpening up as the autofocus kicked in. The men filtered in through an archway. There were twelve or fifteen of them, all wearing black suits. The camera retreated farther behind the pillar.

"Olly, what were you *doing*?" Leigh said with a sob in her voice.

Now the men were arranging themselves in a semicircle around the raised platform. They all stood in the same way, like soldiers standing at attention with their feet together and their arms clasped behind their backs. Their faces were hard to make out. The nearest was standing only a few feet from where Oliver was hiding. The camera hovered on the man's back, traveled up to his neck and his cropped sandy hair. It autofocused on his ear. It was mangled and scarred, as though it had once been half torn off and sewn back on.

Ben turned his gaze on the platform, straining to make out the details. He realized that what he was looking at was an altar. It was the focus of the room, illuminated by dozens of candles set in recesses in the wall. The center of whatever was about to happen. It was like some kind of religious ceremony. But none that he'd ever seen before.

In the middle of the altar was an upright wooden post, maybe a foot and a half thick and about eight feet high, rough and unvarnished. Lengths of chain hung from it, two of them, thick and heavy, fastened to a riveted steel belt around the top of it.

Now there was movement. A tall iron door behind the altar swung open. Three more men came into the large room. Two were wearing black hoods. The third seemed to be their prisoner. They were clutching his arms. He was struggling. They dragged him across the platform to the altar.

The camera wobbled, and the heavy breathing was quickening. In the background, the prisoner's cries were echoing off the stone walls.

"I don't think you should see this," Ben said. He could feel his own heartbeat beginning to race. He reached for the Stop button.

"Let it play on," she snapped back.

The men in black hoods shoved the prisoner against the wooden post and manacled him to the chains. His cries were louder now.

One of the hooded men stepped forward with something in his hand. He went up to the prisoner and raised his hands up to the man's face. He had his back to the camera, and it was hard to see what was happening. The prisoner's screams were becoming shriller, and he was struggling wildly against the chains.

Then the hooded man stepped away. There was something hanging from the prisoner's mouth. It was a thin rope or cable. As the hooded man stepped away the cable was pulled tauter, and Ben realized with a horrified lurch what was happening. The camera was beginning to shake badly.

"Oh, *Jesus*!" Leigh exclaimed in horror. "They put a hook through his tongue!"

The hooded man stopped and turned to face the audience. The cable was pulled as tight as it would go. The prisoner couldn't scream anymore. His tongue was stretched six inches out of his mouth. His eyes were bulging, his body quaking.

The second hooded man came forward. Something glinted in the candlelight. He raised the ceremonial dagger above his head.

It came down in a flashing arc. The prisoner's head was thrown backwards as his tongue was sliced off. The cable snaked away like a bowstring with the glistening tongue attached. Blood spurted from the prisoner's mouth, and his head jerked from side to side, his eyes rolling.

But his suffering was cut short. The hooded knifeman stepped forward again. The dagger came in low and stuck deep into the man's abdomen. The blade sawed and stabbed like a butcher's knife, slicing a path from groin to rib cage.

When his guts began to spill, even Ben had to look away.

14.

It had taken a long time to calm Leigh afterwards. Eventually, the tranquilizers began to take effect, and she lay sleeping on the hotel bed, her black hair spread across the pillow and her body rising and falling slowly.

Ben covered her with a blanket and sat beside her on the edge of the bed, watching over her and thinking hard. Then he stood up, went back to the desk, and watched the video clip again.

He watched it three times, pausing it frequently to study the details. He watched it right to the end. After the victim was disemboweled the cameraman had had enough. The picture went jerky, dark, then jerky again. He could hear Oliver's ragged breathing. He was running.

Ben kept pausing the clip, staring at the screen. Stone walls. Some kind of staircase. The picture was crazy, but by pausing frame by frame he could just about make it out. As Oliver ran on, the rough stone walls disappeared, and he seemed to be in what looked like a very opulent house. A doorway, then a corridor. Shiny wood panels. A painting, brightly illuminated by a lamp above its frame. Ben paused the clip and studied it closely.

It was hard to tell, but the painting seemed to show some kind of meeting. The setting was a big hall. There were columns that looked a lot like the ones in the room where the victim had been executed. The same tiles on the floor. The men in the painting wore wigs and were dressed in what looked like eighteenth-century clothes—brocade jackets and silk stockings. There were symbols around the walls, but he couldn't make them out.

He let the clip run on. Oliver's breath was rasping out of the speaker as he staggered down the corridor. He stopped, swung round as if looking back to see if someone was following him. Nobody was.

Ben paused the clip again. He could see something. An alcove in the wall. Inside the alcove stood a statue that looked Egyptian, like a pharaoh's death mask.

Then the clip came to an end. Oliver must have turned off the camera. Ben was left staring at a black screen.

He struggled to understand what he'd seen. He clicked on the file properties. The video clip had been created at 9:26 on the night Oliver died.

None of this made sense. The official version of the story, that Oliver had been drunkenly messing about on the lake with some woman he'd picked up at a party, was impossible to reconcile with the fact that, not long before his death, he'd witnessed a brutal ritualistic murder. Would Oliver have been capable of putting such a thing out of his mind to go off and enjoy himself? Who would?

Ben ran over what he knew. Oliver had witnessed a crime carried out by some highly organized and very dangerous people. He'd had evidence, and he'd been desperate to hide it. Soon after he'd posted the CD to Leigh, he'd drowned in the frozen lake. The investigation into his death had been a little too rushed, a little too sketchy. And ever since Leigh had mentioned to a TV audience that she was in possession of Oliver's notes, someone had been out to do her harm.

He looked down at Leigh as she slept and resisted the impulse to brush a lock of hair away from her face. Just as she'd been starting to come to terms with Oliver's accident, she was going to have to go through the whole thing again—only this time knowing, almost for certain, that her brother's death had been no accident. He hadn't died messing around in a cheerfully drunken state. He'd died in fear. Someone had coldly and calculatedly ended his life.

Who did it, Oliver?

Ben moved away from the bed and settled into the armchair in the far corner of the hotel room. He reached for his Turkish cigarettes, flipped the wheel of his Zippo lighter, and leaned back as he inhaled the strong, thick smoke. He closed his eyes, feeling fatigue wash over him. He hadn't had a proper night's sleep in four weeks.

His thoughts wandered as he smoked. He recalled fragments of old memories. He remembered Oliver's face as a younger man, the sound of his old friend's voice.

And he remembered the day, all those years ago, when Oliver had saved his life.

It had been the coldest winter he could remember. After three years of army service, Lance Corporal Benedict Hope had traveled to Hereford in the Welsh borders, along with 138 other hopefuls from other regiments for what he knew was going to be the toughest endurance test of his life: selection for 22 Special Air Service, the most elite fighting force in the British Army.

Quite why Oliver had wanted to come along with him, Ben didn't know. For the food, Oliver had joked. The 22 SAS was famous for the mountains of roast beef and lamb chops on which selection candidates feasted before being sent into the hellish Sickener 1, the first phase of selection training.

As the convoy of trucks left the base in Hereford at dawn on day one and headed deep into the Cambrian Mountains of mid-Wales in driving snow, Oliver had been one of the only men able to joke about the long day ahead. Ben had sat in the corner of the rocking Bedford, cradling his rifle and steeling himself for the nightmare of physical and mental torture that would mark the start of the toughest few weeks of his life. He knew that the small minority who survived the initial selection process would be subjected to fourteen more torturous weeks of advanced-weapons and survival instruction, a parachute course, jungle-warfare training, language and initiative testing, a one-thousand-yard swim in uniform, and interrogation-resistance exercises designed to stress a man's spirit past the limits of endurance. Only the very best would get through to be awarded the coveted winged dagger badge and entry into the legendary regiment. Some years, nobody got through at all.

As it turned out, Sickener 1 was every bit as tough as he'd expected, and a bit more. With each freezing-cold dawn the number of exhausted men setting off for another round of torture dwindled a little further. Base camp each night was a huddled circle of silent bodies under dripping canvas. Oliver's expectations of a nightly feast had been quickly dashed, and his morale had plummeted accordingly. That was the idea.

The following week was way beyond even Ben's expectations. Weather conditions were the worst in years. Pain, injury, and absolute demoralization had reduced the 138 men to only a dozen. During a twenty-hour march through a howling blizzard, an SAS major who had volunteered for the course to prove to himself he still had what it took in his mid-thirties had collapsed and been found dead in a snowdrift.

But Ben had willed himself to go on, trudging through the pain barrier and finding new heights of endurance. His only stops were to drink a little melted snow now and then and to take a bite from one of the rock-hard Mars Bars he'd stowed in his backpack. The rush from the sugar gave his depleted body the energy to keep going. In his mind he fought a furious battle to quell the desire to give up this madness. He could end the agony at any time, just by deciding to. Sometimes the temptation was unbearable. That was also the idea, and he knew it. Every moment was a test.

And it didn't get easier. Every night the exhaustion was worse. Back at camp he meticulously soaked his socks in olive oil to ease the torment of blistered feet, and he passed each day in a trance of grim determination as the marches got longer and their packs got heavier. All that mattered was the next step forward. Then the next. He kept his mind clear of the distance still ahead of him. And the pain that was only going to get worse.

By the fourth day of week three there were only eight men left. Pausing for breath on a high ridge near the summit of the notorious Pen y Fan Mountain, Ben looked back and could see some of the others as distant green dots laboring across the blanket of snow between the trees far below.

Oliver was thirty yards behind him. Ben waited for him to catch up. It took a while. He was amazed that his friend had gotten this far, but now Oliver was visibly flagging. His steady trudge had deteriorated to a desperate plod and from there to a stagger. He sank to his knees, clutching his rifle. "You go on," he wheezed. "I'm whacked. I'll see you at camp."

Ben looked at him with concern. "Come on, there's just a few miles to go."

"No chance. I can't fucking move another inch."

"I'll stay with you," Ben said, meaning it.

Oliver wiped snow from his eyes as he looked up. He coughed. "You will not," he said. "You need to keep moving. Go. Get out of here."

Ben's feet were stripped raw, and he could feel his clothes stuck to the bleeding sores on his back where his backpack was constantly rubbing. It was all he could do to support his own weight. There was no way he could help Oliver walk very far, let alone carry him. And the slightest sign of hesitation could mean the humiliation of a Return to Unit order. The rules were brutal. They were intended that way. "You'll be okay," he said. "There's an instructor coming up the mountain. He'll take you back."

Oliver waved him on. "Yes, I'll be okay. Now piss off before you get RTU'd. You want the badge, don't you? Don't wait for me."

Racked with guilt now as well as pain, Ben walked on. The wind tore at his smock. He struggled down a near-vertical rocky slope, his boots slipping in the snow. He reached the ice-crusted rim of a collapsed rock mound and saw a movement through the mist of exhaustion. A hooded figure emerged from a clump of pines.

Ben recognized his face. He was a lieutenant of the Royal Fusiliers. Ben hadn't seen him since setting out at dawn. The tough, craggy Londoner had kept himself apart from the others ever since arriving at Hereford, and Ben detected a cold remoteness in his gray eyes that he mistrusted.

"Didn't think you'd make it this far, Hope," he said.

"No? Then you were wrong. Sir."

The lieutenant was watching him with a faint smile. "Got a light?"

"There's no time to sm—"

Suddenly, Ben felt a broad hand shove him hard in the

chest, and he was tumbling down the slope, the weight of his fifty-pound pack dragging him down. He scrabbled for grip, losing his rifle. His legs crashed through thin ice and into the stinking mud of a stagnant bog.

Above him, the lieutenant stared at him for a moment, then trudged on.

Ben was sinking into the bog. He fought to unsaddle his backpack, but the straps were tight around his shoulders, the weight dragging him down deeper. His fingers closed on a clump of ice-frosted reeds, and he pulled hard, kicking back with his legs. The reeds ripped out of the mud with a gurgle, and he sank down another six inches. He felt the cold, soft clay sucking at his waist, gaining another inch every few seconds. He sank in up to his belt, then to the bottom of his rib cage. He splashed weakly in the mud, his shouts deadened by the wind.

Now the cloying bog was drawing him deeper still. He could feel himself sliding steadily down. It was swallowing him. His legs were starting to feel numb. He tried kicking again, but the mud felt heavy, and his legs were starting to become numb and unresponsive. In a few minutes he would start to go hypothermic unless he could get out. He gave up kicking and scrabbled at the bank, his fingers raking through loose mud and bits of coarse, sharp flint. There was no grip, and his strength was ebbing fast. The mud was up to his chest now, and it was getting harder to breathe.

He wasn't going to get out. He was going to die here, sucked down and drowned in this shitty bog. He kicked again. His legs were too weak to move.

"Ben!"

Someone was calling his name. He looked up. Through the drifting snowflakes he could make out the shape of a soldier scrambling down the slope towards him. He blinked, wiped snow from his eyes with his muddy fingers. The figure came closer.

It was Oliver.

"Grab this." Oliver extended the butt of his rifle, and Ben reached out for it, wrapping the webbing sling around his wrist. Oliver braced his feet against the rocks and grunted with effort as he gripped the rifle barrel with both hands and heaved. Ben felt himself rising out of the bog. An inch, then another. The mud made a loud sucking noise. He kicked with his legs again and gained a foothold.

Then he was out, and he gasped as Oliver helped him to crawl up onto solid ground. Ben collapsed onto his stomach and lay panting hard.

Oliver slung the muddy rifle over his shoulder and reached out his hand. "Come on, brother." He grinned. "On your feet. You've got a badge to earn."

Only half a dozen men made it to the end of that day, the rest limping dejected and exhausted for the railway station at Hereford and back to their units.

One of the six weary survivors to return to base in the now almost empty truck was the lieutenant who had shoved Ben down the bank. Ben avoided his eyes and said nothing. There were no witnesses, and he was outranked. To speak out could mean an RTU, or worse. Anyway, people trying to kill him was something he was going to have to get used to if he made it into 22 SAS.

That night, the eve of the endurance march that was to be the final test of initial selection, Oliver produced a smuggled half bottle of whiskey, and the two friends shared it in the dormitory, sitting side by side on a canvas bunk.

"One more day," Ben said, as he felt the welcome sting on his tongue.

"Not for me," Oliver said, staring into his tin mug. His

face was pale, and his eyes ringed with pain. "No badge is worth this. I've had enough."

"You'll make it. You're nearly there."

Oliver chuckled. "I don't give a shit if I make it or not. I'm done with this madness. I've been thinking. I'm not like you, Ben. I'm not a soldier. I'm just a middle-class kid at heart who wanted to rebel against Dad and all the music shit. As soon as I get the chance, I'm leaving the army."

Ben turned to stare at his friend. "What'll you do?"

Oliver shrugged. "Get back into the music, I guess. It's in the blood. Okay, maybe I haven't got the talent Leigh has—she'll go far."

Ben looked uncomfortably at his feet.

Oliver went on. "But I have my degree. I'm a passable pianist. I'll do the odd recital. Maybe teach a bit, too. I'll make do. Then I'll find meself a good wee Welsh woman and settle down."

"That'll be the day." Ben drank down a gulp of whiskey and lay on the bunk, wincing at the pain in his back.

"And talking of my sister," Oliver continued, wagging a finger at Ben, "you *do* realize that it's my official duty as the elder sibling to beat the shit out of you?" He poured them both another shot of whiskey. "I can't, of course, because you're a better fighter than me and you'd break both my arms. But consider yourself reprimanded, nonetheless."

Ben closed his eyes and sighed.

"She's not a kid," Oliver said. "She's serious about what she does. And she was serious about you, too. You broke her heart, Ben. She's always asking me if I've seen you. She wants to know why you walked out on her. What am I supposed to tell her?"

Ben was silent for a while. "I'm sorry," he whispered, and

meant it. "I didn't want to hurt her. The truth is, Ol, I think she deserves someone better than me."

Oliver slurped back more whiskey and smacked his lips, then turned to Ben. "Listen, I've been thinking about all this," he said. "Why don't you come with me? Forget about this fighting-for-Queen-and-country crap. Who Dares Wins? Who cares who wins? Even if they do take you in, you won't even retain rank—you'll be busted right down to trooper."

Ben nodded. "I know."

"And then what? Get shot to bits in a stupid war that you don't even understand? Die in some stinking jungle? Your name up on the clock tower at Hereford for the sake of a bunch of double-dealing suits in Whitehall?"

Ben had no answer to that.

"Look, man, think about it for a minute. Come back to Builth with me. We're a good team, you and I. We'll set up in business together."

Ben laughed wearily, looking up at the ceiling. "Yeah, I can just see that. Doing what?"

"Details, details. We'll think of something. Something nice and easy that'll make us rich and fat. You can get down on your knee and beg Leigh's forgiveness, then she'll marry you and we'll all be happy." Oliver smiled.

Ben glanced over at his friend and marveled at his view of life. It really was as simple as that for Oliver. "You think she'd still want me?" he asked. "After what I did?"

"Ask her yourself."

Ben raised his head off the bunk. For a few seconds it all seemed to make such perfect sense. He wavered on the brink.

"No," he said quietly. "If I get through tomorrow, I'm going on with it. I want the badge."

• • •

Fifteen years later, Ben Hope stubbed out the Turkish cigarette and looked across the hotel room. Leigh was still fast asleep, with just the occasional flicker of a frown passing over her face that hinted at the unsettled dreams in her mind.

He watched her, and not for the first time he found himself wondering how his life might have been if he'd headed back with Oliver that next morning.

15.

Ben walked into the hotel bar. The place was empty. He leaned against the counter and ran his eye along the row of whiskey optics. The barman appeared. Ben produced his flask. "Any chance you can refill this for me?" he asked. He pointed. "The Laphroaig."

When he got back upstairs to the room, Leigh was awake and talking on her phone. She looked tired, still a little groggy from the sedative. As Ben came in and shut the door she was saying thanks for calling and good-bye. She ended the call and tossed the phone down on the bed in front of her.

"Who was that?" he asked.

"Police."

"You called them?"

"They called me."

"Was it the same guy who called you at Langton Hall?"

She nodded.

"What did he want?"

"Just to know how I was. Don't worry, I didn't tell him anything about what happened, okay? And I didn't mention what's on there, either." She pointed over at the laptop on the table.

Ben looked serious. "How long were you talking?"

"Not long. About two or three minutes. Why?"

"Get your things together. We've got to leave." He ejected the disc from the laptop, clipped it in its case, and put it in his pocket. He quickly packed the computer in its carry bag, threw the Mozart file into his backpack, and used a bathroom towel to wipe down anything they'd touched in the room.

"What's wrong? Why do we have to leave so suddenly?"

"Give me your phone."

She handed it to him. He turned it off and pocketed it. "I'm going to have to dispose of this," he said.

"I need that phone," she protested. "All my numbers are on it."

"You can't keep it," he said. "I'll explain later." He led her briskly downstairs and settled the bill in cash, using his false name.

"Aren't you going to tell me what's going on?" she asked as he guided her out to the car.

Ben started the green TVR. The throaty exhausts rasped, and the wide tires crunched on the gravel. The big car park had two entrances flanked by neat conifers. About to pull out, he glanced in the mirror.

There were two black Range Rovers behind them. They were identical. Private plates, tinted glass, headlights blazing. They turned into the other entrance in a hurry and pulled up right outside the hotel, one behind the other. All four doors opened simultaneously. Ben framed them in the mirror. He counted six men getting out. All six were serious-looking, professional in their movements.

Time to go. He tried to pull away discreetly, but that was hard to do in an ostentatious sports car like the TVR. The rasp of the engine reached their ears. Heads turned. One of the men pointed. They exchanged signals, then headed back to the Range Rovers.

"Is this car registered to you?" he asked quickly.

"Yes, of course it is. You still haven't told me what—"

Ben dumped the clutch, and the TVR spun its wheels,

pressing them back in their seats. He accelerated hard away.

That was twice now. No coincidence. He spoke loudly over the rising pitch of the engine. "They're using your phone to track us, Leigh. They can triangulate the signal to within a few feet."

She looked horrified. "But who? The police?"

"Maybe the police. Or someone on the outside, someone connected. Someone with access to that kind of information."

"Who could that be?" she asked, turning pale.

Ben said nothing. He pressed the accelerator down a little harder.

The Range Rovers were a hundred yards behind them as Ben turned off the quiet country road and joined the lumbering, dense traffic heading towards the city of Oxford. He managed to put a few vehicles between them, but the steady stream coming the other way made overtaking difficult. He saw a gap and nipped past an Oxford Tube coach, but when he looked in the mirror the first Range Rover had gotten past it as well. Horns honked in the distance.

Leigh was gripping the edge of her seat. "Where are we going?" she gasped.

"If we can get into the city, we might be able to lose them," he said. "I know Oxford pretty well."

By the time they reached Headington Hill on the outskirts of east Oxford, the Range Rovers were together again, just a dozen or so cars back. At the bottom of the hill they hit the traffic lights coming into St. Clements.

"There are police cars down there," she said, pointing.

Ben had seen them. "It's not for us." Part of the road had been cordoned off, and there was an ambulance. Traffic was moving at a crawl. The Range Rovers threaded through the tailback as more horns blared.

A policeman stepped into the road four cars ahead of the TVR and signaled to let cars come the other way. Ben twisted in his seat. The Range Rovers were pulling up behind.

"They're coming," Leigh said. Her eyes were wide.

Ben was thinking fast as he watched the passengers' doors of the Range Rovers swing open and three men climb out. Their faces were set as they walked towards the stationary TVR. They were just twenty yards away.

He pulled the car into the side, ripped out the key, and threw open his door. "Come on." He grabbed his backpack and took her wrist, and they ran down the uneven pavement, past shop windows. Paramedics were loading an injured cyclist into the back of the ambulance on a stretcher. There was a twisted bicycle in the gutter. They ran on.

Behind them, the three men quickened their pace.

Leaving behind the mess of congested traffic and running past more shops, Ben could see the big roundabout up ahead called the Plain. He remembered that it led to Magdalen Bridge and the High Street, straight into the heart of the city.

They raced across the road, and the three men followed at a trot, threading through slow-moving cars. Off the Plain was a big wineshop. A young man who looked like a student was parking a scooter on the curb outside. He went into the shop, taking off his helmet and leaving the key dangling from the ignition.

Ben dragged the lightweight machine away from the window and swung his leg over the saddle. Leigh jumped on behind him as he started the engine. The student turned round and ran out of the shop, yelling at them to stop. One of the three men giving chase was talking urgently into a phone.

A hundred yards back down St. Clements the Range Rovers battered through the stationary, honking traffic, smashing aside anything in their way and sending the police running for cover.

Ben twisted the throttle of the scooter. It was like driving a sewing machine. The little bike lurched into a sea of red and green buses, taxis, and cars rumbling away from the Plain and across the Thames over Magdalen Bridge. Leigh's arms were wrapped tightly around Ben's waist as she perched precariously on the tiny pillion seat. He could hear police sirens in the distance behind them. He looked over his shoulder. The Range Rovers were coming up fast. The police cars had given chase, blue lights flashing.

Up ahead the traffic had stopped for a red light. Ben aimed the whining scooter at the curb, and it almost threw them off as it bumped up onto the pavement with a lurching wobble. He opened the throttle again and sent pedestrians scattering as he headed over the bridge. People turned and stared; some shouted. They made it halfway up the High Street, swerving wildly all over the pavement.

A shop door opened and the front wheels of a pram rolled out in front of them. It was carrying a baby wrapped in a blanket. The young mother was looking the other way and hadn't seen the scooter racing towards her. She turned around and stopped, her mouth opening in horror.

Ben squeezed the brakes too hard and felt the scooter's wheels lock up. He kicked out, tried to save it, but it skidded out from under them. He and Leigh tumbled to the ground. The machine scraped across the pavement on its side, hit a signpost, and slid out into the path of a double-decker. The bus couldn't stop in time. Sparks showered across the road as the scooter was flattened and mangled, pieces of smashed plastic bodywork spinning across the tarmac.

Ben sprang to his feet and grabbed his fallen bag while Leigh picked herself off the ground. Her jeans were ripped at the knee. The Range Rovers were speeding up the middle of the honking traffic just fifty yards away.

They ran. Off the High Street and through some metal bollards that blocked the way to vehicles. Up the cobbled lane past the Radcliffe Camera and Hertford College.

The Range Rovers skidded to a halt at the bollards, and all six men jumped out, giving chase. The police sirens weren't far away.

Ben had Leigh by the hand as they ran past the grand Bodleian Library and up Broad Street. Farther up the street was the famous Sheldonian Theatre, a venue for classical concerts. A crowd was queuing for concert tickets as Ben and Leigh ran by. A woman's face lit up with recognition as she spotted Leigh. She pointed, nudged her friend. "Hey, look! It's Leigh Llewellyn!"

The crowd closed in around them as Leigh was met by smiles and requests for autographs. Nobody seemed to notice her flushed face, anxious look, and torn knee. Camera phones clicked and flashed.

The six men were hanging back, watching through the crowd and panting with exertion from their sprint up the street. They scattered as a police car rounded the corner, its blue lights swirling. Two of them crossed the road and pretended to look in the window of Blackwell's bookshop, while another two headed slowly up the Bodleian steps. The last pair stood chatting at the curbside as the police car cruised past, its occupants scanning the busy street with stern faces.

Ben took Leigh's hand again as they slipped away from the crowd and followed the slow-moving police car up the street. They glanced back and saw that the men had regrouped and were gaining on them again.

On the corner of Broad Street and Cornmarket the crowds were thick with Christmas shoppers. Ben spied a taxi rank and quickened his step. Ushering Leigh into the backseat of a cab, he caught a last glimpse of their pursuers' angry faces. He slammed the taxi door, and the car melted into the traffic.

16.

VIENNA

Markus Kinski strode up to his chief's office and barged in without knocking. He took the little plastic bag out of his pocket and slammed it down on the desk in front of him. In it were the handful of jangling, tarnished shell cases from the lakeside.

Hans Schiller looked down at the bag, nudged it with his finger, and frowned up at Kinski. "What is this meant to be, Markus?"

The chief looked harried. His hairline seemed to have receded another inch since yesterday. His face was gray and sallow, and his eyes were sunken deep into a bed of wrinkles. Kinski knew the man was counting the minutes until his retirement.

"I want the Oliver Llewellyn case reopened," Kinski said. He was the only detective on Schiller's team who didn't address him as *sir,* and the only one who could get away with it.

Schiller rested his elbows on the desktop and pinched the bridge of his nose. "I thought we'd laid that one to rest, Detective," he said wearily. "Haven't you anything better to do?"

"There's more to it," Kinski said, not taking his eyes off the chief.

"What've you got?"

Kinski pointed at the bag. "Nine-mil empties."

"I can see what they are," Schiller said. "What'd you do, scoop them off the range floor?"

"I found them just now at the lake. The lake where Llewellyn died."

Schiller took off his glasses and polished them with a tissue. He leaned forwards across the desk and looked hard at Kinski. "What are you trying to say? You've got nothing here. Llewellyn drowned. It was an accident."

"I don't think so."

"So what's with the brass?"

"I don't know yet. I just know that I need to know more."

"But we already know what happened. You were there when they took the witness's statement."

"The witness is a phony."

Schiller leaned back in his chair and breathed out loudly through his nose. He folded his arms across his stomach. "How do you know that?"

"I just do."

"That's a bold statement, Markus."

"I know."

"You can prove it?"

"I will," Kinski said.

Schiller sighed and slumped another few inches in his chair, like a man with an extra burden added to his shoulders. "I want to help you, Markus," he said. "You know I've always stood by you. Not everyone's as tolerant as I am."

"I know that, Chief, and I appreciate it."

"But you'd better keep your mouth shut until you can come up with something concrete here," Schiller said. "Remember who Madeleine Laurent is. I had a whole shit storm of trouble from the Consulate at the time, and I'm not going to start poking around there again." He spluttered and ran his fingers through his hair. "Why don't you just let it drop? Llewellyn was just some rich playboy who got drunk and stupid. Leave it. Do yourself a favor. You've got better things to worry about."

Kinski placed his fists on the desk, knuckles down. "If I find proof, solid proof, will you agree to reopen the Llewellyn case?"

"We'd have to be talking about some pretty solid fucking proof."

"But if I did—"

Schiller gasped and flapped his arms in exasperation. "Yes, Markus. Okay. If—and it's one hell of a big if—you come up with something seriously convincing, then I *might* just consider reopening the case." His eyes were hard. "That's as good as it gets."

"That's good enough for me," Kinski said. Then the office door was flapping in his wake.

The detour to the office had made him even later for picking his daughter, Clara, up from school. The traffic was a nightmare, and the roads through the city looked like a car park. Kinski sat for fifteen minutes in a nose-to-tail jam, drumming on the steering wheel and fighting his rising impatience.

In a nearby department store window, the same channel played on rows of TV screens. Kinski gazed at them distractedly. It was one of those talking-heads shows, some interview with a politician. Kinski knew who he was. His face was plastered everywhere lately. Some rich man's son who thought it was cool to be a Socialist. What was his name? Philippe something. Philippe Aragon. The great new fucking hope for Europe.

Kinski looked at the clock on the dash and sighed. If he

didn't get there soon, Clara would get on the bus and he'd have to double back and try to catch her at the bus stop. She'd be hanging around on the street corner in the dark wondering where Helga was. *Shit.*

What the hell, he thought. He slapped the blue flashing light to the roof and hit the siren. The traffic parted magically, and he sped on through.

As he skidded around the corner and gunned the big Mercedes along the street, he saw the school bus still pulled up outside the high wall of St. Mary's College. Crowds of little girls in their somber gray uniforms and dark blue coats were gathered noisily around the bus, chatting, laughing. Expensively dressed mothers were arriving in their Jaguars and BMWs to collect their daughters.

Kinski screeched to a halt and killed the siren. A group of mothers turned to stare at him as he climbed out of the car and jogged over towards the bus. He looked but couldn't see Clara among the crowd of girls. He recognized some of her friends. "Anyone seen Clara?" he asked them. "Clara Kinski?"

They all looked blank or shook their heads. Kinski stepped up inside the bus, but she wasn't there, either.

He stopped. A group of girls were coming out of the school gate and walking off down the road. They had their backs to him, swinging their schoolbags, laughing, skipping. He looked. He saw a violin case. Fair-colored pigtails hanging out from under the regulation blue bonnet. He ran after them. Called her name. Some of the girls turned to look at the big, panting, red-faced man as he approached. The one with the violin case kept on walking, talking to her friend. She hadn't noticed him. He scattered them and laid a hand on her shoulder. "Clara, where the hell are you—"

She turned and blinked up at him, scared. She backed away.

"I'm sorry," he panted. "I thought you were Clara Kinski. Have you seen her?"

They all shook their heads nervously, big eyes looking up at him. Then they turned and kept walking, throwing glances over their shoulders as he turned away. One of them tapped her head to say, He's crazy, and they all giggled.

He ran through the school gate and down the tree-lined driveway. It was beginning to snow again, heavy flakes in his eyelashes. He wiped them and saw a teacher he recognized coming the other way. "Frau Schmidt, have you seen Clara?" he asked.

The teacher looked surprised. "Is she not on the bus, Herr Kinski? I saw her go through the gate with her friends."

He shook his head. "I checked."

"Don't worry, Herr Kinski. Perhaps she's gone home with a friend?"

"She'd never do that," he said, biting his lip.

A small girl came out of the ivied archway that was the main entrance to the school. She was carrying a little clarinet case. She had dark plaits and big brown eyes that widened in recognition when she saw Kinski.

"Martina, have you seen Clara?" asked Frau Schmidt.

"She's gone," said Martina in her small voice.

"Gone?" Kinski asked.

The girl melted shyly under his look.

"Speak up, Martina," the teacher said kindly, kneeling down and stroking her hair. "Don't be afraid. Where did Clara go?"

"In a car. With a man."

The teacher's expression hardened. "What man?"

"I don't know. Just a man."

"When did you see this?"

Martina pointed up towards the gate, where the bus was pulling away. "I was with her. Then I remembered my clarinet. I came back for it. Just then, a car came. A man got out. He smiled at Clara. He said he was a friend of Herr Kinski." Martina's timid eyes flickered up at him.

Kinski's heart was thudding, and his palms were prickling. "What did he look like?" he asked the child.

"I don't know," she said quietly. "He was big. He was wearing a suit."

"What kind of car was it? What color?"

"Black," she said. "I don't know what kind."

"Which way did they go?"

She pointed down the street. The bus was pulling away. He looked beyond it at the empty road, houses in the distance.

She could be anywhere. She was gone.

17.

OXFORDSHIRE

They switched taxis twice and rode around the countryside in buses until Ben satisfied himself that they weren't being followed. Just as the sun was beginning to set, they boarded a red double-decker in the village of Eynsham heading back towards the city. The top deck was empty, and they sat at the back so they could watch the road behind them.

"What are we going to do now?" she asked.

"I think we both know that Oliver's death wasn't an accident, Leigh." Ben put his hand on hers and squeezed it lightly, looking into her eyes. "I'm sorry. I almost wish it had been."

She nodded sadly. "What was he doing there? What could have happened? He was just researching a book."

He rubbed his temples, thinking hard. "Did the coroner establish time of death, more or less?"

"He died at ten thirty-four p.m. Why?"

"That's too precise," Ben said. "Nobody can pinpoint the moment that accurately."

"Dad's old wind-up watch," she replied. "Oliver always wore it to remember him by. It stopped . . ." It was tough to say it. "It stopped when he went into the water." She sniffed. A tear welled up in her eye, and she wiped it away.

"Are you okay talking about this?" he asked.

"I don't have much choice, do I?"

"Here's how I see it," he said. "Oliver witnessed something. Why, and where, we don't know. We only know what he witnessed, and it looks like some kind of ritual execution. But he must have been seen somehow. They came after him, but it took them a while to catch up with him. Just over an hour's gap from when he witnessed the crime to when he died."

Leigh nodded and said nothing. She dabbed her eyes with a tissue.

"I think he filmed the clip on a cell phone," Ben went on. "Say he still had it with him when they caught him. Say the clip was still on it. They'd have thought they'd retrieved all the evidence."

"But then they saw my TV interview," Leigh said grimly.

He nodded. "Months had gone by. They'd covered all their tracks. Case closed. Then suddenly there's a whole new threat. You announced you had all the research notes Oliver had been sending you, including material posted the day he died that you hadn't looked at yet. What if he'd sent you a copy of the evidence? That's when they knew they had to come after you as well."

Leigh began to cry.

"I'm sorry," he said. "I know this is hard for you. Do you want to stop?"

"What I want is to find out what happened to him," she said through the tears. "But what can we do? Where do we even start? We can't even go to the police."

Ben shook his head. "*We* are not going to do anything. It's too dangerous for you. I'm going to take you somewhere safe, and then I'm going to go to Europe to start retracing Oliver's footsteps. That's the only way we're going to figure this out."

"Where am I going to go?"

"My place."

"Your place?"

"It's in Ireland. Very secluded, out on the west coast. You'll be safe there. I'll rent a car. We'll drive up to Scotland. Ferry from Stranraer to Northern Ireland, and then across the border to Galway. That way, we avoid passport controls. Nobody will know where you are."

Her tears had stopped now, a growing look of defiance on her face. "And meanwhile you hop on a flight and go off on your own?"

"Something like that."

She shook her head. "There's no way, Ben, absolutely *no* way that I'm going to sit this out on some deserted beach in Ireland while you go off to the continent following Oliver's trail on your own. This is my brother we're talking about."

"What if I said you could come with me? You saw what happened today. People recognize your face. I can't move around with you. I'd be better working on my own, and you'd be a lot safer."

"You'd be amazed what a scarf and a pair of shades can do. I'd keep my head down and not mention my name."

"And anyway, you can't travel on your passport. It's too traceable, and if there's someone connected to the police involved in all of this, they'll catch up with us the minute you step into Europe."

"What could the police have to do with this thing, Ben?"

"I don't know yet," he said.

Leigh thought for a while, gazing out of the window at the naked trees flashing by. The bus rocked and swayed on the bumpy road. She nodded to herself, as though a sudden idea had come to her. "There *is* one way we could get out of the country and into France without being noticed."

18.

SOUTHAMPTON

TWO HOURS LATER

Orion's Belt was bright in the east, and the moonlight rippled on the water of the marina near Southampton. On either side of the long jetty, rows of white yachts drifted gently on their moorings.

Chris Anderson stood on the deck of the *Isolde,* his sixty-foot yacht, sipping a hot mug of coffee and listening to the lapping water. A car door slammed in the distance, and a minute later he recognized the unmistakable figure of Leigh approaching down the jetty.

He grinned. He'd been surprised to hear from her earlier that day, and was looking forward to seeing her again. It had been a while.

Chris's jaw tightened as Leigh came closer. She wasn't alone. There was a guy with her. Did he know him? He didn't think so. A good-looking bastard, too, thick blond hair, athletic-looking in jeans and a leather jacket. A couple of inches taller than him, just under six feet. Probably about five years younger than him, too. Chris sucked in his belly. He regretted now that he hadn't played squash for a few weeks and had put on a few pounds. Who was the guy? Leigh hadn't mentioned anything about a guest.

"I'm still not too happy about this," Ben was saying as they neared the moored yacht. He could see Chris's figure under the marina lights, a heavily built man wearing a thick white woolen fleece and a baseball cap, staring at him with a frown. "And I don't think your ex-husband is thrilled, either."

"Relax," Leigh said. "He'll be fine." She skipped lightly over onto the deck and greeted Chris with a broad smile as he put his arm out to steady her. "Thanks for doing this at such short notice, Chris," she said. "I really appreciate it."

She introduced them. Chris nodded curtly at Ben. "You never told me you were bringing a guest along," he said coldly.

Leigh put her hand on Chris's shoulder and gave him a little kiss on the cheek. "*Be nice,*" she warned him softly. She looked up to see the familiar face of Chris's old skipper who was checking the rigging, and smiled. "Hey there, Mick."

"Long time no see," Mick called down. "Good to have you on board. Like old times."

"Hope I haven't put you out too much," she said.

Mick jumped down on deck, wiping his hands. He was a small, hard, wiry man, with dark eyes and a gray beard. "Nah, not a bit. A hop across the Channel's just a stretch of the legs for the *Isolde,* even in December."

"You're a star, Mick. This is my friend Ben. He's coming, too."

"Good to meet you, Ben."

"You, too," Ben said. He looked admiringly at the yacht. "How long's the crossing?"

Mick shrugged. "Hamble to Saint-Vaast-la-Hougue? Nine hours, give or take."

"Traveling a bit light, aren't you?" Chris observed. "No luggage?"

"Just my credit card." Leigh grinned. "I'll do some shopping when we get into Saint-Vaast."

"Whatever you say," Chris replied. "What happened to your knee?"

Leigh reached down to the rip in her jeans. "Oh, that. I tripped."

"You're cut."

"It's just a little graze. It's nothing."

Chris turned to Ben. "Welcome aboard the *Isolde*," he said with the merest touch of warmth. "I'll show you to your cabins." Chris put the emphasis on the plural *s*. He led them down below through the companionway.

The interior of the yacht was surprisingly spacious and plush. "The woodwork is cherry," Chris said proudly, throwing a glance at Ben and stroking the varnished panels as he went by. "Handmade. She's got it all. Oyster Sixty-one, classic model. Push-button everything. Done her share of ocean crossing, too, as Leigh will tell you. We've been everywhere in her: Madeira, St. Lucia, Grenada. Remember that little pad we used to rent on Mustique, Leigh?"

"Wasn't that the place you got bitten on the arse by the monkey, and ended up in hospital?" Leigh said flatly as she followed them down inside.

Chris cleared his throat, and Ben suppressed a smile.

"It'll be strange for you, sleeping in the guest quarters instead of the master cabin," Chris said to Leigh.

"I'll survive," she said.

Chris showed Ben into the smallest of the *Isolde*'s three cabins. "You can put your things over there." In the light of the cabin he ran his eye up and down Ben's scuffed old brown leather jacket and tatty-looking green canvas backpack. It looked heavy. Ben wedged it up on top of a storage unit above the bunk. His jacket sleeve rode up as he raised his arms, and Chris noticed the expensive diver's watch on his wrist.

Within twenty minutes Mick was ready to cast off. The *Isolde*'s sails billowed in the breeze as they left the shore behind and headed into open waters.

Leigh felt obliged to spend time with Chris, so she helped him to prepare dinner. Ben could feel her ex-husband's eye on him, and he took the opportunity to retreat to his tiny cabin. He took down his bag, sat back on his bunk, and opened up the Mozart file.

Oliver's notes were hard to read. Ben gazed for a while at the reference to "the Order of R—." It meant nothing to him, and he tossed the page down in frustration.

On another sheet, Oliver had been writing what looked like some kind of checklist of various historical facts and figures. In red ink he'd scrawled the word ARNO and circled it three times. Beside it was a date in late December, just two weeks before Oliver's death. The writing underneath was burned away, and Ben was unable to read it.

Then there were all the eagles. Oliver was a doodler. The margins that were still intact were filled with little drawings of eagles. Underneath one of them, Oliver had scribbled in capitals:

THE EAGLE?????

He'd gone over and over the words with his pen until they had worn almost through the paper. It was as though he was trying to make sense out of it, make the words speak to him. Had he understood it in the end?

By the time Leigh joined him later on, Ben had given up searching for any meaning in the notes. She handed him a cup of coffee and sat next to him on the narrow bunk.

"How's it going?" she asked in a low voice. The partitions

were thin, and she didn't want Chris to overhear them.

"Not so good," he replied quietly with a shake of the head. He picked up the fallen sheet and showed it to her. "I still can't make out what this 'Order of R—' is about. Then he's scribbled all this stuff about eagles, and rivers."

"Rivers?" She took the paper from him, and he pointed out the word ARNO circled in red. She peered at it curiously.

"The river Arno is in Florence," he said. "Was Oliver there? There's a date next to it."

"He never said anything about it to me."

"Think about it," he said. "It's important. You're the only person who knew where Oliver was going and what he was doing."

She cupped her chin in her hands. "I've no idea."

"Think," he urged her.

"I don't know," she said.

"Did the Mozart letter mention the river Arno? Was there anything in it that could have led Oliver to visit Florence?"

"I don't remember," she replied with a note of impatience. "It was years ago, for Christ's sake."

"Try to remember," he said patiently. "If we can't make sense of it, we've got nothing to go on at all."

"Unless . . ." she said. Her face lit up.

"Unless what?"

"We're getting it wrong. Arno isn't the river. Arno is a name."

"Whose name?"

"The Italian collector," she said, remembering clearly now. "The one who bought the letter from Dad. He was Professor Arno."

Ben remembered the series of digital snaps on the

CD-ROM. The old man with the music books behind him in the background. "So Oliver went to see him?"

"Must have," she said. "Which means Arno can't be dead after all."

"But where?"

"Ravenna," she said. "Remember Dante's tomb? Oliver was there. And Arno taught at a music institute there, if I remember rightly."

Ben thought for a moment. "Oliver must have wanted to see him about the letter. I think we should pay him a visit, too."

"You think he might still have it?" she asked.

"He paid a lot of money for it when nobody else would touch it. It seems to me he'd hold on to it."

"What do you think might be in it?"

"That's what we'll have to find out."

19.

They ate dinner in the yacht's long saloon. Chris poured out chilled wine and served fish chowder with a green salad.

"Leigh tells me you write film music," Ben said.

Chris nodded. "Mostly. You a movie fan, Ben?"

Ben shrugged. "I see the odd thing." He tried to remember the name of the last film he'd seen. It had been in Lisbon, on a job, six months ago. The potential informer he'd been tailing had wandered into a cinema. Ben had sat a couple of rows behind. After an hour the man had looked at his watch and left. Ben had followed, and five minutes later the man was lying in a heap down a backstreet. He couldn't recall a thing about the movie. "What ones have you composed for?" he asked.

"My latest was *Outcast,* with Hampton Burnley. Know it?"

Ben shook his head.

"Maybe you're more of an opera guy," Chris said, glancing at Leigh.

"Ben doesn't get a lot of time for that kind of thing," she said.

"So what do you do for a living, Ben?"

"I'm retired."

Chris looked surprised. "Retired? From what?"

Ben drank down the last of his wine. "Forces."

The bottle was empty. Chris looked at it with a raised eyebrow and fetched another from the cooler. "RAF?"

"Army."

"Soldier boy. What rank were you?"

"Major," Ben replied quietly.

Chris tried not to look impressed. "So what was your regiment, Major?"

Ben threw him a glance across the table. "It's Ben. Nobody calls me major anymore."

"Ben and Oliver were army friends," Leigh said. "That's how we met."

"So you two have known each other for a long time, then," Chris said icily, not taking his eyes off Ben.

"But we haven't been in touch for years," Leigh added.

Chris kept his eyes on Ben a while longer, then grunted to himself and went back to his food. The three of them finished the meal in silence, with just the sound of wind and water outside.

Ben went back to his cabin and sat quietly for a while, thinking. He checked the pistols again, stripping and cleaning them with well-practiced, almost unconscious familiarity. Then he put everything back in his bag and shoved it up on top of the storage unit. He lay on the bunk for an hour, listening to the steady crash of the waves. The wind was rising, and the gentle motion of the *Isolde* was becoming more pronounced.

Around midnight, Leigh was thinking about bed. Across the table, Chris was sitting slumped in his chair glowering at the television. He'd barely said a word since dinner.

"What is it, Chris?"

He was silent. His face darkened.

"Come on. I know that look. What is it?"

He stabbed the remote and turned off the television. "It's him, isn't it?"

"Who?"

"Him. I remember now. *Ben.* The old flame. The one you were madly in love with. The one you wanted to marry."

"That was fifteen years ago, Chris."

Chris laughed bitterly. "I knew there was something going on."

"There's nothing going on."

"No? I heard the two of you whispering before. Alone in the cabin like teenagers." He snorted. "If I'd known what this trip was really about, I'd never have let you sweet-talk me into it. You must think I'm a real fool, a proper soft touch. Getting old Chris to ferry you and your boyfriend over to France for a dirty weekend. Scared the paparazzi will get wind of your little romance? Maybe I should just turn the boat around."

"You're getting it all wrong, Chris."

"I can't believe you'd do this to me. I haven't forgotten, you know. All the stories about this guy who broke your heart so badly it took you years to get over him—now you're running around with the bastard right under my nose, and you expect me to help you? What did I ever do to you? I never broke your heart. You broke my fucking heart." He jabbed his finger several times against his chest. His face was turning red.

"Yeah, when I caught you screwing that bimbo at my birthday party."

Chris rolled his eyes. "One little transgression . . . how many times does a guy have to say he's sorry?"

"I don't call it a little transgression."

"You were never there! You were always off singing somewhere."

"I was there that night," she said. They faced each other, hostility building up between them. Then she sighed. "Please, Chris. I don't want to fight, okay? We've been over this before. You know as well as I do that it wasn't working between us. We're still friends, though, aren't we?"

"Retired," Chris muttered. "How old is this guy? What kind of a bum calls himself retired at his age? You know what army pensions are like? How do you know he's not just after your money?" He thought for a moment. "Did you buy him that watch?" he demanded.

"For Christ's sake. Give me a break. It's not like that."

"So what *is* it like? Why is he here?"

"There are things I can't explain right now. You have to trust me, okay?" She looked at him earnestly. "I swear there is nothing between Ben and me. And I appreciate that you care, and that you're helping me out like this. Really." She hugged him, and he squeezed her tight.

"I miss you, Leigh," he said in a plaintive voice. He kissed her hair. "I think about you a lot, you know," he murmured. Then he moved back a little and tried to kiss her on the mouth. She pushed him away.

Ben had come out of the cabin and stood framed in the doorway.

Leigh abruptly broke away from Chris, and they all stood frozen for a moment, staring at one another.

"Sorry," Ben said quietly. "Didn't mean to interrupt." He turned and headed for the companionway steps to go on deck.

The wind was much stronger than earlier, and he zipped his jacket to the neck. Cold swathes of rain were lashing across the *Isolde*'s bows from the east, and the sails fluttered and rippled loudly above the groan of the wind and the steady crash of waves. Mick was tending the wheel, wrapped in orange oilskins. They exchanged nods. Ben reached for his cigarettes and offered him one. He shielded the flame of his Zippo lighter from the breeze, inhaled deeply, and looked out for a while across the dark, choppy water, narrowing his eyes against the cold spray and holding on to the rail.

The *Isolde*'s prow rose on the unsettled sea, climbing the crest of a big wave, then cleared it and plunged down into a trough with a huge splash of flying foam. Ben steadied himself against the swell as the deck under his feet sloped and settled. The sails crackled like fire.

"Bit of weather up ahead," Mick said, interrupting his thoughts.

Ben looked up at the dark sky. Black clouds raced across the face of the moon. In the dim light he could see the white water of the breaking crests.

He stood on deck for a long time. There was no point in going below. He wouldn't sleep. His thoughts were confused and rambling, switching from one thing to another. Oliver. The Mozart letter. The video clip. The murder. Langton Hall. The call from the police.

But he wasn't just thinking about the mystery. His mind kept drifting to Leigh. The vision of her in Chris's arms lingered stubbornly and perplexingly in his mind. Why did it make him feel so uncomfortable that she might still have feelings for her ex-husband?

What were these feelings he was having? Was he jealous? He resisted the idea. Yet he couldn't stop thinking about the way it made him feel to be around her again.

She must be asleep now. He imagined her lying on her bunk, just a few feet away below deck, with her hair spread out on the pillow.

He smoked more cigarettes and sipped whiskey from his flask, and forgot the rise and fall of the deck under his feet.

He barely noticed the growing storm until the *Isolde* lurched into a broach that made him stagger. The waves were roaring in with fierce intensity. The yacht hit another crest, climbed steeply, and her bows crashed down. A wild turmoil of water and foam blinded Ben for a few seconds as he hung grimly on to the rail. His cigarette fizzled out, and he threw the soggy stub into the sea.

In the cabin below, Leigh was tossing and turning restlessly on her bunk, trying to relax her mind. But it was no use. She couldn't keep Ben Hope out of her head. What was wrong with her?

She checked her watch and saw that it was almost four in the morning. She wrapped herself in a blanket and went to make herself coffee. The yacht was lurching, and it was hard to walk.

Chris heard her moving about and came out of the master cabin, looking bleary-eyed and pale. As she drank her coffee he checked the computer for the latest Met Office weather report. "This blow should be over soon." He shot her a wild look. "Where's your major friend?"

"Leave it alone, Chris. Isn't he in his cabin?"

"His door's open. He's not in there."

"Oh, right. And you thought he was in with me. You really don't trust me, do you?"

Chris grunted and headed up to the deck. As he opened the hatch, a lash of spray caught him in the face, and he spluttered. He cleared his eyes, shook his head, and watched across the deck. Ben and Mick were working together, silently and doggedly, their oilskins glistening with rain. The major seemed to know what he was doing, Chris thought. He swore under his breath, slicked back his dripping hair, and went below again.

Halfway down the companionway steps, Chris had an

idea. The major was out of the way. An opportunity. He sneaked past the doorway of the saloon and quietly slipped into the open door of Ben's cabin. He shut it carefully behind him and bolted it, then looked around the room. He lifted the green canvas bag down from above the bunk and started undoing the straps.

20.

VIENNA

THAT EVENING

Kinski was pacing up and down in his living room. His nerves felt like broken glass, and he could feel a migraine coming on. His hands shook violently, and his stomach churned.

Where was she? Who had taken her? Was this a reprisal for someone he'd put away? He thought of some of the cold bastards he'd dealt with over the past few months. Ran through their names and faces in his head. He knew what they could do to her. He'd seen what they could do.

If they harmed her, he'd kill them. Kill every last one. Kill everybody.

He fell into an armchair with his head in his hands, crying and trembling. Then he paced again and slammed his fists into the wall until they bled. Max the dog watched him nervously from his bed in the corner.

The phone rang, and he leaped at it. This was it. Ransom demand. He lifted the receiver with a shaking hand.

Somebody trying to sell him roof insulation.

"Fuck you." Kinski slammed it down.

He was startled by the noise outside of a car pulling away, then a moment later he heard the doorbell. He raced to the door and ripped it open just in time to see the black

Audi speeding away down the street. He didn't get the registration.

Clara smiled sweetly up at him from the doorstep. "Hi, Daddy. Hey, Maxy." The big dog had jumped out of his bed and was all over her, licking her face, wagging the stump of his docked tail. She turned her face away from him, laughing as she trotted into the house.

Kinski pushed Max away. He threw his arms around Clara and clasped her hard against his chest.

"You're crushing me." She wriggled back and looked at his face, puzzled at his expression. "What's wrong with you?"

"Where have you been?" was all he could say.

He sat her down in a chair and made her tell him everything. She didn't understand why he was so upset, what the big deal was. Franz was nice. He said he was a friend. A cop, like her dad. Dad had asked him to look after her for a while. They had ice cream in a nice café. Franz was funny. He told her stories that made her laugh. No, he didn't touch her. He never touched her at all, except to take her hand to lead her into the café. No, she didn't remember the name of the café or the street where it was. It was just a café somewhere. What was wrong?

Kinski listened to all this, and his head hung lower. "What does Franz look like?" he asked. He tried to keep the fury out of his voice.

She shook her head, as though it was a silly question. "He's big like you but not so fat." She giggled.

"This is serious, Clara."

Clara brushed back wisps of sandy hair and looked serene. "He's old. He must be forty. Probably even more."

"Okay. What else?"

"He has a funny ear."

"What do you mean, a funny ear?"

She made a face. "Kind of horrible. Like it was chewed up or something."

"Scarred?"

"I asked him what happened to it. He said a big old parrot landed on his shoulder and tried to pull his ear off. He acted it out. It made me laugh. I liked him."

He wanted to slap her. "Don't you ever do that again. I mean it, Clara. The only car you get in is our car or Helga's. Do you understand?"

She lowered her head, sniffed, and wiped away a tear. "Yes, Daddy."

The phone rang again. Kinski answered it on the second ring.

"Herr Kinski?"

"Who is this?"

"Just listen."

"Okay, I'm listening."

"This is a warning. Stay away from the Llewellyn case."

"Who are you?"

"Next time that pretty little girl of yours won't be coming home smiling."

Kinski bit his tongue and tasted blood. The line went dead.

21.

Eve checked her makeup in the mirror and sprayed a little perfume on her wrists and behind her ears. He had her wearing the long blond wig today. She made a couple of little adjustments to it. Perfect. She emerged from the en suite bathroom, wearing just her silk underwear, and went into the walk-in wardrobe. The racks of expensive dresses had all been tailored for her.

A voice spoke out of nowhere. She knew that the speakers were all around the room. "*The black one,*" said the voice. It was impassive and controlled.

Eve reached over and took down a Chanel dress—beautiful, black velvet. She hated it, just as she hated all of them. She turned round and held it up against her slender figure.

"*No,*" the voice said. "*The satin one.*" Eve calmly replaced the dress, slid the hangers along the rail, and took down the low-cut satin dress. One of his more recent gifts to her.

"*Put it on,*" said the voice in the same unemotional tone. She did as he said.

"*Now the pearls.*"

She turned away from the racks of dresses. On the opposite wall of the huge wardrobe was an antique glass-fronted cabinet lined with blue velvet and displaying a row of open jewel boxes with glittering gold chains and diamond necklaces. She drew out the long string of pearls and placed it over her head. It hung low down between her breasts, cool against her skin.

"*No. Double them up,*" the voice said. "*And put on the matching earrings.*"

She obeyed mechanically.

In another part of the house, Werner Kroll reclined in his padded chair. He sat with his hands on his lap, his tie as straight and tightly knotted as always. His eyes were fixed on the flat-screen color monitor in front of him. She turned round to let him see her, the way she knew he liked. He nodded approvingly. "Good," he said into the microphone. "Now go to the room." He reached out slowly and pressed a button on the console in front of him, switching cameras. He watched her come out of the bedroom, walk down the long corridor, and climb the stairway.

Eve had made this journey more times than she wanted to remember. What did he want from her? It was always different, but each time it got a little worse. She walked up to a heavy door, turned the gold handle, and went inside. The room was elegant, the ceiling high. The soft lighting cast long shadows on the green silk-covered walls. The furniture was sparse but expensive, and the carpet felt deep and spongy under her feet.

She walked to the middle of the room, glancing around her, feeling uneasy. She caught a glimpse of herself in the high mirror that stretched from floor to ceiling, and looked away quickly.

Someone moaned at the far end of the room, and Eve turned in the direction of the sound. Lying on the broad bed was a woman. She was young and pretty, semiconscious, and almost naked. She was spread-eagled, tied to the bedposts by the arms and ankles.

The voice spoke again from hidden speakers in the corners of the room. It seemed to come from everywhere and nowhere, filling every inch of air. "*Take off your dress,*" it said. "*Slowly.*"

Eve hesitated a moment, then reached behind her back and started undoing the fasteners.

"*More slowly,*" the voice warned. She obeyed. The straps slipped over her shoulders, and the dress slid smoothly down her body. She stepped out of it and left it lying in a satin pool on the floor.

"*Good,*" said the voice. "*Now go to the table and open the case.*"

Eve did as he said. Her legs felt heavy as she approached the gleaming tabletop. She flipped the catches of the soft hide briefcase, raised the lid, and stepped back. When she saw what was inside, she caught her breath.

She looked across at the mirror and shook her head. "Please, I can't do this," she said. "Don't make me."

The voice was silent, but she could imagine the look on his face as he sat in his chair behind the two-way glass.

"This is going too far," she said more firmly, and shut the case.

He spoke quietly. He told her why she had no choice. What he would do to her if she didn't obey him. She listened, her chin on her chest and her eyes shut.

When he finished talking, Eve opened the case again, swallowed hard, and reached slowly for what was inside.

22.

THE ENGLISH CHANNEL
TOWARDS DAWN

The coast of France was a light-speckled haze against the dark blue horizon. The storm had finally blown itself out, and the sea was smooth and gray. Gulls screeched around the *Isolde*'s tall mast as Ben peeled off his waterproofs and made his way below. Mick clapped him on the shoulder as he passed. The skipper looked drawn. It had been a long night.

Leigh met Ben at the hatchway, looking concerned. The smell of frying bacon coming from inside made his mouth water. "I'm making breakfast," she said.

"Where's Chris?" he asked, trudging wearily down the steps.

"I think he's still in bed."

"Some captain," he muttered. Leigh ignored the comment and handed him a steaming plate of bacon and eggs. He sat down to eat it while she pulled on her jacket and went to take another plateful up to Mick on deck.

As Ben lifted the first forkful to his mouth, the door of the master cabin burst open. Chris had a twisted look on his face as he stepped out.

Leigh was coming back down below. She saw Chris and stopped halfway down the steps.

"Don't move," Chris said. In his hand was one of the Para-Ordnance pistols, and he was pointing it straight at Ben.

Ben stared at the gun.

"Pretty surprised, aren't you, Major?" Chris gave a tense little laugh. "Leigh, this is what your boyfriend's really about. Look what I found in his bag. Three of them, and ammunition." Keeping the gun trained on Ben, he reached behind the door of his cabin. He brought out the backpack and chucked it on the floor between them. "Not to mention something like fifteen thousand euros in cash in there," he said. "All tied up in neat little stacks. What's the game, Major? Gunrunning? Dope dealing? Bit of both?" Chris grinned triumphantly at Leigh. "Either way, he's in the shit now. This is a citizen's arrest. I'm calling the police and the coast guard."

"Chris!" Leigh moaned.

"Don't worry, I won't mention your name. It's nothing to do with you—is it?"

"You're being so stupid," she said. "Don't do this. I'll explain everything to you another time. Trust me, all right?"

Chris ignored her and waggled the gun at Ben. "Not so tough now, are you, Major?"

Ben went on eating. "You don't know about the three conditions, do you, Chris?"

Chris flushed, and his triumphant grin faded a little. "What are you on about?"

"I didn't think so. I'm talking about the three conditions of readiness for a single-action semiautomatic pistol."

Chris's smile was wavering, uncertain what to make of this.

Ben went on calmly. "Condition one, cocked and locked.

You only have to flick off the safety, pull the trigger, and I'm dead." He pushed his plate away from him, stood up, and took a step towards Chris.

"Careful, I'll shoot," Chris stammered.

"Condition two, there's a round in the chamber, but you still need to cock the hammer with your thumb." Ben took another step forward.

"I'm warning you—"

"Condition three, there's no round in the chamber at all, and all the weapon's good for is hammering nails." Ben had reached Chris now, and the gun's muzzle was a few inches from his face. It was beginning to tremble.

"You're in condition three, you arsehole. Now give me that before you poke your eye out with it." Ben reached out and snatched the .45 from Chris. He checked the magazine. Eleven cartridges. He picked up the fallen backpack. It was light. The money was still there, but the guns and spare magazines were gone. "What have you done with the other pistols?" he demanded.

Chris rubbed his hand, turning pale. "Tossed them," he said in a low voice.

"Overboard?"

Chris nodded.

"Idiot." Ben tucked the Para-Ordnance into his belt. "Leigh, get me whatever maps there are of the French coast. As for you," he said to Chris, "get back in your cabin and don't let me see your face again, or I swear I'll strap you to the anchor and leave you at the bottom of the sea."

Chris retreated quickly towards the master cabin.

"Oh, and Chris?" Ben added.

"What?" Chris said sullenly.

"I did see *Outcast*. And I thought the score was shit."

It was a lie, but it hit Chris right where he'd wanted it to.

Chris shut his cabin door. He didn't come out again.

"You didn't have to be so hard on him," Leigh said, laying a pile of maps on the table. "He was just trying to protect me."

Ben said nothing. He munched a piece of bacon as he spread a map out and studied the coastline.

23.

The *Isolde* cruised towards the French coast under a clear blue sky as Ben and Leigh brought their things up on deck. Mick the skipper steered the yacht into a deserted little cove a mile or so from Saint-Vaast-La-Hougue, and two hundred yards from shore Ben lowered the dinghy with his and Leigh's things in it. Then he disappeared down below for a minute as she said good-bye to the skipper on the deck.

"I don't know what's been going on with you and Mr. Anderson," the sailor said. "But good luck, love."

"I'll see you again sometime, Mick," she replied, and kissed his bearded cheek.

They climbed down the side, and Ben started the dinghy's outboard motor. He grabbed the tiller and steered the burbling boat away from the yacht. Leigh huddled at the dinghy's prow, drawing her suede coat around her against the chilly sea breeze. Gulls circled and called overhead.

"Do you think Chris will call the police now we're gone?" she asked anxiously.

"No, I don't think there's any danger of that," Ben said, peering towards the shore.

"How can you be so sure?"

"Because I told him just now that if he did, I'd come back and blow his brains out."

She frowned and didn't reply.

A few minutes later Ben was dragging the dinghy up

onto the pebbly shore. Across a stretch of beach, beyond some sand dunes, he could see the rooftops and church spire of a coast village. "This way," he said, grabbing his bag.

They hiked over the dunes and across a piece of rough grassland that bordered a golf course. A winding path led them into the heart of the village, and they soon found a little garage where Ben paid cash for a cheap secondhand Citroën.

They set off. Ben didn't need a road map. His kidnap-and-ransom work had taken him to France on more than one occasion, and he knew the country well. He stuck to the back roads. Kept a sharp eye out for police, just in case, but saw nothing.

It was a thirteen-hour drive across the country and into Italy, and they took turns at the wheel. They stopped only for fuel, and ate on the move. It was cold, and they kept the car heater on high. They were tired and spoke little.

As they crossed the Italian border in darkness a thick fog was coming down, and Ben drove in silence, concentrating on the tunnel that the headlights carved out ahead. Leigh sat with her thoughts, a little drowsy with the heat of the blower. Then she remembered something. "Can I have my phone?"

"It's lying in a ditch in Oxfordshire," he said. "I told you I had to get rid of it."

"Well, can I use yours, then?"

"Who do you want to call?"

"Pam."

"Your PA? Why?"

"I've been gone for days. She'll be getting worried. Pretty soon people will be thinking something's happened to me. I've got to tell her I'm okay."

"Fine, but don't say where you are, and keep it quick." He reached for the phone in his jacket pocket and handed it to her.

Leigh nodded and dialed.

Pam sounded relieved but agitated. Everybody was going apeshit, she said. Where the hell was she? Her agent was in a panic. She'd missed two interviews. *The Magic Flute* production in Italy was coming up in five weeks, rehearsals were scheduled to begin soon, and nobody had heard from her.

"I know," Leigh reassured her. "There's nothing to worry about."

"You're all over tonight's papers," Pam said. "Pictures of you with some guy in Oxford. I'm looking at one here. The headline is 'Who's Leigh's Leading Man?'"

Leigh tutted irritably. "Never mind that."

"Good-looking guy," Pam said. "Wouldn't mind a piece of that myself. You an item?"

"Leave it out, Pam."

"Ask her if everything's okay at Langton Hall," Ben said.

Leigh took the phone away from her mouth. "Why?"

"Just ask. Do it quickly."

Leigh asked, and Pam said everything was fine there. The builders had gone in that morning to start work on the rehearsal studio.

"They didn't find anything . . . unusual?" Leigh asked.

"No," Pam said, sounding confused. "Like what? Oh, by the way. Nearly forgot. Someone else called."

"Who called? Tell me, I can't talk long."

A pause. "It's about Oliver."

Leigh froze. "What about Oliver?"

Ben glanced away from the foggy road.

"Some detective called from Vienna," Pam said. "I've got

his name here—hold on—it's Kinski. Detective Markus Kinski. Wanted to talk to you. What's this all about?"

"Did he say any more?"

"Didn't want to talk to me. But it sounded important. He left a number to call. Said it was safe to call him. Are you in some kind of trouble, Leigh?"

"Just give me the number, Pam."

Pam read it out. Leigh grabbed a pen from her bag and scribbled it. She reassured Pam again then ended the call and switched the phone off. She thought for a minute. "Shit."

Ben looked round. "Well, what did she say?"

"We're in the papers. Someone at the Sheldonian must have sent in their snap of us hoping to make a bit of money."

"The joys of fame."

"It has its downsides."

"This is why I was concerned about traveling with you," he said. "You should have gone to my place." He drummed the steering wheel with his fingers. "Never mind. No use worrying about it. What was that about Oliver?"

She told Ben about the call from the detective. "What do you think he wants?"

"I don't know."

"Maybe instead of going to Ravenna we should drive on to Austria to see him. It might be something important."

"Then again, it might be another trap."

"Come on, Ben, I can't go on avoiding the police forever, can I? At some point I'm going to have to go to them. If someone murdered Oliver—"

"I understand. You want justice."

"Yes. I want my brother's murderer to be brought to trial. Don't you?"

"I want my friend's murderer to pay."

"Meaning what?"

"I don't trust the system. I do things my own way."

"I noticed," she said.

"It's what works."

"My idea of justice isn't a bullet in the head."

"I don't like it any more than you do."

"But that *is* what you do. Isn't it?"

Ben said nothing.

There was silence for a while. Leigh watched the foggy road and listened to the rhythm of the wipers.

It was all so overwhelming, so alien. She felt as though she was spinning away from reality, wandering without a map or a compass. At times she could hardly believe any of this was really happening. She thought about the life she'd left behind, the people and the routine that were back there in the real world waiting for her. They seemed a million miles away. Her life had been hectic, crazy, a constant blur of travel and endless rehearsals and performances, one opera house and hotel after another. But it had been organized and safe.

Now all that had fallen apart. Would things ever go back to the way they'd been? Where was this going to end? She rested her head in her hands.

Ben passed her the flask. "Have some."

"I think I will." She took several long sips. "You get used to this stuff," she said, passing it back to him.

"Tell me about it." He drank some as well.

She felt a little better. "So what about this Detective Kinski?" she asked.

"If you want to see him, we'll see him. But first we need to find Arno. Maybe he can help us to make some sense out of this mess."

• • •

They reached Ravenna sometime after ten in the evening and found a little pensione in the outskirts. Ben checked in as Mr. Connors and let them assume Leigh was his wife. They didn't ask for papers and were happy with cash up front. The landlady took them up the stairs. She unlocked a door, handed them the key, and left them alone.

The room was small and simple. "Only one bed," Leigh said. It was a double, and it took up most of the space.

"I just asked for a room," he said. "I didn't know." He dumped his backpack on an armchair and opened a creaky wardrobe. There were some spare blankets in it. He threw them down in a heap on the floor. "I have to be in the same room as you, Leigh. I can't sit outside your door all night."

"You don't have to sleep on the floor," she said. "We can share the bed. If you want to, that is."

"Chris might not be too pleased about that," he replied, and immediately wished he hadn't said it.

She frowned. "What's *he* got to do with it?"

"Nothing. Forget it. I'll sleep on the floor. It's no big deal. I've slept on a million floors."

"No, what did you mean about Chris?"

"Let's not talk about it."

"You're talking about what happened on the *Isolde,* aren't you? What do you think you saw?"

"Look, it's none of my business what goes on between you and Chris."

"Nothing at all goes on between us."

"Okay, that's fine."

"It's over between Chris and me," she said. "It's been over for years."

"You seemed to be getting on pretty well together." He knew he was saying too much, digging himself into a hole and sounding a lot more like a jealous lover than he cared to admit.

She flushed. "It wasn't what it looked like."

"You don't have to justify yourself to me." He pulled a bottle of wine out of his bag and started opening it. "Want some?"

She shook her head. "You drink it. And I'm not justifying myself." She sighed. "All right, it's true that Chris wants to get back together with me," she admitted. "That's what you saw. But the feeling is definitely *not* mutual, and it's *not* going to happen." She kicked off her shoes and reclined on the bed. "When it's over, it's over. It's never a good idea to go back." She glanced at Ben.

He blew the dust out of a glass on the bedside table and filled it with wine. Knocked it back and filled it up again. "I think you're right," he said. "It's never a good idea to go back."

24.

BORDEAUX, FRANCE

EARLIER THAT EVENING

The auditorium was packed and bustling. The lecture was being held at Bordeaux University's Faculty of Politics and Economics. It was open to the public, and people were standing in the aisles. Attendance figures were unprecedented. The organizers couldn't remember the last time a talk by a rising politician had generated so much intense excitement.

There were police and security everywhere outside under the gentle snow. Barricades had been erected for Philippe Aragon's motorcade to pass through, and massive crowds had gathered to cheer and wave banners. The police had managed to cordon off the estimated two hundred shaved-headed neo-Fascist demonstrators who had come to yell and wave their swastikas in protest. One of them had tried to set fire to an effigy of Aragon before the police had grabbed him and bundled him into a van. A scuffle had broken out, and media crews rushed in to get a shot as three cops were dragged away bleeding and a dozen more battered protesters were arrested.

Now ranks of officers gathered tensely on standby behind riot shields, batons and tear gas at the ready. Well away from the trouble, television crews and newspaper reporters were out in force and hoping for blood.

Henri Juste, the university chancellor, smiled for the

cameras as he walked out from behind the heavy curtains and made his way across the stage. Behind the podium, Aragon's party slogan

L'Europe RedECOuVERTE

stood fifteen feet high on a giant screen. It encapsulated Aragon's policies perfectly. A new Europe, a rediscovered land. Ecological. Green. Filled with hope and promise. The flags of the united European states were on display. In the wings and the control center above the auditorium, armed security personnel scrutinized monitors and scanned the crowd.

Juste reached the podium. He raised his arms, and the hum of excited chatter from the packed theater dwindled. "Ladies and gentlemen," he began. "Our speaker tonight needs no introduction. No modern political figure has ever risen to prominence or gathered such overwhelming public support so surely and so quickly. He has been hailed as the *Brussels JFK*. A pioneering environmentalist architect. A philanthropist who has personally donated millions to protect the underprivileged. A tireless campaigner for the improvement of educational standards. At forty-one, the youngest-ever candidate for the vice presidency of the European Commission. His audacious policies and progressive vision of a truly integrated Europe, and his goal to rid Europe of its dependence on nuclear energy, have placed him firmly at the forefront of European politics. Ladies and gentlemen: Philippe Aragon."

The chancellor stepped away from the podium and extended his arm as Philippe Aragon walked confidently out onto the stage. A hundred cameras focused. Five hundred people were on their feet. Tall and elegant, the young politician was wearing a well-cut suit and no tie. He waited until the applause had dwindled, and then he began his speech.

"Ladies and gentlemen, I thank you for coming here tonight." Behind him on the high screen, the big slogan disappeared, and the crowd murmured as a new image flashed up. It showed the far-right protesters outside. Shaved heads. Swastikas. Ugly faces frozen in expressions of hatred.

Aragon smiled. "And I also want to thank our neo-Nazi friends outside for showing up." He let this register for a beat, and then went on. "By their very presence here tonight, they help me to make my case. Ladies and gentlemen, we are told we already *have* an integrated Europe." He paused again as the crowd laughed. His smile was gone now. He swept the audience with his eyes. "The truth can be seen all around us," he said. "Europe is sinking under a tide of nationalistic fear and greed. But we can recover her. Together we can build a united Europe. A clean Europe. A free Europe. A *people's* Europe."

The crowd roared its approval. Behind Aragon, the image of the neo-Fascists disappeared, and the strident slogan flashed up in its place to mark his words. *L'Europe RedECOuVERTE.* The applause got even louder.

Watching on her monitor backstage in a comfortable reception room, Colette Aragon sipped coffee from a Styrofoam cup and smiled at her husband's perfect control of his audience. Party staff and plainclothes security personnel milled around her. Across the busy room stood Louis Moreau, the former GIGN counterterrorist police response unit commander whom she'd appointed as her husband's private head of security. She didn't have much faith in the government agents. Moreau took his job extremely seriously. The lights glistened on his shaved head as he stood with his arms folded, scrutinizing the bank of screens that showed the crowd from different angles.

Colette stood behind her husband publicly, every step of the way. He was a good man. But privately, she wished he'd give all this up and go back to architecture. It wasn't just the mayhem and madness of constant traveling and press interviews. Even Philippe hadn't been prepared for how fast his political career had taken off. Colette knew that as his popularity grew, he would become more of a target. At public events like this, even the heaviest security presence couldn't guarantee his safety. They couldn't frisk everyone at the door. All it took was a Fascist fanatic in the audience with a pistol in his pocket.

She shivered. She'd never believed that the incident last January in Cortina had been an accident.

25.

NEAR RAVENNA, ITALY

When Leigh woke the next morning, Ben was already into his ninth phone call. The local directory didn't have a listing for a Professor Arno, so he was having to try each Arno in turn. He'd worked his way down half the list before deciding to give up and pay a personal visit to the music institute where the old scholar had taught.

They ate a rushed breakfast in the pensione and drove the Citroën into Ravenna. They parked near the center and walked through a pedestrian zone over the cobbled streets. It was out of season, and the town was quiet.

Past the Church of St. Vitale, the Istituto Monteverdi was a tall and narrow building fronted with white stone columns and a flight of steps. A glass doorway led into a reception foyer. Their footsteps rang off the marble floor and echoed up to a high ceiling. From somewhere above them they could hear a cello playing, and from another room the sound of a woman singing arpeggios to a piano accompaniment. The music mixed together in a discordant swirl that reverberated off the stone walls of the old building.

They approached the desk. The receptionist was a steely-haired woman dressed in black. She scowled at them. "Can I help you?"

"We're looking for Professor Arno," Ben said in Italian.

The woman shook her head. "*Professore* Arno does not teach here any longer. He is retired."

"Perhaps you could give me his phone number?" As Ben asked, he knew he'd be refused.

"We do not give out numbers."

"I understand, but this is very important."

The woman crossed her arms with a severe look. "I am sorry. It is not possible."

Ben was reaching for his wallet. Bribery was always an option, although this one didn't look the sort. Leigh stopped him. "Let me deal with her," she said in English.

The woman was staring at them with a hostile expression. Leigh smiled and spoke in fluent Italian. "Signora, please call your director."

The woman looked shocked. "Why?"

Leigh smiled again. "Tell him Leigh Llewellyn is here and would like to speak to him. It's urgent."

The mention of Leigh's name had an immediate, almost magical effect. The hostile receptionist was suddenly all smiles and apologies for not having recognized the famous soprano before. She led them up a flight of stone stairs to the first floor.

Leigh caught Ben's look. "What?" she whispered.

"Maybe I didn't make myself clear. I thought we'd agreed you were to keep a low profile."

"Can you think of a better way?"

"I'm sure I could."

"Like putting a gun to her head?"

"Wouldn't be a bad idea," he muttered.

The receptionist hammered on a door and stuck her head through. She fired a burst of rapid Italian that Ben didn't follow. A man's voice replied from inside the room. *"La Llewellyn? Qui?"*

The director burst out of the office. He was a short man, plump and round in a dark suit. He greeted them with furious pumping handshakes and ordered the receptionist to bring coffee and biscuits. "I am Alberto Fabiani," he said with a broad smile. He couldn't take his eyes off Leigh. "This is a great honor, *maestra*. What can I do for you?"

They sat at his desk, and Leigh repeated their need to see Professor Arno. Was it possible to be put in contact with him?

Fabiani looked unsure. He breathed in through his teeth.

"He's not dead, is he?" Leigh asked.

"No, no, he is not dead," Fabiani said hastily. "Not yet. He lives in the countryside about ten kilometers from here. I will gladly put you in touch with him. But I feel I should warn you . . ." The director paused. "Francesco Arno is a good man. In his day, he was thought of as one of the greatest Mozartian scholars of all time. But he is old now. Over the years he has become—how should I say it—*strano*."

"Strange? How?" Ben asked.

Fabiani shrugged. "His beliefs. His obsession. He became more eccentric as time passed, and he clashed more and more with his peers until, frankly, my old friend and colleague was becoming something of an embarrassment to the *istituto*. Even the students came to mock him. They would take a delight in winding him up. Once they got him started he would rant on for hours. His lectures became a farce." Fabiani smiled sadly. "I have to say that I was not entirely sorry when he announced his retirement."

"What were these beliefs of his?" Ben asked.

Fabiani rolled his eyes. "If you speak to him, you will find out soon enough."

26.

AUSTRIA

THE SAME MORNING

The man was solid and powerful. He was an inch under six and a half feet tall and weighed two hundred and sixty pounds—none of it fat. He walked naked to the edge of the springboard, feeling it flex under his weight, and bounced a couple of times. His strong leg muscles hardened. He took a breath and launched himself.

His body hit the water in a perfect dive, hardly making a splash, and he knifed deep into the pool, then surfaced and swam fast. He forced thirty lengths out of himself, then heaved himself out of the water and walked to the chair, where his clothes were lying neatly folded. He was barely out of breath. Through the windows of the indoor pool, the snow-covered grounds of the estate swept away to the pinewoods in the distance.

The man scraped back his sandy hair. He reached for a towel, and as he dried himself he admired his trim shape. His muscled arms and torso bore the scars of nine bullet wounds and three knife slashes. He remembered exactly how and where he'd got each of them. Each had its own story. What they all had in common was that none of the people who'd given them to him had lived for more than three minutes afterwards.

The man was forty-three years old. He was a Londoner

by birth and a former British army soldier. His name was Jack Glass.

When he was drunk, he would sometimes boast about his exploits in the legendary SAS. He even had the regimental winged dagger emblem tattooed on his upper right arm. He liked people to see it.

The truth was that he'd been rejected for service in the regiment many years before. A psychological evaluation had exposed certain traits that the regimental heads felt would not be an asset. His unsuitability for the Special Air Service had been confirmed when he'd tried to throttle the officer who'd informed him of his failure to make the grade. He'd been returned to his regular unit in disgrace, court-martialed, and kicked out of the army.

He'd drifted around after that, run out of money. Like a lot of army leavers he'd been forced to take on menial jobs for a while. With his court-martial record he couldn't even get security work.

One rainy London night he'd been at the bar of a pub when he'd met an old contact who had offered him paramilitary work in Africa. The money was excellent, and the work was perfect for Glass. He'd accepted immediately and was on a flight three days later. He'd never returned to Britain.

In the Congo, Rwanda, Liberia, he'd worked for whoever paid the most. Suppressed antigovernment rebels. Burned schools. Destroyed villages. Executed whole families caught up in bloody tribal wars. He did whatever he was told to do, took the cash, and asked no questions.

Liberia was where he'd picked up the scar on his ear. The lobe had been ripped off by a bullet from an AK-47. The person holding the rifle was a black child of nine or ten, a little girl. It was the last round in the magazine of her AK.

When she saw him standing there clutching his ear and screaming at her, she dropped the rifle and ran.

Glass had gone after her. He chased the screaming child deep into the bush. Brought her down, knelt on her chest, pinned her arms over her head with one hand. With the other hand he'd drawn out his bayonet, placed the point against her ribs. When he drove the blade slowly deep inside her little body, he felt the struggles diminish and saw the life leak out of her eyes.

He could still remember it now. Someday, he'd like to do that again.

After Africa came the Bosnian conflict, where Glass had become involved in gunrunning. He quit the battlefields, wore a suit, and carried a briefcase instead of an M16. The case was usually filled with banknotes. He discovered you could make more money getting someone else to pull the trigger. Two years later, now a full-blown businessman with a lot of connections and cash rolling in, he'd met and struck up an alliance with an Austrian called Werner Kroll at an arms fair in Berlin.

At the age of thirty-six, Glass had gone to work for Kroll as a personal secretary and general aide. Glass was used to money by now, but selling Kalashnikovs to warring tribes was nickels and dimes next to the things Kroll was into. He was a little more than just an ordinary businessman. But he took fanatical care to cover his tracks, and only a very select few had any notion of the real scope of his activities.

Glass knew a little about the history of Werner Kroll's family business. It had been around a long time, and had come a long way since its origins. He also knew that Kroll wouldn't hesitate to have him, or anyone else, killed if he betrayed him or informed on him. The old Austrian was small and looked harmless. He was a little odd in his ways, and he had the air of an old-world schoolmaster. But he was the most dangerous man Jack Glass had ever met in his life, and he'd met a great many dangerous people.

Glass pictured Kroll's wrinkled, pinched gray face in his mind. One day, he was going to kill the old bastard and fuck that little whore he kept as his mistress.

He dressed in a white shirt and gray slacks, did his tie up loosely, and put on his blazer. In his office he found a sheet waiting for him on the fax machine. It was from London. He studied it up close. This was interesting.

Werner Kroll was sitting in his conservatory breakfast room with Eve. He ate in silence, with his back to the window and the ornamental lake with the snowy mountains beyond. Kroll had been eating the exact same breakfast every morning for six years: poached eggs with slivers of toast cut into precisely the same sizes, arranged the same way on a porcelain plate. No butter. He ate delicately, almost daintily.

Glass came in carrying a folder. Kroll's fork halted midway between his plate and his mouth. He dabbed his lips with his napkin and glared at him. "I've told you not to disturb me at breakfast," he said in an icy voice. His nose twitched. "My God, man, are you chewing gum again?"

Glass smiled to himself and took the gum out of his mouth. He loved to wind the old man up. "Forgive me, sir," he said. "I thought you might like to see this. It just came through." He opened the file and handed Kroll a sheet of fax paper.

Kroll put on a pair of half-moon spectacles and peered down his nose at the sheet. It was a copy of the front page of last night's *Evening Standard*. It showed a grainy photo of

Leigh Llewellyn surrounded by fans. Kroll recognized the Oxford landscape, the Sheldonian Theatre behind her. To her left stood a man he hadn't seen before. They were holding hands. The headline read "Who's Leigh's Leading Man?"

Kroll lowered the sheet and looked at Glass over the top of his lenses. "Is this the person who killed one of our best men with . . . what was it?"

"A skillet, sir," Glass said.

Eve picked up the sheet and peered at the man in the photo. She liked the look of him, tall and athletic. Glass was watching her face.

"I would also like to find out who Leigh's leading man is," Kroll said. He glanced at Eve. She'd been looking at the picture a moment too long. He snatched it away from her.

"I think I know who he is, sir," Glass said.

"A professional bodyguard?" asked Kroll.

"I think he might be a little more than that," Glass said. "I'll have to check my contacts. It might take a few days. But I'm certain it's him."

Kroll dismissed him and went back to his eggs. They were cold. He pushed them away in disgust.

Eve was heading back to her room after breakfast when she met Glass in the corridor. He was standing at her doorway, leaning casually against the wall with one big hand against the doorframe.

She stopped and looked at him. "Aren't you going to let me through?"

He grinned, eyeing her up and down. She tried to shove past him. His powerful hand gripped her arm, and he whirled her around.

"Get your paws off me," she warned him.

Glass pulled her closer and roughly fondled her breasts through her blouse. "Nice."

She tore away from him and slapped him across the face, felt the hardness of his jaw against her hand. Her palm stung.

Glass smiled. "I'm watching you," he said. "I know what you want."

"Do you really?"

"Once a whore, always a whore. You want to fuck a real man for a change?"

"If I can find one," she said.

"You've got one right here."

"In your dreams."

Glass's smile stretched into a grin. "One day, bitch. One day soon."

27.

ITALY

LATER THAT DAY

Professor Arno invited them into a large, sunlit study and offered them a glass of grappa. His English was heavily accented but fluent. He walked with a stick, and his ancient tweed jacket was two sizes too large for him. His movements were slow, and his frail hands shook slightly as he poured the drinks from a crystal decanter. He motioned them to a cluttered desk that sat in front of a pair of arched windows overlooking the villa's pretty gardens.

The study was filled with a heavy, sickly vanilla-like smell from the three large scented church candles burning in an antique silver candleholder. The elderly professor walked stiffly around the desk and lowered his wiry frame into a button-leather chair with his back to the windows.

Ben and Leigh sat facing him. Ben drank the burning spirit down and put his empty glass in front of him on the desk. Leigh took a tiny sip and cradled her glass nervously on her knee, preparing in her mind what she wanted to say.

The professor leaned back in his chair, his wispy white hair silhouetted against the sunlight streaming in through the glass. He watched Leigh for a few moments with a glimmer in his eye. "I heard you sing *Lucia di Lammermoor* at the Rocca Brancaleone," he said to her. "I thought you were magnificent, the greatest Lucia since Maria Callas."

Leigh smiled graciously. "Thank you, Professor. That's a great compliment, and I'm sure I don't deserve it." She paused. "But unfortunately we didn't come here to talk about opera."

"I did not think you had," the old man said.

"I believe my brother Oliver came here to see you last winter. What can you tell me about his visit?"

"I found him a charming young man," Arno said sadly. "We got on very well. He only planned a short stay, but we talked for many hours. In the end he remained here for nearly two whole days. I was very impressed with his passion for music. He played for me, pieces from the *Goldberg Variations* and some Clementi sonatas. A gifted pianist. His Clementi interpretation was very nearly in the same league as Maria Tipo, in my opinion."

"He was here to discuss the research for his book," Leigh said.

"Yes. Oliver asked me to clarify certain things that were unclear to him."

"Things about the letter?" she asked.

The professor nodded. "The Mozart letter I obtained from your father long ago. Your brother had a photocopy that your father had made of it, but he could not understand its full and true meaning."

"Do you know what happened to Oliver shortly after you saw him?"

Arno sighed. "I know that he went to Vienna."

"Where he was killed. I believe he was murdered."

Arno didn't look surprised. He nodded. "I feared as much."

"Why did you think that?"

"I received an e-mail message from him. He told me he needed very urgently to talk to me, that he had made a discovery, and that there was danger."

"When was this?"

"The night he died, I believe. I was very sorry to hear of his death." Arno shook his head sadly.

"What kind of danger did he say he was in?" Ben asked.

"He did not say. The message seemed to have been written in a hurry."

Ben glanced at the computer on the old man's desk. "Do you still have that e-mail?"

"I deleted it immediately after reading it."

"You realize that information would have been very important at the inquest into the cause of Oliver's death?"

"Yes," Arno said softly.

"But you decided to keep it to yourself that the circumstances might have been suspicious—that it might not have been an accident?" Ben felt his face flush. Beside him, Leigh was staring at her hands on her lap, and he worried that he was pushing the old man too hard.

Arno sighed heavily and ran his fingers through his thin white hair. "I am not proud of what I did. I had my suspicions but no proof. There was a witness to the accident. Who would have believed a crazy old Italian with the reputation of a crank, a conspiracy theorist?" He paused. "And I was afraid."

"Afraid of what?" Leigh asked.

"That I was also in danger," Arno replied. "Soon afterwards, intruders came in the night."

"Came here?"

"Yes. I was in the hospital. My blood—it is not healthy. When I returned home, I found that the house had been ransacked. They were searching for something."

"What were they searching for?" Ben asked.

"For the letter, I believe."

"Did they steal it?"

"No," Arno replied. "After your brother sent me the message, I put the letter somewhere very secret. Somewhere nobody could ever find it."

"May we know where it is?" Ben asked.

Arno smiled. "It is safe," he said softly. "It has gone home."

Ben wondered what he meant by that.

Arno went on. "But for a long time I myself did not feel safe," he said. "I felt I was being watched. It went on for months."

"I think the letter had something to do with Oliver's death," Leigh said.

The professor looked grim. "You may be right."

"Can you explain?"

Arno hesitated as he gathered his thoughts. "I think I had better start at the beginning. As you know, the subject of your brother's book was one that I have been studying for many years."

"Mozart's death," Leigh said.

"Not just Mozart's death, but the events that led up to it, surrounded it, and may have caused it . . . I believe *did* cause it. For this, we have to go back to the eighteenth century—"

"With respect, Professor," Ben said. "We didn't come here for a history lesson about someone who died over two hundred years ago. We want to know what happened to Oliver."

"If you hear me out," Arno replied, "I think what I tell you may help you understand."

"Oliver told me he was doing a lot of research into Mozart and the Freemasons," Leigh said.

Arno nodded. "It is no secret that Mozart was a Freemason himself. He joined his lodge in 1784 and remained a Mason until his death seven years later, during which time it is said he rose to the level of Third Degree, Master Mason. Mozart was so dedicated to Freemasonry he even persuaded his father Leopold to join them. He supplied music for Masonic events, and had many friends who were Initiates."

Ben shifted impatiently in his seat. "I don't understand why this is so important."

Leigh laid a hand on his arm. "Go on, Professor."

"Today we think of Freemasonry as something of a joke, or at best a social club like the Rotarians," Arno said. "But in eighteenth-century Europe it was an extremely important cultural and political force. In 1780s Austria, Freemasonry was a meeting point for the intellectual elite, an important center for ideas of peace, freedom, and equality. The Masonic lodges of Vienna comprised many of the most influential names of the time. Many aristocrats, senior politicians and diplomats, high-ranking military officers, bankers, and merchants. There were also many intellectuals among them—writers, artists, musicians."

"I didn't know they were so powerful," Leigh said.

Arno nodded. "They were, but their power was also their undoing. Other forces, even more powerful, were watching with a close eye. In fact, much of our modern knowledge of the Viennese Masons at this time comes from the intelligence material gathered by the Austrian secret police. Freemasonry was officially condemned in the Austrian Empire on the orders of the pope, and allowed to exist only because of the tolerance of the emperor, Josef II. But in 1785 Josef's sympathy grew thin, and he decided that the Masons had become too powerful and influential. He ordered a drastic reduction of the Viennese lodges, and demanded that the secret police provide him with lists of active Masons. These lists were kept in the files of the court archives."

"Why the sudden sea change?" Leigh asked.

"You have to understand the climate of the times," Arno explained patiently. "Mozart lived in a turbulent age, a revolutionary age. The Americans had only recently overthrown their colonialist British rulers and established a new free nation. Revolution was in the air. By 1789, just two years before Mozart's death, France stood on the verge of terrible bloodshed."

"And the Masons were involved?"

"Masonry was increasingly associated with the growing revolutionary, anti-Royalist current," said Arno. "With its ideals of liberty, equality, and fraternity, it offered a perfect metaphor for the dawning of a new age of free ideas. As the French Revolution gathered steam, some of the revolutionary 'clubs,' such as Robespierre's Jacobins, based their structures on the Masonic lodges, as well as importing Masonic symbolism into their political ideology. In America, when George Washington laid the foundation stone of the Capitol in Washington, he wore with pride the Masonic apron that had been made for him by Adrienne, the wife of the French soldier-revolutionary La Fayette. Thomas Jefferson was another Freemason who drew heavily on those ideals of liberty and equality when he drafted the Declaration of Independence. It was a hugely powerful force with the potential to influence political change across the world."

"And so, naturally, it had to be stopped," Ben said.

"Without question," replied Arno with a bitter smile. "By the late 1780s there were growing concerns in Mozart's Austria that the Masons were going to plunge the country into the same revolutionary, pro-republic spirit as France and America. It was a dangerous time. Many aristocrats who had initially sympathized with Freemasonry's ideals began to worry. Then, as the revolutionary mobs tore through France and the aristocracy went to the guillotine, the Austrian clampdown on Freemasonry began in earnest. By 1791 Masonry in Austria was virtually wiped out. It was a period of severe crisis for Mozart and his lodge brothers." He paused. "A new emperor had taken over, Leopold II. The Masons could not tell what his attitude would be to them, but they were not optimistic. Then Mozart and his close colleague, the theatrical producer and fellow Mason Emanuel Schikaneder, had an idea."

"What idea?" Ben asked.

"They thought that if they could rescue the public image of the Masons, they might help to save the Craft from universal condemnation," said Arno. "What they did would nowadays be called a huge publicity stunt. They conceived of a grand opera that would reach out to an audience of unprecedented scale. A spectacle that everyone would love, written in popular style. A people's opera preaching Masonic ideals of the education of men to a higher morality through wisdom, love, and goodness, heralding the transition to a new social order. Full of mystical symbols glorifying the Freemasons and their philosophy."

"*The Magic Flute*," Leigh said.

Arno nodded. "The new opera had its premiere performance in Vienna at the end of September 1791. It was received with rapturous enthusiasm by the public and the critics, and played to packed theaters night after night."

"It was the most successful thing Mozart had ever done," Leigh added.

"Yes, it should have been the start of a new era for him," Arno replied. "And it was welcomed by his fellow Masons as a new hope for their Craft. But it was the last opera he would ever compose. Within less than three months, he was dead."

"Wait a minute," Ben said. "Leigh, didn't you tell me that Mozart had been murdered by the Masons because he'd given away their secrets in *The Magic Flute?*"

"That's what I thought—"

"Well, that doesn't make sense, does it?" Ben continued. "If Mozart was becoming this great new hope for the Masons, their public relations man at a time when they needed him most, then why kill him?"

Arno smiled. "You are right. This theory is completely illogical. Likewise, the fact that after Mozart's death his fellow Masons gave his widow Constanze a great deal of moral and financial support makes nonsense of the idea that he was murdered by his own." Arno turned to Leigh. "Your brother had noticed these inconsistencies early on in the course of his research. Oliver knew that there was no satisfactory explanation for the strange and sudden death of Mozart."

"Unless he wasn't murdered at all," Ben said. "How do we know there's any truth in this murder conspiracy theory?"

"The official cause of death was acute rheumatic fever," Arno replied. "However, many of those around him at the time found the circumstances of his passing highly suspicious. Towards the end of his life, Mozart often expressed his conviction that he would be poisoned one day—yet the scholars have never bothered to examine this properly. His elder son, Carl Thomas Mozart, also had strong suspicions that his father had died by foul means. The body displayed unusual characteristics consistent with death by poisoning." Arno shrugged. "Based on the medical records of the time, nobody can disprove that Mozart was poisoned. But the single most important piece of evidence is the letter itself."

"What does it say?" Leigh asked.

Arno looked surprised. "You have not seen it?"

"I had Oliver's copy, but it got burned," Leigh said. "All I've seen of it are a few fragments."

"But surely your father showed it to you?"

"Professor, I was only nineteen years old. I had other things on my mind." She glanced at Ben. "I don't remember much about it."

"I see . . ." Arno paused and scratched his chin. "So you are not familiar with the Order of Ra, to which the letter refers?"

Ben remembered it from Oliver's notes. He thought for a moment. "*Ra*, as in the Egyptian sun god Ra?" he asked.

Leigh turned to stare at him.

He caught her look. "Theology," he said. "Student days."

"You studied theology?"

"It was a long time ago."

Arno smiled. "You are correct, and many of the ceremonies and traditions of Freemasonry can be traced back to ancient Egypt. But *Ra* also means king. It is sometimes written as *Re*, and is the origin of the word *Rex* in Latin and your English words *regal* and *royal*."

"So what was this Order of Ra?" Ben asked.

"The Order of Ra was originally a small and obscure Masonic lodge," Arno answered. "Their members were largely aristocratic and pro-Royalist, and they gave their group a name that would reflect their political leanings: for them it signified 'the Order of the King.' They were far divorced from the growing republican spirit within Freemasonry, and became increasingly allied to the establishment powers as the perceived threat from the Masons grew. While Freemasonry stood for freedom, democracy, and the people, the Order of Ra stood for the complete opposite. They were warmongers, fervent capitalists, an agency founded to aid elitist governments in suppressing the people."

"A kind of rogue splinter group, then," Ben said.

"Exactly," Arno replied. "And an extremely powerful one, with lofty connections. The Order of Ra meddled in many political intrigues, not least of which was to put pressure on the emperor of Austria to ban the rest of Freemasonry outright, even on pain of execution."

"Let me get this right," Leigh said. "You're suggesting that the Order of Ra killed Mozart because he was popularizing Freemasonry through his opera *The Magic Flute?*"

The professor's eyes glittered. "That *is* what I believe. And I believe the letter proves it. Mozart was a potential threat to them. If he could restore public support for Freemasonry, he could be dangerous. He was a rising star, a meteoric talent just beginning to shine. The massive success of *The Magic Flute* had given him great prestige. He had only just been appointed to a prominent post at the court, and he had the emperor's ear.

"But his enemies were rising up, too. By 1791 the members of the Order of Ra were fast becoming a major executive branch of the secret services. Their agents were brutal, violent, and ruthless, and their Grand Master was none other than the head of the Austrian secret police. He was a callous murderer, sworn to destroy the Masons."

Ben was about to ask the man's name, but Arno carried on.

"By 1794, just three years after Mozart's death, Masonry in Austria had effectively been obliterated. Many murders were committed—some openly, some less openly. Poisoning was one of their most common means, and would have been the most suited to disposing of someone of Mozart's increasing celebrity status. They had to be careful. Other, more obscure Masons met with a far more violent end. Gustav Lutze, for instance."

"Who was he?" Leigh asked.

"He was the man Mozart wrote the letter to," Arno said. "A member of the same Viennese Masonic lodge, Beneficence. Mozart was writing to warn him of the growing danger. The letter is dated the sixteenth of November 1791, and it is perhaps the last one he ever wrote. Of course, the so-called experts believe that his last surviving letter was the one he wrote to his wife on the fourteenth of October, while she was away taking the waters in Baden. Idiots. In any case, the letter never reached its destination; it was too late."

"What happened to Lutze?" Ben asked.

"He was found dead on the twentieth of November 1791. Just two weeks before Mozart's death. Lutze had been tied to a post and tortured to death. Disemboweled, his tongue hacked out. The secret police blamed a Freemason for the crime."

Ben stood up, reaching in his pocket. "Professor, I want you to take a look at something." He took out the CD-ROM in its plastic case. "May I?" He walked around the desk and loaded the disc into the computer.

"What is this?" Arno asked.

"Something Oliver saw the night he died," Ben said. "Just watch."

Arno blinked bemusedly at the screen. Leigh stayed in her chair, not wanting to see the video clip again.

The images began to play. Ben watched the professor's face as the clip went on. The victim was brought out. The macabre spectacle unfolded.

The old man's eyes widened, and his cheeks drained of color. He pointed a trembling finger at the screen.

Ben reached across and paused the clip just before the victim's tongue was cut out. In the frozen image the man's face was contorted in terror. The blade was held high in the air, where it caught the candlelight.

Arno slumped in his chair. "*Dio mio,*" he breathed, and wiped a trickle of sweat from his brow with a handkerchief. "So it is true."

"What's true, Professor?" Leigh asked.

Arno was about to reply when the window behind him exploded into the room and blood spattered across the computer screen.

28.

Wedged in the crook of a tree eighty yards away, the sniper watched through his high-magnification scope as Arno's body dropped out of view. With his gloved thumb he quickly flipped the select-fire toggle from single shot to fully automatic and fired a long burst through the study windows. Glass shards and chunks of stonework flew as the bullets struck. He smiled.

Ben had hurled himself over Arno's desk, grabbed Leigh's wrist, and dragged her to the floor. He ripped the disc out of the computer. The screen was smoking from a bullet hole.

Another burst of gunfire shattered the rest of the window. It chewed a line of ragged holes in the top of the desk, blew the computer apart, and strafed the book cabinet at the far end of the study. The silver candleholder toppled over as the decanter of grappa shattered. The strong drink burst into flame, liquid fire pouring onto the carpet where it quickly caught hold.

Ben and Leigh pressed their bodies tightly against the thick wall beneath the window, a storm of splinters and glass around them. Ben drew the .45 from his belt and fired blindly through the broken panes.

He could smell burning. He twisted round to see where it was coming from. Black smoke was filling the far end of the room. Fire was crackling up the length of the doorframe.

Arno lay slumped under the desk, blood spreading across the rug. Leigh crawled over to him. His eyes were glazing over. She wanted to do something, stop the bleeding, move him away from the window. There were so many more things she wanted to know from him. "Professor, the letter," she said frantically. "Where's the letter?"

The old man's eyes focused on her for a second. His lips moved almost inaudibly, trickling bloody froth.

The shooting outside had stopped. Ben peered out of the shattered window. He couldn't see anyone, but there were voices and running footsteps down below in the courtyard. The crackle of a radio.

Half the room was on fire now. The bullet-torn books in the bookcases burst alight. The smoke was thickening fast.

Arno coughed, and bright blood appeared on his lips. He tried to speak. Then a long sigh whistled from his lips and his head slumped to the side.

Ben glanced at him. "He's dead, Leigh."

Leigh was shaking the old man. "He was trying to say something."

"There's nothing you can do for him. Let's move." Through the ringing in his ears and the crackle of the fire he could hear the sound of movement downstairs. They were coming. He checked the gun. Three rounds left.

Fire blocked the doorway. They were going to have to run through the flames. He grabbed the dead man's jacket from the stand. He pulled Leigh to her feet and draped the heavy tweed over her head and shoulders. Keeping hold of her arm he took two fast steps into the choking smoke and kicked hard. Flame licked his ankle. The study door juddered open. He shielded his eyes and ran through the fire, pulling her through behind him.

The corridor outside was empty. Footsteps thumped

on the stairs. Ben ran to the right, gripping Leigh's arm. Through a doorway at the end of the corridor there was a short flight of steps and then another door. Ben had a rough idea where he was. On his way in he'd noticed the square clock tower rising up from the center of the house, with shuttered windows on each side overlooking the sloping roofs. He wrenched open the door. He was right.

The winding stair took them upwards. The door to the tower was thick old oak. They ran inside, and Ben barred the heavy door with a wooden beam. He looked around him, getting his bearings. Voices. Someone was thumping at the door. Leigh jumped as shots went off.

"This way." Ben nodded towards the shuttered windows on the next level. The wooden stairway was old and rickety. He guided her up ahead of him.

Down below, the blast of a shotgun boomed through the tower, and splinters flew from the inside of the old door. They'd be through it soon.

Ben kicked open the shutters, and they were looking out across the broad expanse of red-tiled roof. Dusk was falling.

Leigh could feel her legs shaking as she clambered out of the window and onto the roof. The height made her dizzy. Ben guided her along the red-tiled ridge. She kept her eyes pinned to the wooded horizon and the falling sun.

The roof sloped down to the side. He steered her that way, taking them lower. She slipped on the weathered clay tiles and almost fell, but his grip on her arm was firm. He peered over the edge. They were still a long way from the ground.

The tower window shutter burst open, and a man appeared. He was wearing a black jacket and holding a stubby machine pistol. Its muzzle flashed, and bullets whined off the tiles near their feet. Ben returned fire. The man fell back against the tower.

Ben shoved the pistol in his belt and took Leigh's hand. "Trust me," he said, reading the look in her eyes.

Then he took two steps to the edge of the roof and leaped into space, taking her with him.

Leigh gasped as they fell. Then the striped canvas canopy was rushing up to meet her, knocking the wind out of her, and they were sliding down it. There was a crack as the flimsy aluminum frame holding the patio awning to the wall gave way. The taut canvas enveloped their struggling bodies and slowly, gracefully, collapsed in an arc to the outdoor eating area below.

Ben crashed down against a brick barbecue, and Leigh had a softer landing into a circular plastic table. She rolled off it and landed on her hands and knees on the ground, only a little scuffed. Ben staggered to his feet, clutching his back and grimacing in pain. He grabbed her hand again.

They ran through the gardens. Over the rasping of her breath Leigh heard shouts behind. Some shots rang out, and Ben felt a bullet pass close by. They scrambled through dense shrubs and found themselves in wooded parkland. They sprinted on through the trees, branches whipping at their faces. Up ahead, a high stone wall had crumbled to leave a gap they could clamber over.

On the other side of the wall was an old farmyard, overgrown and muddy, dilapidated wooden buildings streaked with green lichen. Ben looked back through the gap in the wall. There were six men running fast towards them. Their faces were hard and determined, and they were heavily armed.

His pistol had only two rounds left. He took aim, then

changed his mind. He could kill two at most, and he'd be left with an empty gun. A fatal tactical error.

They ducked into an old shed. The rotting building was filled with shelves and boxes and tools. Ben snatched up a rake and tried to wedge the door with it, but a heavy body crashed into the door and knocked it open. Ben kicked it shut. The man's arm was trapped in the door. He had a Škorpion machine pistol in his fist. Deafening gunfire strafed the inside of the shed. Leigh screamed.

Ben grabbed a rusty tool from a nearby shelf. It was an air-powered nail gun. He pressed it hard up against the man's thrashing arm and squeezed. With a bang, the arm was pinned to the doorframe with a rusty four-inch nail. Blood spurted. Ben fired three more nails into the howling man's hand, and the Škorpion clattered to the ground. He picked it up. Empty. Useless. He threw it down.

Bullets tore through the shed's thin wooden walls. A pile of crates collapsed and revealed a gap in the planking that was big enough to squeeze through. They ran on across a muddy passage and slipped inside a barn opposite.

The gunmen saw the barn door swing shut and approached the tall wooden building cautiously, exchanging wary looks, their weapons trained. There was a heavy silence in the farmyard, just the sound of two crows calling in the distance.

Then the sudden sound of an engine revving hard. It was coming from inside the barn.

The men didn't have time to react. The barn wall disintegrated into jagged pieces of planking. The old flatbed farm truck burst out into the yard with a roar and went straight over two of them, crushing them into the mud. The other men dived for cover and opened fire as the truck lurched away, but their shots went into the three large plastic-wrapped bales of hay loaded on the back. One of the men swore and spoke urgently into a radio.

The truck skidded out of the farmyard and onto a country road that snaked steeply upwards into the hills. Darkness was falling now, and the truck's headlights cast a weak yellow glow over the craggy rock face on one side of the narrow road and the vertiginous drops on the other.

"Doesn't this thing go any faster?" Leigh shouted over the straining whine of the diesel.

Ben already had his foot flat to the floor, but the needle in the dusty dial wouldn't climb higher than the sixty-kilometers-per-hour mark. In the mirror he saw what he'd been hoping he wouldn't. Powerful car headlights, gaining on them fast. Two sets.

Leigh saw the concern on his face. She wound down the passenger's window and looked back, her hair streaming in the cold wind. "Is it them?" she asked.

The gunshots that rang out answered her question. The truck's wing mirror shattered. "They're going to take out the tires," Ben said. "Take the wheel, will you?"

"What are you doing?"

"Keep the pedal hard down," he said. He opened the driver's door. As Leigh grabbed the wheel, he heaved himself out of the cab. The wind filled his ears and tore at his clothes. The rock wall flashed by only two feet away, brightly lit by the pursuing cars. Ben inched his way along the side of the thundering truck.

More shots boomed from behind. They couldn't see him for the hay bales loaded on the flatbed. The truck was swerving from side to side, veering dangerously close to the rock wall. A protruding shrub almost scraped him off, but he held on desperately. He swung wildly with all his strength and reached the flatbed.

The big round bales were eight feet high, three of them one behind the other, their black polythene wrapping crackling in the wind. They were held in place by strong ropes, taut as piano strings. Ben hung on to the side of the truck with one hand as he grabbed his pistol from his belt.

Four ropes. Only two rounds.

The truck swung away from the wall, its wheels clipping the edge of the precipice on the other side. For an instant Ben was hanging in space, fully exposed and blinded by the lights of the cars behind. He heard the crack of a shot and pain seared through his arm as a bullet passed through his left sleeve and scored the flesh. He pressed the muzzle of the .45 against the nearest rope, said a prayer, and pulled the trigger.

The pistol kicked, and the rope parted. The two smoking ends fell limp. Nothing happened.

Wrong rope.

A burst of bullets screeched off the steel framework of the flatbed by his ear. He pressed the gun to another rope. Last shot.

He fired.

The flailing rope almost whipped the gun from his hand. The bales gave a jerk as they were suddenly cut loose and began to roll backwards. They hit the road and were lit up red in the truck's taillights as three tons of hay leaped like bouncing bombs towards the two wildly braking cars.

Tires screeched as the cars swerved, but the road was too narrow for any chance of escape. The first car impacted with a crunching explosion of hay, glass, and buckled metal. The bale burst all over the road, and the car skidded sideways, rolled, and flipped. Then the second car slammed into it from behind and sent it spinning off the edge of the precipice. Ben caught a glimpse of it tumbling down the sheer drop as the second car skidded violently and smashed into the rock face on the other side of the road, bounced, and lay still.

The truck rumbled on. Ben's left sleeve was bloody. He stood on the flatbed and watched as they left the wreckage behind them in the darkness.

29.

AUSTRIA

Clara was safe. That had been his first priority. Kinski had dealt with it quickly, and there was no way anyone could get to her again. No way anyone would find her at Hildegard's place.

And now, down to business. If they thought this was going to stop him, they could think again. Kinski was a big man, but he could move fast. People stepped aside when they saw him coming down the corridor, eyes front, pressing forward with long determined strides. The look on his face was clear: *Get out of my way.* Kinski wasn't to be messed with when he wore that face. They'd seen it before, but never this intense. They parted like minnows for a shark.

He didn't slow down for the door of the chief's office. He shouldered it aside and marched straight in.

Kinski had marched straight into his chief's office a hundred times before. Every time, he'd been confronted with the exact same thing. The same clutter of piled-up folders and papers, the same stale coffee smell from a thousand cups that never got finished and sat cold around the office. The same gray, harassed, tired-looking chief slumped at his desk. The chief was part of the furniture, almost part of the building itself. It was a tradition to see him sitting there, something you'd never expect to change.

Today, Kinski burst into the office, and everything was different.

The man behind the desk looked about half the chief's age. He had dark hair slicked back, and he wore neat gold-rimmed glasses. His suit was pressed, and his tie was perfectly straight. He was slender and clean-looking. Everything that the chief wasn't.

The office was tidy and smelled of air freshener. The desk was clear of papers, just a small notebook computer whirring quietly to one side. There was a brand-new filing cabinet in place of the rusty, overflowing, scarred old hulk that had sat for the last decade and a half in the corner of the office. Even the windows had been cleaned.

"Where's Chief Schiller?"

The younger man looked up and met Kinski's hard gaze. "Who are you?" he asked.

"Kinski. Who the fuck are you?"

"I'm Gessler. *Chief* Gessler to you, asshole. The next time you come into my office, you knock. Understood?"

Kinski said nothing.

"So what the fuck did you want anyway?"

"Where's Chief Schiller?" Kinski said again.

"He's gone," Gessler replied.

"Gone where?"

Gessler ripped off his glasses and glared at Kinski. "What am I, a fucking travel agent? How the hell should I know where he's gone? Sitting on a beach somewhere south of the equator. Sipping on a long cool drink and watching the girls go by. What else is there to do when you retire?"

"He retired? I just talked to him yesterday. He didn't say anything. I knew it was coming up, but—"

Gessler shrugged. "He got an opportunity, he took it. Now, Detective, did you actually have a reason for barging into my office? If not, I suggest you fuck off and find something useful to do." Gessler smiled. *"Okay?"*

30.

SOMEWHERE IN THE ITALIAN COUNTRYSIDE

They waited until the flames were pouring from the windows of the truck, paintwork blistering on the doors and black smoke rising through the trees. Then they turned and walked away from the forest clearing.

It was getting dark, and the air was cold and damp. Ben's bandaged arm was beginning to hurt badly, but the bullet had only creased the flesh. He'd been lucky.

They walked in silence for some distance along the empty country road. Below them in a valley were some lights from a building. A little way along the road they came to a gate and a sign on a post.

It was low season at the Rossi pony-trekking center. Gino Rossi and his wife had five empty cabins that were rented out in summer to horse riders exploring the local countryside. It was a pleasant surprise to be offered cash from the two strangers in return for accommodation for the night. Rosalba Rossi prepared a big dish of tagliatelle with tomato sauce that filled the farmhouse with the scent of basil and fresh garlic, while her husband dusted out the cabin and fired up the heating system.

After dinner Ben bought two bottles of Sangiovese from Gino, and he and Leigh said good night and retreated to their cabin. The accommodation was rustic, but warm and comfortable. There were two single wooden beds with patchwork quilts, and a crucifix hung on the whitewashed wall between them.

Ben had noticed that Leigh had only picked at her food. She slumped down on one of the beds, looking pale and exhausted. Ben sat with her and poured some wine. They sat in silence for a while, letting the wine relax them.

"I can't take much more of this," she said. Her voice sounded strained.

He gently put his arm around her shoulders and pulled her to him. Their closeness felt a little strange. She rested her head against him and moved closer. He could feel her body heat, her thigh pressed against his, and her heart beating against his arm. Then he realized that he was tenderly stroking her hair, enjoying the soft silky feel of it, letting his hand run down her neck and the curve of her shoulder without even thinking about it.

Suddenly self-conscious, he shifted away from her. He reached for the bottle and poured himself more wine. "It'll be all right," he said.

"How did they know we were there?" she asked softly.

He didn't reply.

She seemed to read his thoughts. "It was my fault, wasn't it? They were tapping his phone."

"It wasn't your fault. I tried to call him, too. Don't think about it. You need to rest."

"But I gave my name," she went on. "You told me to keep it quiet, but I used it. I didn't listen to you, and now because of me that poor old man is dead."

"You didn't pull the trigger," he said.

"I might as well have." She sighed. "Who *are* these people? They're everywhere." She looked up at him with frightened eyes. "They're going to kill us, too. I know it."

He reassured her, and his voice was calm, but his mind was working hard and fast. They'd come about twenty kilometers from Arno's place. There was no way anyone could have followed them, and they were safe for the moment. But they wouldn't be safe for long, and he had no idea where to go next. They still didn't know where the letter was. Oliver's trail seemed to have gone cold.

Arno's words echoed in his mind. *It has gone home.* He'd put the letter somewhere safe—but where? Where could be home to the Mozart letter? Maybe the place it had been written. Austria?

Leigh slept eventually, her fingers still curled around the base of her empty wineglass as her chest rose and fell gently. Ben took the glass away, covered her with a blanket, and watched over her for a while as he sat on the other bed and finished the second bottle of wine with the last of his cigarettes. His mind was a swirl. All questions. No answers.

It was after eleven thirty when he stepped outside to clear his head in the cold night air. The frost was hard under his feet, making the grass crunch. He looked up into the night sky, orientating himself with the North Star out of long habit.

Across from the row of cabins, on the far side of the moonlit yard, was a range of stone outbuildings, stables, and ramshackle corrugated-iron sheds. A dog barked in the distance. One of the sheds had a light on in its dusty window, and Ben could hear the metallic sounds of someone working with tools inside. He approached and peered through a gap in the rust-streaked corrugated sheets. The shed was a rough workshop filled with battered farm equipment and racks of tools. A young curly-haired man was working on an old Fiat Strada, clattering around under the hood.

Ben walked round to the open doorway. "*Ciao*," he said. "I'm Steve."

The young man turned. He was a younger version of Gino Rossi, about nineteen or twenty.

Ben pointed at the car. "Problems?" he asked in Italian.

"*Ciao*, Steve. Sandro." Sandro grinned and waggled a spark-plug wrench to show the foreigner. "Changing the plugs, that's all. I'm selling her, and I want her to go well." He finished tightening up the plugs, replaced the caps, and slammed the rusty hood shut, then walked around to the open door and fired up the engine. Ben listened. There were no unhealthy rattles, and the exhaust note was clean. No gaskets gone, not sucking air. No blue smoke.

"How much are you asking?"

Sandro wiped his hands on his jeans. "She's old, but good. Say a thousand and a half."

Ben took cash from his pocket. "Is she ready for a run right now?" he asked.

He drove quietly out of the farmyard and up the rutted drive, then turned right to follow the winding country road back the way they'd come. The yellowed reflectors of the old Strada picked out the lopsided road signs and the landmarks he remembered from earlier. He passed the forest where they'd dumped the farm truck, and he wished he had a weapon.

He hated going back to Arno's place. It was tactically sloppy and possibly dangerous. But it was the only way. He bitterly regretted not having pressed the old man to say more about where he'd hidden the letter. He was making too many mistakes. Was the damn thing even worth finding? Maybe not, he thought, but clutching at straws was his only option right now. He had to hope he was clutching at the right one.

It was half-past midnight by the time he found Arno's villa. The front gates were set back from the road, across a neat border. He slowed. The driveway and gardens were lit up with the swirling lights of police cars and two fire engines.

As he swore and accelerated past the gates, he looked past the vehicles at the house.

It wasn't there anymore. Hardly a wall was still standing. The villa was a leveled mess of blackened rubble and smoking timber, the collapsed roof lying like the twisted spine of a giant carcass, tiles and charred woodwork and smashed windows scattered over a wide circle.

The fire had obviously raged a long time. The crews were calling it a night, packing up their equipment. There was nothing left worth saving.

Ben drove on, thinking about the options left open now. Either the blaze in the study had spread, or someone had made sure the place was thoroughly torched. It was more likely to be the latter. Whoever they were, these people liked their tracks to be covered. And fire was the best cleanser.

After a kilometer or so he turned into the farm entrance and followed the bumping, stony lane as far as the deserted yard where they'd stolen the truck earlier that day. Other than the shattered barn, there was no visible trace of what had happened there.

He turned off the engine and stepped out. He waited in the dark for a while. There was nobody around. He searched the buildings by the thin beam of his Mini

Maglite but found nothing, not a single shell case left uncollected. They'd even cleaned the blood off the toolshed door where he'd nailed the man to the frame. The nails had been pliered out too, leaving four neat holes in the wood.

There was a sudden movement behind him, and a crash of something falling. He whirled around in the darkness, every muscle tensing.

The black cat leaped down from its vantage point on a high shelf, landed next to the old nail tin it had knocked over, and darted out through a hole in the planking.

Ben cut across the dark farm and found the gap in the crumbled stone wall leading into Arno's rambling parkland. He stayed back among the trees, watching the fire crews leave and the police strolling up and down the sides of the gutted villa. He knew he was wasting his time here. It was worthless.

He turned to go, heading back for the gap in the wall, picking his way between the slender tree trunks by moonlight. A cloud passed across the face of the moon, casting the woods in shadow.

He stopped. Lying among the leaves, half hidden behind a mossy knot of tree roots, a man's body was lying crumpled and gray on the ground with his arms flung out to the sides.

There was no head on the body.

He waited, perfectly still, watching it until the cloud passed and the moonlight brightened. He went over to it and nudged it with his foot. It wasn't a body. It was something the clean-up team had missed.

Arno's tweed jacket. He remembered Leigh dropping it as they ran across the grounds.

He picked it up. It felt cold and damp, and it was empty apart from an oblong shape in the left inside pocket.

He fished it out. It was a slim wallet.

• • •

"Who's there?" Her voice sounded frightened in the darkness.

"Relax," he said. "It's me." He shut the door of the cabin behind him.

"Where were you?"

He told her.

"You went back?"

"The place has been torched, Leigh. There's nothing left. But I found something." He held up the wallet. "It's Arno's."

Leigh sat up in bed as he flipped on a bedside light. He sat on the edge of the bed next to her, and she brushed the thick black hair out of her eyes. "Where did you find it?" she asked sleepily.

"Where you dropped his jacket, in the woods," he said. He opened the slim calf-leather wallet and unzipped one of the internal pockets. "There's not much here," he said. "A library membership card, out of date. A couple of old cinema tickets. Fifteen euros in cash. And this." He took out a small slip of paper and showed it to her.

She took it and looked at him quizzically. "What's this?"

"It's a receipt."

"The Museo Visconti in Milan," she said, reading the crumpled print.

"Ever heard of it?"

She shook her head.

"This is an acknowledgment of something Arno donated to the museum," he said. "The receipt doesn't say what it is, but it's dated last January, just a few days after Oliver's death."

She looked up from the slip of paper. "You think—"

"The letter has gone to Milan? I don't know," he said. "We'll soon find out. Get some sleep. We're moving on at five."

31.

The kid had been right about the car. It was old, but it was dependable. It took them to Milan in a little over four hours. On the way they stopped at an autostrada service station, where Leigh picked out a head scarf, a pair of wide sunglasses, new jeans, and a warm jacket.

The Milan traffic was insane, and it was midmorning by the time they found the Museo Visconti, an imposing eighteenth-century museum of music in the city suburbs. Its high porticos overlooked a walled garden away from the street and the traffic rumble.

They went inside and breathed the old museum smell of must and wood polish. The place was almost empty, with just a few middle-aged visitors strolling quietly around the exhibits, talking to each other in subdued voices. The parquet floors were varnished and waxed to a slippery mirror sheen. Classical music played softly in the background. The doorways to each room were flanked by thick velvet curtains. The security guard on patrol looked about eighty.

They walked from room to room under the sweeping gaze of cameras, past displays of period brass instruments and a collection of magnificently ornate antique harps. Ben peered through a doorway into a large gallery space filled with old oil portraits of famous composers. "Nothing in here," he said. "Just a bunch of dead men in powdered wigs."

"Philistine," Leigh whispered at him.

From the main hall a curved flight of wooden stairs led up to the next floor. Ben went up, and Leigh followed.

The creaking stairs took them to a long room whose walls were lined with tall glass cabinets displaying period opera costumes and other exhibits. Leigh stopped at one of them and read the small brass plaque. "This is the gown that Caruso wore in his first-ever public appearance in 1894," she read out. She walked along and stopped at another. "Wow. Look. The dress that Maria Callas wore when she sang *Norma* in Milan in '52. Incredible. How come I never knew about this place?"

"Leigh. Please. We're not here to gape at some old dress. The letter, remember?"

Back in the entrance foyer, the old security guard shook his head. "We do not have any letters or documents."

"Is there another Museo Visconti?" Ben asked. He knew what the answer would be.

The old man shook his head again, like a mournful bloodhound. "I have been here for fifty years," he said. "There is only one."

They walked away.

"I had a feeling this wouldn't lead anywhere," Leigh said.

"But Arno donated something. The receipt proves it."

They walked down a long corridor. On either side were rows of antique violins, violas, and cellos behind glass. "He was a collector," she said. "He could have donated anything. A painting, an instrument." She pointed at the violins behind the glass. "Could have been one of these, for all we know."

He stopped. "We're idiots."

"What?"

"It's gone home," he said.

She stared at him in confusion.

"It's gone home," he repeated. "Arno said the letter had

gone home. It's gone back to where it came from. He didn't mean the museum itself. It's never been here before."

"We're in the wrong place?"

"Maybe not," he said, looking up and down the corridor. "We need to find the piano exhibit."

Understanding dawned on her face. "Shit, I think you might be right."

"Would you recognize your dad's old piano if you saw it?"

"You bet I would."

Their footsteps rang fast off the parquet as they hurried back up the corridor to find the keyboard instruments section. Through an archway to the side, flanked with red drapes, they found it. The big room was full of old keyboard instruments, pianos, spinets, and harpsichords, all highly restored and gleaming. They stood on plinths, cordoned off with DO NOT TOUCH signs on them.

Ben walked in among them. "Can you see it anywhere?" he asked.

"This is it," she said, pointing. She ran over to the old instrument near the window. It was big and ornate. Its woodwork gleamed dully under the museum lights. She circled it. "Christ, last time I saw this it was half restored, all stripped down to the bare wood and bits chipped off everywhere. But it's definitely the one."

"You're sure?"

"I'd know it anywhere."

Ben studied the piano carefully, running his eyes over the heavily varnished surface, the mother-of-pearl inlays and the gleaming ivory and ebony keys. Over the top of the keyboard, in gold letters, was the maker's name: JOSEF BOHM, VIENNA. It had three intricately carved legs, two at the front and one holding up the long tail at the back. It was about twelve feet long, solid and heavy. "So remind me," he said. "Which leg was hollow?"

Leigh put her finger to the corner of her mouth, thinking. "It was one of the front ones."

"Left or right?"

"Right, I think. No, left."

Ben leaned over the security cordon, but he couldn't get close enough to examine the piano properly. He glanced around. There was nobody in sight. He could hear the footsteps of the old security guard pacing through one of the adjacent rooms.

"Right," she said. "Definitely the right front leg."

"You don't sound too certain."

"I'm certain."

Mounted on a bracket high in a corner, the small black eye of a security camera was watching them. Ben stepped away from the plinth and looked casual as he slipped into the camera's blind spot and along the wall beneath it. He looked up. Then he walked back to the piano and stepped straight over the cordon. "The camera's useless," he said to Leigh with a smile. "It's almost as old as these pianos, and half the wires are disconnected at the back."

"That's so typically Italian," Leigh replied.

"Don't knock it." He knelt down next to the piano and examined the front right leg up close. The instrument had been carefully restored and was in such perfect condition that it was hard to believe it was almost two centuries old. Ben couldn't see anything. But then his eye picked out a small crack in the varnish three-quarters of the way up the leg. He scratched with his nail. Tiny scales of varnish flaked away to reveal what seemed to be a hairline saw mark. He scratched a bit more. The saw-line extended right round the leg, but it was barely visible. Had someone been at the instrument since the last restoration, removed the hollowed-out leg, replaced it, and then painted over the join with clear varnish?

There was only one way to find out.

32.

BELGIUM

THE SAME DAY

Philippe Aragon had been reading policy documents and signing letters at his study desk all morning, and the stack of papers at his elbow was a foot high. He liked to work from home whenever he could. He'd designed and built the house himself, back in his architect days. The Aragon family home near Brussels was simple and modest by his billionaire father's standards, not at all like the fabulous château in which Philippe had spent his childhood. But Philippe was tired of opulence. Opulence was anyone's for the money. It meant nothing.

As he worked, his eyes drifted from time to time to the framed pictures that sat on his desk. He had a whole collection of them, clustered together. His parents; his wife, Colette. Vincent, his boy, riding the bicycle he'd gotten for his tenth birthday. Delphine, their beautiful four-year-old daughter, swinging on her swing with a glittering smile. And Roger. Dear old Roger.

Philippe was suddenly filled with sadness all over again as he thought about him. He laid down his pen and picked up the framed picture, studying it. His old friend and mentor looked up at him. He'd had such kind eyes. It was still hard to accept what had happened. Or to understand it.

To the political world, the man in the photo had been

the Swiss-French former politician and highly respected statesman Roger Bazin. To Philippe, who had known him all his life, he was like an uncle. He'd taught Philippe a great deal, even though their political stance had radically diverged as Philippe got older. Roger hadn't ever been completely comfortable with his protégé's Socialist and environmentalist leanings, and they'd spent many a night debating over a bottle of cognac. They might have agreed on less and less as time went by, but those intellectual wrestling matches with the elder statesman had proved an immensely valuable training ground for the young politician, shaping and sharpening his mind for the battles to come. Philippe had always considered Roger as part of the bedrock of his life, something that would never go away, like the old oak tree he could see from his study window.

It still hurt that he was gone. It hurt a great deal. And it hurt even more to think that Roger might have been involved in what had happened that night.

Those events of the previous winter were still, and would always remain, fresh and sharp in Philippe Aragon's mind. He remembered the chalet in Cortina as though he'd been there just yesterday.

It had been one of those rare moments in his hectic new political career when he'd been able to reserve a whole six days to get away with Colette and the children. He'd been so happy to see the kids looking forward to it. He'd been planning to teach them to ski. More than anything, he'd been looking forward to spending time with Colette, the way they used to before things had gotten so crazy.

The nineteenth-century chalet was perfect, something out of a fairy tale. Far away from anything, total silence, nothing around except mountains, forests, and clean, clean air.

On the second day he'd had the phone call. Few people had his private cell phone number—just Colette, his secretary, and a handful of family members and close friends.

It was Roger Bazin on the line. It had been the first time in a while that Philippe had heard from him. He'd sounded odd, his words a little slurred as though he'd been drinking. That was peculiar in itself, but there was something else, something stranger. It was the note of fear that Philippe had picked up on instantly. A tortured edge to Bazin's voice that the younger man hadn't heard before. What was wrong?

"Philippe, where are you?"

"I'm on vacation. Remember?"

"Yes, but where are you now? This moment?"

Philippe had frowned, confused. "I'm in the chalet. We're just about to have dinner. What's wrong, Roger?"

A hesitant pause. Heavy, stressed breathing. Then: "Get out of there."

"What?"

"Get out of there. All of you. Run. As far as you can. Now."

Philippe was left gaping at a dead phone. He turned to look at his family. In the next room, Colette was opening a bottle of wine, ready for dinner, and laughing at something Delphine had just said.

He'd hesitated for a few seconds. It seemed absurd, insane. But then he ran over to her and grabbed her by the shoulders. The wine smashed on the floor. He'd yelled for Vincent to come quick, and he'd scooped the little girl up under his arm, and they'd all run out into the garden, Colette asking what was wrong, *what was wrong.*

They had all run like lunatics. At the bottom of the garden, deep in snow, they'd reached the edge of the pine forest and stood looking back at the house. The kids had realized it wasn't a game from the look on their father's face. Colette was screaming at him now: *What's wrong, have you gone nuts?*

As he stood there in the cold, still clutching his cell phone, he thought that maybe he *had* gone nuts. Or that Roger had gone nuts. Or was this some kind of stupid, reckless, tasteless joke? That wouldn't be like Roger.

"It's freezing out here," Colette said. "The kids—"

He blew out his cheeks, exasperated with himself. "I must be insane," he said. "Shit, your shoes." Colette's suede moccasins were soaked, snow clinging in clumps to her ankles.

"What did you think was happening?" she demanded.

"I don't know," he sighed. "Christ, maybe the stress is getting to me or something. I'm sorry. It was stupid. Let's go back."

"Daddy's crazy!" Vincent sang. "Daddy's crazy!" Delphine had started to cry, and Colette picked her up, shooting fierce looks at her husband.

Aragon took his wife's hand apologetically. They started walking back to the house.

And were thrown backwards by the force of the explosion.

The chalet had just disintegrated in front of Aragon's eyes. The night sky was lit up as the house erupted in a massive rolling fireball that mushroomed upwards and sent wreckage spinning for hundreds of yards around. He saw the roof lift off and the walls burst outwards. Bricks and wrecked timbers and flying glass rained down across the snow. He'd tried to shield Colette and the children with his body as secondary explosions ripped through the shattered building, leveling it.

Nothing had been left of the house or anything standing

nearby. The outbuildings, the garage, and the car were reduced to smoking shells.

Colette and the children had been hysterical. They'd taken shelter in a hut in the garden and called the emergency services. After that, things really had gone crazy. Police, security, fire brigade, television, and press had all descended on this quiet mountain valley. Aragon had gotten his family away from the place as quickly as he could get the private plane in the air.

He had said nothing to anyone about the phone call. Time had passed. He'd waited until the results from the investigation, but they'd turned up nothing except signs of a gas leak.

He'd tried and tried to contact Roger Bazin. He didn't know what to think. He needed to talk to him. How had he known about the explosion?

But Roger seemed to have disappeared. Days went by, and there was still no answer on his phone. Philippe left messages, and none were returned. He'd been just about to get on a train to visit Bazin personally at his home in Geneva when he got another call.

Roger's old Alfa Romeo Spider had gone out of control in an empty tunnel and hit a pillar at 120 kilometers an hour. The sports car had been pulverized, and the flaming wreckage had blocked the tunnel for hours. By the time the fire crews could get inside, there had been little left of Roger Bazin. There were no witnesses to the crash, the only testimony the gruesome photographs that the paparazzi had rushed to print in the glossy gutter press.

The distraught Bazin family testified that the old man had been suffering from stress for some weeks before the accident. He'd seemed depressed and agitated, frightened of something. Nobody knew what. His doctor had prescribed antidepressants, and they knew he was drinking, washing the pills down with brandy. There hadn't been enough left of Roger to run tests, but the medical people all agreed on the obvious conclusion. The coroner's verdict was death by misadventure.

For six months afterwards, the private firm hired by Philippe put thousands of man-hours into the investigation of Bazin's death. Aragon baited the hook with a million-euro reward for anyone who could come up with information that would reveal the truth. They found no sign of anything suspicious.

Car accidents happened. So did gas explosions.

33.

MILAN, ITALY

The Museo Visconti closed for lunch at one p.m. Visitors filed quietly out through the portico entrance. When the last ones had left, old Domenico Turchi, the security guard, pushed the entrance door shut behind them. With a shaky hand he reached for a jangling ring of keys on his belt and locked it, then threw the heavy iron bolt. He was sharing a joke with Signora Bellavista, the receptionist, as he hung his uniform jacket and cap on a hook behind the desk. They headed through a side door leading to the staff exit. He flipped open a panel on the wall and punched numbers to activate the alarm system, and he and Signora Bellavista left the building still laughing. Luca and Beppe had already left the workshop downstairs, and Domenico knew he'd find the two men drinking Peroni beers over lunch in the café around the corner where they all congregated every day.

The rooms of the museum were still and quiet. Down in the basement, among the honeycomb of gloomy passageways and corridors, there was the sound of a door creaking open.

Ben peered out, listening, then stepped quietly out of the disused store cupboard.

Leigh followed. Her legs were cramped after the long wait in the darkness. They made their way through a door and up some shadowy steps, tracing their way back to the main part of the building.

Ben recognized the workshop where they'd sneaked past the two men earlier. It was empty now, tools left in a disordered pile on a restoring bench. An old violin lay on a chisel-scarred table with its face removed. Two frameless oil paintings were propped up against the wall awaiting restoration. The workshop smelled strongly of wood glue, wax polish, and varnish.

Ben picked up a handsaw. He ran his eye along the sharp blade and nodded to himself. Leigh gave it a puzzled look. She didn't even want to think what he was planning to do with it.

There was still no sign of anyone around. Ben pushed softly through another doorway and found what he was looking for. The main fuse box was an ancient Bakelite affair with big clunky switches. He pushed them all to Off, then flipped off the master switch. He pulled out all the fuses and hid them in a crate under a pile of packaging material.

They emerged from a staff-only doorway into the main hall. Dull sunshine filtered in through the windows. All the lights were dead, and the blinking red LEDs on the security cameras had gone dark.

They made their way back through the long corridor where the violins were displayed. The keyboard instruments exhibit was just around the corner.

Germana Bianchi had been dusting the frames upstairs in the portrait gallery and listening to Mina on her battery radio when the lights cut and her vacuum cleaner died. She was a heavy, ponderous woman, and it took her a moment to register what had happened. She reached down with a fat hand to switch the vacuum cleaner off and on several times. "*Cazzo*," she swore. The power had cut out once before. She'd been alone in the building just like today, doing her lunchtime cleaning, when the fuses had tripped and she'd had to make her way down to the basement to flip the switch on the box. It was a long way down for her, and she didn't like the empty feeling of the place when it was closed.

She munched on her sandwich for a moment or two, hoping the electricity would come on again on its own. It didn't. She heaved a sigh, picked up her radio, and started towards the stairs.

Ben examined the piano and decided on his plan of action. The front right leg had to come off as quickly and cleanly as possible. He might not have a lot of time. A member of staff might be back any minute. If he could lift the right corner of the piano an inch or two and jam something underneath the lip of the keyboard to keep the leg raised up long enough to saw it off . . . He grabbed a double piano stool, flipped it up on end, but it was too high.

He stepped up on the plinth, laid the saw down on the piano, and tested the instrument's weight. He could barely move it quarter of an inch, and he didn't think that Leigh's extra strength would make the difference. He gazed at the saw, then down at the leg. It was going to take a good fifteen minutes to cut through the solid wood. He might not have fifteen minutes.

Think of something, Hope.

Leigh tensed. "Ben, there's someone in the building."

Ben heard it, too. Footsteps, slow and heavy, on the creaky stairs leading down to the main hall. In the quiet building the echo carried softly but clearly. There was another sound, too. It was music, growing steadily louder. Someone with a radio was coming down towards them.

This wouldn't do. It was now or never. He looked around him desperately.

The rope cordon around the piano was supported by six brass pedestals, three feet high on broad circular bases. Yes, that was the only answer. He used the saw to cut the rope, then picked up one of the pedestals. It was solid and heavy. He turned it upside down and held it like an ax. The brass was cold in his hand.

"Fuck it," he muttered. He caught Leigh's horrified look as he swung the pedestal back over his shoulder and then smashed it sideways into the piano leg with all his strength.

The crashing noise shattered the stillness of the room. There was a huge crunch of splintering wood. The piano gave a juddering groan, strings vibrating in unison. The leg gave a little, and the front end of the instrument sagged, creaked. Then stopped.

Halfway down the stairs and puffing with the exertion, Germana heard the terrible sound over her music. She turned the radio off. *What the hell was that?* Her heart gave a flutter. She grasped the banister rail and started walking faster.

Ben hit the piano again. The pedestal hummed through the air. Another shuddering crash. The leg gave way and folded out from underneath the keyboard. The front corner of the instrument tipped downwards, and he stepped quickly out of its way.

A ton of iron frame and heavy wooden casing toppled over and smashed through the plinth it stood on. Splinters flew. The massive ringing chord of the fallen piano filled the whole museum with a cacophony of sound.

• • •

Germana was getting very scared now. There were thieves in the place. She reached the bottom of the stairs and waddled across the hall to the ladies' toilets. She wedged herself into a cubicle and bolted the door. Her heart was pounding, and her breathing came in rasping gulps. She felt the shape of her cell phone in her pocket. *Yes. Call the police.*

Leigh was standing over the wrecked piano with her mouth hanging open. All her father's work, hundreds of hours he'd spent restoring the valuable instrument. The loss of this piece of musical heritage. It was terrible, sickening.

The strings were still resonating as Ben picked up the smashed leg. He hoped it had been worth it. He pulled away at splintered bits around the broken end. "I can't see anything," he said. He picked up the saw and hacked frantically at the end of the leg. The sharp blade skipped off a splinter and sank into his hand, biting at the flesh and drawing blood from a jagged gash. He swore and ignored the pain. He sawed harder. Leigh was standing at his shoulder, her eyes widening.

He blew sawdust away, wiped blood off the wood. Nothing.

"This wood is solid," he said. "There's no hollow."

Germana spoke in a flurry to the police switchboard. There were thieves in the Museo Visconti. Relief spread over her face as the man's voice on the other end of the line reassured her. The police were on their way.

Ben glared up at Leigh. "You said you were sure."

"I . . . Maybe it was the left leg."

"For fuck's sake," he muttered. He jumped to his feet, glancing at his watch.

"I'm sorry," she whispered.

"I will be, too, when someone walks in on us." He grabbed the pedestal and raised it up again. The devastated instrument was lying like a beached whale with its remaining front leg sticking out at an angle. Ben brought the pedestal down hard. Another tremendous crash filled the museum. Leigh covered her ears.

Ben stood back. The leg had broken cleanly away. He dropped the pedestal with a clang on the wooden floor and fell on his knees. He picked up the severed leg.

It was hollow. His heart jumped. He pushed two fingers inside the smooth cavity and felt something.

There was a roll of paper inside. He turned the leg upside down and shook it out. The tight roll was old and yellowed, tied neatly around the middle with a ribbon. It fell on the floor among the wreckage of the smashed piano.

Leigh knelt and snatched it up. She picked at the ribbon and unfurled the single sheet, handling it as though it could break apart at the slightest touch. "My God, this is it," she said, staring at it. The ink was faded, but there was no mistaking the handwriting and the signature.

She was holding her father's prize. The Mozart letter.

When she heard the sirens, Germana Bianchi ventured out of the toilet and opened up the front door to let the police in. She pointed and jabbered and led them through towards the piano room where the robbers had been. A whole gang of them, vicious, armed. She was lucky to be alive.

They rounded the corner. The keyboard exhibit room was empty. They all gaped speechlessly at the wrecked piano. Who would do this? It was senseless.

The thieves were far away by then, the old Fiat lost in the crazy sea of Milanese traffic.

34.

Ben drove fast out of Milan, wanting to put as much distance between the city and themselves as possible. He checked his mirror every few minutes. Nobody was following them. Sleet and hail hammered the Fiat's windscreen for two hours as they headed northeast towards the Austrian border. Beside him, Leigh was bent over the old letter, deep in thought. Signs flashed up for autostrada services.

The motorway cafeteria was half empty. They bought two coffees and headed for a corner table that was far from the other diners and close to an emergency exit. Ben sat facing the room and kept an eye on the entrance.

Neither of them had eaten anything since the night before, but the letter came first. Leigh unrolled and flattened it carefully across the plastic table, using the salt and pepper mills to weigh down the edges and stop it from springing back into a tight curl.

"This is so precious," she said, running her fingers over the aged, faded paper.

"Fake or no fake, it's only precious if it can teach us something." Ben took Oliver's file out of his bag and opened up his notebook. "Let's see what we've got. How's your German?"

"I can sing it better than I can translate it. How's yours?"

"I can speak it better than I can write it." He ran his eye over the handwriting. Was this really Mozart's original hand? It looked authentic enough, but then, what did he know? He studied it up close. The writing was scratchy in places, and it looked as though the letter had been dashed off in the back of a carriage.

The best place to start was from the top. *"Mein liebster Freund Gustav,"* he read. "My dearest friend Gustav."

"Good start."

"That's the easy bit," he said.

They worked for an hour, and the coffee cooled untouched on the table. The translation came together very slowly, piece by piece. Ben glanced over his shoulder around the room every few seconds, checking for any unwelcome company.

"What's *Die Zauberflöte?"* he asked.

"That's easy. *The Magic Flute.* What about this word?" she asked, pointing. "I can't make it out." She chewed her pen thoughtfully.

"It's *Adler."*

"Adler?"

"Adler is *eagle,"* Ben said, biting his lip. It didn't mean anything. He filled the word into his patchy translation. Understanding could come later. First, get it all down.

It took another three coffees and several pages of crossed-out notes before the translation had taken shape. Ben turned the notebook sideways on the table so that they could read it together.

Vienna
16 November 1791
My Dearest Friend Gustav,

It is in great haste that I pen this letter to you, and I hope with all my heart that it may reach you in time. I so wish I could write to you with only good tidings about the magnificent reception of The

Magic Flute. *But alas I have more pressing things to relate to you. There is nothing more pleasant than the freedom to live peacefully and quietly, and how I wish that could be for our Brethren! However, God seems to have willed it otherwise.*

Yesterday I was taking my favorite walk near the Opera when I met our friend and brother "Z." He was most distressed and agitated, and when I asked him what was wrong he told me of new developments. As you know, "Z" is privy to certain information that has been discussed at the meetings of the Order of Ra. Thanks I am sure in no small part to the favors that our emperor has placed upon the Eagle, our enemies grow stronger and more influential with each passing day. I fear that the success of my opera has angered them exceedingly and that our Craft may be in greater danger than ever before. Our friend advises great caution in all our movements. I urge you to be most careful, my dear Gustav. Do not trust strangers. The Order of Ra has agents everywhere, and not only in our beloved Austria.

I am sorry for the brevity of this letter, but I will sign off now in the deepest hope that my warning may reach you before the forces pledged to destroy us can do greater harm. Keep yourself safe and well. I send my love to your dear Katarina and am always

Your Brother,
W. A. Mozart

"What do you make of it?"

"Let's talk about it while we eat. I'm ravenous."

The lasagna was hot, tasty, and plentiful. They ate as

they talked, with the letter carefully tucked away in Ben's bag. He had the notebook open in front of him, next to his plate.

Leigh looked disappointed. "There's nothing here that we didn't already know from Professor Arno. Mozart was warning his lodge friend about these Ra people who were out to get them. That's it. It's a waste of time."

"*Adler*," Ben said through a mouthful of pasta. "Eagle."

"What about it?"

He pointed at the notebook. "It looks from this as though the 'Eagle' is important, and connected with the Order of Ra."

"How, though?"

"I don't know," he said. "Oliver's notes mentioned eagles a lot."

"Might Eagle be a code for something?"

Ben nodded. "Could be. Eagle. Maybe a symbol."

"Imperial eagle?"

"It can't be that. Read it. The Eagle is something or someone the emperor paid favors to."

"If we knew what the favors were—"

"But we don't." He scanned the letter again. "There's nothing more."

"Basically we're back where we started." Leigh sighed. "We're no closer to knowing what happened to Oliver." She let her fork clatter down and rested her head on her hand. "Maybe this is all a wild-goose chase. Maybe the letter has nothing to do with any of it. And what if it really is just a fake?"

Ben shook his head. "I'd be inclined to agree," he said. "But there's one thing that's puzzling me. The room where the murder took place—do you remember the ram?"

She'd been trying to forget what she'd seen in the video clip. "Ram?"

"On the wall, up above the altar or whatever it was, there was a gold ram's head with long horns."

She hesitated. "Rams. Goats. Idols. Horns. You're talking about devil worship now."

"No. Something a lot older than that. Remember I said I studied theology?"

"That *was* a surprise, Ben."

It was a chapter of his life that he didn't like to talk about, so he moved on quickly. "Ra was the sun god of the ancient Egyptians. Arno confirmed it."

Leigh didn't see where this was going.

"He didn't always go by his name," Ben said. "He was depicted in symbols, too. Usually the sun, but often also as a ram. You see him in Egyptian art as the body of a man with the head of a ram, or sometimes just the head on its own."

"Are you sure? Why a ram?"

"The horns. They symbolized rays of light coming from the sun. It's an old, old symbol, and it became pretty universal through the centuries. The Hebrew word *karan,* meaning rays, is a close match with *keren,* meaning horns."

She took a moment to digest this, then nodded. "Go on."

"Something about that gold ram on Olly's film struck me at the time," he said. "I couldn't think what it was, but now I have an idea. You're going to think this sounds crazy."

"Nothing sounds crazy to me anymore, believe me."

"Try this on. I think the Order of Ra still exists."

"That *does* sound crazy."

"Yes, but think about it. What did Oliver witness? They cut the guy's tongue out and then disemboweled him. What did Arno tell us about Lutze? The exact same thing happened to him. Coincidence? I don't think so."

She pulled a face. "I'm listening."

"Now remember what Arno told us before he was shot? He said, '*So it is true.*' "

"I remember. So what was true?"

"He never got a chance to finish. But he was pointing at the ram's head as he said it. I think he knew something. Don't ask me what. But whatever suspicions he had, hearing the news of Oliver's death must have confirmed them. He got frightened enough of the letter to want to keep it far away. You saw how well he hid it."

Leigh thought for a while, poking at her food absently. "If the letter is so dangerous, why didn't they come after Dad? He had it for years."

"First, your dad was more interested in the signature at the bottom and its historical value," Ben said. "Oliver was the one who went deeper. Second, until Oliver began to investigate it and found what he found, I don't think anyone cared about the letter at all. It only became important when it led him to them."

"But how could it have?"

"I don't know that yet," he replied.

She was silent for a minute. "Say you're right and these people still exist. Who would they be? Where would you find them?"

He shook his head. "You wouldn't find them, not easily. Remember who they were. This wasn't just some silly cult of men with funny handshakes. They had links with the secret police. They were deep in the heart of politics, not just in Austria. Those were uncertain times. The powers of the day were so scared of a Europe-wide revolution that they'd have been very happy to encourage them. Think how big they might be now, two centuries later. Not only big, but tight into the establishment."

"But this is modern democratic Europe. Surely that kind of repressive organization doesn't exist anymore."

"I know you're not that naïve, Leigh. The new order is built on top of the old. Nothing ever really changes."

"I thought Arno was the conspiracy theorist."

"Maybe he was right," Ben said.

"You're serious, aren't you?"

He nodded, paused. "I haven't told you much about things I did in the forces. I don't talk about it. I don't *want* to talk about it. But there's a lot that happens that ordinary people don't get to hear of. Ever. We fought whole wars that the history books will never mention. We operated far from the main battlefields, and we carried out operations that even we didn't understand. We had no idea what we were doing. We were just given targets and orders. We destroyed places without ever knowing their names. We were pawns in a game. We were fools. Oliver knew that years ago, but I didn't have the sense to listen to him. And the men pushing the pieces, the players who actually control things, are people you've never heard of. Hardly anyone knows who they are."

"So who are we dealing with here?"

Ben shrugged. "Who knows? People right inside the infrastructure, hidden behind layers and layers of fronts. People with connections. People who come after you when you show your face, use your passport or credit card, or try to talk to the police. This goes very deep. That's why we need to tread carefully if we're going to come out of this. And we're going to do it my way."

There was a long silence.

"All right," she said. "What do we do now?"

35.

VIENNA

LATE THAT NIGHT

Markus Kinski sat up in bed, blinking. His cell phone was screaming near his ear. He planted his feet on the floor. The clock on his bedside table glowed 1:09 a.m. He snatched up the phone. Was it Clara calling him so late? How could it be? He'd been sure to take her phone away. Panic rushed through him. What was wrong?

It wasn't Clara. The woman on the other end introduced herself as Leigh Llewellyn. He listened, waking up fast. "So where can I meet you?" he asked her.

Leigh covered the phone with her hand and looked questioningly at Ben.

They'd talked about this. Her idea had been a public place in the heart of Vienna, somewhere that offered the safety of bustling crowds. It was a smart idea, but Ben wanted to put this Kinski to the test. The best way to do that was to set up an initial rendezvous that would offer a good opportunity for an ambush. Ben nodded, and she gave Kinski the reply they'd agreed on.

"Meet me at the lake," she said.

Kinski didn't need to ask which one she meant. "Okay. When?"

"Tomorrow morning, nine o'clock."

• • •

Kinski was there at quarter to. The Mercedes turned off the road and crunched on the thin snow as it lurched towards the lakeside in four-wheel-drive mode. He got out, checked his watch, and walked up and down the edge of the lake for a while. Minutes passed. His breath billowed, and he clapped his hands to keep them warm. In the pocket of his heavy greatcoat he had a Thermos of hot black coffee, and he slurped back three scalding cupfuls. This winter was a cold one, colder even than last year, and the lake was fully frozen over now.

He heard a car in the distance and tensed. He shielded his eyes from the low sun. Through the scattered pine trees he could make out bits of the road that swept around the lake, three hundred yards away. There was a bright yellow hatchback moving along it. He watched. It kept going. He looked at his watch again. It was well after nine. Where was she?

He kicked his heels and walked around. This was stupid. She wasn't going to turn up. He flapped his arms, skimmed some stones across the ice, drank some more coffee, and then he had to go and piss in the bushes. By half-past nine he was freezing, and the coffee was all gone. By ten he decided to give up.

He went back to the Mercedes, muttering to himself. "What the fuck's the matter with her? Okay, fine, if she doesn't want to know what I know, I've got better fucking things to do with my time . . ." He turned the key in the ignition, and the heater started blasting cold air. Kinski swore again and turned the blower down.

And froze as he felt the cold steel against the base of his skull. The click of the safety resonated through his head. "No sudden moves," said a voice from behind him.

Raising himself up onto the backseat, Ben reached forward with his free hand and drew Kinski's SIG Sauer out of its holster. Now, at least, he had a pistol with something in it.

He watched Kinski. He was a bear of a man, somewhere shy of fifty, weathered and ruddy, with the features of a prizefighter and a nose that had been broken more than once. He looked like he could be dangerous, but he was built more for strength than for speed. If he could land a punch, it would be over. But Ben was faster.

Kinski snarled. "What the fuck do you want from me?"

Ben didn't reply.

The detective wanted to whirl round in his seat and rip this guy's head off. "If you're the motherfucker who took my daughter, let me tell you that she's safe now. You won't get her again."

"Why would I want your daughter?" Ben asked.

Kinski hesitated. It was a strange question. The gunman's German was good, but he spoke with a foreign accent. What was it? American? British? He rolled his eyes round as far as he could, trying to get a glimpse of him. Trying to get a look at his ear. But the guy was careful to keep out of sight. Who was he?

"Because I know you murdered Llewellyn," Kinski replied, probing, testing. Now for the big bluff. "And I'm not the only one who knows, so kill me if you like, but it won't end there."

"Oliver Llewellyn was my friend," Ben said. "Someone murdered him, but it wasn't me. I'm here to find out who did it, and when I find them, I'm going to kill them." He withdrew the empty .45 and shoved it back in his belt. The police SIG Sauer 9 mm was well cared for and fully loaded. He didn't think he was going to need to use it.

He'd been there half an hour before Kinski arrived, hiding in the trees. The big cop's behavior hadn't been that of a decoy with hidden cronies waiting to pounce. No man would chuck stones, flap his arms like a kid, or take a piss in the open knowing his friends were watching. He would have been glancing around him at their hidden positions, looking hunched and nervous with the anticipation, trying too hard to seem cool. And Kinski's reaction to the gun at his head inclined Ben to trust him.

Though not too much. It was Ben's nature to be cautious.

"You got any coffee left in there?" he asked.

Kinski had felt the pressure of the gun disappear. He turned round slowly and looked at Ben, his heavy brow knitted. His own 9 mm was in the intruder's hand, but only loosely.

"I'm sorry I had to do that to you, but I needed to check you out." Ben pointed at the Thermos. "And I would appreciate some of that coffee." The air from the heater was beginning to warm up, but his long wait in the snow had chilled him to the bone.

"It's finished."

"Then it'll have to be this," Ben said. Keeping one hand on the SIG, he reached for his flask and unscrewed it. He took a swig and then handed it to Kinski.

The cop shook his head. "I'm on the wagon," he muttered.

"Good man." Ben put the flask away.

Kinski relaxed a little. At least it didn't look as though he was going to die. Not today, anyway. "So what's your relation to Leigh Llewellyn?" he asked. "Boyfriend? Husband?"

"Neither. Like I said, a friend of the family."

"Do opera stars usually have friends with guns?"

Ben smiled. "I was in the army with Oliver."

Kinski nodded. Ex-military. That made sense, from the way this guy had sneaked up on him so easily. "What's your name?" he asked tentatively.

"You can call me Ben."

"Markus Kinski."

"Good to meet you, Markus. Now perhaps we could drive awhile, and you could tell me what you know about Oliver's death. And then, if I'm satisfied that I can trust you, I'll take you to meet Leigh."

36.

Kinski parked the Mercedes on a side street in central Vienna, and they walked to the Hotel Sacher on Philharmonikerstrasse, opposite the imposing Vienna State Opera. Ben wanted a busy place, as public as possible, for their talk with the detective, and the Sacher was about the most public place in the middle of the city. Even if someone spotted Leigh here, they'd be less likely to come running for autographs. Music stars were nothing new in Vienna.

The Sacher Café was bustling with people taking a break from their Christmas shopping for a morning coffee and a piece of the café's famous cake. Ben guided Kinski to a table in the corner.

"Where is she?" Kinski asked, sitting down, expecting Leigh to be there. Not another damned tearoom, he was thinking. He hated these places.

"You sit here and keep yourself occupied for an hour," Ben said. "And I'll be back with her."

Kinski grunted. "Great."

"I've got people here watching you," Ben lied. "If you make any phone calls or try to make contact with anyone, I'll know about it and you won't see me again until I come to kill you. Is that very, very clear?"

"Absolutely clear. Thank you."

Ben smiled. "Nothing personal, Markus."

Left alone, Kinski glowered at the menu. When the surly waiter arrived, he ordered enough black coffee and buttery Malakoff torte to keep him going for the next hour.

Then he sat back and waited and thought hard about this guy he'd just met.

Ben walked across the busy Philharmonikerstrasse, heading in the direction of the Albertina Palace. He saw a sign marked Strassenbahn and boarded a tram. Leigh was waiting for him at the cheap bed-and-breakfast on the other side of the Danube Canal.

Kinski was into his fourth coffee when Ben and Leigh walked into the Sacher Café just over an hour later. Kinski rose to his feet as Leigh approached the table and greeted her politely. He turned to Ben. "I was beginning to think you weren't coming."

"Another coffee?"

"Forget it," Kinski said.

Leigh took off her sunglasses and laid them on the table. Her hair was tied up in a ponytail, and she was wearing a woolen hat. Ben sat down beside her.

She studied Kinski carefully. "I believe you have some information about my brother."

"Tell her what you told me," Ben said.

Kinski spent the next few minutes going back over it, explaining in detail what he knew. Leigh listened carefully as he talked. He described how he'd accidentally stumbled across Madeleine Laurent, who had then turned out to be Erika Mann, which was almost certainly another false name. The whole Laurent episode had been an elaborate cover. Then he took the little plastic bag of spent 9 mm cases out of his pocket and laid them on the linen tablecloth in front of Leigh. "I found these by the lakeside," he said.

She studied them, recognizing what they were. "I don't understand," she said. "My brother drowned. He wasn't shot."

"They weren't shooting at him," Ben said. "They were shooting at the ice."

Leigh closed her eyes for a moment. He patted her hand, gave it a brief squeeze.

Kinski went on. He explained how he'd tried to reinvestigate Oliver's case. How someone had taken Clara from her school and used her to silence him; how his old chief had been suddenly removed, and with him any chance of reopening the case.

Leigh looked concerned. "Where is Clara now?"

"Somewhere safe. She's okay."

"Tell her what you told me about the guy with the ear," Ben said, tapping his own earlobe.

Kinski related what Clara had told him about her abductor. Leigh turned and looked at Ben with wide eyes. "The ear," she said. "The man on Oliver's video clip. He had a mangled earlobe."

"What video clip?" Kinski asked.

"We need somewhere private with a computer," Ben said.

"Shouldn't be a problem," Kinski replied. He got up and approached the counter. He asked for the manager, produced his police ID, and within five minutes they were being shown to a small conference room at the back of the hotel. They sat at a long table, and Ben loaded the CD-ROM into the computer's drive.

Kinski watched the clip in silence. His brow furrowed at the end, but he didn't take his eyes off the screen when the victim's tongue was hacked off and his guts were slashed open. Leigh had turned away and was standing at the window watching the traffic go by.

Kinski sat back in his chair when it was over. He exhaled deeply. "And you think this happened here in Vienna?"

"Look at the times," Ben said. "The film was shot not

long before Oliver's death. It had to be somewhere nearby. It looks like a big house, an old house, and part of it is a cellar or a crypt of some kind."

"The victim looked familiar to me," Kinski muttered. "I've seen him somewhere, but I can't place him."

"What about this other guy, the one in the foreground, with the ear?"

Kinski nodded. "From what Clara said, it could be the same guy who took her, yeah."

"One more question," Ben said. "Does *Adler* mean anything to you?"

"Common enough name. What about it?"

"I don't really know," Ben said. "Never mind."

"Anything else on this disc?" Kinski asked.

"Just some photos."

"Show me."

Ben clicked out of the video file and brought up the images. Kinski shook his head at each of them in turn. Then he said, "Wait a minute. Stop. Go back. I saw something."

The shot of Oliver playing the piano duet at the party came back up on-screen, and the big detective's eyes narrowed. He pointed with a stubby finger at the second pianist sitting beside Oliver. "I know him," he said. "That's Fred Meyer."

Kinski had seen him only once before, and he'd been a corpse dangling from a rope. But it was the same man, no question.

"Tell me more," Ben said.

"Meyer was a music student," Kinski said. "I didn't know he was a friend of Oliver's."

"Can we speak to him?" asked Leigh.

"Tricky," Kinski said. "There might be an issue with availability."

"Dead?" Ben asked.

Kinski nodded. "But that's what's interesting. He died on the ninth of January."

"The same day as Oliver," Leigh said quietly. She sat heavily down on a chair. Kinski could see the hurt in her eyes, but he went on. She needed to know this. "Supposed to have been suicide," he said. "But I've never been happy with that. Didn't check out at all. Suspicious."

"Suspicious how?" Ben asked.

"I've seen a lot of suicides," Kinski said. "There's always a reason why a person makes that decision. Fred Meyer had none that I could find. He had everything to live for. Plus, I don't like those kinds of coincidences. Two musicians both die on the same night, around the same time, just a few kilometers apart. One dies in an accident that doesn't add up. The other dies in a suicide that nobody can explain. Tell me that's not strange."

"And now it turns out he knew Oliver," Ben said.

Kinski nodded. "So now it's even more suspicious. There's another link, too. Meyer had a pair of opera tickets." He pointed at Leigh. "For the first night of your performance in *Macbeth* last January, here in Vienna."

"The one I canceled," she said. "I was just about to fly over for rehearsals when I got the news that he was dead."

"These tickets were for a private box at the Staatsoper," Kinski went on. "And they cost a bomb, far more than a student can afford. I checked. Meyer was on a budget, and big-time opera tickets were way out of his league. His family didn't have a lot to spare, either, so it wasn't like someone got them as a present. So where did he get them?"

"Oliver could easily have gotten them," Leigh said. "He could get free tickets for any of my performances, because he was my brother. No mystery there."

"So they must have known each other well, these two," Kinski said.

"Olly never mentioned him." Leigh's brow creased. "But what does it mean that they knew each other?"

"If Oliver died because he knew something," Ben said, "why did Meyer die?"

"Maybe they both witnessed this together?" Leigh said.

Ben shook his head. "It's clear that the clip was filmed by one person. Oliver was on his own in there. If there'd been two of them, we'd have heard them talking. We'd have seen flashes of the other guy as Oliver was running."

"So what did Fred know, and how?" Leigh asked. "Did Olly tell him what he'd seen, show him the clip?"

"I don't know," Ben said. "I don't think he'd have had time to show him the clip. Maybe he called him."

"Or they were planning something together."

Ben thought about it. "We need to know more. I'd like to talk to the Meyer family."

"They won't tell you anything they haven't told the police," Kinski said.

"I'd still like to talk to them." Ben paused, thinking hard. "Now, this place you've hidden your daughter Clara. Where is it?"

Kinski smiled. "We're trusting each other now, then?"

"I wouldn't have brought you here if I didn't. I'd have left you dead in the car."

"Thanks," Kinski grunted. "Okay. She's in a convent. An old friend of mine is the Mother Superior there."

"Nearby?"

"No, it's out of the country," Kinski said. "Over the border into Slovenia, about five, six hours by car. In the mountains."

"Secure?"

"Totally. Nobody could ever find her there, and nobody knows about it, not even the few cops I still trust."

Ben looked Kinski in the eye. "Could Leigh go there, too?"

Leigh exploded. "What?"

Kinski thought about it and nodded. "I could arrange that, sure."

"Good," Ben said. He turned to Leigh. "Because I think it's getting far too dangerous for you. I want to put you somewhere safe until this is over."

"We've had this discussion," she said hotly. "I'm not going anywhere."

Ben looked hard at her. "I wanted you to go to Ireland. You wouldn't go. I gave in to you and look what happened."

"You won't dump me like that," she said. "I want to be involved, not out on a limb somewhere waiting for you to call."

"Make a choice," Ben said. "Either you let me do this my way, or I walk. Hire another bunch of steroid users to look after you. You'll be dead in a week."

Kinski glanced at him. Ben was playing tough tactics, but it worked. Leigh sank her head into her hand. She let out a long sigh.

"I'll go crazy," she said. "I'll be worried all the time."

"But you'll be safe," Ben replied. "And if I know you're protected, I can work better."

"He's right," Kinski said.

She let out a long sigh. "Okay," she said reluctantly. "You win."

Ben nodded and turned to Kinski. "So now you need to tell me the way to this place."

Kinski smiled. "I can do better than that."

37.

Kinski drove the Mercedes fast on the autobahn. They headed south past Graz, then Wolfsberg, Klagenfurt, and finally crossed over the border into Slovenia. Kinski's police ID got the Mercedes waved through the border with no paper checks.

By the time they were approaching Lake Bled, night had fallen and it was snowing hard. The forests were heavy with a canopy of white, and every so often a fallen branch blocked the road, snapped off by the weight of the snowfall. The roads became narrow and twisty, and Kinski had to concentrate hard as the windscreen wipers slapped quickly to and fro with a hypnotic beat. Leigh was asleep in the backseat. As Kinski drove, Ben went through everything he knew, telling it calmly, slowly, methodically.

"The Order of Ra," Kinski snorted. "Give me a break."

"I knew an African dictator," Ben said. "He put a tin crown on his head and declared himself a deity. That sounded funny, too, but people stopped laughing pretty fast when he had their arms and legs cut off and forced them to eat them in front of him."

"Holy shit," Kinski said.

"I don't care what these bastards call themselves. It doesn't make them any less real or any less dangerous."

Kinski didn't say anything for a minute. Then he asked, "What happened to the dictator?"

Ben smiled in the darkness. "Someone ate him."

• • •

Their destination was deep in the heart of the Julian Alps, situated in a long valley between snowy mountains. The only road leading to it was a rutted track, and the snowdrifts were deep. They had to stop and fasten snow chains to the wheels of the Mercedes. Soon afterwards, Kinski pointed to a pinprick of light in the distance. "There it is."

The old convent was almost in total darkness as they approached. The Mercedes's headlights swept the craggy walls as they passed through a crumbling arch and pulled up in a little courtyard. The convent consisted of a rambling complex of buildings that looked as though they had grown up out of the valley and changed very little in the last five or six centuries. The main entrance was an iron-studded oak door, black with age and framed with ivy.

A warm glow of light appeared in an arched window as the Mercedes pulled up. The old door creaked open, and little Clara Kinski came skipping out over the snow. Behind her stood a tall woman in a nun's habit, carrying a lantern. She looked more than seventy, but she stood straight and walked with a firm step.

Kinski turned off the engine, and they climbed out of the car, stretching after the long drive. Clara flew excitedly into her father's arms. Max the Rottweiler also came running from inside the building and made a big fuss over him, jumping up and licking his hands.

The nun approached with the lantern. Kinski greeted her warmly and introduced Ben and Leigh. "This is my old friend, Mother Hildegard."

The Mother Superior welcomed them and led them across the courtyard, showing the way with her lantern. Ben and Leigh followed her. Kinski trailed along behind with Clara hanging on his arm and Max trotting happily in his wake.

They went through a dark cloister and under another arch. Ben could hear the soft lowing of a cow in a stall, and the rustic smell of fresh hay and manure wafted on the cold night air. Beyond the sprawl of convent buildings was a little farm with dry-stone outbuildings and enclosures. Mother Hildegard led them through a gateway to a simple cottage. "This is where you will stay, my child," she said to Leigh.

Leigh thanked her. "You're sure it's all right for me to stay here awhile?"

"Karl, the groundsman, lived here for many years." Mother Hildegard smiled. "But he is very old now, and has gone to live in a retirement home in Bled. His cottage is likely to be unused for a long time. The simple life we lead does not appeal to all."

"As long as I'm not imposing," Leigh said.

The nun laid a hand on Leigh's arm. "Any friend of Markus's is more than welcome here," she said.

She showed them inside the simple cottage. It was warm and cozy, and a fire crackled in the log stove. "I lit the fire for you, but you men will have to split some logs in the morning." She pointed to a cupboard in the small entrance. "In there you will find rubber boots and heavy jackets for the cold," she said. Keeping warm on top of the stove was a cast-iron tureen of delicious-smelling mutton stew, and the simple wooden table was laid with earthenware plates and cups.

The old nun was watching them closely. She knew all too well that they were in some kind of trouble, but she wasn't about to ask questions. "And now, I will leave you. Clara, you may stay here for an hour, and then you must come straight back and be ready for bed."

They were all tired, and Clara did a lot of the talking

over dinner. They passed around the pot of stew until it was empty. Ben drank one of the bottles of the nuns' homemade dandelion wine. Clara took a lantern and went running back to the convent building. Max wanted to stay with Kinski, refusing to leave his side. "You don't mind if he shares the attic bedroom with you and me, Ben?" Kinski asked.

Ben eyed the huge, slavering dog. "As long as he doesn't sleep in my bunk."

"Well, I'm beat," Kinski said, yawning. He headed up the wooden stairs with Max at his heel.

Ben and Leigh were left alone. "I feel like walking," she said. "Want to come along?" They found pairs of boots that fitted them, and went out into the night.

The moon's reflection on the snow made it almost like day. The place was completely still, the scenery breathtaking even in semidarkness. Leigh felt more relaxed than she had in days. "I didn't want to come here," she said as they walked over the crisp snow, their boots crunching. "But I'm glad you insisted. I feel protected here."

Ben nodded. Kinski had chosen well. There was no way anyone could find this place. He was glad that Leigh was happy. Tomorrow, he'd be able to head back to Vienna with a clear mind, knowing that she was safe.

They walked on awhile. She clapped her hands together. "I wish I had some gloves. My hands are freezing."

"Let's go back."

"No, it's beautiful out here. And so nice to be free to walk about without worrying that someone's going to start shooting at us."

Ben took her hands and clasped them in his own. "My God, they're so warm," she exclaimed. "How do you do it?"

Their eyes met, and she suddenly realized they were

standing there in the snow facing each other holding hands, and he was smiling at her in the moonlight. She drew back quickly and put her hands in her pockets. "Thanks," she mumbled. "Maybe we should get back now."

The nuns were up and about at six the next morning, attending to the animals and starting their morning chores before prayers and breakfast. Clara ran over to the cottage and thumped on the door.

Ben had risen early, and he was tending to the stove when he heard the child knocking. "Your father's still asleep," he said as he let her into the cottage. She was wearing a quilted anorak and a pair of heavy woolen trousers.

"Daddy always sleeps late when he can," she said brightly, hanging her anorak on the back of a chair. She sat down and swung her legs.

"So you thought you'd come and wake him up before sunrise?"

She giggled. "I want to show him Sister Agnes feeding the piglets. They're so cute!"

"He can see them later, okay? He needs to sleep."

"Can I stay here with you?"

"Sure. Want some breakfast?"

"Mother Hildegard left some eggs in the cupboard," she said, pointing. "They've got so many chickens here that there's always piles of eggs to eat."

"I guess we're having eggs, then."

"I like them boiled, just a little bit runny with a piece of Schwarzbrot to dip in them. Please," she added.

"How come your English is so good?" he asked as he filled a saucepan with water.

"Because I go to St. Mary's College."

"What's that, a bilingual school?"

She nodded. "Most of our lessons are in English. Daddy says it's the most important language to learn nowadays."

"By the time you're twenty, kids your age will all be learning Chinese."

She leaned her little elbows on the table. "Why's that?" she asked.

"Because the world changes all the time," he explained. "That's grown-up stuff you don't want to know about."

"Does your friend Leigh sing in Chinese? They have Chinese opera, don't they? I saw it on the TV."

He laughed. "I think that's a little different."

"I've seen her on TV, too. She sings in Italian and French and German."

"She's very clever."

"Daddy bought me her Christmas album last year," Clara said. "It's called *Classical Christmas with Leigh Llew—Llew—*" She smiled. "I can't say it right."

"It's a Welsh name. They speak funny in Wales."

"Wales is part of England, isn't it?"

"Don't say that in front of Leigh." Ben smiled.

"Is Leigh your girlfriend?" Clara giggled, dimples appearing in her cheeks.

He turned and looked at her. "You ask a lot of questions."

"That's how I learn things."

"You're too young to learn about things like that."

"She *should* be your girlfriend," Clara said seriously, playing with a wooden spoon. "I think she wants to be."

"Oh, really? And how might you know that?"

"Last night at dinner she was looking at you. You know. Like this."

Ben laughed. "She was looking at me like that? How come I didn't notice?"

"And when she speaks to you, she does this with her hair." Clara sat back in her seat, raised her chin, and brushed her fair hair back with her fingers. "That's a sign that a woman likes a man."

Ben nearly choked. "I can see I have a lot to learn from you. Where did you get that from?"

"I read it."

"Not in one of Mother Hildegard's books, I hope."

She laughed. "No, it was in one of Helga's magazines."

"Helga?"

"My sitter. Daddy likes her, I think."

The eggs were ready. Ben spooned one out into an egg cup and put it down on the wooden platter in front of her. "Anyway, little lady, I think you think too much." He smiled. "Now shut up and eat."

"That's what Daddy says, too." Clara shrugged and cracked the top of her egg.

38.

Leigh emerged from her room half an hour later to the smell of coffee, toast, and eggs. There was animated talking and laughter coming from downstairs. Peeping down the narrow stairway, she could see Ben and Clara sitting at the table together building a house out of cards. Ben was delicately putting the last card on the top. He took his hand away tentatively. The house wobbled slightly but remained standing. Clara watched it, entranced, then her cheeks puffed out and she blew it down. Cards scattered across the table.

"Hey, that's cheating," Ben said. Clara giggled and rocked in her chair.

Leigh stood quietly at the top of the stairs. She watched Ben play with the child. For a man who had never settled down and would probably never be a father himself, he had an amazingly easy way with kids. Clara obviously liked him a lot. That hardness Leigh had seen in him was completely gone. Suddenly, she was looking at the Ben she'd known from years ago.

Never go back, Leigh.

Clara saw Leigh coming down the stairs and smiled shyly. "I think Daddy's awake, too," she said, cocking her head at the clump of footsteps above. "Leigh, you'd better get off the stairs."

"Why?"

"Because if Daddy's getting up, Max will get up, too. And when he runs down the stairs, he won't stop for anyone, and he'll send you flying. He does it all the time." Her eyes filled with delight as the dog came thundering down like a huge black cannonball. "Here he comes!"

Leigh quickly stepped aside to avoid being bowled over. Clara jumped down from her chair and ran out of the room with the dog. "Come on, Maxy. I'll get Sister Agnes to fix your breakfast." The door banged, and she was gone. The cottage was suddenly much quieter.

"Nice kid," Leigh said.

"She's great."

"She likes you."

"I like her."

"You never wanted kids, Ben?"

"Wrong life," he said.

He made her coffee. Last night's tension was gone, and she was smiling and relaxed. They sat and drank the hot coffee. They could hear Kinski thumping about upstairs.

"Are you and he leaving today?" Leigh asked.

Ben nodded. "Later, maybe in the evening."

"It's going to seem strange without you around."

"It's better this way."

Leigh sipped her coffee. "What are you going to do?"

"First port of call, the Meyer family."

"You think they'll talk to you?"

"I can only try. Hey, look at that," he said suddenly, looking up above the door. "I didn't notice it before." A wooden rack over the low doorway cradled an old double-barreled shotgun. He went over and lifted it down. "Nice," he said.

"Looks old."

"Probably a hundred years. Good condition, though." He ran his eye along the elegant lines, the hand-checkering on the stock and the hammers. Modern weapons were brutish and functional. They did their job efficiently, but they lacked grace. This had been crafted with loving artistry and skill. Hand-finished wood and engraved steel, not hard black rubber and polymer plastic.

"I wonder if it still works," Leigh said.

"These things were built to last forever," he replied. "The old groundsman here probably used it to pot a rabbit now and then." He tested the action. The hammers clicked back with a sound like winding up an old clock. Three loud clicks. They locked back solid. There were two triggers, one set behind the other. He tried each one in turn. They had a light, crisp let-off, a little under two pounds. The action was well oiled, and the twin bores were smooth, unpitted, and clean. He flipped the gun over in his hands. "I have to have a go," he said. He searched around and soon found a box of cartridges in a drawer.

The sun was shining bright on the snow outside. "Mind if I come, too?" she asked.

"Be my guest."

Ben carried the gun over his shoulder as they trudged away from the convent in their snow boots. The sky was clear and blue, and the air smelled fresh. When the convent was sinking out of sight behind a snowy ridge, he looked back. "We should be okay here. I don't want to give the nuns heart attacks." He looked up at the mountains in the distance. "I don't think we're going to start any avalanches." He propped the shotgun against the trunk of a pine tree. "Here, help me."

"To do what?"

"Make a snowman." He crouched down and started gathering up armfuls of snow, heaping it in a pile. She joined him, clapping handfuls of snow onto the heap. "I haven't done anything like this for years," she said, laughing. "I remember when Olly and I were kids and we used to lark about in the snow. But it always ended up with him shoving a load of it down my back and me clobbering him with the spade."

Ben smiled and gathered up more snow.

Leigh watched him with a curious look. He saw her face. "What?" he asked.

"I still find it hard to believe," she said.

"Find what hard to believe?"

"You and theology."

He paused, rubbing snow off his hands. "Really?"

"You studied it where?"

"Oxford."

"Impressive. What were your intentions?"

He stopped what he was doing and looked at her. "You mean, was I going to make a career out of it?" He smiled. "Maybe. At the time, I thought about it."

"You were seriously going to become a clergyman?"

He clapped another handful of snow onto the growing snowman. "It was a long time ago, Leigh. Before I knew you."

"How come you never told me?"

"That part of my life was already over. It didn't seem relevant."

"Did Oliver know about it?"

"Why should he?"

Leigh shook her head. "You, in a white dog collar, living in a little ivy-fronted vicarage somewhere in the south of England, shepherding your flock. The Reverend Benedict Hope. What made you change your mind?"

"Life happened," he said. "I drifted away from it."

"An angel," she said.

He laughed. "What?"

"You didn't drift that far," she said. "You just found a different path to do the same thing. You became an angel.

You're the guy who comes down and saves people, looks after the weak."

Ben didn't reply.

When the snowman's body was about four feet high, Ben rolled him a head and stuck it on top. "We need a carrot for a nose, a woolly hat, and an old pipe to stick in his mouth," Leigh said. Ben stuck two finger holes in the head for eyes. "That'll do. Come away from him now."

"I get it," she said as they trudged back towards the tree where the shotgun was propped.

"What do you get?"

"You're going to shoot him, aren't you?"

"That's the idea."

"Honestly. You men."

Ben loaded a cartridge into the right-side breech and snapped the action shut. He shouldered the old gun and pointed it at the snowman from thirty yards away. Leigh stood with her fingers in her ears.

He thumbed back the right-side hammer, pointed, and fired. The stock of the gun kicked back against his shoulder, and the booming echo rolled around the mountains.

Leigh took her fingers out of her ears. "An *exterminating* angel," she said.

Ben looked at his target. "I don't know about that," he said. "Looks like the snowman lives to fight another day." The shot had scooped a channel out of the side of the snowman's head. He frowned at the shotgun. "Throws to the right a bit. Barrels could be slightly out of true."

"Let me try the next one," she said. "That looked like fun."

"I thought only immature men liked this kind of thing," he replied, handing her the gun.

"Immature women do, too. How do you work it?"

"Like this." He showed her how to break open the action and eject the spent cartridge from the smoking breech. She loaded a second round, and he placed her hands on the gun, making sure the stock was well pressed into her shoulder.

"Does it kick a lot?"

"Not too much. Go for it." He stepped back.

She clicked back the hammer, aimed, wavered a little, took a breath, and squeezed the trigger. The snowman's head exploded into a shower of powder snow.

"Good shot," he said.

"I got him!" she yelled. She spun round, dropping the gun and hugging him. It had been so spontaneous, so natural, that she hadn't even realized she was doing it.

Ben was caught off balance. They tumbled into the snow together. She was laughing. For a carefree instant they were back to the way they'd been fifteen years ago. She brushed her hair away from her face. Her cheeks were flushed and rosy, and there were snowflakes on her eyelashes.

They stopped and looked at each another. "What are we doing?" she asked softly.

"I'm not sure," he said. He reached up and stroked her face.

They came together slowly, and their lips touched. Their kisses were uncertain and quick at first, then he put his arm around her shoulder and drew her nearer. They embraced for a long time. She ran her fingers through his hair, pressing her mouth hard against his. For a moment everything else was forgotten, and it was as if they'd never been apart.

But then Leigh broke away and scrambled to her feet. Ben stood up with her. They dusted the snow from their clothes. "This can't happen, Ben," she said. "We can't go back, you know that."

They stood for a few moments, feeling awkward in the

silence. Ben was angry with himself. The old shotgun was lying deep in the snow. He picked it up and wiped it clean, then touched her arm. "Come on, let's head back to the cottage."

That kiss hung over them for the rest of the day. There was a strained atmosphere between them—neither of them knew what to say. They'd crossed an invisible line, and they were stuck. They couldn't undo it, and they couldn't move forward. Ben blamed himself. Unprofessional. Undisciplined. Stupid.

He avoided thinking about it by spending time with Clara and Max outside. The big dog was quick-witted, and Ben taught him to sit while Clara ran and hid. If he had been a few years younger, Max would have made a perfect police or military dog. He learned wait in three goes. He would sit trembling with anticipation on his haunches, eyes alert and completely keyed into his surroundings. Ben would wait two, three whole minutes, longer each time to build the dog's concentration span. Then he would give the quiet command "Find Clara," and Max would be off, hurtling through the snow. Wherever she went, he knew exactly where to find her. He loved the game as much as the little girl did.

Evening came. Ben was strapping up his bag when he sensed a presence behind him. He turned quickly and saw Leigh there. She had a sad smile, and her eyes were a little moist.

"You take care," she said. She put her arms around him and drew him close. She pressed her cheek against his ear, her eyes tightly shut. He was about to stroke her hair. He patted her shoulder instead.

"I'll see you again soon," he told her.

"Make it sooner?" she replied.

• • •

Kinski headed back along the snowy roads. Ben liked the way he didn't feel the need to talk all the time. Military and police guys, guys who spent a lot of time with each other waiting for things to happen, shared that quality of being able to stay quiet for long periods. It was a good atmosphere. They said little for an hour. Ben blew cigarette smoke out of the car window, deep in his own thoughts. He left the whiskey flask untouched.

"What's the story with you and Mother Hildegard?" he asked as they crossed the border back into Austria.

"I knew her long before she was a nun," Kinski said. "Funny how you never think that nuns were women once. Back then she wasn't Hildegard, she was Ilse Knecht. She was a writer in East Berlin."

"How does a cop get to meet a writer?"

"You know, friend of a friend of a friend. I met her at a party and thought she was okay. Intelligent, aggressively intellectual. I like women like that. But that was her problem."

"How so?"

"She was a little too smart, opened her mouth a little too wide, and got in a heap of shit," Kinski said. "She wrote Christian stuff for newsletters, magazines. The Communist authorities didn't like her. Then she wrote a novel. They decided it was subversive. They had her followed for a while. Found out she was hanging around with a bunch of people from their files. Names that had red circles around them. Dissidents, activists, people on the margin. That didn't help. East Berlin was a fucking snake pit."

"Before my time," Ben said. "I joined up after the wall came down."

Kinski nodded. "Lucky you. It wasn't pretty. Anyway,

that gave them the excuse they needed to vanish her. I heard through a contact that they were coming for her. I didn't think it was right to magic her away to some fucking camp in Manchuria just because of what she wrote."

"So you helped her."

"I knew some people. We got her out. She came to Austria, did whatever it is women do to become nuns. Then, after the wall came down she got the post at the convent. She still writes, under another name. A tough old trouper."

"You saved her life."

Kinski waved that away. "Well, I just pulled a few strings, you know. It was hard, though. You never knew who you could trust."

"I know the feeling. Who do you trust now?"

"In the police?" Kinski had already given it a lot of thought. "Three guys for sure. My own guys. Others I'm not so sure about."

"What about your superiors?"

"I knew my chief for nearly eight years. I don't believe he's mixed up in this. Someone got to him. Or else they just fast-tracked his retirement, and he took their offer. That could be it. He was tired."

The road flashed by. More quiet time passed. "I'm going to need some new kit," Ben said.

"Like what?"

"Ammunition for my Para," Ben said. "Forty-five auto. Copper jacketed, in clean condition. Two hundred rounds at least. No military surplus. Something quality, a good brand like Federal or Remington. Can you arrange that?"

"I'll see what I can do," Kinski replied.

"Or else another pistol," Ben said. "Nothing fancy, no unusual calibers, no revolvers. Nothing smaller than nine millimeter, nothing bigger than forty-five."

"I know a guy."

They drove on for a while. Then Kinski asked, "So what's the story with you and Leigh?"

Ben hesitated. "There's no story."

"I can see there is."

Ben shrugged. "I've known her for a while. She and I were close once, that's all." He didn't say anything more.

"Okay, I'll back off," Kinski said. "None of my business. I just wanted to say—"

"What?"

"That if you and Leigh have something going between you, don't waste it."

Ben turned to look at him. The cop's face was hard as he drove.

"Just don't fucking waste it, Ben," Kinski said again. "Don't throw something like that away. Make the most of it." He was quiet for a minute. His hands gripped the wheel in the darkness. He added in an undertone, "I lost my wife."

39.

AMSTETTEN, AUSTRIA

THE NEXT MORNING

Freezing rain was spattering hard on the pavements by the time Ben found the place. It was a plain terraced house in a winding street, ten minutes' walk from the railway station at Amstetten.

He knocked. Dogs barked inside. He waited awhile and knocked again. He heard the sound of someone coming. A figure appeared through a dimpled-glass inner door. It opened, and a man stepped into the entrance porch. He unlocked the outer door and stood in the doorway. He was heavyset, bleary-eyed, with puffy cheeks and straggly gray hair. An odor of cheap cooking and wet dogs arose from the hallway.

"Herr Meyer?"

"*Ja?* Who are you?" Meyer peered at Ben suspiciously.

Ben flashed the police ID he'd stolen from Kinski's pocket. He kept his thumb over most of it. He held it up just long enough for the word POLIZEI to register, then he jerked it away and tried to look as officious as he could. "Detective Gunter Fischbaum."

Meyer nodded slowly. Then his eyes narrowed a little. "You're not Austrian."

"I've lived abroad," Ben said.

"What's this about?"

"Your son, Friedrich."

"Fred's dead," Meyer said in a sullen voice.

"I know," Ben replied. "I'm sorry. I have a couple of questions."

"Fred's been dead almost a year. He killed himself. What more do you people want to know?"

"It won't take long. May I come in?"

Meyer didn't say anything. Down the hallway, a door opened. A scrawny woman appeared behind Meyer. She looked worried. "*Was ist los?*"

"*Polizei,*" Meyer said over his shoulder.

"May I come in?" Ben repeated.

"Is this a criminal investigation?" Meyer asked. "Did my son do anything wrong?"

"No, he didn't," Ben answered.

"Then I don't have to let you in."

"No, you don't. But I'd appreciate it if you did."

"No more questions!" the woman yelled at him. "Don't you think we've suffered enough?"

"Go away," Meyer said quietly. "We don't want to talk any more about Fred. Our son is dead. Leave us alone."

Ben nodded. "I understand. I'm sorry to have disturbed you." He turned to go. The rain was hammering down, and he felt it trickling coldly across his scalp.

The tickets. Two opera tickets. One for Fred. Who was the second one for? Oliver? No, that didn't make sense. Why would Oliver have given him both tickets? He'd have kept his own and given just one to Fred. Two guys going to the opera together wasn't Oliver's style anyway. Oliver wouldn't go out anywhere without a girl, usually a nice one. Maybe it wasn't Fred's style, either. So who was the other ticket for?

Ben stopped on the bottom step. He turned back to the door. Meyer had half closed it, watching him with a guarded look.

"Just one question, then," Ben said. "One question and I'll leave you alone. Can you do that?"

Meyer creaked the door an inch wider. "What?"

"Fred had a girlfriend, didn't he?"

"What about her?" Meyer asked. "Is she in trouble?"

Ben thought for a moment and then said, "She might be, unless I can help her."

That was his final shot. If Meyer shut the door now, he had nowhere else to go. That worried him.

Meyer stared. There was a long silence. Ben waited. Cold rain dribbled down his neck.

"We haven't heard from her lately," Meyer said.

"Where can I find her?"

He took a taxi to the place. He pushed open the door and went inside. The cybercafe was quiet, almost deserted. There was a long stainless-steel counter, with a till and a bubbling espresso machine. Cakes and doughnuts sat in a row behind glass. The place was neat and clean. There were framed movie posters on the walls: *Ocean's 13, The Bourne Ultimatum, Pan's Labyrinth, Outcast.* Ben smiled at that one. In the back of the room, a couple of teenagers were giggling over something they were typing up on a computer. Soft music was playing in the background: modern classical, minimalist.

The young woman behind the counter was perched on a stool reading a book. As Ben approached, she laid it down and looked up at him. She was about twenty, twenty-one, plumpish and pleasant-looking. Her auburn hair was tied up neatly on her head under a little white cap. She smiled and spoke in fast German.

Ben didn't show the police ID this time. "I'm looking for Christa Flaig," he said.

The young woman raised her eyebrows. "That's me. What can I do for you?"

"I'm a friend of Oliver Llewellyn," Ben said. He watched her eyes.

She flinched a little. Looked down. Painful memories flashed behind her face. He was sorry to bring it all back for her.

"Has this got something to do with Fred?"

He nodded. "I'm afraid so. Can we talk?"

"Sure, if you like. But I don't know what you want to talk about."

"Can I have a coffee?"

She nodded and served him an espresso, pouring herself one, too. "So what's this all about?" she said. "What's your name?"

"Ben."

"What do you want to know, Ben?"

"Were Fred and Oliver friends?"

"You think there's something strange about it, don't you?"

He looked up from his coffee. She was sharp. He made a quick decision to trust her. "Yes, I do think that."

She sighed, a sigh of relief mixed with sadness and bitter anger. Her face was tense. "So do I," she said quietly. "I thought I was the only one who did."

"You're not the only one," he said. "But I can't tell you everything. Maybe one day I'll be able to. Until then, I just need your help. Ten minutes, and I'll be out of here."

She nodded. "Okay, I'll tell you. They weren't really friends. They only met a couple of times."

"The first time was at a party?"

"That's right. Some student party. I wasn't there. Fred told me he met this good fun English guy, a pianist. Fred was one, too."

"I know," Ben said.

"Musicians always talk to each other," she continued. "Fred loved music. It was his language. He told me Oliver loved it, too."

"He did."

"They talked for hours. They got on really well."

"You and Fred didn't live together, did you?"

She shook her head. "No, I work here full-time. I'm the manager here. Fred had cheap digs in Vienna. We were saving to get married after his graduation from music school."

"I'm sorry to put you through all this again."

She sniffed and wiped a tear away. "No, it's okay. If something bad happened, people need to know. I need to know."

"Can you tell me about the opera tickets?" Ben asked. "Fred had two tickets for *Macbeth*. They were for him and you, weren't they?"

"Yes, they were. He was so excited about it. He couldn't have afforded the tickets himself. He couldn't wait. He loved Verdi." Christa gazed into the middle distance. Her face darkened. "Like he would have killed himself. It's crap. I always said it was a pile of crap. But nobody would listen to me. People thought I was just this hysterical girl with issues, who couldn't face up to the idea that her man had killed himself. Like I was in denial or something. They told me to see a shrink. And Fred's parents just accepted it. I mean, how *could* they?"

"People tend to take the path of least resistance," Ben said. "It's easier to believe someone committed suicide than to start looking for a killer."

"Are you looking for the killer?"

"Yes, I am."

"What'll you do if you find him?"

He didn't answer that. "Did Oliver give Fred the tickets?"

Christa nodded.

"Tell me about it," Ben said.

"I don't know all the details," she replied. "Fred used to play piano gigs here and there to make a bit of extra cash. Mostly it was bars, restaurants, anywhere with a piano. He gave classical recitals, too—he had a little circuit going. He was such a great player, and he had a good reputation. One day he landed this really important gig at a private party, some big house outside the city. It was a real prestigious thing, tuxedo job. Anyway, the night he met Oliver was the week before the gig. He told him about it, but Oliver didn't say much at the time. Well done, congratulations, good luck, all the things one player would say to another if they weren't jealous." She paused. "But later that night, hours after the party was over, Fred got a phone call. It was Oliver. He said he'd been thinking about what Fred had said. He'd found out something. Suddenly, he was all excited about the gig at the big house."

Ben listened hard.

Christa went on. "He wanted to know everything about it, and he wanted to go with him. He was desperate to get into the place."

"Why?"

"I don't know. But Fred told him there was no way he could get him an invite. It was very exclusive. Politicians, people like that. Major bigwigs. A lot of security."

"I don't understand why Oliver would have been so keen to meet those kinds of people," Ben said. "They weren't his favorite kind."

"From what Fred said, it wasn't the party he was interested in. It was the house itself. He was asking lots of questions about it."

"Why was he so interested in the house?"

"I don't know," she replied. "He kept talking about his research."

"He didn't say more?"

"If he did, Fred never told me."

"Never mind," Ben said. "Go on."

"When Oliver called up late that night, he made Fred a weird offer. He said he could get him a private box for two at his sister's performance of *Macbeth* at the Vienna State Opera. The last box, the last tickets. Worth a fortune. But there was a condition."

Ben got it. "If Fred agreed to change places with him? Oliver wanted to get in there as the pianist for the night?"

She nodded.

"And Fred agreed to the deal?"

"He didn't really want to give up the date, and the whole idea seemed nuts. But Oliver was totally serious, and the opera tickets were too tempting. Oliver said he'd let him have the gig fee, too. Fred knew that Oliver was a good player, that he'd do a good job and wouldn't spoil his reputation. So he went for it."

"And Oliver gave the recital?"

"You tell me," she said. "According to the papers, he was somewhere else. Didn't they say he was at a party and got drunk with some woman, then drowned in a lake?"

"So the night of the recital was the night Oliver and Fred both died," Ben said.

Christa let out a long sigh. "Yes, it was."

"Where was the recital?"

"I don't know where the house is," she said. "Just that it's not that far from Vienna. It's some seriously expensive, fancy place. A real palace. An aristocrat owns it. Old Viennese money, going back centuries."

"Do you know who the aristocrat is?"

She nodded. "Von Adler. He's the Count von Adler."

40.

SLOVENIA

THE SAME DAY

Clara carefully wrote down the right answer to question ten and folded her notebook inside her math textbook. Mother Hildegard didn't have a calculator, but that didn't matter. Clara's arithmetic was pretty good.

The child left the schoolbook lying on the desk, slipped down from the hard chair, and went off to potter about the nun's office, looking for something else to do. She looked along the bookshelves at the rows of leather spines. Most of Mother Hildegard's books were religious, and Clara wasn't too tempted by them. There were a couple of tatty old jigsaw puzzles in the cupboard, but Clara had already done them both. Puzzles were for kids, and Clara didn't think of herself that way. The pope's left eye was missing, anyway.

She looked out of the window for a while, watching the mountains in the distance. It was lovely here, and it was a nice holiday, although she couldn't understand why her daddy couldn't be with her more of the time. The nuns were kind to her, and Leigh was a lot of fun, too. But she missed her friends, her school, and most of all she missed her sitter Helga. Helga was like a big sister to her. She wondered whether Daddy would ever marry her, and they could have a real family again.

On the Mother Superior's desk was an old phone, the only phone in the convent. It was like no other phone she'd ever seen, and it fascinated her. It was heavy and black, with a funny-shaped receiver that sat sideways on top and was connected to the heavy part by a braided cord. But the strangest thing about it was the round dial in the middle, with little holes in it. She knew from watching old movies with her daddy that you were meant to put your finger in the holes and turn the dial. Her fingers went in the holes easily. She wondered whether her daddy's big stubby fingers would fit.

It was weird to imagine that people used to use this kind of thing all the time. She amused herself dialing 1-2-3-4-5 and watching the dial whirr back a little farther each time until it reached the stop.

Then she had a thought. She suddenly wanted to talk to Helga, to tell her about her new friend Leigh, the famous singer who was on CDs and television. She looked around. She could hear singing coming from the chapel. Just a little call, nobody would mind.

She picked up the heavy receiver, remembered the code for Austria, and dialed the number. Her face lit up at the sound of her friend's voice. "Helga, it's me," she said.

Leigh sipped a coffee and watched the crackling fire. It was so quiet here. Ben had been gone less than eighteen hours. They'd hardly spoken when he left, and the memory kept playing back in her head. There was a lot she wanted to say to him. She knew she was lying to herself when she tried to tell herself she didn't still love him. Over the last few days she'd begun to wonder whether she'd ever really stopped. But she'd been selfish with him, and that was the biggest regret she had. She'd initiated the kiss, and then she'd pushed him away. It wasn't fair to play with his emotions.

She heard the cottage door open, and Clara appeared in the doorway. "Hi, can I come in?" She came and sat on a chair, kicking her feet.

"What have you been doing today, Clara?"

"Oh, stuff. Mother Hildegard gave me some math to do." Clara decided not to mention her fifteen-minute call to Helga. "Then I helped Sister Agnes feed the piglets and collect the eggs. I want one."

"You want an egg?"

"No, a piglet. But I don't think piglets are allowed in Vienna."

"They don't stay so small and cute for long, you know. You'd soon have a great big smelly pig living in your house."

Clara grinned. "I already have one," she said. "My daddy."

"That's a terrible thing to say, Clara." But Leigh couldn't help but laugh.

"Leigh?"

"Hmm?"

"Can I have a look at your gold locket?"

"Yes, of course you can." Leigh reached behind her neck and undid the slim chain. The shiny oyster-shaped locket dangled from her fingers as she handed it to the child.

"It's beautiful." Clara turned it over in her hand, admiring the delicate engraving of Leigh's initials. She found a little catch on the side and pressed it, and the halves of the oyster sprang open with a click. Set into the two halves, facing each other, were tiny miniature photographic portraits of three people. "Who are they?" she asked.

Leigh leaned across and pointed. "These two people here together on this side are my parents," she said.

"Your mummy's pretty," Clara said. She studied the

other picture. "The man on the other side looks like you."

She nodded. "My brother, Oliver."

"Where do they live?"

"In heaven," Leigh replied, after a pause.

Clara understood. "All of them?"

"Yes, all of them. I'm the last one left of the whole family."

"My mummy's up in heaven, too. Do you think maybe she knows your brother and your mummy and daddy?"

Leigh smiled sadly at a child's notion of death. "I'm sure they probably do all know each other very well."

"What do you think people do in heaven?"

"They play, and have fun, I suppose."

"That's not so bad. I like playing."

"You want to play now?"

Clara nodded enthusiastically. "Let's go out and play the find game Ben taught me and Max."

Leigh was glad of the excuse to quit moping and get out of the cottage. She slipped on a pair of boots and a quilted jacket, and they walked out into the snow. The sky was the clearest blue, and the sun was sparkling off the mountains. They walked through the farmyard, towards the main convent buildings. Max loved the snow and was cavorting about in it, sending up a fine spray. From the little stone chapel Leigh could hear the nuns doing their choir practice. She knew the piece they were singing, one of Palestrina's choral chants.

"You hide first," Clara said. "Let's see if Maxy remembers the game."

Leigh ran around the corner of a woodshed and squatted down behind an ornamental shrub. She heard Clara finish counting to ten and saying, "Max, go find Leigh! Find Leigh!" Max instantly responded and came bounding over to her. He licked her face, and she patted his big head.

Over the sweet, harmonious sound of the nuns' singing came the steady thud of helicopter blades. Leigh looked up, shielding her eyes from the sun. There were two of them, high over the convent. They seemed to be moving slowly, hovering. "Someone must have got into trouble in the mountains," she said. But as the choppers grew nearer, the thump of their rotors filling the air, she could see they didn't look like mountain rescue aircraft. They were black, unmarked. What did they want?

Clara followed her gaze for a moment, then shrugged her shoulders. "Anyway, now it's my turn to hide. You hold Maxy by his collar and count to twenty."

The child ran off. Leigh was still watching the two black helicopters as she counted. *Eight, nine, ten, eleven . . .* They were circling, descending, drowning out the nuns' choir.

They were coming awfully close.

Leigh shivered. She didn't like it. *Fourteen, fifteen, sixteen . . .*

Enough. She stopped counting. "Clara!" she called out. "Come back!"

Clara didn't hear and kept running. The dog was pulling hard against Leigh's grip, yearning to be set free. The helicopters were now only a hundred feet off the ground, and the sound was deafening. They vanished from view behind the convent roofs. They were landing.

Something was wrong. Terribly wrong. Leigh let go of Max's collar, and the big dog streaked across the snow towards where Clara had just disappeared round the side of one of the buildings.

• • •

Clara ran on, counting as she went. Any minute now, Maxy was going to come galloping after her She glanced over her shoulder to see if he was there.

And gasped as she collided with something hard. She fell backwards into the snow.

A tall man she'd never seen before was looking down at her. His eyes were cold, and he wasn't smiling.

41.

VIENNA

Black clouds scudded across the sky, and the wind was icy. Ben bought a copy of *Die Presse* from a newspaper stand. It was nearly midday, but he wasn't hungry. He was leaning against a wall reading it on the corner of Bankgasse and Löwelstrasse opposite the towering facade of the Burgtheater when he spotted Kinski's car pull out of the traffic. The cop barely slowed to pick him up. Ben got in, and the big car powered away.

"Might want this back." Ben tossed the police ID onto Kinski's lap.

"You bastard. I've been looking for that everywhere."

"Did you get the stuff?" Ben asked.

Kinski nodded. "Backseat. Little blue bag."

Ben turned round to grab it. He saw the black Audi Quattro through the rear window, three cars back. "Someone's tailing us," he said.

"You're good. It's okay. They're my guys."

"How much do they know?"

"No more than they need to know, if that," Kinski said.

Ben nodded. He grabbed the small flight bag off the backseat, turned back round, and unzipped it on his lap. There were five identical oblong card boxes, six inches long and four wide. They had FEDERAL emblazoned in bold letters across the top and .45 ACP 230 GR. FMJ CENTERFIRE

PISTOL CARTRIDGES printed on the side. He opened one of the boxes. Inside it was a red plastic tray with fifty half-inch round holes, ten rows of five, a gleaming cartridge in each one. Fifty rounds a box, two hundred and fifty rounds. He was pleased. "All untraceable?"

"Come on, what do you take me for?" Kinski said.

"You'll tell me what I owe you?"

"Forget it. I don't need your money. Did your train ride pay off?"

Ben reached into his backpack and took out the empty Para-Ordnance. He thumbed the magazine release. The mag dropped out. He locked open the action of the pistol and laid it on his lap. "It certainly did."

"You found out something?" Kinski asked.

"I know everything." Ben quickly ran through what Christa had told him.

Kinski listened hard. His coarse features were puckered in concentration as he pushed the 4x4 through the aggressive Vienna traffic. "But why was Oliver so interested in getting inside the house?"

"I'm coming to that," Ben said. "Christa's place is a cybercafe. After I spoke to her I went online. I did more research. I cross-referenced everything. It all checks out. I found out a lot. Remember I asked you about Adler?"

Kinski nodded.

"Adler is the key," Ben said. "It wasn't a code. It was a name. Von Adler. *Count* von Adler."

"I've heard that name."

"What about the name Kroll?"

Kinski shook his head.

"Same family," Ben said. "Here's what I found out. Viktor Kroll was head of the Austrian secret police from 1788 to 1796. He was awarded land and title for services to the empire by Josef II. He became Count von Adler and was given a palatial house and estate near Vienna."

"The same house?"

"The same house. It's been in the family ever since. The current Count von Adler is the great-great-great grandson. That's as far as the historical record goes. But the house and title weren't the only things that got handed down."

"I'm not getting it."

"This is the bit the history books don't mention," Ben said, "because the letter that Richard Llewellyn discovered never made it into the historical record. Von Adler was the Eagle mentioned in the letter. We know from Arno that he was also Grand Master of the Order of Ra. A big part of those services to the empire was the order's dirty work in helping to wipe out the Masons. He used his estate as his base."

"So?"

"So they're still there, Markus. Oliver found them."

Kinski chewed it over for a moment. "Oliver knew?"

"He was halfway to the truth," Ben said. "He knew about the historical connection with his Mozart research. Who knows what he thought he'd find in the house? Perhaps he thought he was opening up a hidden chapter of history. He had no idea what he was really walking into. He witnessed the execution by pure chance."

"This would explain why Meyer died the same night," Kinski said.

Ben nodded. "He was the hired pianist for the night, so his name was on the list. As soon as Oliver was out of there, they were already searching for the address of Meyer's student digs. They got to him within minutes. But they'd have realized immediately that he wasn't the same guy. With a gun to his head, he must have blabbed Oliver's name pretty fast. They probably told him he was buying his life if he talked."

Kinski scowled. "But the fuckers killed him anyway, just to keep him quiet. Then they went after Oliver."

"Faster than that," Ben said. "They're not short of people. There would have been a team on its way for Oliver even while Meyer was still breathing."

Kinski frowned. "Wait. How did they—"

"Know where to find him? Police computer. They've got the right connections, remember? Oliver was a foreign visitor. He would have needed his passport to check into the boardinghouse. There couldn't have been too many Oliver Llewellyns in the area. They picked him like an apple."

Kinski grunted.

"He just had time to burn the video clip to CD and post it to the only person he could trust," Ben said. "Then they caught up with him. They took him out to the lake. Probably made him walk out onto the ice and then let loose with the nine millimeter to crack it up around him. He never had a chance." He took a fat, shiny .45 Federal round from one of the cartridge boxes and used his thumb to press it into the magazine. It snicked into place.

"So what now?" Kinski asked.

Ben loaded the second round into the magazine, pushing down against the stiff spring. "I know where the house is," he said. "I'll take care of it. It ends here."

"Where's the house?"

"Let me deal with it. You can read about it in the papers."

"You need my help."

Ben loaded the third round. "No," he said. "That's not how it works. I don't use partners, Markus. You'll get in the way."

"You really are crazy."

"I've been crazier." He pressed the fourth round in on top of the first three.

The traffic was heavy. Kinski flipped on the indicator at a busy intersection, cutting across into the Burgring. His eyes darted from road to mirror and back, concentrating on the traffic. "I believe you," he said.

Ben didn't reply. He took a fifth cartridge from the box and loaded it into the magazine.

Neither of them saw the dark blue truck until it was almost on them. It was a security vehicle, massive, heavily armored, unmarked. As Kinski's Mercedes cut across the street the truck surged through a red light and came on hard. Horns blared. Kinski saw it half a second after Ben. He hit the brakes an instant too late.

The truck caught the Mercedes broadside at fifty miles an hour and cut it in half.

42.

SLOVENIA

From where Clara had fallen in the snow, she could see the two black helicopters sitting side by side in the field on the other side of the convent buildings. There were more men getting out of them and striding quickly among the buildings. They wore some kind of white overalls and carried small black things. She gaped.

The small objects were guns. Like the one that the man standing over her was pointing at her head.

He grabbed her by the hair and hauled her to her feet. She let out a cry of fear and pain. He clamped his hand over her mouth.

A big black shape came streaking around the corner. Max's eyes were alert, and his body stiffened as he saw the man clutching Clara. He growled, advanced, and charged at the man. He grabbed the man's arm and dragged him off the little girl, pulling him to the ground and shaking him like a rag doll. Clara was screaming. Two more men appeared through an archway. They aimed their guns at Max and fired. The dog howled and thrashed on the bloody snow.

Leigh saw it all from a distance as she ran through the snow towards the convent. The running figures vaulted the wall into the grounds and circled the buildings, kicking open doors and cocking their weapons. Over the noise of the helicopters she could hear a new sound. The nuns had stopped singing, and now it was their cries of terror and panic that were coming from the chapel's arched windows. A sound that was cut short by the chattering of suppressed gunfire.

One of the men bundled Clara roughly under his arm and carried her kicking and thrashing and screaming towards the waiting choppers. Leigh's heart was hammering furiously. As she watched, one of the nuns burst out of the chapel, her face contorted in horror. She made it halfway across the courtyard before she was cut down by a blast from a gun. She collapsed on her face, the black-and-white habit stained with red. They got her by the ankles and dragged her body towards the chapel, leaving a thick trail of blood on the snow. Through the open chapel door Leigh could see the men throwing dead nuns in a bloody, twisted heap at the foot of the altar.

She would have done anything to help Clara, but there was nothing she could do except run the other way. She sprinted back to the cottage. Nobody had seen her. She crashed through the door and ran inside. She was shaking violently.

The shotgun on the rack. She looked up at it for an instant, then grabbed it down. Her hands trembled as she rummaged in the drawer for some cartridges. She thrust a fistful of them into her jacket pocket, opened up the gun's action the way Ben had shown her, and slipped a round in each barrel.

She burst out of the cottage.

Run like hell, Leigh.

She dashed through the passageway leading to the farm. She let out a cry as a man stepped out pointing a gun at her head.

His face was hard, his eyes serious as he stared down the twin bores of the shotgun. "Drop the weapon," he warned, leveling his own.

Leigh didn't have time to think. She wrapped her fingers around the two triggers and let off both barrels. Right in his face. The gun kicked violently back, making her stagger.

The impact of the gun at extreme close range was devastating. The man's features disintegrated. Blood flew up the wall. She could taste the thick saltiness of it on her lips. She spat and ran on again, jumping over him and away from the convent. As she stumbled through the snow, she feverishly reloaded the shotgun the way Ben had shown her.

Another man saw her and gave chase. She reached the low perimeter wall and vaulted over it, making for the cover of the trees.

He had orders not to kill her unless necessary. He fired a warning spray at the snow around her feet as she ran. Passing the snowman she'd built with Ben the day before, she turned and let off a barrel. The boom echoed across the valley.

He felt the sharp bite of stray pellets in his thigh, slapped it, and saw blood on his fingers. Angry now, he raised his weapon, this time to bring her down. Orders be damned. He'd seen what the bitch had done to Hans.

She was zigzagging across his line of fire, feinting left and right to put him off. He squeezed the trigger. The chatter from the weapon churned up the snow and gouged the bark off a tree to her left. Then his magazine was empty. He slung the gun behind his back and drew the combat knife from the sheath on his belt.

Twigs and branches raked at her clothes and whipped her face as she darted through the dense forest. The long shotgun caught on a branch and was torn from her grip.

She started to run back for it, but he was gaining on her. She gasped and staggered on. But where could she run to? The steep drop down to the river was just up ahead. She'd run herself into a trap.

The man saw the fallen shotgun and picked it up. There was a hammer cocked. One barrel gone, one to go. He smiled to himself. She was just twenty yards away, and the brightly colored quilted jacket was an easy target against the forest.

He took aim and fired.

The shotgun kicked back against his shoulder with a rolling boom. The double barrel jerked upwards with the recoil, and through the smoke he saw her go down.

She staggered and went down on one knee. For a moment she clutched at a sapling, trying to stay upright. Then she pitched headlong into the thicket and tumbled head over heels down the slope, crashing down with a crackle of twigs.

The man walked coolly up to the edge of the thickly wooded drop. It was a long way down. He could hear the rush of the river below. He looked down at his feet. Where she'd fallen, the snow was stained red.

He craned his neck, peering down. He saw her, far below. She was lying tangled in the snowy reeds near the water, one arm outflung, her black hair spread across her face. There was blood on her lips and her exposed throat, and all down the front of her torn jacket. Her eyes were open and staring up at the sky.

He watched her for ten seconds, fifteen, twenty. She wasn't moving. No breath. Not a flicker in the eyes. He unzipped a pocket and took out a small Samsung digital camera. He switched it on and zoomed in on the body until it filled the frame. He took three shots of it and then put the camera back in his pocket.

Something glinted gold in the corner of his eye. He reached out and snatched the little gold locket from where it had snagged on a naked twig. He held it out on his palm. It was spattered with bright blood.

The convent was burning now, and the screams had been silenced. The first chopper was already rising up into the sky, rotors beating through the black smoke.

He turned and started walking back.

43.

VIENNA

Wreckage spun across the busy intersection as the massive truck plowed through the Mercedes and tore it apart. Cars skidded and crashed into one another. The front and rear halves of Kinski's vehicle spun in opposite directions. The rear half flipped and rolled and came to a rest upside down, while the front half rolled into the curb with sparks showering from its dragging underside.

The road was scattered with broken glass, slick with engine coolant. Horns blared. There were screams and yells from the crowds of people that lined the boulevard. Cars were strewn everywhere at crazy angles. The intersection had suddenly transformed from an everyday street scene into a wild, chaotic sea of vehicles and terrified people all scattering in panic. An icy rain began to fall. In seconds it became a hailstorm.

Ben shook pieces of smashed safety glass out of his hair. The Mercedes was a mess of twisted, buckled metal, crumpled plastic, shattered windows. Behind the front seats was a gaping hole where the rest of the car should have been. His ears were ringing from the impact, and he was disorientated. One of his ammunition boxes had burst open and there were pistol cartridges rolling around everywhere inside the car. He could smell burning. The door next to him was hanging off its hinges.

To his left, Kinski was groaning, semiconscious, blood on his face. Ben could hear screaming and mayhem from outside in the street. Hail cannoned off the roof of the Mercedes.

He twisted groggily round in his seat. The armored security truck had skidded to a halt fifteen yards from the wrecked car. Now the back doors burst open.

Five men spilled out. They were wearing black flak jackets and carrying Heckler & Koch assault rifles. Military weapons, fully automatic, high-capacity magazines filled with high-velocity ammunition that could tear through steel and brick. Their faces were hidden behind black hockey masks. They strode purposefully through the hailstorm, rifle stocks high against their shoulders, barrels trained on the Mercedes. There was the deafening bark of high-powered fire. Bullets punched through the Mercedes door and ripped into the dash inches from Ben. Sparks flew from deep inside the electrics.

Through a haze, Ben looked down at his hand. It was still clutching the partly loaded pistol magazine. Things seemed to be happening in slow motion. He could see the shooters getting closer, but his senses weren't reacting.

Focus. He slammed the mag into the pistol grip of the .45 and hit the slide release. By the time the first round had chambered he'd already found his first target. The man staggered back a step, stayed on his feet, shouldered his weapon, kept coming. Bulletproof armor.

The black Audi Quattro swerved through the chaos, bumping cars out of its path. Three men climbed out, ducking down low, drawing pistols. Kinski's officers. They crouched behind the open doors of their car and fired on the masked rifle shooters. The pistol shots were poppy little things compared to the massive bang of military rifles. Fully automatic fire strafed the Audi. Supersonic rifle bullets chewed effortlessly through steel. One of Kinski's men sprawled backwards, chest torn open, gun clattering across the road. People ran screaming. There was mass panic on the pavements. Sirens in the distance.

Ben's vision was too hazy to see the sights on his gun. He relied on instinct. This time he hit high of the armor. One of the rifle shooters went down, clutching at his throat, slipping on the icy road. A rifle bullet tore through the window frame of the Mercedes, and Ben felt the stunning shock wave ruffle his hair. He fired blind, two more rounds. Supporting fire came from the Audi. The four remaining riflemen fell back. The sirens were getting louder, cutting through the mayhem and the screaming.

Kinski had come round. He was writhing in pain and clutching his leg. Ben kicked open the Mercedes door and rolled out onto the road, grabbing his bag as he went. He saw the riflemen falling back. They hadn't expected this much resistance, and Kinski's guys had been a surprise.

Beyond the ocean of abandoned cars were the flashing lights of the police. The four rifle shooters started to run. One of Kinski's officers leaned across the perforated hood of the Audi and let off a burst of three rounds of 9 mm. A shooter staggered and collapsed on his face on the wet road, his rifle spinning out of his grip.

The other three made it to the pavement and dashed away down a narrow side street. Kinski's guy raised his badge as armed police burst out of the wailing fleet of cars and sprinted between vehicles to the scene, guns ready.

Ben looked back at Kinski. The cop's face was white and

twisted in agony. "Leg's bust," he grunted. "You go. Get after them."

Ben knew he couldn't be discovered with Kinski. Too many questions and complications that wouldn't be good for either of them. He gave the big German a quick nod that said, Till next time. Then he ran low between the abandoned cars, moving quickly away from the smashed Mercedes.

The cops didn't see him. He reached the pavement, staggering a little, still stunned. He slipped into the alleyway where he'd seen the three escaping shooters disappear seconds ago.

44.

Ben sprinted away down the side street, leaving the sirens and the devastation behind him. The hail had softened to sleet. He leaped over an icy puddle, came down on the edge of it, and almost fell. His head was still bursting from the impact of the truck, and his breath rasped in his ears.

He stumbled around a corner and saw a cobbled alleyway to his left, narrow and winding, carving deep into the ancient backstreets of the city. He could see three black running shapes fifty yards ahead, their racing footsteps echoing up the walls of the buildings on either side.

The men were running to a waiting brown Volvo saloon. Brake lights blazed through the sleet. The engine revved, and Ben gave chase. The escaping riflemen piled in, doors slammed, and the Volvo took off, skidding away out of sight.

Ben stood in the middle of the wet road, his heart pounding, the gun hanging limply at his side as he listened to the noise of the car engine fade. But then it changed. There was a screech of tires. The engine note began to rise.

The car had U-turned. It was coming back.

It rounded the corner, heading back up the alleyway towards him, accelerating hard. He could see faces behind the rain-spattered windscreen. Four, perhaps five men inside the car. He raised the Para-Ordnance and fired at the screen.

His bullet punched a web of cracks in the glass. The

Volvo kept coming, faster, aiming to run him down. He brought the pistol back to aim.

But the gun was empty. He'd had time to load only five rounds into the magazine. Those five rounds were gone. The slide was locked back, and the ammunition was still in the Mercedes. Two hundred and forty-five rounds, enough to hold off a small army, and he couldn't get to a single one of them.

The Volvo was gaining on him—he could see the grinning faces behind the cracked glass. Ben turned and ran. The engine roared behind him in the narrow alley, drowning out the echoing clap of his footsteps as he half sprinted, half staggered over the slippery, glistening cobbles.

He wasn't going to make it. The car crash had knocked the energy out of him, and he could feel his strength giving out. Then he saw another alleyway entrance to the left. It wound sharply downhill between old walls and uneven houses, its entrance blocked by three old iron bollards. You could barely squeeze a large motorcycle between them, let alone a car.

Ben raced between them and heard the Volvo slide to a halt behind him. He hurtled down the steep alley, the downward slope giving him more momentum. The Volvo's doors opened. A shot cracked, and a bullet sang off a wall.

Ben ran on. The alley curved round to the right, taking him out of sight of his pursuers. He could hear their running footsteps coming down the hill. He rounded the lip of a crumbled wall, and suddenly the alley opened up into a little square. There was an old fountain in the middle.

He leaned against it and paused for breath, stuffing the empty pistol in his belt. He looked around him. From the square, a whole network of tiny streets ran off in different directions. There were six ways he could go. He stole a glance over his shoulder and chose one at random. It was even steeper. He ran as fast and as lightly as he could, to mask the sound of his footsteps. There was nobody following him. They must have gone a different way, but he still had to hurry. They could split up; they knew the city better than him, and he was unarmed.

Ahead of him, the downhill alleyway opened up onto what looked like a bigger street. Thirty yards, twenty. As he approached the bottom, he looked over his shoulder to check if they were following. He couldn't see—

Brakes screeched. He couldn't stop in time. He ran straight out in front of a red Peugeot.

45.

The car knocked the wind out of him. He flew across the hood, cracked his head on the windscreen, and tumbled to the ground.

The driver's door burst open, and a young woman with a look of horror on her face got out. She rushed over to where Ben was slowly picking himself off the ground. She spoke in a flurry of German, apologizing profusely.

Ben staggered to his feet and rested against the side of the car. His head was spinning badly. He tried to focus his vision up the alleyway. They would be here any second. "It's okay," he muttered. "It wasn't your fault."

Her eyes widened. "You're American?" she said in English.

"British." He tried to formulate his thoughts. "I was mugged back there."

She looked confused.

"Robbed," he explained.

She nodded. "Bastards. I'll call the police," she said, taking out her phone. "You get in the car. *Setzen sie hier.* You must rest."

"*Nein.* No. *Keine Polizei.* There's no need for the police. Just get me out of here, please. Quickly." He picked up his fallen backpack and slumped on the passenger's seat. The alleyway was still empty, but his pursuers couldn't be far away.

"Then I have to take you to the *Arzt*—to the doctor. To the hospital. You're hurt." She looked at his bleeding head with concern, biting her lip as she started the car and pulled away over the cobbles. "I'm so sorry. I've never done anything like this before. I—"

"It's not your fault," he repeated. "Look, I don't need a doctor. I'll be all right. I need to rest a bit somewhere. If you can drive me to a cheap hotel, that'll be fine."

She looked perplexed, then nodded hesitantly. "Whatever you want," she said. She drove out into the main street and filtered into the traffic. Ben struggled to twist round in his seat. There was no sign of anyone following. He hoped Kinski was okay.

She drove in silence, looking uncomfortable and distressed, then shook her head. "Listen, my flat is just half a kilometer from here. I have some stuff I can put on that graze, and you can rest there. Please, it's the least I can do."

Ben's head was throbbing. Maybe it wasn't a bad suggestion. Staggering into a hotel with a bleeding head was a little too public. "All right."

"I'm Ingrid," she said. "Ingrid Becker."

"Ben," he said. "Jesus, my head."

Ingrid's phone rang. "*Ja?* Hello, Leonie. Yes . . . I can't talk now, I'm with a friend . . . Maybe see you later, okay? *Tchüss.*" She switched off the phone. "Sorry about that," she smiled. "My cousin. Here we are." She flipped on her indicator and turned the Peugeot into a basement car park.

Ingrid helped Ben into the lift and pressed the button for the second floor. He slumped against the lift wall and watched her. She was in her mid-twenties or so. Her hair was short and dark with a few reddish highlights. She was dressed in jeans and combat boots, an Afghan coat over a checked shirt, but for all that she still managed to look strikingly attractive.

The lift opened, and she carefully took his arm to walk him to her door. "You okay?"

"I'll be fine."

Ingrid's flat was small but comfortable. She directed him to a two-seater sofa in the main room. It was warm in there, and he took off his leather jacket and laid it on the arm of the sofa. He sat down then leaned back onto the sofa as she hurried to the bathroom to fetch cotton wool and disinfectant. "This will sting a little," she said. She leaned over him and dabbed his head with a ball of moist cotton.

"Ouch."

"Sorry. I feel so terrible about this. Can I get you something to drink?"

Ben took out his flask. "You have some as well," he said. "I think you need it more than me."

Ingrid fetched two tumblers and sat with him on the sofa. He emptied what was left of his Scotch into them. He looked at her face. She had a nice smile and soft, dark eyes. He could see sadness in them, too. "Cheers."

"*Prost.*"

They clinked and drank. "It's good," she said. "You like schnapps? I have a bottle."

"I'd love some." His head was spinning a little less now, and he was beginning to feel more composed. Concussion wasn't going to be a problem—but fatigue was. It was coming over him in waves.

"Do you want a painkiller?"

"I'd rather have the schnapps," he said wearily, and she laughed. "I'm so glad you're okay, Ben. I was worried I'd killed you or something."

Ben drained the Scotch, and she uncapped the schnapps. She poured some of the clear liquor into the glass, and he sipped it. It tasted about twice the strength of the whiskey. "Don't worry," he said. "I'm not that easy to kill."

"Smoke?" She pulled a crumpled pack of untipped Gauloises out of her pocket. Ben took one and reached for his Zippo. Her long fingers clenched his hand as he lit hers first. He leaned back on the sofa and closed his eyes.

"You're a rare breed," she said, watching him, exhaling a cloud of smoke.

"In what way?"

She jiggled the cigarette and pointed at the glass of schnapps in his hand. "I don't know any men who smoke proper cigarettes and drink proper drinks anymore." She smiled. "They're all so concerned about their health. Wimps."

"My Irish grandmother smoked over a million cigarettes in her life," he said.

"A million!"

"Sixty a day, from the age of fifteen to the day she died. You do the math."

"*Mein Gott*. What did she die of?"

"She got drunk on her ninety-fifth birthday, fell downstairs, broke her neck." Ben smiled at the memory of the old lady. "She died happy and never felt a thing."

"That's it, I'm going to start drinking and smoking more," Ingrid said. She laid a warm hand on his knee. It stayed there for an instant longer than normal. "Hey, you like music?" She jumped up and went over to a hi-fi on a sideboard.

"You haven't got any Bartók, have you?"

She laughed. "No way. Music to chew your fingernails to. Far too intense for me."

"I like intense."

"You're an interesting one," she said. "I like jazz. What about some jazz?"

"How about Don Cherry or Ornette Coleman?"

"You *do* go for intense," she said. She ran her finger along the rack and plucked out a CD. "I've got *Bitches Brew*. Miles."

"Miles is good," he said. They sat for a while and listened to the music, drinking their schnapps and talking. She asked him what he was doing in Vienna, and he told her he was a freelance journalist. It made him think of Oliver.

His eyes were burning with fatigue, and his head nodded a couple of times. He'd been hoping the frenetic Miles Davis fusion jazz might help to keep him awake, but it wasn't working.

"You look exhausted," Ingrid said, looking concerned. "Perhaps you should sleep awhile."

"Perhaps," he muttered.

"Lie down here on the sofa," she said with a smile.

He was too tired to refuse. She turned off the music, laid cushions under his head, and fetched a blanket from her bedroom to cover him. He drifted off.

He awoke as though it were seconds later. She was sitting on the edge of the sofa, watching him with a tender expression. He propped himself up on his elbow, blinking. "How long have I been asleep?"

"Just over an hour. I'm hungry," she said, getting up. "How about you?"

He stretched, got to his feet, and followed her to the kitchen. It was small and clean. "I shouldn't stay here too much longer," he said. "I don't want to put you to any trouble."

"No, really, no trouble. I'm glad of some company. And anyway, I'm using you."

"Using me?"

She giggled. "To practice my English."

"I've been sleeping most of the time. And your English is fine."

"You like wurst?" She opened the fridge. "And I've got some cold roast chicken."

She took out two plates and served him some pieces of chicken with sliced sausage and some bread and salad. They sat on two high stools at the kitchen worktop, and she poured him a glass of mineral water. As he ate he could feel his strength beginning to return. "I never asked you what you do," he said.

She made a sour face. "I work for a big company, as a personal assistant."

"You don't like it?"

"No, I despise it," she said emphatically. "I wish I could leave."

"Sounds pretty bad. What do they make you do?"

"You have no idea," she replied. Her smile was gone.

"Maybe you should think about changing jobs."

"It's not that easy," she said. Their eyes met for a second. She liked him. She could barely remember when she'd last spent time with a man she actually liked. She looked away.

"I'm sorry you have problems," he said.

She shrugged. "Everyone has problems." She paused. "Here, why don't we have another schnapps?"

"Why not?" he replied.

She smiled at him, slipped off her stool, and went to fetch the bottle from the other room. She came back a moment later with a glass for each of them.

"One for the road, then," he said, taking his glass from her.

She watched the glass travel to his lips. He sipped a couple of sips. Bitch's brew, she thought to herself.

Ben looked at his watch. He had things to do, and his

headache had eased. "I should be getting on," he said. "It was good to meet you, Ingrid. Take care, won't you?"

"Good to meet you, too, Ben." She hated herself. She felt like screaming.

"Leave that job if it makes you so unhappy," he advised. "Find something you love."

"I wish I could."

"Don't worry so much, Ingrid. You're one of the good guys, remember." He touched her arm affectionately.

She pulled it away, avoiding his eyes.

"What's wrong?" he asked, seeing her look.

"It's not the way you think."

"What do you mean?"

Why hadn't she listened to her better judgment and let him go? He wasn't like the others. She wanted to take back the last few seconds and tell him to run, run like hell.

But it had gone too far for that. He'd had six drops of the drug, and in a few more seconds it was going to kick in. It was tasteless and odorless, and he had no idea what was happening. He smiled, but his eyes were beginning to glaze.

She knew what they were going to do to him. She'd signed his death warrant.

He slipped down from his stool. The strange feeling was spreading fast through him, and he barely had time to register it or fight it. His knee wobbled under his weight. His leg seemed to shoot out in front of him, and he felt himself going down as if in slow motion. He hit the floor and watched numbly as his glass shattered beside him.

His vision began to cloud. He looked up at her standing over him. She was talking on the phone. When she spoke into it, her voice sounded deep and booming and far away.

"You can come and get him now," Eve said, looking down

at him. He was losing consciousness. His head slumped on the floor.

She knelt down beside him and stroked his hair. "I'm so very sorry, *Liebchen*."

Four minutes later, the men came for him. They burst into Eve's flat, picked him up off the floor, and carried him out to the waiting van.

46.

Consciousness returned to Ben in staggered layers. First, he was dimly aware of the vibration pulsing through his skull where his head was resting against the hard metal of the wheel arch. His vision was blurry, and he felt sick. Suddenly, he was aware of being terribly, terribly cold. His body was racked with shivering, and his teeth were chattering.

He was sprawled across the floor of a rattling truck. The tin walls around him resonated loudly with the engine and transmission whine. He groaned and shifted, trying to get to his feet. His head was still spinning.

Memories came back to him in fragments. He remembered Ingrid's flat. Being hit by the car. Before that, the running chase through the streets. Kinski injured.

He remembered now. He'd been drugged.

He grabbed hold of one of the reinforcing braces inside the metal shell and dragged himself upright. The truck was lurching and bouncing, and it was hard to stand. There were no windows. He looked at his watch. It was nearly six o'clock. He must have been on the road for over an hour and a half. Where were they taking him?

The rattling, juddering journey lasted another quarter of an hour, the truck slowing as the road got rougher. He staggered across from one wall to the other as it swerved violently into a turning, then stopped. He heard the sound of doors slamming, and at least three different men's voices, all speaking in rapid, harsh German. He felt the vehicle reverse, and its engine sound was suddenly echoey and reverberating, as though the truck was inside a big metal space.

The doors opened, and he was dazzled by the lights. Powerful hands gripped him by the arms and hauled him out of the van. He dropped to his hands and knees on cold concrete and looked around him, blinking. Around him were seven, eight, nine men, all armed with either pistols or Heckler & Koch machine carbines. They all had the look of ex-military, serious faces, eyes cold and calm.

The prefabricated building looked like an old air-base hangar, stretching out on all sides like a vast aluminum cathedral. The concrete floor was painted green. The only furnishings were a tubular chair and a metal table. A fire blazed in a glass-fronted stove with a long steel flue that rose to the ceiling.

Standing in the middle of the huge open space, warming his hands over the stove, was a tall man in black. Sandy hair, cropped short.

Ben narrowed his eyes against the bright lights. He knew this man. Who the hell was he?

One of the men with guns got too close, and Ben saw a crazy chance. He lashed out with the rigid edge of his hand, fingers curled. The man let out a choking squawk as his throat was crushed, and fell squirming to the floor clutching his neck. The stubby black H&K was spinning in midair when Ben snatched it. It was cocked. He flipped off the safety. He was faster than these men, and he could bring them all down before they got him.

Maybe.

The gun clattered from his hands, and he fell to the floor along with it, his whole body quaking in a spasm. Curly plastic wires connected the dart in his flesh to the

Taser gun that one of the guards was holding—the one Ben hadn't seen, the one who had come out from behind the truck. The strong electric current flowed through him, controlling his muscles, rendering him completely helpless.

"That's enough," the tall man in black said.

The pulsing shock stopped. Ben gasped for air, lying flat on the concrete. One of the guards had his canvas backpack. The guard walked over to the tall man and handed the bag to him. The man emptied the bag out on a steel table, spilling out Ben's roll of spare clothes, his first-aid kit, the Para-Ordnance .45.

But the man was more interested in the box file. He flipped open the lid and thumbed through Oliver's notes, nodding to himself. This was the stuff. His instructions were clear.

He bunched the notes up in a big fist, opened the stove door, and slammed the papers inside. Ben's head sank to the floor as he watched his friend's notes burst into yellow flame, curl, and blacken. This time, they burned away to nothing. Tatters of ash fluttered up the stovepipe.

Now the man picked up the rolled-up Mozart letter. He jerked away the ribbon and tossed it over his shoulder. He unfurled the old paper and ran his eyes up and down it cursorily, a look of derision on his face.

For a moment Ben thought he was going to burn it, too. But then he rolled it back up and dropped it in a cardboard tube. He set the tube to one side, and started sifting back through the stuff on the table. This time his hand came up clutching the CD case. He nodded to himself, checked the disc was there, then snicked it shut and stuffed it in the side pocket of his combat trousers. He looked satisfied. "Bring him over here," he said to the guards.

Ben groaned as they picked him up by the arms and half

dragged him across the hangar. A length of heavy chain hung from a steel beam high up in the ceiling, stopping about seven feet above the concrete floor. There was a gun to his head. His arms were jerked outwards, and he felt the cold metal bite of cuffs on his wrists. Two pairs of cuffs, one pair for each wrist. They raised his arms up and clipped the other end of the cuffs to the dangling chain. Then they backed off, eight men standing in a wide semicircle around him. Gun muzzles were trained on him from every direction. He could just about stand, taking the weight on his feet instead of his wrists.

The big man walked up closer. His head was cocked to one side, his face cracked into a smirk. Ben knew what was coming next.

The man planted his feet, curled his meaty right hand into a fist, and put his back into it. He was powerful, and he'd done this before. The punch was a good one. Ben flexed his abdominal muscles for the blow, but it wasn't enough. The wind whistled out of him. His knees sagged, and he hung from his chained arms.

"Good to see you again, Hope. Remember me? I *want* you to remember me."

Ben got his breath back and rolled his eyes up to look at him. He remembered now.

Small world. Jack Glass. The psychopathic bastard who'd nearly killed him fifteen years earlier in the Brecon Beacons.

Ben's mind was struggling to put it together. Why Glass, why here, why this?

Glass grinned, flicked a bead of sweat from his brow, and started rolling up his sleeves. "It's been a long time," he said.

Ben watched him. He was much heavier than he'd been

in SAS selection days, but the extra bulk wasn't flab. His forearms were thick and muscular, as though he'd been working out with weights for hours every day, year after year. That wasn't the only physical change Ben noticed in the man. His right ear was badly scarred, the lobe gone, looking like melted wax.

As Ben stared at that ear, connections flew together in his dazed brain. The video clip. Clara Kinski's abductor.

"What are you doing here, Hope?" Glass sneered. "Come to check up on your girlfriend's dead brother? He's dead, all right. Trust me, I know." He drew back his fist and slammed it hard into Ben's side.

This time, Ben was ready. He tensed his muscles harder and twisted a little to catch the blow in the middle of his stomach instead of the kidney. But it still hurt, badly. The pain exploded, driving the air back out of him. He wheezed and saw stars.

Glass stepped back, rubbing his fist. "You don't have to answer," he said. "This isn't an interrogation. You know what that means." He tapped the CD case through the fabric of his pocket. "I've got everything I need from you. I don't need you alive, you understand?"

A thought came into Ben's mind, and it worried him. *Why weren't they asking him about Leigh?*

Glass reached over to the table and picked up something dull and metallic. It was a heavy steel knuckle duster. He held it in his left hand, fanned out his right fingers, and slipped the knuckle duster over them. He clenched it in his big fist, looked Ben in the eye, and smiled. "I'm going to take my time with you," he said. "Nice and slow. First, I'm going to soften you up. Then—" He paused and looked round at the other men with a smirk. "Well, hey, why don't I show you?" He gestured to one of the guards, the short fat one with the gray hair scraped back in an oily ponytail. The guy lowered his MP5, slung it behind his back, and stepped over to a holdall that was on the floor. He unzipped.

There was a chain saw inside. The fat guy primed it with a squirt of gas in the tiny carburetor. He hooked his fingers around the end of the start cord and jerked it. The chain saw buzzed angrily into life in the echoey hangar. The guy gunned the throttle.

Glass nodded to him to kill the saw's motor. The hangar went quiet again. The guard laid the chain saw down on the table.

Glass turned back to Ben. "Like I said, this isn't an interrogation. So now here comes the fun part." He grinned. "I'm going to take you apart one bit at a time, and I'm going to enjoy it." Glass pressed his face up close to Ben's. His skin was pallid and sweaty. "Just like I enjoyed killing your friend Llewellyn. That's right. He was easy, too."

Ben blazed at the words. Glass had just marked himself for death.

If he could get out of this. Right now, it wasn't looking very certain.

He jerked on the chain. It was solid. The ring of guns was centered steadily on his head. No way out.

He looked past Glass at the chain saw, imagined the blade coming closer, whirring, gnashing. It would only have to touch him lightly to cause irreversible damage. Where would they cut him first? Not the shoulder or the abdomen—major trauma to a vital organ would kill him too quickly. They wanted sport. A leg, maybe. But not too high up. The blade would come at him sideways, below the knee. The first soft pressure would tear through clothing and split the flesh. More pressure and the saw would bite hard into the bone. It would slice through like nothing.

First one leg, then the other. His limbs would drop off him like fruit off a tree. Irreversible, whatever happened afterwards. He'd be swinging from the chain, spinning round and round, screaming, stumps thrashing, blood jetting out all over the concrete. He'd see them laughing at him.

That wasn't going to happen to him. No way.

He jerked the chain again.

The knuckle duster caught the light of the overhead fluorescents. Glass swung his fist a couple of times theatrically, grunting. He paused, grinned, then drew it back, eyes scanning Ben's face for his best mark.

Hanging from the chain, Ben kept his eyes on the steel-clad fist and resigned himself to the brutal blow that was going to break his nose and smash his teeth into his throat. There'd be worse to come. He started to close himself down in readiness.

But you could never be ready for this.

47.

The sharp command halted Glass's fist before it could make contact. Ben let out his breath, and his muscles slackened.

Glass lowered his arm and turned as a small man in his sixties walked into the hangar. Ben watched him approach, flanked by four guards carrying MP5s. He was well-groomed, immaculately dressed in a dark suit, sober tie, and long tweed overcoat. The black patent-leather shoes clicked on the concrete floor. His face was long and pale, with a hooked nose and unblinking eyes that gave him the penetrating look of a bird of prey.

"Change of plan," he said curtly to Glass. "Bring him into the office." His accent was German, his English perfect.

Glass looked sullen and disappointed as he barked orders at the guards. He slipped off his knuckle duster. Two men stepped forward and released Ben from the cuffs. He wasn't going to fall on the floor, not in front of them. He stayed on his feet, swaying a little, trying hard to focus.

A gun jabbed him in the back, and they walked him across the hangar. Through a steel door at the far end was a dark corridor. Glass led the way and opened another door to a sparsely furnished office. The desk was bare, save a computer hooked up to a pair of screens facing in opposite directions.

The guards threw Ben down into a tubular steel chair facing the desk. He fought the pain and the dizziness, blinking to keep his mind clear.

The smartly dressed old man walked calmly around the

desk and sat in the swivel chair opposite Ben. He spoke softly and deliberately. "My name is Werner Kroll," he said.

Ben knew who he was. The current Count von Adler.

Kroll watched Ben for a minute. His eyes were sharp and intelligent, and Ben could only guess what he was thinking. His wizened face had a look of detached curiosity, and there was a glimmer in his eyes that could have been taken for mild amusement. He dismissed the guards with a small gesture. They responded like well-trained dogs and filed out without a word. They all knew better than to hesitate when Kroll gave them an order.

Glass took the CD-ROM case from his pocket and handed it to Kroll. "He was carrying this on him, sir."

The old man took out the disc and turned it over in his hands. His fingers were long and thin. He popped open the CD drive of the computer on his desk and inserted the disc. There was silence in the room as the CD loaded up. The old man leaned back pensively in his chair and watched the video clip without a word. Ben could see the flickering images reflected in the lenses of his spectacles.

Then Kroll calmly ejected the disc. He turned it over in his hands again, looked coolly at Ben, and snapped it in half. "Thank you for bringing that to me," he said. He scattered the broken shards on the desk in front of him.

Then he picked up the cardboard tube containing the Mozart letter. He reached a finger inside and took out the rolled-up paper. "Interesting," he said as his eyes darted across it. "Very interesting. I begin to understand what this is all about. Mr. Llewellyn's research." He sighed and folded the letter in half, then again in quarters. He held the yellowed paper between his slim fingers and ripped it suddenly in two. He kept on ripping until Richard Llewellyn's prize was lying in tiny tatters across the desk. He reached for a wastepaper basket and carefully swept the pieces into it. Ben sat still and didn't speak a word.

Glass stood behind Kroll's chair, with his arms folded behind his back. There was a twisted half smile on his face. He'd been looking forward to killing Ben Hope. Maybe he still would, if the old man let him. SAS. He could eat SAS for breakfast.

Kroll reached calmly into a briefcase and took out a file. "I believe you two gentlemen have a long acquaintance," he said conversationally. "It must be nice to meet again after so many years."

Every time I meet him he tries to kill me, Ben thought, and it almost made him smile. "I don't know what you're talking about," he said. "My name's—"

"Paul Connors," Kroll cut in. "Yes, we know what your papers say. My compliments to your forger. Very convincing. I wonder why you didn't use your Harris or Palmer identity this time?"

"You've got the wrong man. I'm a journalist."

A crease deepened in Kroll's wrinkled brow. "Games? Must we? We know exactly who you are. No point in pretending." He held up the pieces of the CD. "And we know precisely why you're here." He flipped open the file. "You are Benedict Hope," he said quietly. "An interesting life. Private education. Attended Christ Church, Oxford, where you read theology." He looked up and raised his eyebrows quizzically. "Unusual choice of subject. Evidently the Church was not your true vocation. You terminated your studies after two years to join the British Army. You were officer material, but you enlisted as a private. You displayed great aptitude and rose rapidly through the ranks. Selected for Twenty-second Regiment, Special Air Service. Something of a reputation for being a maverick, a little rebellious against authority, and the medical reports highlight a recurring drinking problem. But it seems that none of that marred your career too badly. Decorated for bravery in the second Gulf war, left the army with the rank of major."

Ben said nothing. His eyes were fixed on the old man.

Kroll smiled. "No need to be modest. Your impressive record is the only reason I haven't allowed my friend here to dispose of you as he saw fit." He looked back down at the file. "I see here that for the last several years you have been working freelance as a crisis response consultant. Rather an interesting euphemism for what you do, wouldn't you say?"

There was no point in keeping up the pretence any longer. "What do you want?" Ben asked quietly.

"An opportunity has just arisen. I have a job for you."

"What kind of job?"

"The job you were trained to do."

"I'm retired."

"Come now, Major," Kroll said. "I know everything, and I do mean everything, about you, so please save yourself the trouble of lying to me. I can even tell you the name of the client who hired you for the Turkish assignment from which you were returning home when you went to meet Leigh Llewellyn. You escorted her to Langton Hall in Oxfordshire, where you damaged some precious equipment of mine. You've been a trouble to me ever since. Now—let me show you how I deal with people who are a trouble to me."

"I think I get the picture," Ben said.

"Indulge me, please." Kroll reached out to a remote keyboard and tapped with a long, thin finger. Images flashed up on the screens. "This was broadcast on the ORF2 television news earlier today," Kroll said.

The female reporter was dressed in a heavy coat and fur hat. Snow was streaking down as she spoke. Behind her, the ruins of a gray-stone building were smoldering and smoking. Black timbers littered the burned-out shell, and little patches of flame still flickered here and there. Emergency vehicles bumped across the rough terrain with lights flashing, and a helicopter was thudding overhead.

The building was so completely devastated that it took Ben a moment to recognize it.

Kroll saw the horror in his face and smiled. His bony hand touched the remote, and the volume rose.

" . . . *disaster. It is believed that the blaze, in which at least twenty-five Dominican nuns perished, may have been caused by a spark from an open fire. The tragedy has already prompted a demand for new health and safety regulations across* . . ."

"What have you done with Leigh and the child?"

Kroll hit the remote again, and the picture cut to black. "I was coming to that. I have some bad news for you. I am afraid the beautiful Ms. Llewellyn did not survive the incident."

Behind him, Glass suppressed a snigger.

"I would have preferred to take her alive," Kroll went on. "I was looking forward to meeting her in the flesh. But unfortunately for her, it appears that someone taught her how to operate a firearm. I wonder who that might have been?" He smiled. "She took it upon herself to open fire on my men, and they were obliged to take her down."

Fingers of ice curled around Ben's spine and held it tight. "You're a liar."

Kroll reached into his briefcase and laid something on the desk. It clunked on the wood. "Is this familiar to you?"

It was a gold locket. Dull, dirty, and spattered with russety spots of dried blood.

Glass's shoulders quaked, and a grin spread across his

face. Kroll shoved the locket across the desk. "Look more closely."

Ben picked it up and turned it over in his hands. They were beginning to shake. The letters *LL* were finely engraved on the back.

"Open it," said Kroll.

Ben pressed the little catch with his thumb, and the locket popped open. His heart was pounding, and when he saw what was inside, all hope left him and he closed his eyes. The miniature photos faced each other inside the opened locket. On one side was Oliver, on the other Richard and Margaret Llewellyn.

The last time Ben had seen it, it had been hanging around Leigh's neck.

He slowly snapped the locket shut and let it fall back on the desk.

He swallowed. His mouth was dry. "That's no proof."

"Very well. I wanted to spare you this, but you are stubborn." Kroll tapped another key, and suddenly Leigh was on the screen.

She was lying sprawled in a thicket.

Her eyes were glazed and dead. There was blood on her face and all down her front.

He sat still for a moment. It was impossible. But his eyes were telling him it was true. Screaming it. She was dead. Leigh Llewellyn, gone like smoke.

There was so much he'd wanted to say to her.

He felt faint, drifting in a black void. He swayed in his chair. His eyes clamped shut.

"Beautiful even in death," Kroll said, gazing at the screen. "But she won't remain so for long, after the wild animals have found her. They may have done already."

Ben couldn't speak. Then, out of the emptiness inside

him, a massive wave of rage came surging up. He snapped open his eyes. The first thing he saw, the only thing he could see, was Kroll sitting there with that impassive look on his face. It was the look of a scientist observing the death throes of a laboratory animal and calmly noting the details.

Ben hurled himself across the desk. The blow he aimed at the old man's neck would have crushed his windpipe against his spine. They could have done what they wanted to him after that, but he would have had the pleasure of watching Kroll die a panicked and tortured death within about fifteen seconds.

But Glass was quick, and the frame of the 9 mm came down hard on Ben's head before he could reach the old man. Kroll kicked out with his shiny shoes, and his executive swivel chair rolled out of range. The door burst open, and the guards stormed in. They grabbed Ben and threw him back in his chair. His wrists were cuffed roughly behind his back with the chain through the steel tubing.

Kroll wheeled himself back towards the desk and straightened his tie. "Evidently, you cannot be trusted to behave in a civilized manner."

Ben shook blood out of his eye. "You're a dead man, Kroll."

"I doubt that," said Kroll. "We haven't finished yet. There was one survivor of the incident in Slovenia." He pressed another key and brought up another image.

Ben's shoulders dropped.

It was Clara Kinski. They'd taken her.

The cell looked small and dank. She was tied down to a bare mattress on an iron-framed bed, her small wrists and ankles strapped to the bars with duct tape. She was blindfolded and struggling weakly, as though her strength was giving out.

"That is a live webcam image," Kroll said. "I can prove it to you by sending an e-mail order this very moment to have one of her fingers removed as you watch. Would you like that?"

"No," Ben said. "I wouldn't. But I know what I *would* like to see."

A strange, wild light in the prisoner's eyes disconcerted Kroll for an instant, but he hid it with a smile. "You are in no position to be defiant, Major," he said. "I am about to make you a proposal, and I suggest you consider it carefully. Based on your decision, the child either lives or she dies. It's as simple as that."

Ben shut his eyes for a long moment. In his mind, Leigh was looking at him. She smiled. He opened his eyes again, controlling his heartbeat and his breathing. "I'm listening," he said quietly, after a long pause.

"Tell me if you recognize this person." Clara disappeared from the screen and was replaced by a picture of a handsome man in his early forties. He was well tailored but casual, and the photo looked as though it had been taken at some kind of VIP function.

"I don't know who he is," Ben muttered truthfully.

Kroll watched him closely, as though assessing whether or not to believe him. He nodded. "You should follow politics, Major. That is Philippe Aragon. The candidate for the EU Commission vice presidency. He is your target."

"I'm not an assassin."

"That is precisely what you are. And you like to keep your skills well practiced. It isn't long since you gunned down five men in cold blood on your little mercy mission in Turkey." Kroll waved that aside. "Anyway, I didn't say I wanted him assassinated. We want you to bring him to us. We will take care of him."

"I imagine you will," Ben said. "I've seen the sick things your Order of Ra does to people."

"The Order of Ra!" Kroll's wrinkled face split into a yellow smile, and he twisted his neck to grin up at Glass. Glass smirked.

Kroll wiped his mouth and his grin faded. "It has been a long time since anyone has called us by that ridiculous old name. The Order of Ra is part of history, my young friend. It is as much a relic as its founder, my great-great-great-grandfather Viktor Kroll."

"But I see you keep up some of your traditions," Ben said. "Bullet in the head too modern for you people?"

"Some people are worth no more than a bullet," Kroll said. "For men like Philippe Aragon, we reserve a special kind of reception."

"Like ritual execution," Ben replied.

Kroll shrugged. "Some traditions are worth keeping."

"What are you going to do, cut his tongue out the way you did to that other guy—whoever he was?"

Kroll said nothing. He watched Ben for a moment, again as though assessing the truth of his words. Then he gave that icy smile once more. "The punishment fits the crime," he said. "Men who cannot keep their tongues from wagging have them removed. In Aragon's case we have something a little different in mind. This will take place in precisely two days from now, after you have acquired him and delivered him to a prearranged rendezvous with my agents." Kroll reached out and pressed another key. The image of Aragon was replaced with a picture of a house.

Ben ran his eyes over the unusual building. The house was a radical design of curved steel and glass, cut into the side of a sweeping embankment. It was a peaceful setting.

The sky was blue, the grass was green, and there were rolling hills in the background.

Cuffed in his chair, blood running down his face, Leigh dead, Ben wanted to be in that peaceful scene more than anything in the world. Anywhere but here.

Kroll's finger clicked rapidly, and multiple images flowed in a slide show, of the house from different angles, front and overhead views, lakes and hills in the background. Architect's plans and design blueprints flashed up, and Ben took them in as Kroll went on: "The house is in Belgium, an hour from Brussels. An hour ago my sources informed me that he will be alone there for three days as of tomorrow, while his wife and family attend a wedding in America. Aragon was planning to travel with them, but due to work pressures he changed his mind. This presents a perfect opportunity for a man with your skills and in your particular predicament. It's the only reason I have decided to keep you alive. For the moment, I should add."

The screen went blank. Kroll leaned back in his chair. "If you complete the task successfully, we will let the girl go back to her father, and you will also have your freedom. You can go back to freelance assassination in the name of rescuing the needy, or however you like to justify what you do." Kroll paused again and knitted his long fingers together under his chin. "If you refuse, or if you try to double-cross us in any way, you will first watch the girl die, and then you yourself will die. I hope I make myself clear. There will be no second chances."

Ben said nothing.

Kroll went on. "Now, I know what kind of man you are, Major Hope. I know perfectly well that if we let you walk free, it's in your nature to attempt a reprisal against us.

However, please remember that we can get to the child and her father at any time. Not only that, but we can also put a very quick end to your operation. If you ever show any sign of playing tricks with us, you will immediately be taken and transported to Turkey. Our contact there would be very interested in acquiring you for the murder of five men."

"I'm not a murderer," Ben said quietly. "I save people."

"Really? Yet you consider it fair exchange to expend five lives to free a single child."

"Two children," Ben said. "They were innocent. The men running the pedophile ring weren't. And they weren't going to stop doing it."

"What a noble calling you have, Major. Perhaps you were unaware that they were police officers? Corrupt officers, granted, but nonetheless, the authorities do not like it when a vigilante takes it upon himself to kill their agents."

"I did know that. All the more reason to kill them."

Kroll waved his thin hand dismissively. "Perhaps so. But we are not discussing ethics here. It's you we are talking about. Imprisonment in Turkey is not a pleasant experience. There would be no trial, and no possibility of parole. You would spend the next three decades or so in great discomfort, and if you ever saw freedom again, it would be as a very old and broken man. I want you to bear all this in mind as you make your decision, Major. We own your life. We control you completely. You have no options, other than a coward's death here today if you refuse to cooperate."

"You've really got this sewn up, haven't you?"

Kroll chuckled. "We should have by now, after two centuries of practice."

Ben let his straining muscles relax against the chair. "Why me?" he asked wearily. Blood trickled into his mouth.

"It's very simple," Kroll said. "Aragon has many

bodyguards. We have tried to get him before, and he has become very suspicious. He is well protected. We need someone with proven expertise in the art of stealth, who can slip in and out of heavily guarded places undetected. Second, you cannot be connected to us. If you get caught or killed, the newspapers will report that a loner, a neo-Fascist, tried to assassinate the great man." He smiled. "Naturally, I need not remind you that if you *are* caught, you will keep your mouth shut. Or else the child dies, and it's a one-way ticket to Turkey for you."

"I should go with him," Glass said, watching Ben intently from behind Kroll's chair. "Make sure he doesn't get up to any tricks."

Kroll smiled and shook his head. "No need for that," he replied. "I believe we can trust our finder of lost children not to misbehave. He knows what will happen to our young guest if he does." He sat back, satisfied with himself. It was a perfect plan, an opportunity he'd been waiting for for a long time. Aragon dead, Hope neutralized and pressed into service, Kinski silenced—all at a stroke.

Ben hung his head. He searched for a way out.

There wasn't one.

48.

THE VON ADLER MANSION

LATER THAT EVENING

Kroll had laid out some more clothes and jewels for her. As Eve slipped into the low-cut dress, his voice in the speakers told her quietly that she was to come upstairs. Not to the mirror room this time, but to a place she hadn't been inside for over a year. He wanted her in his bedroom.

As she climbed the stairs to the second floor, she wondered what he had in store for her this time. The relationship had never been sexual, not in any normal sense, since that first time. The idea of getting physical with him made her cringe.

She walked the wide corridor and arrived at the double doors. She could hear Kroll's voice on the phone inside the room. She listened.

"The whole committee will be in attendance, as usual," he was saying. "If all goes according to plan, and I'm confident it will, we'll be in a position to conclude our business matter on the night of my little Christmas soirée." A pause. "Yes, I'll keep you informed." Another pause. "Very well. I will see you in two days, then." Silence.

She waited a minute or so before she knocked on the door.

He was waiting for her inside the vast bedroom, sitting

primly in a wing chair beside a crackling fire. There was champagne in an ice bucket on the table near the four-poster. He was wearing a silk robe. He greeted her with a smile. "Champagne?"

"What's the celebration?" she asked. She accepted the crystal flute he passed her and sipped a little.

"An opportunity has arisen to dispose of a certain little problem that has been bothering me for a long time," he said. "But don't let me bore you with such details, my dear." Kroll walked around behind her. She closed her eyes as he laid his bony, cold hands on her naked shoulders. She could feel his thumbs rubbing on her skin. "You're tense," he said softly.

She was repulsed by his touch. She put down her glass and moved away quickly.

"Why do you hate me?" he asked.

"I don't hate you, Werner."

"You find me repellent," he said. "Don't think it escapes me. Nothing does." He watched her. "You've changed somehow. There's something different about you."

She looked away. "I don't know what you mean."

He thought for a moment, rubbing his chin and observing her in that birdlike way of his. "Something has been perplexing me, Eve," he said. "You were alone with Hope for a long time. Much longer than usual. I did wonder why that was."

Eve measured her reply cautiously. "I had to be careful with him. He was more dangerous than the others."

"Very dangerous," Kroll agreed. "Yet you didn't seem too anxious to get away from him. You were alone for nearly three hours. A lot can happen in that time."

"I had to find the right moment."

"What were you doing?"

"We talked," she said.

"You talked. About what?"

"Just things. Music. Life. Nothing special. Then he slept for a while. Why are you asking me these questions? I got him for you. I did what you told me to do. Finished. It's over."

Kroll raised one eyebrow. "He slept? In your bed?"

"On my sofa," she said impatiently. "I suppose you think I was fucking him, is that it?"

"It had crossed my mind," he said. "I understand that you have needs. I saw the way you were looking at his picture. He's young, and not entirely unattractive."

"You mean *was?*"

He smiled coldly. "Oh, he isn't dead, if that's what you think. He's far too useful to me for that."

Eve's pulse quickened, but she was an expert in covering her reactions. "I don't care either way," she said. "I just don't like these questions." She turned away from him. *Ben Hope was still alive.*

Kroll took a tiny, dainty sip of his drink, watching her. "It's not your place to challenge my questions," he said. "Remember who and what you are."

Who and what she was. The words bit into her. She spun and glared at him. "You're jealous, aren't you? You think I felt something for him, and you can't stand it."

His smile slipped. "Don't fence with me."

"You can't stand it because you know that deep down you're just a frightened, weak old man who can't get it u—"

His hand caught her hard around the face, and her head spun. His eyes bulged in the bony skull, and his white hair was in disarray. "All it takes is one phone call," he warned in a trembling voice. "And I can erase you. I will *end* you."

"I'm already officially dead," she retorted. "You might as well finish the job."

"I wouldn't make it that easy for you. Your life would become a living hell."

"I'm already there."

He turned his back on her and walked across the room. He laughed bitterly. "I should have let them lock you away forever six years ago."

There wasn't a day when she didn't wish he had. He'd owned her completely for those six years.

She'd been twenty years old when it had happened. Back in those days, she'd had a proper identity, for what it was worth. There'd been nothing more than a violent, abusive father and a drunk of a mother to hold Eva Schultz in Hamburg. She'd hitched a ride and somehow ended up at the other end of the country. Men were drawn to her pretty face and striking figure. She'd quickly learned you could make money out of that. As time went by, she got very good at doing things that very few of the girls would do. She was popular and attracted a particular clientele—a lot of the clients were rich men who turned up with bodyguards and limousines.

Kroll had been a client once, just once. The sex had been a disaster. Ever since then, he'd just wanted to watch. He barely slackened his tie.

The fat Russian was different. He was a slob who loved dirty sex and went at it like a slavering mastiff to a plate of meat. That was fine, she could cater for that. He'd hired her for the whole night, and she'd kept him going for most of it. Outside the door, the two guards with Uzi submachine pistols had waited quietly, listening. They were used to hearing what was coming through the door.

In the morning the guards were gone. Eva Schultz woke up and rolled out of bed. She'd felt strangely drowsy, but she put it down to the vodka he'd brought with him. It had never occurred to her that she'd been drugged. The moment she'd realized something was wrong was when she'd placed a bare foot on the floor and felt something sticky. She'd looked down. The room was a sea of blood. The Russian had been stabbed. Later, she'd learn he had sixty-seven stab wounds in him. His bloated body was lying at the foot of the bed.

She'd still been staggering about the room in shock when the men in dark coats had found her. One of them was someone she knew. It was Werner Kroll. The ID he showed meant nothing to her. He'd said something about the secret service, but her mind had been too full of horror and the aftereffects of the drug to take it in properly. She'd been bundled into a car and taken to a room with no windows. They'd told her the deal, told her how lucky she was that the police hadn't found her first.

They sympathized. Yes, they knew she was innocent. But who would believe a whore? Her prints were all over the knife, and it didn't look good. Her client was a very important man, and the courts were going to crucify her. She'd go to jail for the rest of her life.

And there was more. Kravchenko had connections. They didn't tell her what those connections were. It was enough for her to know that she wouldn't be safe in prison. Someone would get to her sooner or later. But if she let them deal with it, they could help her. They told her some of the ways she could do that.

She'd been too scared to refuse Kroll's offer, and with her prospects in tatters there'd been no real reason not to clutch at the lifeline he was giving her. She'd grabbed it with both hands and said yes to everything.

She'd never seen the inside of a jail or a courtroom. Instead, they'd taken her away to a compound somewhere. She didn't ask what was going on, and she didn't care. All she knew, over the next few months, was that she was safe. She'd been given a set of rooms to live in, simple but comfortable. She'd accepted the confinement, the guards outside the door, the total lack of communication with the outside world. Kroll had come to see her once a week, checking that she was all right and was being looked after. He told her nothing about the Kravchenko incident. She'd wondered if he was going to ask her for sex. He never did.

Eva Schultz had officially died in the same accident that killed the Russian. Eva had become Eve. Eve nobody. A nonperson, a ghost. She never asked who really killed the Russian. She never asked whose body had doubled for hers, or how it had been obtained. She just wanted to forget the whole thing and start afresh.

Of course, there'd been a price to pay.

After six months, with a new nose and a different look, she'd left the compound and come to live at the big house. Now she was directly, personally, under Kroll's wing. She had jewels and beautiful clothes. He'd taught her how to pass herself off as a lady—how to talk, how to walk, how to dress. Her acting ability surprised even her.

She was suffocated in his care. The more she'd found out about who he really was and what he really did, the deeper he'd sucked her into his world. Information. Manipulation. Power. She was the honey trap that none of the carefully selected targets seemed to be able to resist.

One day, he'd taken her into a study, opened a safe, and asked her to look inside. Stored in a plastic bag was the knife that had killed Kravchenko, still smeared in the dead man's dried blood and with her fingerprints on the handle. He had said nothing. Just showed her, so she understood.

There were more crimes to add to the list now, and some of them she really had been involved with. She could never get out of here, never tell anyone the truth. If she did, she knew she probably wouldn't even make it as far as jail.

She watched him now as he walked across the room and stood near the crackling fire with his back to her. Her face was livid and tingling where he'd slapped her.

"You were right, Werner," she said. "I *do* hate you."

He turned with a wrinkled yellow grin. "I've never doubted it," he said. "But you'll always stay close to me."

"What choice do I have?"

"None whatsoever," he said. "By the way, I have a little job for you."

She grimaced. What was it this time?

"You might enjoy this," he said, seeing her expression. "You can learn to exercise your underused maternal instincts. Clara Kinski is coming to stay with us. I want you to look after her, keep her quiet. If necessary, subdue her."

Even Kroll had never descended to anything like child abduction before. Her heart began to pound harder. "How long are you keeping her here?" she asked.

Kroll smiled. "Oh, not long," he said. "Just for the rest of her life."

49.

Ben lay and stared at the dark, gray ceiling above him until it swam in front of his eyes. He looked at his watch. Only five minutes had gone by since the last time he'd checked it. His mind had been working so furiously that it seemed like hours.

He had checked the cell a hundred times for weak spots. The only light filtered in through a high barred window. He'd jumped up, scrabbled up the wall, and grabbed the cold, black steel bars, wedged his knees against the wall and jerked them with all his strength. There was no give in them, no movement at all. They were solid. It would take a tractor to tear them out of their concrete bedding.

Dropping back down into the shadows, he'd run his fingers along the contour of every stone block. The walls were in perfect condition and at least double-skinned. Nothing to work on. Then he'd tried the door. It was sheet steel, the hinges were concealed and the rivets were flush. Finally, he'd turned to the bunk, looking for something he could use as a lever or a hammer. But the steel frame was welded solid and its feet cemented into the floor.

Worse than the prison walls around him, he was trapped inside his own thoughts.

Leigh was dead. Leigh was dead.

And it was his fault. He'd left her on her own. She'd died alone, unprotected, in fear.

Just as Oliver had died. *It was his fault.* And now the

little girl was a hostage. That was his fault, too. He'd get her out, or he'd die trying.

Tomorrow, his mission would begin. He'd have the equipment he'd asked for, a vehicle, some clothes, some cash, a weapon, and a phone to call them on when he'd acquired his target. They were going to let him go free, and he already knew what his first move would be. But he'd never felt so powerless in his life.

There was no use in hammering on the steel door until his knuckles were a mess of blood. No use in screaming his frustration until his vocal cords were in tatters. No use beating his own brains out against the stone walls. He dropped to the floor, down on his fists and the tips of his toes, and pressed thirty push-ups out of his tortured muscles. Then another thirty. The pain purged his thoughts for a few minutes. It helped him to focus on what he was going to do next.

He started at the sound of jangling keys against the steel door. The lock turned. A sliver of light shone from the corridor outside as a figure slipped inside the cell.

It was a woman, furtive, nervous. He knew her.

"What are you doing here?" he demanded.

"I had to come," she said. Her eyes were moist and caught the light.

"How did you get in?"

The ring of keys glinted in the shadows. "Kroll keeps a spare set in his study," she whispered.

"What do you want, Ingrid? Or whatever your name is today."

Eve winced and put her finger to her lips. "*Shhh*. Glass is out there. They'd kill me if they knew I was here."

"Then I'll call them," he said. "They might let me watch."

"I'm sorry," she said.

"That's what you said last time we met."

She crept across the cell towards him. In the light of the window her eyes were wide and bright with terror. "I'm Eve," she muttered. "Eve's my real name. That's the truth. I promise it."

"I don't care what your name is," he said. "What do you want?"

"They have the little girl," she said.

"You came here to tell me that?"

"I want to help," she whispered. Her voice was husky and urgent.

"I don't trust you," he said.

"I'm sorry about what happened. I had no choice. You have to believe me."

"You won't fool me twice."

"I can help," she protested. "Please listen to me. I know things."

He could smell her fear. That couldn't be faked. She was telling the truth. "Tell me," he said.

"They're planning something," she said. "Kroll is holding a party. Those men will all be there. They're going to kill someone."

"Who?" He already knew the answer.

She shook her head. "Someone important to them. I don't know. I just know that every time they have one of their gatherings, someone dies. There's a signal. It's usually between nine and ten, when the party's in full swing and the guests are distracted by the music. The men leave one by one and go down to a special part of the house. That's where it happens."

"Who are these men?" he asked.

"They're in business with Kroll. That's all I know. Old men in suits who kill people. Politics. Money. I don't know. I just know they make people disappear."

"Where does it happen?" he asked.

She glanced nervously at the cell door. "The house has its own private church," she said. "I think that's where they go. I've never seen it. Kroll keeps it all locked up."

"Would it have a vaulted ceiling, pillars? A tiled floor with a checkered pattern."

"I don't know," she said. "Maybe. But I wanted to tell you something else. The little girl."

"Clara?"

She nodded. "They're going to kill her. Afterwards, by lethal injection."

He glared at her. "Why are you telling me all this?" he asked. "Why wait until now?"

"Because I want to get her out of there," she said. "They've got to be stopped. It's gone too far." Her eyes were earnest, pleading, searching his. She glanced over her shoulder at the door. "I'm sick of this whole thing," she went on. Her words were a gushing whisper. "When he told me about the child, I had to do something. You've got to believe me. It was hard for me to turn you over. But I had no choice. They have a hold on me, like they have on you now. That's what they do: they trap people and then use them."

Ben said nothing as he worked through it all from every angle. "Where are we?" he asked.

"An old military base near Ernstbrunn, north of Vienna. Kroll owns it."

"Where are they holding Clara?"

"At the house."

"The von Adler house?"

Eve gave a quick nod. "They've got rooms for her, secure and guarded."

"Tell me exactly where the place is," he said.

"About five kilometers south of Vienna. I'll take you there. I'm getting you out. I have a car."

Outside, there was the loud clang of a steel door and the sound of heavy footsteps echoed off the walls of the narrow corridor. Eve gasped. "It's Glass. He'll kill me."

Ben froze. There was nowhere to hide her.

The footsteps had almost reached the cell door. They were out of time.

"Kiss me," he said. He put his arms around her.

Eve looked startled, then she understood. It could save them both. She wrapped her arms around his neck and drew her body up close to his. Her lips were warm and soft on his mouth.

The cell door clanged back against the wall. The tall, broad figure of Jack Glass stood silhouetted in the doorway. He laughed when he saw them. "My, how romantic. So the old man was right—you *were* fucking him this afternoon. You come back for some more?"

"I had to see him," Eve said. "I love him." She stepped away from Ben. Glass walked into the cell, ducking his head at the entrance. He grabbed Eve's arm and jerked her away. "You're in deep shit now," he said.

"Don't hurt her for this," Ben said. "It's my fault."

Glass sneered.

"Please don't tell Werner," she pleaded. "He'll kill me."

"Oh, I know that," Glass said. "And *then* he'll go to work on you." He paused. There was a light in his eye as the possibilities began to flash up in his mind. He had her now. This was what he'd been waiting for. "But maybe you and I can come to an agreement," he said. He turned and winked at Ben.

Ben's eyes were on the Beretta 92 in Glass's belt. It was only four steps away. Ben could break his neck before he knew what was happening. Take his pistol and use it to kill the other guards.

It was a crude plan, but it appealed to him.

He took the first step, then the second. Eve was struggling in Glass's arms.

Five more guards came through the doorway. They weren't taking any chances, and all the guns were aimed steadily at him. Suddenly, the odds had shifted. He stopped and stood still.

"See you later, cowboy," Glass said.

Ben caught a last imploring glance from Eve as Glass dragged her out of the cell. The guards followed. The steel door clanged shut, and he heard the turn of the lock. He was alone again.

50.

THE VON ADLER MANSION

NEXT MORNING

Clara raised her face from the pillow. Her head was still spinning, and she had a horrible taste in her mouth. How long had she been sleeping? She remembered now. It hadn't been a nightmare. She'd been screaming and banging at the door. After a few minutes, when her hands were sore, the door had opened.

It had been the old man, the one who looked like a hawk. He was smiling, but not in a friendly way. His eyes were cold, like black pebbles. The one she'd called Franz had been there, too. He wasn't really called Franz, she knew that now. She hated him. She hoped his ear wasn't scarred at all, but that it was the start of some awful disease that was going to spread all across his face until he had to hide himself away in a hole for the rest of his life. She remembered how he'd held her down on the bed, pinning her arms down. She'd kicked and fought, but he was too strong.

Then another man had come in. He was a doctor. Or maybe he just wore a doctor's white coat. He had a smile on his face she didn't like. In his hand was a little leather bag. He'd opened it and taken out a syringe. She'd wriggled and squirmed, but they held her tight and she couldn't move. Then, pain as the needle went in, and after that she couldn't remember anything.

Clara felt her arm. It was sore where they'd injected her. She wiped her eyes and looked around her small, bare room. There was a mess of food on the floor from where she'd upended the tray they'd brought her earlier. They'd brought her a toy, some stupid little rag doll, as though that would keep her happy. She'd flung it in the face of one of the men who'd brought her here and shut her in the room. It was still lying there near the door, untouched.

How long had she been in here? It seemed like forever. She wanted to see her daddy. Where was he?

She cocked her little head and listened. Was that a voice outside her door, speaking low? She knew there was always someone out there, keeping watch over her. Maybe it was Franz. Or it might be the blond lady who checked on her from time to time. She seemed gentler than the others. She had a look about her, like she was sad or upset. Clara didn't trust her, though, and wouldn't speak to her.

Sitting up straighter in the bed, she looked up at the window. It was little more than a skylight, high up in the ceiling above her. All she could see out of it were dark clouds scudding across the gray sky. This place was quiet. There was no traffic noise from outside. Still, there might be people walking past down below. If she got their attention, maybe someone would help her.

She dragged herself off the bed. Her legs felt heavy. She realized only then that they'd changed her clothes, and that she was wearing a pair of blue pajamas a size too large for her. Her own clothes were folded neatly on a chair. She walked slowly across the room and dragged the chair over beneath the window. She dropped the folded clothing on the floor, grasped the wooden backrest with one hand, and put one foot on the chair, then the other. She wobbled as she straightened up. She reached up with one arm, as high as she could. Her straining fingers brushed the window catch but couldn't get a purchase. She strained harder.

Four hundred yards away, Ben rested his weight on the thick branch and adjusted the knurled focusing ring on the 20x50 Zeiss binoculars. The cold wind rocked the tree in a lazy arc. He was a long way up and hoped the groaning branch would hold.

The palatial mansion hadn't been very hard to find. That had been the one detail Kroll was missing—he didn't know that Ben knew where he lived, and where they were keeping Clara. From the moment he'd been let out of the cell and provided with the things he needed for his mission, Ben had had only one plan in mind. Forget about going after Philippe Aragon. He was going to find Clara and get her out of there. Nobody had better get in his way. And once she was safe he was coming back for Kroll, Glass, the lot of them.

But now, seeing the place for the first time, he knew that plan was impossible.

It was a fortress. The high stone wall encircling the estate must have been several kilometers long, with towers every few hundred yards along its length and a single enormous arched gateway. On each massive gatepost was a bronze eagle. The tall iron gates were gilded and spiked. Through them he could see security guards pacing up and down by a gatehouse. A broad private road led to a huge sprawl of tiered steps and fountains and gardens and sweeping stone balustrades. The house perched majestically above it all, glittering white stone against the pinewoods and the mountains beyond. Ben scanned the towering baroque facade, picking out dozens of little skylights and garret windows. There had to be a hundred rooms in the place at least, and the girl could be in any one of them.

Clara stood on the backrest of the chair. Wobbling precariously, she reached up as high as she could, and her little fingers closed around the catch of the window. She shoved it. It gave an inch or two with a grating of a rusty hinge. If she could open it farther, maybe she could stick her head out and shout for help. She pushed again.

The window opened a little wider. She shoved a hand through it and felt the cold wind on her fingers. Then the sudden roaring thud of helicopter blades filled her ears.

Ben saw the Bell 407 chopper come in to land, sleek, black, unmarked. It disappeared behind the ornate facade, coming to rest on top of the house. The undulating roofs blocked his view of the helipad and of whoever might be getting out or getting in.

He swept the binoculars downwards and watched the rows of vehicles at the front of the house. There were more guards down there, at least fifteen men. He knew they would be armed. There was no telling how many more would be inside. He scanned the grounds. Trees and bushes provided good cover inboard of the wall, but closer to the house the terrain was open, a cleared zone that would be hard to cross unseen. By night the lawns, flower beds, and concreted areas would all be illuminated and almost certainly watched by security cameras as well as regularly patrolled.

Ben took the Zeiss glasses away from his eyes, and the house was suddenly tiny and white in the distance. Letting the binoculars hang from his neck, he lay prone on his branch for a few minutes, thinking hard.

He thought back to all the places he'd raided alone. He was good at what he did, and he knew it. But to go up against something this size was a suicide mission, not just for him but for the kid. It couldn't be done. There was no use. He had no choice but to go after Philippe Aragon and give him to Kroll.

He backed along the branch and started climbing downwards, agile and silent. He reached the ground, wiped his hands, and made his way towards the road, lighting a cigarette as he walked to the nondescript gray van, shoulders hunched against the biting wind. He sighed as he opened the van door and slid into the driver's seat. He laid the Zeiss glasses on the seat next to him, leaned back behind the wheel, and finished his cigarette. Then he crushed the stub into the ashtray and twisted the ignition. The diesel rasped into life.

It was a long drive to Brussels. He'd better get moving. But before that, he had one other stop to make.

51.

PHILIPPE ARAGON'S RESIDENCE
NEAR BRUSSELS
THAT EVENING

It was late, and the two private bodyguards were sitting relaxed in armchairs at opposite ends of the large open-plan main reception area. They had nothing to do but leaf through back issues of *The Economist,* astronomy magazines, and architecture books while their charge came and went, filled out paperwork, and made phone calls.

They weren't complaining. Their two colleagues were out in the freezing cold patrolling the grounds, while they stayed inside the comfortable building soaking up the warmth from the solar heating system. In two more hours they'd have to put on their coats and exchange places with them, and they weren't looking forward to that.

Philippe Aragon was feeling mentally drained after working all day. He had four major addresses to prepare and stacks of files and reports to sift through. His PA, Adrien Lacan, had left him a whole pile of letters to check and sign, and that alone had taken up a big piece of his day. He prepared a cup of organic cocoa with a pinch of cinnamon, said good night to the two bodyguards, and headed up the spiral staircase to his private quarters at the top of the house, carrying the steaming mug.

The electronic security system sealed him inside the

reinforced door. He kicked off his shoes and slipped his feet into a pair of soft slippers, then walked through his private sitting room. Here at last he felt as though he was in his own tranquil space. He tried to forget about the armed men who were watching over him, sitting in his home, and walking about his garden. The place was beginning to feel more and more like a fortress. It was mostly down to Colette's insistence. Ever since the chalet episode she'd been edgy about safety. Maybe she was right, but it was tough living like this, looking over your shoulder all the time. He knew it was stressful for her as well, and he was glad that she'd been able to have a break and get over to Florida for her cousin's wedding.

He pottered around his sitting room, sipping his cocoa, feeling mentally tired but restless. He sifted through a rack of CDs and slid out the Mischa Maisky recording of Bach's suites for solo cello. The warm, woody tones of the cello breathed through the speakers and soothed him. He sat in a soft armchair and closed his eyes, listening to the music and tapping gently with his fingers against the armrests. But Philippe wasn't a man who could switch off his active mind that easily. He jumped up. For a moment he thought about going into his private study next door, firing up the computer, and checking to see if Colette might have e-mailed him from the States. But he knew that once he was sitting behind the keyboard, he'd only start tinkering with his speeches for next week again. It could wait till the morning.

Through the patio doors, moonlight cast long inviting shadows in the sunken rooftop garden. It was his favorite part of the house, and one of the designs he was most proud of. The garden was surrounded by a ring of stone pillars and filled with plants and shrubs. It smelled of fresh earth and greenery. A little fountain in the center splashed and burbled softly under the big glass dome.

It was a beautiful starry night, clear and still. He wondered if he could see Saturn. He pulled a cardigan over his shirt and wandered out into the garden, enjoying the stillness and beauty. On the wall near the doorway was a panel with buttons, and he pressed one. With a subtle whoosh of hydraulics, a glass panel in the dome above him began to slide back. He went over to where he kept his Celestron CGE 1400 refractor telescope permanently set up on an electronic mount. The cold night air flooded in through the open dome. He let the scope cool for a while to get a sharper image, then set the coordinates for Saturn. The telescope automatically whirred across and up, aiming through the gap in the roof. Philippe took off the lens cap and looked into the eyepiece. The ringed planet was a thrilling, surreal sight that had captivated him since childhood. He never stopped marveling at it.

A sudden lancing pain at the base of his neck crippled him. He staggered away from the telescope, disorientated and stunned. A heavy kick to the back of his leg crumpled him to the floor, and he felt a knee between his shoulder blades, crushing him to the cold flagstones. Hard steel pressed against the back of his head. A quiet, calm voice in his ear said, "Any noise, you die."

Aragon was helpless. He tried to roll over on his side and look up. The man towering over him was dressed in black. Eyes looked at him impassively through the slits in the ski mask. Moonlight glinted on the steel of the gun pointed at his head.

52.

"Who the hell *are* you?" Aragon said in a daze. He lay back in the armchair, his chest heaving fast with panic and shock. The intruder had marched him into the house and made him sit. His first thought had been that the man was an assassin come to kill him. Why hadn't he? The gun was back in its holster. The intruder reached up a black-gloved hand and pulled off the ski mask. Aragon winced at the pain in his neck and rubbed his shoulder. Why was the man letting him see his face?

Ben sat opposite him in a matching armchair. Between them, a polished pine coffee table shone in the dim light. "Someone who needs your help," he said.

Aragon was taken aback. "You break into my house and point a gun at me, then you say you need my help?"

"That's how it is."

"People usually approach my office for that kind of thing," Aragon said.

Ben smiled. Aragon had guts. He liked him. "When you hear what I have to say, you'll understand why I couldn't see you the normal way."

Aragon's brow creased. "I don't know if I want to hear it."

"I don't know if you have a choice," Ben said.

"You won't get away with this. There are security cameras watching this room right now."

"No, there aren't," Ben said. "This apartment is the only

bit of private space you have left. You relish it. You wouldn't let them put cameras in here."

"How the hell did you get past the guards?"

"Never mind that," Ben said. "Just listen to me. If you help me, I'll help you in return."

Aragon laughed. "You'll help me? By doing what?"

"By giving you the people who murdered Bazin."

Aragon stopped laughing and went pale. "Roger?"

Ben nodded. "Your mentor. Your friend."

Aragon was quiet for a few seconds. He gulped. "Roger wasn't murdered," he said in a low voice. "He died in a car accident."

"Politicians are usually good liars. You're not."

"I had it investigated," Aragon said. "They didn't find anything. It was an accident."

"I don't think you believe that," Ben said. "I know about the chalet explosion. Was that an accident, too?"

"How the hell do you know all this?"

"I always research my targets," Ben said.

Aragon was sweating. He bit his tongue. "So what is it you want to tell me?"

Across the room was a drinks cabinet. Ben stood up and went over to it. The soles of his black combat boots were silent on the wooden floor. "You want a drink?" he asked. "Something stronger than that cocoa you were drinking before."

Aragon thought about running.

"Don't try," Ben said. "You wouldn't get halfway to the door."

Aragon sighed and leaned back in the armchair. "Get me a glass of Armagnac."

Ben took out two bottles and two cut-crystal glasses.

He poured a double shot of brandy in one, and a triple shot of Aragon's eighteen-year-old Islay malt in the other. He handed Aragon the brandy and sat down again. "It's a long story," he said. "I'm going to start from the beginning." He sipped the Scotch. Opposite him, some of the color had returned to the politician's face. His glass was on the coffee table in front of him. He sat with his arms folded, his brow creased with doubt.

"Last January a friend of mine witnessed something by chance," Ben said. "Something he shouldn't have. He was murdered for it, but the evidence fell into someone else's hands. His sister. You might have heard of her. Leigh Llewellyn, the opera singer."

Aragon nodded. "I know who Leigh Llewellyn is."

Ben went on. He told the whole thing in detail. It took a long time. Aragon listened carefully. "They killed her?" he said quietly.

Ben nodded.

"I haven't heard anything in the news."

"You will," Ben said. "There'll be another staged accident, or a disappearance."

Aragon thought for a few moments. "If what you're saying is true," he said, "I'm very sorry to hear it. But you haven't given me a shred of proof, and you still haven't told me about Roger."

"I was coming to that. It was your friend's murder that Oliver witnessed."

"You mentioned evidence."

Ben nodded. "Oliver filmed the whole thing. It was recorded on a disc."

"And where is the disc?"

"Destroyed," Ben said.

"So you can't show it to me? That's very convenient."

Ben pointed at the study door. "Can I use your computer?"

"What for, if you've nothing to show me?"

Ben led Aragon into the dark study. The laptop on the desk was already on. "What are you doing?" Aragon asked.

"Checking my e-mail," Ben said.

"Your e-mail. This is ridiculous."

Ben ignored him. There was just one message in his web mail in-box. He didn't have to read it—it was a message he'd sent to himself from Christa Flaig's cybercafe.

At the time, it had been an afterthought, an insurance policy. He almost hadn't bothered. Now he knew he couldn't have done a better thing.

There was an attachment with the message. A big one. He clicked on it. The laptop was brand-new, fast, and powerful, and it downloaded the file in under five seconds.

"What's this?" Aragon asked.

"Just watch."

Aragon sat. Ben nudged the glass of brandy across the desk towards him. "Drink this. You're going to need it." He moved away from the desk and sat on a chair in the corner, sipping his Scotch.

By the time the clip was over, Aragon's glass was dry, and his head was on the desk. Suddenly, he lurched to his feet. "I'm going to be sick," he muttered. He staggered out of the study into a bathroom. Ben heard him retching into the toilet.

A minute later, Philippe Aragon emerged from the bathroom. His face was gray and his hair was plastered across his forehead. He wiped his chin with his sleeve. His fingers were trembling. "They killed him," he murmured. "They killed him, and then they rigged the car accident." His voice sounded weak and shaky.

"I didn't know who he was until today," Ben said. "I didn't recognize him before. I don't follow politics. It's bullshit." He paused. "But like I said, I always research my targets."

"You kidnap a lot of people, then?"

Ben smiled. "I'm on the other team. But the reconnaissance is the same whatever side you're on. With you, it was easy. You're all over the media. Before I left Vienna I paid a visit to the university library. There's enough material on you in their political science section to write ten books. There was a picture of you with your family on a tennis court. Bazin was there. That's when I recognized his face from the video clip. There was a caption saying who he was."

"That was taken two years ago at Roger's place in Geneva," Aragon said sadly.

"Then there was another photo of you at his funeral," Ben said. *"Europolitician pays last respects to his political mentor."*

"He was like a father to me," Aragon said. He sat heavily in a chair. "He tried to warn me that time."

"Cortina?"

Aragon nodded. "He phoned me just before it happened. I don't know how he knew about it. I don't know what he was mixed up in. I just know that if it hadn't been for him, my family would be dead."

Ben remembered what Kroll had said. *Men who cannot keep their tongues from wagging have them removed.*

"He was my best friend," Aragon continued. "And they murdered him as punishment for warning me."

"Join the club," Ben said. "They murdered mine the same day, because he saw them do it."

Aragon looked up at him. "And now his sister," he said.

He could see the expression on Ben's face. "You loved her?"

Ben didn't reply.

"You know who did it?"

Ben nodded. "Who they are and where they are."

"I'll have them arrested. One call."

Ben shook his head. "There isn't enough proof." He pointed at the computer. "You can't make out the faces. And I want to get them all together in one place, round them up, and catch them in the act. There's only one way to do that."

"How?"

"That's where you come in," Ben said. "You're going to have to trust me. You'll have to do everything I say."

Aragon paused, wavering, then let out a sigh. "I must be crazy. But all right. I trust you. What do you need me to do?"

"There isn't much time," Ben said. "I'll have to make some long-distance calls."

"No problem."

"We'll need to move immediately. You'll have to drop everything you're doing, right this moment."

"I can do that," Aragon said.

"And it's going to cost money. Maybe quite a bit."

"That's easy," Aragon said. "Whatever it takes."

"How fast can you scramble a private jet?"

"Fast," Aragon said.

"It's going to be dangerous," Ben said. "Very high risk. I can't guarantee your safety."

"He was my friend," Aragon replied without hesitation.

"Good," Ben said. "Then let's get on with it."

"What are you going to do?"

"I'm going to kidnap you."

53.

OUTSIDE VIENNA

THE NEXT MORNING

He wondered if Glass's choice of a meeting point was his idea of a joke.

A thick icy blanket of mist had descended over the lake. He could barely make out the frozen surface from here. He wiped an arc in the condensation on the window, his fingertips squeaking on the cold glass. He leaned back in the seat. There was no sign of them yet. Behind him, on the other side of the plywood partition, his cargo was silent and would be for a few more hours, until the effect of the dope wore off.

Ben didn't have to wait long. He saw them coming from far away, the headlights of two big cars slicing through the mist. They turned off the road and bumped slowly across the mud and slush and patchy reeds towards where he was parked. As they emerged from the mist he could see them more clearly. Two Mercedes, black, identical. The cars pulled up on either side of his van, blocking it in. The doors opened. Glass and five others stepped out, their breath billowing in the cold.

Ben narrowed his eyes. He couldn't see Clara in either car. He hadn't fully expected to. He jerked the handle of the van door and went out to meet them. He tossed his cigarette in the snow, and it hissed. Glass stood with his arms folded, watching him. His face was flushed from the chill. "Well?" he said. His voice sounded flat in the mist.

"Well?" Ben echoed.

Glass scowled. "You got him?"

"I did what I agreed to do. Where's Clara Kinski?"

Glass glanced over his shoulder and nodded at his men. For an instant Ben thought they were going to pop open the boot of one of the cars and bring her out. Instead, they stepped forward and grabbed his arms. He let them. They spun him round and slammed him against the side of the van. Hands frisked him, lifting his pistol. "Where is she?" he repeated, keeping his voice calm and low.

One man held a gun to his head while two others opened up the back doors of the van. Glass peered inside.

Aragon was covered with a blanket. His wrists and ankles were bound with plastic cable ties, and there was a length of duct tape over his mouth. He was unconscious.

One of the men pulled a photo from his pocket. He studied the prisoner's face long and hard, then nodded to Glass. "It's him."

A fourth man reached inside one of the cars and brought out a leather case. He carried it to the van, unzipped it, and took out a stethoscope. He listened to Aragon's heartbeat and looked satisfied. "No problems."

"Good work," Glass said.

"The girl," Ben said again, keeping his eyes on the side of the van.

Glass grinned. "You'll get her when we decide."

"That wasn't the arrangement," Ben said.

"Fuck the arrangement. You don't make the rules, you cocky bastard."

"So what next?"

Glass reached inside his coat, and his fist came out

clutching a 9 mm. He stepped up to Ben and stuck the muzzle of the gun roughly under his chin. "If it was up to me," he said.

"Except it's not," Ben replied. "Is it?"

Glass flushed. "You'll be contacted. There'll be more jobs for you."

"I don't think so," Ben said.

"No? You're working for us now." Glass pointed at the frozen lake. "Or maybe you'd rather take a swim?" He chuckled. "You'll do as you're told. Lie low and wait for our call. Any funny business and the girl dies. Don't forget."

Ben looked him in the eye. "I never forget anything," he said.

Glass's grin wavered. He holstered his pistol with a grunt and motioned to his men. They slammed the van doors. One of them climbed into the driver's seat and started the engine. The rest of them walked back to the cars. The two Mercedes threw up mud and slush as they accelerated away. The van followed, taking Philippe Aragon with them.

Ben stood and watched their taillights disappear into the mist. Silence fell over the lake again. He started walking, then took out a phone. He dialed a number. A voice answered.

"We're on," Ben said.

He turned off the phone and walked faster.

No going back now. *But what if he was wrong?*

54.

THE VON ADLER MANSION

THAT NIGHT

Light poured from the windows of the mansion and floodlights illuminated its facade and the snowy grounds for a hundred yards. A steady stream of guests was arriving. The cars were opulent, the curves of Ferraris and the coachwork of stately Bentleys glittering under the floods. Doormen in uniforms greeted the guests and ushered them inside, while the chauffeurs parked their vehicles along the side of the enormous house.

Inside the mansion, the huge marble-floored entrance hall was milling with people. Waiters in white tuxedos circulated carrying silver trays of champagne glasses or poured cocktails and dry martinis at the bar. Long tables were covered with selections of canapés and gourmet finger food.

The guests were dressed for the occasion, the men in sober evening wear while the expensively decked women on their arms took the opportunity to show off their jewels. Diamond necklaces glittered like wet ice. The sounds of popping corks, laughter, and music rang up to the high ornate ceiling. Through the tall double doors to the magnificent ballroom, the string quartet for the evening was into its first set of waltzes, and a few couples were out on the dance floor.

Far from the house, the guards at the gate were strolling up and down in the snow, kicking their heels and clapping their gloved hands to keep warm. One laid down his radio handset as the lights of another car lit up the icy road. The black Jaguar stopped at the gate. The guard stepped forward as the driver's window whirred down. He bent and looked inside the car. There were four men inside, all looking appropriately dressed under their overcoats. They were a little younger than most of the male guests, all in their late thirties or early forties.

"Guten Abend, meine Herren," the guard said, waiting for them to produce their invitations.

Hands reached inside pockets. The guard collected the four invites and moved away from the car, closer to the light from the gatehouse so he could inspect them. He shook his head. There was a problem. These were wrong.

He turned back towards the Jaguar.

That was the last thing he knew.

Ben caught his limp body before it could leave any marks in the snow. There was a muffled shout from the side of the gatehouse. The second guard was reaching for his radio when the Jaguar's rear door opened. The passenger stepped out and shot the second guard through the head with his silenced pistol. The guard fell back through the open gatehouse doorway.

The rear passenger's name was Randall. He was an ex-regiment man, quick-witted and built like a fox. Ben had trained him years before and trusted him completely. His accentless German had come from his mother's side and made him the perfect choice to take over the gatehouse and wave through any straggling guests. Bryant, the lean dark ex-para from Lancashire, had been chosen to back him up.

Working fast, they laid the guards out on the floor of

the hut. Ben nodded. Randall and Bryant quickly removed their overcoats and tuxedo jackets and started pulling on the guards' clothes.

Ben walked briskly back to the Jaguar and slipped in behind the wheel. In the passenger's seat was Jean Gardier, one of Louis Moreau's former GIGN guys, the youngest of the team they'd hastily but carefully assembled in Aragon's office. Gardier was smooth and handsome, with a head of thick black curly hair and a broad white smile that he flashed freely. He'd mix well with the party crowd. From what Aragon's head of security had told him, Ben knew enough to know Gardier would be excellent at his job.

The tall gates glided open with a dull mechanical whirr, and the car purred on through and down the driveway towards the incandescent mansion in the distance.

The house towered into the night sky as they drew up outside. Every leaf of ivy on its massive facade was lit up like daylight. Ben opened up a slim case and took out a pair of oval wire-framed glasses with plain lenses. He slipped them on.

He did a last check of his subvocal earpiece before he stepped out and handed the keys to a valet. Gardier followed him towards the house. The doormen greeted them at the entrance. Ben let one of them take his long black coat. They walked inside and instantly split up without a glance at each other, mingling with the crowd.

It was warm inside the reception hall, and the air was filled with music and bright chatter. A waiter came wafting by, carrying a tray of glasses. Ben snatched one without stopping and brought it to his lips, sipping the ice-chilled champagne. He stood in the corner of the huge entrance hall, catching a glimpse of himself in one of the tall gilt-framed mirrors that lined the walls. The black tuxedo fitted him well, and he barely recognized himself with the spectacles and this darker brown hair tint. Subtle changes were enough to alter a man's appearance very effectively and naturally. Kroll and Glass would know him if they got close, but if he was careful he'd go unnoticed. For the moment, at least. He still had to get deep inside the place.

He chewed on a canapé from a side table and wiped his mouth delicately with a napkin. "Check," he said quietly behind the napkin. Gardier's voice responded instantly in his ear.

He looked casual as he scanned his surroundings. The hallway alone was large enough to accommodate a small jet aircraft. From its center the broad red-carpeted marble staircase swept up to a landing with a high domed ceiling, satin drapes, and a huge dramatic painting that he thought he recognized as a Delacroix.

Beyond the landing, the staircase split into two, climbing in a majestic double curve to the first floor. The landing was cordoned off with a length of silky gold rope. There were two guards hanging around at the foot of the stairs, very discreet with their weapons and radios well out of sight.

He circulated, strolling calmly through into the ballroom and pausing to hear the string quartet. He'd lost sight of Gardier.

He looked around him at the guests. Most of them were high society, wealthy businessmen and their wives just here for the party. They had no idea of the real reason for the gathering, the bloodthirsty ritual murder due to take place right under their noses as they sipped their champagne and nibbled their canapés.

A waiter came by with a loaded tray, and he turned to pick up another glass of champagne. Just then he saw Kroll walking quickly his way. For an instant he thought he could feel the old man's dark eyes on him. Ben turned slowly away, controlling the surge of adrenaline, sipping his drink, and feeling completely naked as Kroll came close. As he pretended to be admiring the artwork on the wall he felt Kroll pass within a foot of him. Ben breathed again as the old man's narrow back disappeared among the crowd.

As he watched Kroll go, Ben had another sudden uncomfortable sensation that he was being watched. He turned. A woman was standing by herself across the dance floor, drink in hand. Their eyes met for an instant through the throng of waltzing couples. She seemed to frown, as though scrutinizing him uncertainly.

Her long blond hair was piled up with a diamond clasp, and a shimmering backless ball gown clung to her figure. But there was no doubt who she was under the makeup and the wig.

Eve turned away, and he lost sight of her. He wondered if that had been a flicker of recognition in her eyes. Whether he could trust her. Whether he could do anything about it either way.

He glanced back through the double doors into the hallway. The guards had moved away from the foot of the stairs. He checked his watch. It was 8:51. He coughed lightly into his palm as he headed from the ballroom. "Diversion," he said softly into his cupped hand.

Two seconds later there was a loud crash from the back of the ballroom. A waiter had tripped and a whole tray of glasses lay broken and spilled on the floor. One of the guests, a young man with thick dark curly hair, was apologizing for his clumsiness as two more waiters came running with a broom and wads of paper towels. There was a buzz of conversation around the scene. The waiters got to work cleaning up the mess, and then it was over. But it had given Ben the time he needed. He smiled at Gardier's act as he headed quickly for the stairs and trotted up to the first landing. He glanced over his shoulder. Slipped under the rope cordon. Nobody saw him. He took off the spectacles and slid them into the pocket of his tuxedo jacket.

He hoped that O'Neill, Cook, Lambert, and Delmas would be in their assigned positions outside. How many guards would they have to neutralize? Everything seemed to be going all right—for the moment.

"How are we doing with the church?" he muttered into the subvocal as he reached the first floor.

Silence. A tiny crackle in his ear. Then: *"No way in from the outside."* He recognized the throaty voice of Delmas, another of Moreau's ex-GIGN men. He'd been expecting that.

He explored the corridors, looking for the landmarks he'd memorized from Oliver's video clip. This was familiar, he thought, as he paused at an alcove in the wall, domed at the top, just a little taller than him. It housed an Egyptian artifact on a marble pedestal, the black and gold pharaoh's mask Oliver had accidentally caught on camera. He was moving in the right direction.

But the place was a maze. To his left, a doorway opened up into another long corridor that was flanked with delicate antiques and more paintings in gold frames. He checked his watch again. Time was passing fast.

The chilling thought entered his mind again. *What if he was wrong?*

He tried a door. It was locked. He moved down the corridor to the next one and found it open. He turned the gilded handle. The door creaked as he stepped inside. He left it slightly ajar. Letting his eyes adjust to the darkness he walked through the room. Something heavy and hard caught his hip, and he put his hand out to feel it.

It was a billiard table. He made his way around its edge to the moonlit French window and unlatched it. He stepped out onto the stone balcony, feeling the sudden bite of the freezing cold air. He scanned the snowy grounds. There was no sign of his team—but then, there wasn't meant to be. These men were trained to be invisible.

He took the Mini Maglite from his inside pocket and flashed twice.

At the signal, four dark shapes broke cover and crept across the lawn to the side of the house. They gathered under the window. There were no guards to surprise them. Ben knew it was the guards who must have had the surprise.

The rubber-sleeved claw of the grappling hook flew over the edge of the balcony and gained a hold. Ben secured the rope and gave it a tug. He felt it go taut as the first man tested his weight on it.

Light flooded into the room behind him. A man's figure stood silhouetted in the doorway. "*Was machen Sie da?*" said a harsh voice.

55.

Ben walked away from the window. The guard's arms were folded across his chest and there was a severe look on his face. His bald crown gleamed in the light from the corridor, a fuzz of dark stubble over his ears. Another man came up behind him, smaller than his companion, scowling as he saw Ben.

"Pardon me," Ben said in German. "I was looking for the bathroom."

"This is a private room," the bald guard said. "What are you doing in here?" He peered past Ben's shoulder, looking at the open window. "Did you open that window?" he demanded, his eyes narrowing suspiciously.

The rope scraped on the balcony handrail. The guard took a step closer to the window. He had one hand on his radio.

"I needed some air," Ben said, grinning. "Too much wine."

"There are bathrooms downstairs," the smaller guard snapped.

"Guess I got lost," Ben said. "Big place."

The wiry guard didn't look convinced. The bald one kept moving towards the window.

Ben glanced at the balcony. The black claws of the grappling hook were plain against the white stone. The bald guard saw it and tore out his radio. The wiry one dived a hand inside his jacket.

Ben was two feet away from the edge of the billiard

table. In the shadows his fingers closed on something smooth, tapered, and hard.

The bald one was about to signal the alert when Ben smashed the cue across his head. The guy dropped the radio and crumpled to the floor.

The wiry guard went for his pistol. Even if he missed, the sound of a shot was going to alert the whole house. He moved fast, but Ben was faster. The billiard cue was a broken spike in his hand. He rammed the jagged point hard and deep into the guard's eye, penetrating the brain and killing him instantly.

The first one was by then back up on his feet, teeth bared in the shadows. He lunged. Ben sidestepped and felt the wind from a swinging punch that just missed his head. He moved inside the arc of the blow and crushed the bald man's trachea with the web of his hand. The guard went down. Ben stamped on his neck and snapped it.

There was a movement at the window. Ben turned to see the black shape of a man hauling himself up and swinging his legs over onto the balcony. It was O'Neill, the Irish SAS sergeant who'd been Ben's first choice for the team.

"Glad you could make it, Shane," Ben said.

O'Neill stepped into the room. He pulled the black woolen hat down tight and grinned through his straggly salt-and-pepper mustache. He looked down at the two dead guards. "Looks like you started without us."

Ben was already dragging the bodies towards a cupboard. By the time they were hidden and the bloodstained carpet covered by moving a rug, the three other black shapes had scrambled up the rope and had joined Ben and Shane O'Neill in the billiard room. Cook, Lambert, and Delmas were all in place. The six remaining team members would be well dispersed on the grounds by now, moving in pairs, neutralizing any security staff they came across.

The four black-clad men did a last check of their silencer-fitted submachine carbines. O'Neill handed Ben a high-capacity 9 mm with a long silencer.

"We haven't got much time," Ben said. He cocked and locked the pistol and stuck it in his belt.

The corridor outside was clear. Ben stepped out first, looking carefully around him. The other four followed, padding over the thick carpets in their combat boots, carrying their weapons silently. Any chance of passing themselves off as lost party guests was gone now.

They had to act fast. There was still no word from Gardier downstairs, but Kroll's associates could be moving any time now. Ben led the way, concentrating hard to remember the layout from Oliver's video clip. Another corner. Another doorway, another decision.

He stopped and studied a painting on the wall. It was the one Oliver had caught on camera, showing an eighteenth-century scene of men meeting in a large hall. Masonic symbols, columns. He knew what it meant now.

He pressed on, feeling a cold rage building up inside him. They must be close.

A door burst open ahead of them. They threw themselves tight back against the wall. A giggling young couple staggered out, clasping each other and fooling about. There was a mirror on the opposite wall. The girl broke free and sauntered over to it on her high heels, checking her makeup and her hair. "I look like someone who's been screwing," she said in a slurred voice.

"You look fine," said the young man, doing up his tie. "Let's get back to the party."

The girl straightened up her dress in the mirror. She had to take only half a step to her left and she would see the reflection of the men hidden in the corridor behind her. Ben tensed.

The girl smiled in the mirror, pursed her lips, and teetered off to join her partner, taking his outstretched hand as she caught up with him. Their giggles disappeared with them around a corner.

Ben glanced at O'Neill, who let out a long sigh. Ben was about to whisper something when his earpiece crackled and he heard Gardier's voice. "*Things are moving down here.*"

Ben checked the time. 9:12 p.m.

56.

Werner Kroll rolled back the sleeve of his dinner jacket and peered at the gold Longines on his wrist. He signaled to Glass on the other side of the ballroom. Glass nodded. It was time.

Dr. Emil Ziegler was standing on the edge of an animated conversation near the grand fireplace when he felt the tap on his shoulder. Ziegler turned, looking over the top of his spectacles. "Sorry to disturb you, sir," Glass said, bending down to speak in his ear. "You're wanted on the phone."

Ziegler's chubby face registered no surprise. He nodded, walked stiffly over to a nearby table, and put down his champagne flute. He smoothed back his thin gray wisps of hair, made his excuses to the group, and started making his way to the door.

Glass did his rounds. Nobody noticed as the twelve men left the party. Their exit was discreet and casual. They all knew exactly where they were going.

Eve watched them slip away. In six years she'd witnessed this seven times. Or was it eight? It was always the same polished, well-orchestrated performance. The party guests would barely notice the absence of the gray-haired men, and nobody else had the slightest idea of where they were going. Or what was about to happen. As the last of the twelve left the room, Kroll and Glass exchanged brief glances. Kroll checked his watch again and looked satisfied. He headed for the doorway, Glass following a few feet behind.

Eve sipped her champagne and felt sick.

• • •

Nobody but members of the group had ever walked down the hidden corridor, one of the many secret passageways that honeycombed the old house. It was long and stark, lit by fluorescents, the walls plain white and the floor bare concrete. At the end of the corridor was a waiting area. There were twelve wooden chairs, a low table with a jug of water, and some glasses.

The twelve men gathered in silence, exchanging little more than a few nods. Emil Ziegler cleared his throat and poured himself a glass of water. Thomas Blochwitz glanced at his watch, mopped sweat from his pale forehead, and took a puff from an asthma inhaler. Peter Gienger paced the waiting room. Ziegler watched him irritably. "Do you have to pace like that?" he snapped. Gienger sat down.

They had little to say to one another. Their association wasn't based on friendship. It was a business relationship that went deeper than loyalty, deeper even than money. When this was over, they wouldn't see or speak to one another for a while. Until the next time. None of them knew when that would be. The signal would come, sooner or later. It always did. The decisions were not theirs, but they knew and trusted that every time they met here like this, it meant a consolidation of their collective business interests. Tonight's event was, for some of them, a very considerable consolidation indeed. It was the removal of a serious threat that had caused all of them a good number of sleepless nights over the past months.

Some of the men looked up as footsteps echoed down the bare corridor. Kroll appeared in the doorway. Glass stood behind him.

"Gentlemen," Kroll said softly. A thin smile tugged at the corners of his lips. "I believe we are ready."

57.

Ben had seen these stone walls before. They were deep in the heart of the house now. The classical decor was behind them. In front of them was an arched bridgeway that Ben knew would take them where it had taken Oliver almost a year earlier.

He led the way through the arched passage and laid a hand against the heavy wooden door at its end. It was open. He pushed gently and stepped through.

They were standing on a high gallery overlooking the interior of the private church below.

Gardier's whispered voice buzzed urgently in his earpiece. "*Subjects have left,*" he said. "*Presume heading your way. I have no visual contact. Repeat, heading your way.*"

Just a little moonlight seeped through the stained-glass windows, throwing long shadows across the church's interior. The flagstones were plain and gray. Polished wooden pews gleamed dully.

Ben's mouth went dry, and his heart began to pound. He didn't want to believe what he was seeing, but it was undeniable. It wasn't the room Oliver had captured on film. This was a completely different place.

He glanced around him. There were no doorways leading off anywhere, just the one they'd come in.

He could sense O'Neill and the others behind him, watching him and wondering what was wrong. His mind started to race, filling with thoughts that swelled his fears.

Kroll's associates were heading for a completely different

part of the house. Kroll had anticipated him, double-bluffed him. Eve had tricked him a second time. He'd walked right into it. He'd given Aragon away to them on a plate. He was out of time. And he was leading his team into a trap.

"What now?" O'Neill asked.

Ben said nothing.

"What do we do, sir?" There was an edge of worry to the Irishman's whisper.

Ben said nothing.

Down below them, there was a grating sound of stone on stone. In the shadows of the church, in the middle of the aisle between the rows of pews, something was moving. A flagstone scraped sideways. A dark figure of a man seemed to emerge from the floor.

58.

The crypt was filled with flickering golden candlelight and the scent of hot wax. The wavering light lined the edges of the ancient symbols carved into the stone walls and the three massive columns that dominated the space. Around the stone walls hung intricate tapestries depicting the esoteric emblems of the Order of Ra. Up above, the golden ram's head glinted, and its spiral horns threw eerie shadows across the vaulted stone ceiling.

A line of men filtered through an arched entrance. They walked silently, solemnly, in single file, their heads slightly bowed as though out of reverence for a church service or a funeral. Each man knew his mark, and they quickly assembled in a semicircular formation in the center of the floor between the columns. Like a line of elderly soldiers they stood and faced the strange platform. The sacrificial altar was ready for them, as always. Chains hung from the high wooden post erected in the middle.

Kroll and Glass entered the crypt last. They stood at the end of the line, slightly to one side. Nobody spoke. Kroll threw a last quick glance at his watch. It was about to begin.

Deep in the shadows, the heavy iron door swung open. Three men stepped into the flickering light. Everyone recognized the face of the man in the middle. Philippe Aragon's shirt was stained and crumpled, and there was a cut across his left eyebrow. His arms were held tight by the two hooded men flanking him. There was a leather gag tied across his mouth. His eyes were wild and staring, darting up and down the row of black-suited men who had come to see him die.

They walked him slowly to the wooden post. He struggled as they cuffed his arms behind it and wrapped three lengths of the heavy chain around his waist. He sagged weakly at the knees. Once the chains were secure, the hooded men turned and walked solemnly back into the shadows behind the altar, one either side, half hidden in the darkness.

The only sound in the crypt was the echoing clinking of the chains as Aragon struggled feebly to get free. All eyes were on him.

Glass smiled to himself. He always enjoyed this moment. He didn't give a damn one way or the other about Aragon or what he might represent, any more than he'd cared about the others. He just liked the idea of what they were going to do to him. Maybe one day, he thought, they'd get to do a woman this way. That would be good. Maybe the old man would let him do it himself.

The iron door creaked again, and the executioner walked out across the platform. His black hooded robe hung down to his feet. In his hands was a long object wrapped in a piece of scarlet satin. He drew the cloth away, and firelight danced down the blade of the ceremonial knife. He stepped up to the prisoner.

Kroll spoke out, and his voice echoed in the crypt. "Philippe Aragon, have you anything to say before your sentence is carried out?" He gestured to the executioner. The hooded man reached out and tore away the gag from Aragon's lips. Aragon hung from the post, breathing heavily. He fixed Kroll with red-rimmed eyes and spat in his face.

Kroll turned to the executioner. "Cut his heart out," he said quietly.

The executioner didn't hesitate. The razor-sharp blade glittered as he raised it above his head.

The twelve men in the line watched as if hypnotized. Glass grinned in anticipation. Kroll's lips stretched into a thin smile.

The knife came down in a blur. Aragon let out a cry as the sharp blade buried itself deep.

Into the wooden post by his head. The executioner let go of the knife handle, and it stuck there, juddering.

Kroll took a step forwards, his brow creasing, mouth opening. Something was wrong.

The executioner moved away from the prisoner. His hand darted inside his robe and came out with a silenced 9 mm pistol. The fat cylindrical muzzle swung towards the assembled spectators.

Glass reacted instantly by reaching for his own gun. A rattle of silenced gunfire raked the black-and-white flagstones at Glass's feet, and he dropped his weapon.

The hooded guards emerged back into the light. Candle flame glimmered on their stubby black automatic weapons. O'Neill and Lambert. Two more figures appeared from behind the stone columns on either side. Delmas and Cook. Lambert stepped up to the wooden post and undid Aragon's chains.

Ben ripped back his hood and shrugged the executioner's robe off his shoulders. It slipped down to his feet, and he kicked it away.

Kroll's associates were panicking, wide-eyed, looking to their leader for an explanation. Kroll's jaw had dropped in amazement. Ben met his eye with a cold smile. *Figure that one out,* he thought.

The improvised plan had worked well. It hadn't been difficult to disable the guards and take control of the crypt beneath the church, minutes before Kroll and his people had come in. The real executioner was now lying dead in a back room with the rest.

Jack Glass stared up at Ben with burning hate in his eyes. Even disarmed, he was still the most dangerous man in the room. Ben kept the sights of the Heckler & Koch square on him, watching him down the pistol's barrel. The hammer was back, the safety was off. His finger was inside the trigger guard. He had only to squeeze lightly and the hammer would punch down on the round in the chamber, igniting the fulminate in the primer and sending the 9 mm hollow point spinning down the short barrel. It would reach Glass's body in less than a hundredth of a second. The bullet would mushroom inside him, exploding into a million razor splinters of lead alloy and copper that would blast out a wide tunnel of lifeless jelly.

His finger caressed the smooth, curved face of the trigger. His eyes were fixed on Glass's. He let the sights blur out.

A bullet in answer for Oliver. Another for Leigh. And he had fifteen more in the magazine. He wouldn't stop until the last spent case was tinkling across the floor and the hot gun was locked back in his hands and Glass and Kroll were lying broken and twisted and sprawled in a lake of their mixed blood. His heart quickened at the thought. He felt his eyes burn. He saw Leigh's smile in his mind. His throat ached.

"Ben," said a voice to his left. He darted a glance sideways, still aiming the gun at Glass.

Aragon was looking hard at him. "Don't do it," he said.

Ben shook his head. His fingertip ran down the trigger blade. One pull.

"This wasn't what we agreed," Aragon said softly. "We're not murderers."

One pull. The gun began to shake in Ben's hand.

"They'll be arrested and spend the rest of their lives in jail," Aragon said. "That's what you promised me. A bullet in the head is not the same thing as justice."

Ben let out a long sigh. He took his finger out of the trigger guard and flipped on the safety. He let the pistol down.

Glass smiled. Kroll was still staring at Ben in disbelief, his wrinkled mouth half open as if the words were stuck.

Kroll's associates stood frozen as the four team members moved forwards out of the shadows, weapons shouldered. The old men's faces were drawn and pale, eyes wide, foreheads thick with sweat.

Emil Ziegler suddenly staggered. His face was twisted in agony as he clapped a hand to his left shoulder. He collapsed, convulsing. Heart attack.

Cook was a trained medic. Slinging his MP5 behind him, he ran to the stricken man's side and dropped down to his knees.

Ziegler's arm lashed out. Cook fell back, the last expression on his face one of complete surprise. Then the blood started spurting from his slashed throat. Ziegler's chubby fist was still clutching the stiletto knife.

Suddenly the air was filled with yelling and panic. O'Neill and Lambert looked ready to empty their MP5s into Ziegler. Aragon was commanding them to hold fire, *hold your fire.*

In the corner of Ben's vision, the edge of a tapestry fluttered in the shadows. He looked away from Cook's body.

Glass and Kroll weren't there anymore.

59.

Ben leaped down from the platform and tore the gold-threaded tapestry away from the wall. He saw the entrance to a small hidden archway, dark against the shadowy stone. A cold breeze wafted from it. He stepped inside the dimly lit stone stairway and saw that it spiraled upwards. He could hear the sound of running footsteps echoing off the walls above him.

He threw a glance over his shoulder. The crypt was secure. There was nothing anyone could do for Cook. Aragon was propped wearily against a pillar, pressing numbers into a phone. The other three team members had the old men firmly cornered. They were Philippe Aragon's responsibility now.

Ben had other business. He started up the spiral steps, two at a time. The staircase wound round and round. Over the sound of his own rapid footsteps he thought he could hear the two men running ahead of him. He was gaining.

A second later he heard the flat report of a pistol. Followed by another. They were just up ahead.

The instant she'd recognized Ben Hope in the ballroom, she'd known that her moment was approaching fast. It was the endgame, the culmination of all these years of fear and duplicity and self-loathing that Werner Kroll had put her through. She didn't care anymore. It had to stop here. Whatever happened.

She hadn't lived as Werner's prisoner all this time

without finding out a few of his secret routes. The enormous rambling house was riddled with them, enabling him to slip unnoticed from one place to another. Even though he'd always kept the private crypt locked to her, she knew about the hidden stair and had thought he'd come that way. He always had a surprise card to play. He was like that. Too clever to let anyone catch him so easily.

Now it was time for her to surprise him. She'd gone to her room, changed out of the party dress into jeans and an old sweater, taken that detested wig off for the last time, and fetched her purse. Then she'd come here to this dark, dusty part of the old house to wait for him, crouching in the shadows of the passage, staring at the iron-studded door that she knew he was going to emerge from sooner or later. Through a dark passage to her right, the stairway wound right up to the top of the house. She wasn't going to let Kroll up there.

As she heard the footsteps and the rattle of keys in the lock of the old door, she slipped the Black Widow out of her purse and firmly snicked back the hammer with her thumb. The door creaked open, and she stepped out of the gloom to meet them.

Kroll stopped in the entrance and stared at her. Glass was with him. Kroll's eyes flicked from hers to the muzzle of the little pistol and back up again. "Eve—" he began, raising a hand.

She'd never pointed a gun at a living person before. But she didn't hesitate. The rubber grip filled her palm. Her finger curled around the little spur trigger and squeezed.

The .22 Magnum fired a very small bullet at a very high velocity. The report of the supersonic round was vicious in the enclosed space, and she almost cried out at the lancing pain in her ears.

Glass twisted and clutched at his neck. He swore and staggered back two steps. There was a spray of blood on the stonework behind him.

But he didn't go down. He swayed on his feet, and for an instant Eve thought he was going to come at her. She struggled with the little gun. Her hands had started to shake violently, and she couldn't get the hammer cocked for a second shot.

Glass staggered across the landing towards the next flight of stairs. She was still fumbling with the gun as he disappeared round the corner. She heard his footsteps racing unevenly up the wooden steps.

Kroll stood still in the middle of the landing. His eyes were wide.

The Black Widow's hammer clicked back into place, and she brought it to bear on him. "Eve," he said again, raising his eyebrows. "Think what you're doing."

"It's over, Werner," she said. "I can't let you go on with it anymore."

His eyes pleaded. "Look into your heart, Eve." He took a step towards her. "You know that you don't want to kill me."

She saw the stubby little automatic in his hand an instant too late. His face tightened. He fired from the hip, without aiming. His first shot went through her hand. The .22 spun out of her grip. She screamed.

He fired again and caught her in the shoulder. The searing agony sliced through her. She fell back, slumped against the wall, and slid down slowly to the floor.

Kroll smiled as he stood over her, his legs planted either side of her body. He aimed the little Colt auto between her eyes. "Good-bye, Eve," he said.

Then he went tumbling forward with a spasm.

Ben Hope was in the doorway. Through the pain and the ringing in her ears, Eve heard the muffled cough of his gun repeating in a rapid staccato as he emptied it into Kroll. The old man crumpled bloodily onto his face with nine bullets in him and lay half on top of her.

Ben grabbed Kroll's dead body by the collar and rolled it aside. He knelt down beside Eve. He could see that not all the blood on her was Kroll's. He ripped the neck of her sweater, searching for the gunshot wound.

The bullet had hit high on the right shoulder, between the collarbone and the upper chest muscle. He probed gently, fingers slick with blood. She was near to fainting as he ran his fingers over the back of her shoulder and found the small-caliber bullet lodged under the skin. It had passed through the shoulder without fragmenting. He breathed more easily. It wasn't as bad as it looked.

The hand was worse, quite a bit worse. He winced when he saw the jagged bits of bone protruding whitely through the flesh. Her fingers were twisted in a way they shouldn't be. She might never recover the full use of that right hand.

But she'd live. She'd been lucky. Kroll had been a bad shot. The sign of a man who had always paid others to pull the trigger for him. Or maybe just a sadist who wanted to take his time and cause as much pain and peripheral damage as he could before he killed her. Either way, it was over now.

"You'll be all right," he said. "You'll be taken care of."

"*Thank you,*" she mouthed weakly. She tried to smile, and then passed out.

He looked at her for a moment, then reached out and caressed her cheek, leaving a smear of blood.

He stood up and looked down at Kroll. The old man lay twisted like a broken doll. The von Adler line had just ended, and with it two centuries of murder and corruption. Werner Kroll's lifeless eyes were staring like oily porcelain. The thin wrinkled lips seemed to smile mockingly at him. For an instant Ben wanted to shoot him again.

But he had other things to worry about. Where was Jack Glass?

There was a spatter of blood on the wall. Splashes of it across the floor. They led towards the stairs. A slick red footprint on the first step. A big red splash on the second. Another footprint on the third. A bloody handprint on the banister rail. The blood led all the way up. But it was just a trail. Glass himself was nowhere.

Ben's mind suddenly filled with a single thought.

Clara.

60.

Jack Glass had been shot before, plenty of times. As long as he was still functional and on his feet, he was still in the game. It was going to take more than a bullet from a woman's gun to stop him. He knew his collarbone was broken, but he was prepared to ignore the pain if he could do what he wanted to do now.

He pounded up the stairs, his hand pressed hard against his shoulder to stem the blood. He reached the third floor, leaned against the banister rail, and looked down. He could see a dark shape two floors below, moving fast up the winding staircase. Hope was after him again. Fucking blood trail was giving him away. Nothing he could do about that. He had to keep moving. Forget the pain.

He grinned. Hope and him in the running together. It was like SAS selection all over again. But this time he had an edge, and he meant to use it. The old man was fucked: the ship was going down. But there was no way Jack Glass was going down with it.

He made it to the top floor and thundered stiffly along the corridor, soaked in sweat and blood. The doors to the garret rooms were on his left. Paper was peeling off the walls, and the carpets were threadbare. It was cold up here, cooling the sweat that was pouring off him. He ripped open one of the doors to his right and staggered into the room. He found what he was looking for and tucked the small leather case under his arm.

"Boss, you okay?"

It was the Swede. His dull face registered mild alarm as he saw the blood on Glass's shirt.

Glass turned. "Never better," he grunted painfully.

He had to look down at most men. But the Swede, Björkmann, towered over him by nearly three inches. That made him a very big man indeed. His neck was wider than his head, as thick as Glass's thigh. Three hundred pounds of solid muscle with an arrowhead haircut and very little brains. The kind of man Glass loved to have on his team. The big Ruger revolver was dwarfed in his meaty fist.

"Everybody's going ape shit down there," Björkmann said in his broken German. "What's going on?"

"Somebody crashed the party," Glass replied. He wiped the cold sweat out of his eyes and felt the ends of his broken collarbone grate. He clenched his teeth. "I need you to watch my back, Christian. There's a guy on his way up here. You know what to do. I'll come back for you. Okay?"

The gigantic man nodded slowly. "Sure, boss."

Glass watched Björkmann lumber down the corridor. He grinned and left the outline of a bloody hand on Clara Kinski's door as he shoved it open.

The child was crouched in the corner, pressed against the wall, looking up at him with terror in her eyes. Glass took the syringe out of the leather case. He plucked the cork off the end of the long needle and fired a squirt of the lethal poison into the air. "Your uncle Jack's going to take care of you now," he said.

Clara started to scream as he walked into the room.

61.

Ben's eyes were on the blood trail as he sprinted up another flight of stairs. His left hand grasped the polished banister rail as he climbed, his right holding the pistol ready.

The splashes of bright blood on the stairs were frequent. Glass was badly hurt, but he was running like a maniac and he was still extremely dangerous. He was heading for the top floor.

Ben cleared the final flight, his heart hammering in his chest. The blood trail led onwards down the corridor. He followed it, sweeping the gun left and right.

At the end of the long passage, a door was banging open. Through the doorway he could see curtains fluttering in the cold wind and snow blowing in through an open French window. He went into the room. All his senses were blazing. Over the thudding of his heart he heard an unmistakable sound. As he crept into the room it got louder.

It was the high-pitched whine of a powerful engine, revs building to a roar. It was coming from outside, on the roof. Someone was firing up the helicopter. He moved towards the window.

His vision exploded white, and suddenly he was on his face. The gun slid away across the bare floorboards. He felt fingers curl around his collar, and he was yanked to his feet with brutal force. He had a glimpse of a broad forehead and two small, fierce eyes staring down at him, and then a massive fist slammed into his jaw and sent him reeling backwards as though he weighed nothing. He crashed into a desk, sprawling over the top of it and sending papers and files, an ashtray and a telephone flying.

One of the biggest men he'd ever seen walked calmly towards him around the edge of the desk. "You are dead," the giant said simply. His English was heavily accented. In his hand was a stainless-steel Ruger .44 Redhawk with an eight-inch barrel. He tucked it into the back of his belt. "I no need this," he said. He raised his fists.

Ben staggered to his feet. The whine of the helicopter outside was getting louder. There was blood on his lips from the punch. His head was spinning. But even the biggest bastard could be brought down. He moved in fast and aimed a heavy blow at the solar plexus. He put all his strength into it and pain lanced up his arm as it impacted. It was a good punch. It would have crippled most men.

The giant barely seemed to feel it. A fist the size of a pineapple flew at Ben's head and only just missed. If it had landed, it would have killed him.

This was getting serious. Ben aimed a kick to the groin. The giant blocked it. He jabbed at the throat. Another block. Ben retreated, aware that he was running out of space in the room. Through the open window he heard another sound, the high, keening, terrified sound of a child's scream. He followed the sound with his eyes. The windows opened out onto a wide, flat expanse of rooftop. The helipad was surrounded by sloping gables and towering chimneys. Snow flurried on the rising wind. Thirty yards away, the lights of the Bell chopper cut a white beam through the drifting snowflakes, its rotors turning faster now. Jack Glass had Clara by the arm and was trying to bundle her into the open door of the helicopter. She was struggling and kicking. His teeth were gritted in pain, and the front of his shirt was dark and clinging with blood.

Ben looked a fraction of a second too long. A heavy boot caught his ribs, and he felt something crack. He cried out, rolled to the floor, clutched his side. He crawled under the desk. The giant grabbed the edge of the desk with one hand and hurled it over. He ripped out a drawer and crashed it down over Ben's head. It shattered into pieces, showering him with bits of office equipment. Something glinted on the carpet. It was a letter-opener in the shape of a dagger. His fingers closed over it, and as the giant came on again Ben plunged the blade downwards into the man's boot.

It was a solid heavy-grain leather boot. The blade was blunt. But Ben stabbed it so hard that it went through the leather into the foot inside. Through the foot into the sole. Through the sole into the wooden floor. It pinned him like an insect to a board.

The big man threw his head back and howled in pain. Ben struggled to his feet and lashed a foot into the man's groin. That had an effect. The man doubled up. Ben grabbed the giant's tiny ears and slammed a knee into his face.

Outside, Clara broke away from Glass. Her hair streaming in the blast from the spinning rotor blades, she ran towards the windows. She slipped on the snow and fell, then scrabbled back to her feet. Glass went after her and grabbed her by the hair. He yanked her back, and she screamed.

The giant was teetering, moaning, trying to stagger away from his pinned foot. Ben tore a fire extinguisher off the wall and rammed the heavy metal cylinder down on his head. The man crashed to the floor and rolled onto his back. Ben brought the base of the extinguisher down on his face and almost vomited as the man's skull caved in. The giant convulsed and twitched for a second and then lay still.

Bloody and hurt, Ben ripped the .44 Ruger from the dead man's belt. The cylinder was loaded with six fat magnum cartridges. He staggered towards the open French window. Glass was dragging Clara back towards the helicopter. He picked her up and stuck her under his arm. Her little legs kicked wildly.

Ben ran out onto the roof, ignoring the pain from his cracked rib. He aimed the heavy revolver and yelled Glass's name over the roar.

Glass jerked Clara's body round in front of his. He pressed something against her neck. His thumb was on the plunger of the syringe. "I'll kill her," he screamed. "Put the gun down."

Ben dropped the revolver and kicked it away from him. Glass grinned through his pain and dragged the child inside the helicopter. Still holding the syringe to her neck, he handcuffed her to the frame of the seat. Ben watched helplessly. Glass slid behind the controls. He'd learned to fly in Africa, and he was a good pilot. Crazy enough to take off in the snow, but then Jack Glass had always been crazy. He was proud of that.

The helicopter began to lift off. Ben could see Clara's pallid face through the Perspex window. Her mouth was open in a scream that was drowned out by the huge noise and the wind.

He ran across the helipad. The chopper was in the air, driving the snow into a storm of flakes that stung Ben's eyes. He picked up the fallen .44 but didn't dare to fire.

He looked around him in desperation as the hovering chopper spun slowly round on itself. Along the edge of the roof was a stone parapet, about four feet high. He ran to it and leaped up on top of it. He shoved the long barrel of the revolver through his belt and steadied himself with his hands. It was a long way down. The chopper dipped its nose as Glass hit the throttle.

Ben launched himself. For an instant he was weightless. The floodlit grounds of the mansion were below him. He saw the flashing lights of police cars swarming down the driveway. The party was in chaos.

He began to fall. Then his flailing hand clasped the cold metal of one of the chopper's skids. The craft veered to the right, moving away from the house. The thudding wind tore at Ben's hair and clothes as he dangled in space. He reached up and clapped his other hand onto the skid, kicking with his legs to haul himself up. Below him, the ground spun dizzily.

Glass felt the chopper unbalanced with Ben's weight. From the cockpit he could see him hanging there, desperately trying to climb up to the side door. He smiled and turned the chopper towards the house. He couldn't shake him off, but he could scrape the bastard off.

In the darkness a chimney stack loomed large. Glass banked hard towards it. Ben had a glimpse of brickwork rushing towards him. He raised his legs clear, and the chopper roared over the roof. Glass brought it round again, the g-forces stretching Ben's arms as he hung on to the skid.

Glass headed for the roofs again. Ben's flailing legs raked violently up an incline of tiles, some of them coming loose and tumbling down to the ground below. Glass banked the chopper another time, laughing. One more pass and he'd leave Hope smeared like a bug across twenty feet of stonework.

But he banked too early. The tail rotor caught the side of the roof with a crashing shower of sparks and twisted metal. The helicopter juddered. The controls went crazy as the craft began to spin away from the house and towards the trees.

Ben had a foot on the skid now. Reaching out with an effort he clasped the handle of the side door and ripped it open. He threw himself inside the cockpit as the chopper gyrated out of control over the treetops, its lights tracing a wild circle over the snowy green pines and the naked branches of oaks and beeches.

Glass lunged at him with the lethal syringe. Ben dodged the stab and drove Glass's wrist against the controls. The needle clattered to the floor. The two men wrestled over the seats, gouging and punching. Ben dug his fingers into Glass's cropped hair and slammed his face against the dials, and again, and again, until Glass's forehead was streaming with blood.

The helicopter was going down, spinning faster and faster. Glass's fingers clawed at his face. Ben hammered him against the door, punched him in the teeth, slammed his head against the controls again. Glass flopped limply in his seat as the chopper banked violently to one side and twisted downwards towards the treetops.

Ben heaved on the controls, but there was nothing he could do. The chopper spun wildly for another hundred yards before it hit. The rotors disintegrated and flew apart as they sliced into the treetops. They tumbled down: snapping branches raking and tearing at the fuselage, engine stalling, pieces of twisted rotor crashing down with them. Ben was hurled against the floor, and the roof as the craft flipped over and over.

Thirty feet from the ground, the Bell tore free of the lower branches. Through shattered Perspex Ben glimpsed the snowy forest floor rushing up to meet them. The impact flung him hard against the instruments. The chopper buried its nose in a snowdrift. Splintered branches and pieces of aircraft rained down.

Glass was lying slumped across the control console. Sparks crackled from somewhere behind the dials, and the strong scent of aviation fuel reached Ben's nostrils.

He hauled himself painfully upwards through the dark, smashed cockpit. Above him, Clara was wedged on the back of the front seats. Her lip was bleeding. She desperately tugged at the chain that connected her wrist to the steel tubing of her seat.

Ben heard the *crackle* and *whoomph* and looked over his shoulder. Flames licked at the inside of the glass, searing across the controls and the front seats. In seconds the helicopter was going to blow.

He yanked at the handcuff chain, glinting in the flames. It held fast. Clara's eyes were bulging, her hair plastered over her face. She strained to tear her little wrist out of the steel bracelet, but it was tight against the skin.

The flames were catching. Ben clambered down towards Glass's slumped body and felt in the pocket of his bloody tuxedo for the key to the cuffs. It wasn't there. The heat was unbearable. A tongue of fire licked Ben's back, scorching his jacket. There wasn't time. The chopper was going to explode.

Over his pain and fear he remembered. *The gun.* He jerked it out of his belt and pressed the muzzle against the handcuff bracelet that was locked around the seat tube. Fire seared his sleeve. He squeezed the trigger.

The stunning noise of the .44 revolver cut away all sound. For an instant Ben was disorientated, lost in a surreal world of silence with the high-pitched whine in his ears filling his head.

Another rolling wave of liquid flame poured across the blackened interior of the chopper, and he came to his senses. Clara was free, the broken chain dangling from the cuff around her wrist. They struggled across the cockpit. Ben kicked against the door with all his remaining strength. The door buckled open, and he grasped the little girl's arm and somehow they crawled through the gap just before the fire engulfed the whole cockpit.

He dragged her stumbling across the snow. Before they'd staggered twenty yards, the forest behind them was suddenly filled with white light. Ben dived behind the trunk of an oak tree, shielding Clara's little body with his as the fuel tanks ruptured with the heat and the chopper exploded into a massive ball of searing flame. The whole night sky was lit up. Trees burst alight. Burning wreckage spewed in all directions. Clara screamed, and he held her tight.

62.

THE HOTEL BRISTOL, VIENNA
THREE DAYS LATER

Ben walked in off the Kärtner Ring and entered the lobby of the luxury hotel. His clothes felt too new and stiff, and every time he moved a stab of pain jolted his side.

The place was milling with journalists and photographers. He already knew that Philippe Aragon and a small army of his people had occupied a whole floor as their base for the series of press conferences that the media was screaming everywhere. The police raid on the von Adler mansion was the biggest news event for years, and Aragon was right in the center of the frenzy. Ben had deliberately avoided TV and radio for three days, but even so he hadn't been able to escape it.

Behind the scenes, Aragon had been pulling more strings in those last three days than most politicians pulled in a lifetime. He had the kind of high-level influence that enabled certain details to be smudged for the media. The deaths at the mansion had been attributed to Kroll's own people. As for Ben and his team, they had never been there.

It had taken forty-eight hours to clear up the carnage. Nothing remained of the burned-out helicopter except blackened fragments scattered across the forest floor by the explosion.

No trace remained of Jack Glass, either. At the kind

of temperature generated by blazing aviation fuel, human tissue—even teeth and bones—would be reduced to fine ash. Ben had seen it before.

He pushed through the throng filling the hotel lobby and was met by a man in a pin-striped suit. He was around the same age as Ben, but balding and on the scraggy end of thin. He offered his hand. "I'm Adrien Lacan," he said over the buzz. "Philippe Aragon's personal assistant. Glad you could make it, Monsieur Hope."

Lacan escorted Ben through the lobby to the lift. Some cameras flashed as they walked. Ben kept his face turned away. Security men pushed back the journalists who had started crowding them, and they stepped into the lift alone. Lacan punched the button for the top floor and the lift whooshed quietly upwards. "It's insane," he said, shaking his head. "I've never known it like this before."

Aragon's plush rooms were bustling noisily with his staff, people coming and going, talking into headsets, the sound of more phones ringing in the background. TV screens were set up on desks playing different news channels while people clustered around to watch. A tall stack of newspapers sat piled on a table, two women sifting through them and scrutinizing the front pages. Ben walked into the busy room and felt several pairs of eyes on him wondering who he was.

In the middle of it all, Aragon was perched casually on the edge of a desk, flipping through some papers while talking to someone on a cell phone. His shirt was open at the neck, and he looked fresh and energetic even with the bandage over his eyebrow covering up his stitches. He smiled broadly as Ben approached, ended his call, and snapped his phone shut. He laid the sheaf of papers down on the desk and greeted Ben warmly.

"Don't forget you have a press interview at quarter past," Lacan warned him. Aragon waved him away and took Ben's elbow.

"I'm sorry for all this chaos," he said. "It's quieter in here." He guided Ben through the milling crowd of staff and into a smaller room to one side. He closed the door, shutting out the noise. "Thanks for coming," he said.

Ben watched the politician. He'd bounced back like a fighter. He looked relaxed and confident, but there was an edge to him now, a competitive fierceness Ben hadn't seen in him before. He looked primed and ready for battle.

"You said it was important," Ben replied.

"It is. A matter I need to clear up with you before you leave. Your flight's today?"

Ben nodded. "In a few hours."

"Ireland," Aragon said. "I've never been. What's it like?"

"Green," Ben said. "Empty. Quiet."

"There's a part of me that would love to be able to retreat to a tranquil place," Aragon said, nodding towards the door and the crazy bustle on the other side. "Right now, I'd probably never want to come back. You're a lucky man."

Ben didn't feel much like a lucky man. "You could always just give it all up, Philippe," he said. "Go back to your old career. Architects don't attract the wrong kind of attention. They don't get kidnapped or executed."

"You talk like Colette, my wife."

"Sounds like a sensible lady," Ben said.

"You like to live on the edge yourself, though."

"I do what I do."

"You've been a big help to me," Aragon said. "I won't forget it."

Ben smiled. "I didn't do it for you."

"I appreciate your candor. But I'm grateful to you,

nonetheless." The politician reached into the inside pocket of his jacket and drew out a small white envelope. "Which brings me to the reason I asked you to meet me here," he said. "I wanted to give you this."

Ben took the envelope from Aragon's outstretched hand. His name was printed in neat writing on the front.

Aragon waggled a finger at it. "Open it." He leaned on the back of a chair with a look of amused anticipation as Ben tore it open.

There wasn't much inside, just a slip of paper. Ben took it out. It was a signed check from Aragon's personal account, and it was made out to Mr. Benedict Hope. He ran his eye along the figure. A one with a whole line of zeros after it. "I don't understand," he said, looking up. "What's this for?"

"I never told you about the reward I was offering," Aragon said. "One million euros for whoever helped me to find Roger's killers." He smiled. "You helped me. We got them. It's yours. Enjoy it."

Ben stared at the check. "Thanks, Philippe," he said.

Aragon smiled. "That's settled then. Have a pleasant journey home. I expect we'll meet again."

"But no thanks," Ben finished. He handed the check back to Aragon.

"You won't accept?"

Ben shook his head.

"You earned it," Aragon said.

"Take care of Sandy Cook's widow and kids," Ben said. "Give the rest to charity. Do something good with it. I don't want it."

Kinski was at home. It took him a while to hobble to the door on his crutches. "Good to see you on your feet,

Markus," Ben said as he stepped inside the hallway. He was carrying something in a plastic bag.

Kinski was in a dressing gown. His hair was a mess, and he had four days' stubble growth on his face. His skin was pallid, and there were dark bags under his eyes.

Ben looked around him at the small, modern suburban house. It didn't look like the home of a big rough guy like Markus Kinski. Everything was too orderly and cared for, neat little vases of flowers on the tables. A woman's touch about the place. Helga, Ben guessed.

The detective looked happy to see him. Ben looked down at the heavily plastered leg, stubby bare toes sticking out from the end. The plaster was covered in the autographs of well-wishers.

Kinski caught his gaze. "Itches like crazy," he said. "The fucking thing can't come off soon enough."

"How is she?" Ben asked as Kinski hobbled down the hallway.

"A little subdued," Kinski said. "But she'll be fine. She's a tough kid." His eyes wandered to the plastic bag Ben was carrying. "What've you got there?"

"I brought her something," Ben said. He reached inside the bag and pulled out the big floppy teddy bear he'd picked out in a hurry on his way across town. "I hope she likes it."

"Why don't you ask her yourself?" Kinski suggested. He limped to the bottom of the stairs and leaned on his crutches. "You've got a visitor, Clara," he called.

A door opened on the landing, and a little face peeped out. Her eyes lit up when she saw Ben standing there. She ran down the stairs and hugged him tight.

He was happy to see her smiling again. That lost look had faded from her eyes since the last time he'd seen her.

She'd been through a hell of a lot, but maybe her father was right. She was a tough kid.

"I suppose you're far too grown-up and mature for this," he said, handing her the teddy bear.

She clasped it to her chest. "I'll call him Ben." She beamed. "I have another new friend, too," she said brightly. She turned. "Can I show Ben, Daddy?"

Kinski nodded. Clara ran happily up the hall, clutching the teddy. "Muffi!" she called. A Rottweiler puppy, a black ball of fur no bigger than a rabbit, flopped out of the sitting room on clumsy oversize paws and cocked his head to one side, watching Ben with big curious eyes. He had a patch of tan above each one, just like Max.

"Go and play with the puppy," Kinski told her. "Ben and I need to talk."

He led Ben into the kitchen and propped his crutches against the table. He opened a cupboard and took down two tumblers and a bottle of Jack Daniel's. They sat, Kinski's plastered leg sticking out in front of him. He poured out two full glasses and shoved one towards Ben.

Kinski groaned, tried to shove two fingers down inside his plaster. Frustrated, he gave up and knocked back half a measure of the bourbon.

"I thought you were on the wagon," Ben said.

"Fell off. Takes my mind off this goddamn itching."

"Aragon told me you're heading the investigation."

Kinski nodded. "I get the feeling it's going to drag on for months. They say it's the shit-hottest team of defense lawyers anyone's ever seen." He grunted. "The fuckers are going to need them."

"You can cut down the weed," Ben said, "but the roots go deep. You can't destroy it."

Kinski shrugged. "Maybe you're right. Personally,

I'll be happy to see some bastards take a fall. That'll satisfy me."

They drank in silence.

"I'll never forget what you did for Clara," Kinski said quietly. "I wish I could have been there to help you."

"I'm sorry about your friend Hildegard," Ben said.

Kinski raised his tumbler to his lips. When he put it down, it was empty. He let out a long sigh. "Ben, when they told me about Leigh . . ." His voice tailed off. His stubbled chin sank to his chest.

Ben laid a hand on the cop's arm. "Thanks, Markus."

Ninety minutes later he was leaning back in a soft armchair and looking around him at the luxurious decor of the private clinic's lounge area. The warm room was filled with plants and flower arrangements. There was a pretty Christmas tree in one corner. Snow pattered lightly against the windows.

Hidden speakers were playing some kind of music-box stuff that sounded to Ben like Mozart. He couldn't name the piece, and he didn't care. He didn't want to hear any damn Mozart. It made him think of Leigh and Oliver. Suddenly, he missed his old drinking flask.

"Hello, Eve," he said.

She paused in the doorway before she smiled self-consciously and crossed the room towards him. She was wearing a navy tracksuit with a sleeve cut away, and her arm was in a sling. She was in plaster from her elbow to her fingertips. There were no autographs on her cast.

"How's the hand?"

"I don't think I'll play the guitar anymore," she said as she lowered herself into the armchair next to his. "They operated on it. We'll see. Doesn't hurt too bad, though.

As long as I keep dosing myself stupid on painkillers." She smiled. Her face looked tight and pale.

He shifted round in his chair and winced a little at the sharp pull on his ribs.

"Look at the state of us," she said. "All banged up. Are you okay?"

"I'll live," he said. "Just a little stiffness, that's all."

"I was surprised when you called. I didn't think I'd see you again, Ben. Thanks for coming to visit me."

"I'm glad Aragon's looking after you," he said.

"Real VIP treatment in this place." She paused. "I've a lot to thank Philippe for. It's more than I deserve," she added.

"He's a good man," Ben said. "For a politician."

"He's taken good care of me. I might have to be on probation for a while, but I can handle that. It's a fresh start for me."

He nodded. They both knew she'd been cut a lucky deal. Ben knew more than she did about the strings Aragon had pulled to make things work out for her. Aragon had a lot of compassion in him. He made Ben wonder about his own compassion.

"I'm ashamed of all the things I've done," she said, looking down.

"You never had a lot of choice. You made it right in the end."

"Yes, we made it right," she said. "So what about you . . . you sticking around awhile, or what?"

"I'm catching a flight to Dublin this afternoon."

"Shame," she said. "I'd have liked to get to know you."

He smiled sadly and said nothing.

"Planning on ever coming back this way?" she asked.

"Maybe one day."

"You won't be at the hearing?"

He shook his head. "I was never here."

"I'm the star witness," she said.

"I know. You'll be fine," he told her.

He went to leave. She followed him into the hallway. "Wait," she said. "I just remembered something. I had them bring it here from my place after you called." She climbed the stairs and disappeared through a door on the first floor. When she reappeared a moment later, she was holding something very familiar in her good hand. It was his old brown leather jacket.

"I thought I'd never see that again," he said.

She flushed. "You left it in my flat that day."

He took it from her and slung it over his shoulder. It felt good. "Thanks," he muttered. He turned for the door.

"You're sure you can't hang around for a while?"

"I'm sure."

"Can I call you sometime?"

On the twenty-kilometer taxi journey southeast towards Wien Schwechat airport, Ben took off the new jacket he'd bought and slipped on the old leather one. He felt a little happier with it on. He found his drinking flask in one pocket, and his phone in another. He turned the phone on to check if it still had any battery life. It did.

He used it to call Christa Flaig. She listened in silence when he told her that Fred's death had been answered for. He didn't say too much. "Watch the papers," he said. "And you might be getting a call from a cop called Kinski. You can trust him."

He had an hour to kill after check-in, and he knew exactly how he wanted to use that time. He took a stool at the departure-lounge bar and bought a triple whiskey. That didn't take too long to finish, and he ordered another. He didn't get drunk often, not properly drunk. But today didn't feel like a bad day for it, and now didn't seem like a bad time to get started. He slipped the pack of Gitanes out of his leather jacket and thumbed the wheel of his Zippo. He clanged the lighter shut, took a deep lungful of the strong smoke, and let it trickle out of his nose. He closed his eyes. Immediately, he was seeing Leigh's face in his mind.

The barman eyed him and came over. *"Rauchen verboten,"* he said, pointing at the NO SMOKING sign. Ben shot him a look that made him back away. A woman in a pinstriped trouser suit sitting along the bar tutted irritably but said nothing. He finished the whiskey, twirled the empty glass on the polished surface of the bar. He thought about ordering another one.

His phone rang. He ignored it. It rang a few times then stopped.

He ordered the whiskey. The barman poured it curtly.

The phone started ringing again. The woman along the bar was staring at him, as if to say, *Either answer the damn thing or turn it off.*

He sighed and pressed to answer. The line wasn't good. The voice was female. He listened for a moment and then said, "What do you want, Eve?" She'd said she would call him sometime. But not this soon.

"Who's Eve?" asked the voice.

"What?" he asked, confused. He put a hand over his other ear, shutting out the noise of the bar and the music and the flight announcement, which were drowning out her words.

"It's Leigh," she shouted down the phone. *"It's Leigh."*

63.

THE MOUNTAINS OF SLOVENIA
A FEW HOURS LATER

It was a long drive from Ljubljana airport to Bled in the northwestern corner of Slovenia. Ben pushed the rental Audi hard and fast. He was eager to see her again. The awful image of what he'd taken to be her dead face was still lodged in his mind.

The little town was nestled deep in the pine forests. The road took him around the Lake Bled shoreline under a heavy gray sky. Across the water was a tiny wooded island with a baroque church steeple poking through the trees. The snowy mountains towered in the background. The road was virtually empty, and rain had washed it clear of ice.

As he reached the outskirts he checked his map. The directions she'd given him on the phone led him to an elegant chalet-style villa at the end of a quiet street. Rain pattered on the windscreen as he drew up outside the house. A polished brass plaque on the wall was inscribed with the name ANJA KOVAK in heavy black lettering. Beside the name was a title he didn't understand, but it looked like the kind of plaque a doctor or lawyer would have. A professional person. He checked the address again. It was definitely the one Leigh had given him, but it didn't seem right. What was she doing here?

He sat in the car for a minute to clear his mind. He'd

been doing a lot of thinking since her call. He watched the raindrops run down the outside of the screen. Then he reached for the handle, opened the car door, and swung a leg out.

That was when the door of the house opened and he saw her standing there at the top of the steps. She was wearing clothes a size too big for her—a heavy black woolen pullover and a pair of black baggy trousers. They looked borrowed. Whoever had lent them to her liked black.

He climbed out of the car and walked slowly through the gate. It began to rain harder. Leigh came towards him. They started moving more quickly as they got nearer to each other. She hugged him tight when they came together.

He held her. He didn't want to let go. The pain in his ribs didn't matter. He suddenly wanted to kiss her again—but he didn't know if it was the right thing.

They held each other for a long time, and then she pulled away from him, clasping his hands tightly. Her hair was wet with the rain. She was crying and laughing at the same time. "It's so good to see you," she said.

"I thought you were dead" was all he could say. "The last few days have been a torture."

She looked up at him. "You said it was over. Is it, really?"

He nodded. "It's over. You're safe. You can get on with your life again."

"You found them?"

He nodded again.

"What did you do?"

"Don't ask me that."

"Where's Clara?"

"At home with her father. She's fine. They're both fine."

Leigh glanced up at the sky, hugged herself and shivered. "It's raining," she said. "Let's go inside."

She led him into the house. There were terra-cotta tiles on the floor, and the walls were painted white. It looked clinical and clean. He heard a cough and looked to his left. There was a sign on the wall that he couldn't read. Through the open doorway next to it he could see some people sitting on chairs. A couple of them were reading magazines. Someone coughed again. The air smelled of chlorine disinfectant. It was a doctor's waiting room.

"What are you doing here?" he asked Leigh as she led him past the door and up the corridor towards another one.

"Anja's consulting room," she said. "We can talk in here."

She pushed open the door, and he followed her into a kitchen. It was small and practical. There was a percolator bubbling on a gas cooker, and the smell of real coffee.

She poured coffee into two cups and handed him one. "You look different. What happened to your hair? It's darker."

"You look different, too. You look alive."

"I'm definitely not dead," she assured him, smiling.

"I know what happened at the convent," he said. "I should have been there for you."

"I've been trying to call you for days. Your phone was never on. I was really worried about you."

"I didn't have my phone," he said. He didn't tell her why. "What happened to you? What are you doing here?"

"It's a simple story," she said. "The helicopters went away. They took Clara. There was nothing I could do." She paused awhile, remembering. "I waited until the men were gone. I could see the smoke. I guessed what was happening. I was scared they might come back. I wanted to get away, as far and as fast as I could. I was covered in blood."

"Whose blood?"

"Not mine," she answered.

"The old hammer gun?"

She nodded. "I had to use it." She shuddered, closed her eyes for a moment, sipped coffee. "I couldn't bear the feel of his blood on me. I found a stream where I scrubbed it all off. I wandered for a long time in the snow. I just walked. I didn't know where to go. Everything was wilderness and trees and hills. I don't remember too well, but they said I was staggering and near to collapsing when they found me."

"Who found you?"

"Anja."

"The doctor?"

She nodded. "I was lucky. Anja doesn't get too many days off. She was skiing with some friends. They found me and took me to a ski cabin in a valley. At first Anja said she wanted to take me to the hospital. She was the only one in the group who spoke English. I pleaded with her not to take me there. She agreed to bring me back here to her office, and I've been here all week. I'm fine now."

"I'm thankful to Anja," he said. He stroked her arm. It felt warm and soft. "There's something I have to tell you, Leigh. Your father's letter. It was destroyed. I'm sorry."

"I'm not sorry," she said. "I wish he'd never found it. I would have destroyed it myself."

"Something else," Ben said. "I think your father was right. So was Arno. I don't think it was a fake."

"We'll never know, will we?"

He shook his head. "No. But I'm glad it's gone, too."

"And so this is definitely over?"

"It's definitely over."

"I feel I should know more."

"I don't think you should. People died."

She was quiet.

"I'll take you home," he said.

"I've got no papers. I lost everything."

"You won't need them. We're going back by private jet."

She raised an eyebrow. "Whose?"

"It belongs to Philippe Aragon."

"Aragon?" She shook her head, puzzled. "The politician?"

"Don't ask," he said. "Will you be ready to leave here in the morning?"

"I'm ready now."

"Dinner first," he said.

"You're taking me out? I've nothing to wear."

"You look great," he replied, and smiled.

Dinner was in the restaurant of the Grand Hotel Toplice on the shores of Lake Bled. They sat at a small table for two in the corner. He'd ordered the best bottle in the house. He couldn't take his eyes off her. He had to keep reminding himself that she was really here, really alive.

"You're still looking at me like I'm some kind of apparition," she laughed.

"You didn't see the photo of you. You scared the hell out of me. I still stop breathing every time I think of it."

"That's what comes with years of playing tragic heroines onstage," she said. "I've died a thousand times. Opera's full of gruesome deaths. Carmen gets stabbed. Tosca jumps off the battlements. Lucia di Lammermoor stabs her husband, gets covered in blood, goes mad, and then dies herself. You soon learn to look very dead. And they sometimes film the performances, so there are cameras zoomed right on your face. I can hold my breath like a pearl diver, and I can keep my eyes open forever without blinking."

"Well, you had me convinced."

She sipped some wine. "It hardly seems real to me now."

"Let's not talk about it."

"I still can't understand how he missed me," she said. "When I heard that shot, I thought I was finished. It was only after I fell down the bank that I realized I was all right. It was a miracle."

"It was no miracle," he said. "Don't thank God, thank the patron saint of bent barrels. Remember the snowman?"

She raised her glass and smiled. "Such a skeptic, especially for a former theologian."

"I told you the gun was throwing to the right."

"Yeah, well, *I* hit the snowman dead center, no problem."

"You did," he admitted. "But if the gun had been straight, you'd have missed."

She laughed. "That is some logic."

He let the laughter die away. His smile faded. He fingered the stem of his wineglass. There was something he wanted to say, and he thought about the best way to say it.

She noticed the change in his face and looked at him curiously. "Something on your mind?" she asked.

"Leigh," he said seriously. "I've been thinking."

She looked up at him attentively.

He paused, not meeting her eye.

"What?" she said.

"I don't want to do this anymore."

She blinked. "Do what anymore?"

"I'm retiring."

"I thought you already were retired?"

"I mean I'm stopping what I do."

She leaned back in her chair. "Why?"

"It isn't what I want to do anymore."

"Why?" she asked again.

He looked up and met her eye. "Because of you."

"Me?"

"I want a life, Leigh. I threw so much away when I walked away from you that time. I'm sorry. I should have listened to Oliver. I should have married you when you wanted me to. I was stupid."

She said nothing.

"When they told me you were dead, I realized something. I realized how much I still love you. That I never really stopped." He reached out across the table and took her hand. "Will you give me a second chance?"

She looked at him.

"I want to be with you," he said earnestly. "Is there room in your life for me?"

She looked at him.

"I want to marry you, Leigh. Will you have me?"

"I'm stunned," she said.

He let go of her hand and fiddled with his glass. "You don't have to answer now."

"Are you seriously asking me?" she said.

"Yes, I am. I'm seriously asking you."

"I travel around a lot," she said. "My work's important to me. I'm not that easy to live with."

"I can deal with that."

"What about your home in Ireland?"

"I'll sell it," he said without hesitation.

"You want to live with me in Monaco?"

"I like France," he said. "I like the wine and the food. I have a place in Paris. France is no problem for me."

"You'll get bored with nothing to do."

"I'll find things to do," he said. "I already know what I'll do."

"And you hate opera."

He paused. "You've got me there," he said. "I do hate

opera. Especially German opera, and especially Mozart."

She laughed and then went quiet and serious, watching him. "Fifteen years," she said. "A long time since we left off. A lot of catching up to do. We've both changed."

"I know," he said. "But I mean it. Will you think about it?"

64.

THE BAHAMAS

A FEW WEEKS LATER

Chris Anderson sipped on his martini and looked out across the white sand. A warm breeze ruffled the palm fronds over his head as the *Isolde* bobbed slowly on the shimmering water. There was sand between his toes. He reached out from the sunbed and picked up the newspaper.

The copy of the *Times* was three days old, dated the nineteenth of January. Yesterday's news, but he liked to catch up on what was happening at home, and what could happen in three days? He rustled through the pages. Foreign news. More assassinations in the Middle East. Storms lashing the U.K. Same shit as always. Chris stretched and shot another glance at his yacht on the calm blue water, then grinned to himself.

He flipped randomly through a few more pages.

A small headline caught his eye. He did a double take.

"I knew it," he muttered under his breath. "That bitch. Lying bitch."

"Opera Star Weds."

He read it three times. It wasn't a long article. There was a small photo to go with it. The wedding had taken place a week ago in Venice, where the bride, Miss Leigh Llewellyn, was in rehearsals for the much-anticipated new production of *The Magic Flute.* Chris stared long and hard at the face of the groom in grainy black-and-white. He looked down at the name in the article, then back up to the photo. "Bastard," he muttered. Just as he'd thought. It was Major Benedict Hope.

Chris rumpled the paper up in disgust, tossed it away, and took another swig of his drink. Then he hurled the glass away, too.

THE GRAN TEATRO
LA FENICE OPERA HOUSE,
VENICE, ITALY

Everything in the box was red velvet. Ben's seat was upholstered with it; the wall behind him and the partitions on either side of him were draped in it. He loosened his collar, leaned back in the seat. He was as casually dressed as he could get away with in this place, just a dark suit and a plain navy tie. Most of the men in the audience were in tuxes, but dressing in a tux twice in the space of five weeks was a little too much for Ben.

Perched up in the private box, he had a great view of the Gran Teatro La Fenice. The Phoenix, the legendary opera house. Aptly named. He'd read in the program that the place kept burning down. The last time had been in '96. In 2003, the program said, it had been restored to its former grandeur.

Grandeur was the right word. He looked around him. He'd seen some sumptuous decor in his life, but this was going a stage and a half further. The ornamentation of the place was beyond belief. It was like a cathedral built in the name of music.

He sighed. So here he was. Venice. His first opera. Leigh was an old hand here—half the audience was here especially to see her. The Queen of the Night was the big diva role. The media were all over her, and all over her new husband by extension.

He'd gotten used to being a very private man, and his first encounters with the hordes of journalists and paparazzi had been a bit disquieting. He might have been a little surly with them. Especially the overinsistent camera hound he'd threatened to ditch in the Grand Canal.

This was all something he'd have to adjust to. He wondered if he'd ever get to like opera. Maybe one day. For now, all he wanted was to see her on the stage. He'd never heard her sing live. He couldn't wait to see her in her element.

Down below, the orchestra was tuning up and the audience was animated; the theater filled with the hum of chatter. Ben sprawled in his seat and drank it all in. It was a heady feeling. He could begin to understand the appeal for the performers who devoted their lives to this moment.

Then the conversation began to die down, and the audience started applauding loudly. The conductor was coming up through the orchestra pit. He was a tall man in a black tuxedo, white tie, a thick mane of black hair swept up from his high forehead. His expression was severe, focused. He bowed to the stage, turned, and bowed to the audience and the musicians, then took to the podium. Dead silence fell over the theater for a moment before the overture began.

A huge orchestral chord sounded, the instruments all coming in together. Then a pause for four beats, and another two big chords. Another pause, followed by two more stabs. It was the composer's way of grabbing the audience's attention by force, and it worked perfectly. The theater was suddenly filled with sound as the whole orchestra chimed into the main theme.

The overture over, the audience applauded again, and the house lights dimmed. This was it. The heavy curtains glided apart across the stage, and Ben settled back.

The set was breathtaking. It was a wilderness strewn with ruined buildings, broken-down temples, bushes, and huge rocks. It looked completely real, and the lighting effects were as good as in any movie he'd ever seen. He could see the Masonic influence in the Egyptian look of the ruins, a pyramid in the background. He stifled the memories they brought up. That was all over now.

A man emerged from stage left and ran across the set, chased by a giant snake, then stumbled and lay still at the foot of the giant pyramid. While he was unconscious, three women in strange costumes came out and killed the snake with silver spears. Ben watched. It all seemed very odd to him. He was taken aback by the volume of the singing. No microphones. He checked the libretto on his knee and tried to follow the storyline, but quickly lost the thread. He wasn't that interested. He wanted only to see Leigh, and she wouldn't appear until some way into the first act.

Until then, he drifted and let the spectacle wash over him. It was huge and impressive and fantastically staged, but it didn't captivate him.

However, the Queen of the Night's entrance did, completely.

She was wearing a long silvery-black robe and a wild crown, both covered in glittering stars. He could feel the impact she had on the audience the moment she stepped out onto the set. The lights followed her to center stage. She looked totally at ease, in command of the whole theater. Someone threw a red rose from a box across the opposite side. It sailed over the orchestra pit and landed on the stage.

Then she started to sing. The power and depth of her voice blew him away. He watched her. It was hard to believe it was the Leigh he knew. It was as if the music wasn't coming from her, it was coming through her from some other source. She filled the room with an awesome kind of beauty he'd never experienced before.

So this was what it was about. Now he suddenly knew who Leigh really was, what she lived for. It was something you had to understand. Nobody could explain it to you, and if you couldn't feel it, you were soulless, dead inside. It gave him goose pimples.

Her aria was over far too quickly. He was left stunned by it. There were cries of "Brava!" as she exited. More flowers landed on the stage. Another scene started.

Ben knew from the libretto that she wouldn't be on again for a while. He had plenty of time to get down to the bar and grab himself a drink before her next appearance. He quietly left his box and started down the red-carpeted passageway.

That was about the same moment that the latecomer wandered into the lobby. He looked around him. He avoided the ticket office. That wasn't what he was here for. He kept his head low and walked fast. He aimed for a side door. The sign read PRIVATE. He pushed through it and walked on.

65.

The latecomer had never been in this place before, but he'd been reading about it very recently. He kept his coat collar turned up and drew the peak of the baseball cap down lower over his face. He walked quickly, a little stiffly, turning right, left, right again. Here, away from the public areas, the walls were plain, and some parts still looked unfinished since the last restoration. He passed some stage assistants carrying a wooden prop that looked like part of a stone battlement; some performers in costume, looking nervous and checking sheets of music notation. There was activity and bustle around him—everyone too distracted and psyched up about the show to notice him. He avoided eye contact and pushed on. He could hear the sound of the orchestra, muted and damped in the background.

Suddenly, he was backstage, and the music was much louder. It was hectic here in the crowded wings, people everywhere, a million things going on at once to keep the huge show rolling. A stage director was hissing orders in Italian at some flustered-looking crew members. Everyone was tense and high on adrenaline.

Too many people. This wasn't a good place to be. He walked on quickly and pushed through another door and followed the red carpet. This was more like it. Decorative plants in tall porcelain vases lined the walls on both sides with doors between them. At the end of the corridor, a good-looking woman in a long yellow dress was talking to two men. He slipped into a room with a sink in one corner and some mops and buckets in another. He pulled the door to, and through the crack he watched the people leave.

He stepped out of the cleaner's room.

"What are you doing here?" asked a voice.

The man turned round slowly. The usher was a good few inches shorter than him. The man looked down at him and said nothing. He kept his face low, so the visor of the cap covered a lot of it.

"This area is for stage personnel and performers only," the usher said. "You'll have to leave."

The man didn't understand the usher's quick-fire Italian, but he got the message. He raised his head a little. The usher's eyes opened wider. He couldn't help himself. Most people had that same look of revulsion when they saw his face. That was why he wore the cap.

The usher was standing there gaping at him. The man laid a hand on his shoulder. "Let me explain something to you," he said in English. He moved him out of the middle of the corridor to where it was a little shadier, near to the door of the cleaner's room.

He killed him quickly and quietly. It was easily done, and there was no blood. He propped the body against the inside wall of the cleaner's room and snicked the door shut. He turned the key, slid it out of the keyhole, and dropped it into a plant pot.

He walked on until he found the door he was looking for. It had her name on it. He slipped to one side. He took a phone from his pocket, pressed a preset number, and spoke quietly to the person on the other end. Then he waited.

66.

Ben glanced at his watch and downed the last dregs of his whiskey. He was alone in the bar. He suddenly felt a little guilty about sneaking away from the opera. He'd stayed away too long, and Leigh should be back onstage any minute now. That was something he didn't want to miss.

He made his way back along the red-carpeted passage, up the flight of steps he'd come down, and along the curved corridor that led to the doors of the private boxes. They all looked the same, red velvet inset into the red velvet wall. He found his number. Settling back in his seat, he looked down at the stage and saw that he'd been just in time.

The opera was into its second act. An aria was just finishing as the Queen of the Night reappeared. She hit center stage and began to sing about love, death, and revenge. It was powerful.

But something was wrong.

The voice was wrong. It was a strong, vibrant soprano. It was good enough for world-class opera, but it didn't have anything approaching Leigh's passion or depth, the things that had made his skin tingle.

He frowned. On the seat beside him were the tiny opera glasses Leigh had given him. Their magnification was scarcely military grade, but they were enough to see the faces of the performers up close. He put the little eyepieces to his eyes and focused in on the queen.

She was wearing the same costume, and she was made

up to look just the same. But she wasn't Leigh. She was another woman.

Everyone was elated. Leigh had had to see a million people backstage after her first aria. She had costume check, hair check, makeup retouches. Some TV guy had sneaked in on a pretext and wanted to talk to her about chat-show bookings, but she turned him away. Then one of the opera producers wanted to lavish praise on her. People wanted to give her flowers. And the show wasn't even over yet.

A breathless runner found her as she stood talking in the wings with the overflowing producer. There was a message for her. Her husband had called the front desk and needed to speak to her. It was something important. He hadn't said what. But he wanted to meet in her dressing room. He couldn't see her backstage. It was a private thing. And it couldn't wait. The runner was apologetic. That was what Mr. Hope had said.

She made her excuses and broke away from the producer. It was strange. What did Ben want to see her about? She was in a rush. She didn't have time to run back to her dressing room. It was miles away through the maze of corridors. But if he'd said it was urgent—

"You've got exactly four minutes," the stage manager warned her.

"I'll be here, Claudio."

"Three minutes, fifty-nine seconds."

"I'll be here."

She'd run. The long, flowing costume wasn't easy to run in. The corridors were empty. She was a little out of breath by the time she reached her dressing room.

She'd expected to find him standing outside the door. Aside from that, she didn't know what to expect. Had he been taken ill? Received bad news? The car was stolen? The house was on fire? It wasn't like him to panic.

But he wasn't outside the door. There was nobody there. The passage outside her door was deserted. It was in shadow. A whole row of the wall-mounted lamps had gone dark. She stepped over to one of the lamps to check it. There was nothing wrong with the switch. Someone had taken out the bulb. She checked the next one. Someone had taken the bulb out of that one as well.

She walked back across the darkened red carpet and tried the handle of her dressing room door. The door was locked. She'd locked it before the start of the performance. He didn't have a key anyway. So where was he?

She had only a couple of minutes to get backstage. No time to wait. He'd have to catch her later. She turned to start running back.

That was when the cold leather of the gloved hand had clapped over her mouth and strong fingers had gripped her arm.

67.

Ben pressed through the crowd backstage. The Queen of the Night's aria was over, and he caught sight of her coming through the wings. He moved quickly towards her. "Who are you?" he asked her. She looked surprised.

A hand on his shoulder. He turned and saw a heavyset man with long graying curly hair tied in a ponytail, looking at him nervously. "Claudio," he said, recognizing the stage manager.

Claudio was biting his lip. "Where is she?" he asked. His English was perfect.

"I came to ask you that," Ben said.

Claudio looked confused. "Your message—"

"What message?"

"You called the desk and asked for Leigh to meet you at her dressing room."

"When was this?"

"Just five minutes ago. She went to meet you. She hasn't come back. We've been going crazy looking for her. We had to fill in for her." He motioned towards the young soprano in the Queen of the Night costume. She was still standing there uncertainly. "This is Antonella Cataldi, her understudy."

"I have to go," Antonella said. Claudio nodded to her and she filtered away through the crowd with a last glance at Ben.

The stage manager looked irritated. "Where did she go? She's never done anything like this before."

"I never left that message," Ben said.

Claudio's mouth fell open. "Then who did?"

Ben said nothing. He was already pushing back through the crowded wings towards the performers' dressing rooms.

The corridor was half dark. He tried her door. It was locked. There was nobody around. Claudio caught up with him, out of breath, sweat shining on his cheeks. "This is crazy," he said. "Where did she go?"

Ben stood back from the door. He took two quick steps forwards, bounced on his left heel. The flat of his right shoe crashed into the door, five feet from the carpet. It burst open, tearing a long splinter out of the frame. It juddered against the inside wall.

The dressing room walls were lined with rich blue satin. There was a cluttered dressing table surrounded with lights. A chaise longue with Leigh's clothes neatly folded on it. Her coat was hanging from a hook on the back of the door. Her handbag was slung from its strap over the back of the dressing table chair. Her shoes were neatly lined up on the rug. The book she'd been reading was propped open on a side table. But the dressing room was empty.

"So where the hell did she go?" Claudio asked. He was looking more worried every second.

Ben walked fast out of the room. He ran up the corridor. Something was lying on the red carpet up there. He knelt down beside it. It was black, silvery, soft. He picked it up. It was the starry crown from her Queen of the Night costume. He examined it. Nothing unusual. Except that it was here and she wasn't.

"There must be an explanation," Claudio was saying. He was sweating heavily.

"The message is the explanation," Ben said.

"Who could have left it, if not you?"

"I didn't leave it." Ben pointed up the corridor, past where he'd found the crown. "What's up there?"

"More dressing rooms. Some storage areas. Offices. A fire exit. The way down to the basement."

"Who was the last person to see her?"

"I was," Claudio said. "I told her to be quick. She said she'd be right back. I don't unders—" His phone rang in his pocket. It was a classical music ringtone. He flipped the phone open. "Barberini," he said. He listened for a moment. His eyebrows rose. His eyes flickered over to Ben. Then he handed Ben the phone. "It's for you," he said.

68.

Ben hadn't thought he'd ever hear that voice again. But it was right there in his ear. It sounded a little different, indistinct, garbled, like there was something wrong with the man's mouth. But it was definitely Jack Glass on the other end of the phone.

"You know who this is," Glass said.

Ben didn't reply.

"You know what I'm calling about," Glass continued.

Ben stayed silent.

"I have something of yours. Meet me outside."

"When?"

"Now. Right now, Hope."

Ben shut the phone. "I might need this," he said. He dropped it in his pocket. Claudio didn't argue.

Ben ran up the corridor. A side door was flapping open, and he stepped out into the night, into the icy fog hanging over Venice. There were no stars. His footsteps echoed up the pitted walls of the narrow street. He could hear the swish and gurgle of the canals, the water lapping at the old stone banks and the sides of the buildings.

He ran out onto the piazza, the white stone steps and columns of the Teatro Fenice behind him. Ahead of him was a stone quay.

Jack Glass was standing near the edge. There was a streetlight above him, mist drifting in its glow.

He had his arm around Leigh's neck. A black hand

clapped across her mouth. Her eyes were dilated with fear, her hair plastered over her face.

Glass's other hand clutched a knife. It was a Ka-Bar U.S. military killing knife. It had a seven-inch blackened carbon steel blade with a double-edged tip. Its sharp point was pressing hard against Leigh's stomach.

Ben took a step closer. He looked at Glass's face under the peak of the baseball cap he was wearing.

He was disfigured. He had no nose. He had one eye. His skin was bubbled and yellow and black, still raw and seeping in places. One side of his mouth was stretched downward, the skin puckered and loose. His lips were mostly gone.

In a cold rush of horror Ben remembered the helicopter explosion. He and Clara had gotten out and run across the snow to safety. Two seconds later the chopper had gone up. Two seconds. Maybe just enough time to scramble out of the cockpit. Not enough time to escape entirely from the blast.

He took another step. As he came closer Glass's mouth twisted into what used to be a smile. "Here we are again," he said. His voice was lumpy and fleshy.

"Let her go, Jack. It's no use."

Glass smiled. He pressed the point harder into Leigh's stomach. She struggled in his arms.

Ben winced. He took a step back. "What do you want?" he asked.

"You took my life away, Hope," Glass said. "Now I'm going to take something away from you."

"You want a ransom," Ben said. "I'll pay you whatever you want. I'll give you the money to get your face fixed up. Whatever it takes. Let her go."

"You don't get it," Glass shouted. "I don't want *money*!"

Ben felt ice in his heart. This wasn't a kidnap. "Kroll's dead," he said. "It's over. Let her go and leave now. I won't come after you."

Glass just smiled.

"Please," Ben said. He took a step forward again. "Let her go."

Glass just smiled.

"I promise you'll be left alone," Ben said. "I'll help you. I'll help you get whatever it is you want. But you've got to do the right thing. You've got to let her go."

Glass grinned.

"Take me," Ben said. "I don't care. Take me instead. Let her go."

Across the misty piazza he could see people walking. A young couple. Behind them, a family. Someone pointed. There was a yell. Then another.

That was what scared him most. That Glass just didn't care anymore.

"Let her go!" he shouted. Desperation was starting to rise.

Glass was still grinning. Leigh struggled.

Their eyes met. Ben looked into hers, and he made her a promise he prayed he could keep.

"This is for you, Hope!" Glass screamed.

Ben saw the intent flash across the man's mutilated face, and he knew what was coming. He saw the black-gloved fingers tighten on the leather handle of the Ka-Bar. He saw the muscles of the right arm and shoulder tense under the heavy coat.

"No, no, no—"

The arm pushed. The knife drove in. Glass's knuckles pressed against Leigh's belly. She went rigid and drew in a sharp breath, the gasping sound of surprise people made when a cold blade pierced deep into their body. Ben had heard it before.

Glass let her fall. She dropped like a puppet with the strings cut. Her knees folded under her. She hit the hard ground with the knife embedded in her stomach. It was in up to the hilt.

A woman's scream echoed across the piazza.

Glass gave Ben a last look and ran. His footsteps echoed away down one of the backstreets.

Ben rushed to Leigh and sank to his knees beside her. She was lying on her back, sprawled across the stone quay, coughing gouts of blood. It was leaking out all over her costume. He held her. His hands and face were sticky with it. There was so little he could do. The passersby were running over. Someone screamed again. A young woman held her hand over her mouth.

"Call a doctor! Ambulance!" Ben yelled at them. Ashen faces peered down at him. Someone pulled out a phone.

She was trying to speak to him. He pressed his face against hers. She convulsed. Her eyes were rolling in fear. He held her tight. He didn't want to let her go.

But she was going.

"I love you," he said.

She mouthed something in reply.

He held her as her pulse became weaker and slower. Then weaker still. Then nothing.

He shook her. There was blood everywhere. He was kneeling in a spreading pool of it.

"The ambulance is coming," someone said in a hollow voice.

Nothing. No pulse. Her eyes were open. There was no breath coming from her lips.

He shook her again. "Fight!" he screamed at her. "Fight it!" The tears were mixing with the blood on his cheeks. They streamed down and dripped on her face.

"She's gone," said a voice overhead.

He buried his face against her shoulder. She was soft and warm. His shoulders heaved as he clasped her tightly. He rocked her.

"She's gone," the voice said again. He felt a gentle hand on his shoulder. He looked up. A young blond woman was gazing down at him. Her face was contorted. She was crying, too. She knelt down beside him and took his hand. "I'm a nurse," she said in English. "I'm sorry. She's gone. There's nothing more to be done."

Ben knelt there with his head hanging. The nurse reached out and closed Leigh's eyes. Someone laid a coat over her. People were crying. An elderly woman blessed herself and muttered a prayer.

People were coming out of the opera house. A crowd gathered quickly. There were cries of horror. A couple of voices said her name. Claudio ran out of the building. His hands were clutched to his face. There were sirens in the distance, growing louder.

Everything faded. Ben's mind became still. He couldn't hear the noise. He could see only one thing. He opened his eyes. They were white against the streaks of blood. He stood up and looked down at Leigh's shape under the coat.

The crowd moved aside for him. Eyes followed him. Hands touched him, lips moved.

He walked away. He looked up and saw someone at a window, waving to get his attention. It was an old woman. Her face was wild. She was gesticulating. Pointing down the shadowy backstreet. He understood what she was telling him.

He began to walk, and then his walk quickened to a run, and then his footsteps were hammering under him and clapping off the walls of the twisty, murky alleyway.

69.

Glass couldn't run that fast. His injuries from Vienna were still too fresh to have healed, and the pain in his shoulder was grinding.

The backstreets of Venice were dark and deserted. The fog was coming down, settling heavily over the city. That was good. The fog would help him to slip away. He'd wait awhile, hole up somewhere and try to heal, become strong again. He wanted Ben Hope to hurt during that time. Then he was going to come back and finish him. Do it right, slowly and properly. The way he would have, if that stupid old bastard Kroll hadn't stopped him.

The water slopped against the side of the canal. He limped on. Through the drifting mist he saw the arched bridge across the water. There were some steps leading down. He hobbled down them. They were slippery. Down near the waterline, the old pitted stone walls were slimy with green-black mossy scum.

The little boat was moored down there, rocking gently in the shadow. He climbed into it and fired up the outboard motor. The boat burbled into life. Glass gripped the tiller and cast off. He turned the boat around, leaving a churning white wake in the darkness. A few hundred yards up the narrow canal he would pass Piazza San Marco, and then he'd be heading for the open water of the Grand Canal.

After that, he could disappear. Five minutes—and he would be gone.

• • •

The dying echo of the outboard reached Ben's ears. He got to the arched bridge. His heart was pounding, and his sides were aching. He saw the ghost of the wake in the water, already breaking up, the foam dissipating against the scummy, streaked edges of the canal.

He ran on. He could see only one thing. He was sharp and focused. It would be different later, when the pain and the grief hit him. There'd be a lot of pain. But there was no room in his mind for that now.

Glass had to be in the boat. There was nowhere else to run. If he got out of the narrow canals and into the broad waters, he could vanish all over again.

A light cut through the fog. The purr of a powerful twin-prop motor. A fiberglass hull bumped gently on rubber buffers against the canal wall. Ben walked that way.

The guy was in his late twenties or early thirties. He was well dressed, well-groomed. He looked like someone who drove a fast boat, took a pride in it, took good care of it. He stiffened when he saw Ben approach out of the fog. "I need your boat," Ben said in Italian. "I'll bring it back when I'm done."

The guy didn't argue. Thirty seconds later the speedboat kicked up a foaming wake, and Ben powered hard down the dark canal.

He reached the mouth of the canal. No sign of Glass anywhere. Through the fog the lights blinked and reflected like stars on the wide, dark expanse ahead of him. Hundreds of boats out there, all going their own ways. Even on a cold winter's night, Venice was a busy marine thoroughfare.

He motored out into the open water. A bank of fog drifted in, and suddenly he couldn't see more than a few yards ahead. The water was black, and the icy fog stung his skin. The boat drifted.

Glass was nowhere.

From the darkness he heard the revs of an outboard and the whoosh of bows slicing water. He was dazzled by a bright light and put his hands up to shield his eyes.

The crash almost knocked him out of the boat.

Glass slammed across his bow. Fiberglass splintered under the impact as the prow of Glass's boat sliced through. The crippled boats fused together, lying transverse. Engine revs soared as Glass's propeller rose out of the water.

Then Glass hurled himself at Ben, attacking like a wild animal. A slamming punch threw Ben down in the boat, winded. Glass towered above him.

The two locked boats were tacking in a tight circle. White foam churned. The airborne engine screamed. Water gushed in through the shattered bow of the speedboat. In three seconds it was closing over Ben's chest as he lay on his back. They were sinking fast into the freezing water.

"I was going to let you live a little while longer," Glass shouted over the engine roar. "Looks like I made a mistake."

Ben fought to get his wind. Glass bent down, picked him up by the collar of his jacket, and hauled him to his feet. The man's burned face was twisted like a nightmare in the boat lights.

Then the broad puckered forehead was heading for Ben's face. Ben dodged it and punched a knee into Glass's groin.

Glass staggered back. "Pain?" he yelled. "You can't hurt me with pain." He stood upright and came on again, throwing himself bodily at Ben. Ben was driven backwards towards the exposed outboard propeller. He felt the scream of the spinning prop in his ear and the wind of it in his hair. A stab of agony as the blades sliced his shoulder.

He kicked back and heard Glass grunt from the blow.

They went down, wrestling frantically in the bottom of the sinking boat. Then Glass was on top, forcing him down into the water, fingers around his throat, thumbs pressing deep into his windpipe.

Bubbles exploded from Ben's mouth as he fought desperately to wrench the hands from his throat. But Glass's strength was wild, and his was failing. He wasn't going to make it. He was going to drown.

So he prized the two little fingers away from the black fists, and he snapped them. Left and right, snap, snap, both together.

Glass let go with a scream. Ben's arm flailed up out of the water and smashed what was left of Glass's nose.

Then Ben was back on top, up to his waist in water as he pinned Glass down with his knees. He drove the man's head against the splintered fiberglass side of the boat. Felt a crunch. He did it again. He felt another crunch, saw the blood spurt.

Jack Glass was a hard man to kill. This time Ben was going to make sure. He didn't want to hear that Glass was dead. He wanted to see Glass dead. He hit him again. "You killed her!" he was screaming. "You killed her!"

The floor of the boat slid another foot into the black water. The spinning propeller hit the surface and foam flew. Then the boats slipped completely under, and Ben was suddenly swimming loose, treading water. His suit and shoes made it hard to stay afloat.

Glass's head reared up out of the water two feet away, gasping for air, his mangled lips drawn back from his teeth.

Ben forced Glass's head under the icy water. Glass kicked, struggled, surfaced.

Ben punched him and drove him down again, a hand on the top of his head to keep him under. Bubbles streamed up to the surface. Glass's arms and legs thrashed, but more slowly now.

Ben held him under a little longer.

Glass's struggles began to diminish. The stream of bubbles lessened.

Ben held him under a little longer.

Glass's hand burst out from the water. The glove was gone. Melted fingers clawed at the air. Then the arm went limp. It flopped down with a splash.

Ben felt the tension go out of Glass. His inert body drifted with the heave of the swell. He seemed to blink once with his remaining eye. His mouth opened, and a single bubble rolled out. It rose slowly to the surface and popped.

Then another bubble, a smaller one.

Then none at all. His face was relaxed. His arms were splayed outwards to the sides, floating loose in the water, fingers limp and curled. His eye stared upwards.

Ben let him go. Watched the body slip into the shadows.

The siren of the police motor launch was closer now. Torch beams swept and searched the water.

Glass was finally gone. Ben floated in the freezing water, barely moving, staring down into the murky depths. The chill was numbing his body.

He thought about Leigh. His beautiful wife. The pain began to take him.

Then he kicked out and swam towards the quayside.

Author's Note

Having trained as a classical pianist and having had a deep interest in music all my life, I have always been intrigued by the story of Mozart and thought that the mysterious circumstances surrounding his death would make a great basis for a novel.

Over the last two hundred years there has been much speculation as to what might have actually killed Mozart. The official, and apparently cast-iron, medical view is that he died of acute rheumatic fever, and that there is "no basis whatsoever" to the idea that he was poisoned.

Case closed? I don't think so.

In fact, it takes only a little probing beneath the surface to reveal that this version of events is far from conclusive. Over the years, different medical hypotheses have varied wildly. The fact alone that medical records from the time were so sketchy makes it very hard to support the sweeping statement that "Mozart could not have been poisoned." The fact is, nobody can make such a claim.

Modern medical experts conveniently overlook Mozart's own conviction that he had been given "*aqua toffana*." This was a blend of three lethal poisons—arsenic, belladonna (deadly nightshade), and lead. The colorless, tasteless, and water-soluble formula gets its name from the infamous seventeenth-century Italian poisoner Giulia Toffana, who sold it to women ostensibly as a beauty treatment but also as a neat means of liberating themselves from unhappy marriages by dosing their husbands with it.

The symptoms of Mozart's fatal illness included painful joint swellings in his hands and feet, terrible stomach pain and colic, renal failure, vomiting, and skin rashes. He also suffered from mental symptoms such as personality change, paranoid delusions and hallucinations, obsessive preoccupation with death, and severe depression. Loosely speaking, these symptoms *could* point to a diagnosis of rheumatic fever, streptococcal infection, or any of the other conditions that doctors have proposed.

But they *also* match with uncanny precision the collective toxic effects of *aqua toffana*'s three deadly ingredients: hallucinations and delusions, extreme worry and agitation, an obsession with death, depression and personality change, violent stomach pains and colic, renal failure, painful swelling of joints and extremities, skin rashes, and so on. Small doses, given over time, could bring about exactly the kind of lingering death that Mozart suffered. The composer himself believed he was being poisoned up to six months before his death—hardly consistent with an acute illness that would have run its lethal course within days. His son Carl Thomas Mozart also later claimed that his father had been deliberately poisoned.

Nobody will ever know the truth for sure. But I leave it to you to speculate. . . .

If there *are* reasonable grounds to suppose that Mozart might have been poisoned, who should we be pointing the finger at? The popular theory expounded in Peter Shaffer's play and hit movie *Amadeus* is that Mozart may have been poisoned by rival composer Salieri. The notion that Salieri poisoned Mozart was around long before *Amadeus*, however—Pushkin composed poetry about it, and Rimsky-Korsakov even wrote an opera on the subject, called *Mozart and Salieri.*

So did he do it? Nobody can be certain that he didn't; however, the historical fact is that although the mentally ill Salieri later confessed to the crime, he was never punished for it and changed his testimony so often that nobody took his confession seriously.

Another popular theory, as Leigh Llewellyn tells Ben Hope in the book, is that Mozart might have been murdered by the Freemasons for giving away Masonic secrets in his opera *The Magic Flute.* However—as Professor Arno tells us later in the story—this is inconsistent with the fact that Mozart was a star of the Masonic movement, a major public relations figure for Freemasonry at a time when it was coming under political fire.

The Mozart Conspiracy is only a story. But as I was researching the historical background I became increasingly convinced that more sinister and far-reaching political forces could potentially have been involved in the composer's demise. It is a fact that Freemasonry's strong associations with the revolutionary movements taking place in France and America in the late eighteenth century were a source of great concern to aristocratic rulers across Europe. It is also a fact that the Viennese secret police were under Imperial instruction to spy on, and ultimately eradicate, the Masons. As a rising celebrity very much in the public eye and openly championing the pro-revolutionary ideology of Masonry, it is perfectly feasible that Mozart would have been targeted as a major threat.

It's only a story. Did it really happen this way? Again, I leave it up to the reader to decide.

I know what I think.

Acknowledgments

The author wishes to express special gratitude to Stacy Creamer and Lauren Spiegel at Touchstone, without whom this book would not have been possible. Many thanks also to the rest of the editorial, design, and publicity team at Simon & Schuster for their invaluable contribution: Cherlynne Li, Renata DiBiase, George Turianski, Martha Schwartz, David Falk, Meredith Kernan, and Marcia Burch.

Last but not least, special thanks to my literary agent, the inimitable Noah Lukeman.

1.

CORFU, GREEK ISLANDS,
JUNE 2008
THE FIRST DAY

It was night when they took her.

They'd found her living on the lush island and watched for three days in the sun before they figured out their move. She was staying in a rented villa, isolated and shaded by olive trees, high on a cliff above the crystal-clear sea.

She was living alone, and it should have been easy to snatch her. But the house was always filled with party guests, and the dancing and drinking was virtually round the clock. They watched, but they couldn't get close.

So the team planned. Right down to the last detail. Entry, acquisition, extraction. It had to be subtle and discreet. There were four of them, three men, one woman. They knew this was her last day on the island. She'd booked the flight from Corfu Airport next morning and was flying back home—where she'd be far, far harder to take.

So it was tonight or never. Strategically, it was the perfect time for her to disappear. Nobody would be looking for her in the morning.

They waited until evening, when they knew the farewell party would be well under way. Their car was a rental sedan, bland and inconspicuous, paid for in cash from a local hire firm. They drove in silence and parked off the road, unseen in the shade of the olive grove a hundred yards from the villa.

And watched quietly. As expected, the villa was lit up and the sound of music and laughter drifted through the trees and across the cove. The white stone house was fine and imposing, with three separate balconies where they could see couples dancing and people standing around drinking, leaning out over the railings, taking in the beauty of the evening.

Down below, the sea glittered in the moonlight. It was warm and the air was sweet with the scent of flowers, just the gentlest breeze coming in from the shore. Now and again a car would pull up outside the house as more guests arrived.

As 11 p.m. approached, the team put their plan into action. The two men in the front seats stayed where they were, making themselves comfortable for what might turn out to be a long wait. They were used to that. The man and woman in the back exchanged a look and a brief nod. She ran her fingers over her glossy black hair, pulled it loosely back, and fastened it with an elastic tie. Checked her makeup in the rear-view mirror.

They opened their doors and stepped out of the car. They didn't look back. The man was carrying a bottle of wine—something local, expensive. They walked out of the shadows and up to the villa, through the gate, and up the steps towards the terrace and the front doors. The two in the car watched them as they went.

The couple walked into the villa, adjusting to the light and the noise. They said nothing to each other and moved casually but expertly through the crowd. They knew how to blend in. Many of the guests were already too out of it to notice them anyway, which suited them perfectly. There were a lot of empty bottles lying around and a lot of the smoke wasn't tobacco.

The couple wandered through the cool white rooms, gazed around them at the expensive décor. They located their target quickly and kept her carefully in sight the whole time.

She suspected nothing.

She was very much the center of attention, and she looked as though she loved it. They knew that she'd been spending the money freely, carelessly, the way a person does when they're expecting a whole lot more of it. There was plenty of champagne on offer. People milled around the self-service bar in the corner of the main room, helping themselves to as much as they could drink.

The couple watched her the way a scientist observes a rat in a tank, knowing exactly what will happen to it. She was young and attractive—just as in her photographs. Her blond hair was a little longer now, and her deep tan made her eyes stand out a bright and startling blue. She was wearing white cotton trousers and a yellow silk top that had many of the men glancing appreciatively at her figure.

The woman's name was Zoë Bradbury. They knew a lot about her. She was twenty-six and had carved out a remarkable career for her age as an author, a scholar, a historian, and a biblical archaeologist with a solid reputation among her peers. She was single, though she had a crowd of men around her and liked their company. The couple could see that much for themselves from the way she was flirting and dancing with all the good-looking guys at the party. She was English, born and raised in the city of Oxford. They knew the names of her parents. A whole raft of information about her. They'd dug deep, and they were good investigators. It was what they were getting paid for.

The plan was simple. The woman would drift away after a few minutes, and the man would get closer to the target. Offer her a drink, maybe flirt a little. He was in his early thirties, toned and handsome, and he was pretty sure he could get close enough to slip the dope into her drink.

It was a slow-acting chemical whose effects looked exactly like those of too much wine, except that it made the victim sleep for hours. The way she was knocking back her drinks, nobody would make a big deal of it when she had to retreat to her bedroom to sleep it off. The party would wind down, people would leave, then they'd move her out to the waiting car. The motor launch was already waiting at the rendezvous point.

As they'd anticipated, it wasn't hard to get close to her. The guy introduced himself as Rick. Chatted and smiled and flirted. Then he offered her a martini. She wasn't about to say no. He walked to the bar, mixed her drink, and quickly added the contents of the vial. All very professional. He was smiling as he brought it back to her and placed it in her hand.

"Cheers," she giggled, raising the glass in a mock toast, the gold bracelet on her wrist slipping down her tanned forearm.

And that was when the plan started going wrong.

They hadn't noticed the man standing in the corner of the room until he suddenly strode across, moved in fast, and took Zoë's arm, asking her if she wanted to dance. They knew his face. They'd seen him a few times while watching the villa. He was about forty-five, slim and well dressed, a little graying at the temples. A good bit older than her other boyfriends. They'd paid him little heed—until now.

She nodded and put the glass down on the table untouched. Then the man did something strange for someone who looked so sober. He nudged the table with his knee, a clumsy sort of movement, but almost as if he'd done it deliberately. The glass toppled and the drink spilled to the floor.

And they had only one vial of the stuff. They watched as the older guy led her onto the terrace, out into the starry evening where the people were dancing to the slow jazz beat.

So the couple did what they were trained to do: they improvised. Their communication was all in the eyes and the minute gestures undetectable to anyone who didn't know why they were there. In seconds they had a new plan. To hang around, merge into the background. Slip through a door and stay hidden in the house until the guests left and she was alone. Easy. They were in no hurry. They moved quietly out onto the crowded terrace, leaned against the wall, and sipped their drinks.

They observed some kind of tension between the target and the older man. The two of them danced for a while, and he seemed to be attempting to persuade her of something. He was whispering in her ear, looking anxious but trying to keep it discreet.

Nobody noticed except the couple. Whatever he was saying, she refused. For a second, it looked like an argument was brewing. Then he backed off. He ran his hand down her arm in some kind of conciliatory gesture, pecked her on the cheek, and then left the party. The couple watched him walk to his Mercedes and drive off.

It was 11:32.

By quarter to midnight, they saw her glancing at her watch. Then, unexpectedly, she began making moves to usher the remaining guests out of the villa. She turned the music off, and the quiet was abrupt. She made her apologies to them all. She had an early flight in the morning. Thank you all for coming. Have a great night. See you sometime.

Everyone was a little surprised, but nobody was too upset. There would be plenty of other parties going on across the island on a warm summer night.

The couple had no choice but to leave with the others. There was no chance to slip away and hide. But they hid their frustration well. It was only a minor glitch, nothing to worry about. They walked quietly back to where the car was hidden under the shade of the olive trees and got in.

"What now?" said the driver.

"We wait," the woman replied from the backseat.

The fair-haired man scowled. "Enough of this bullshit. Give me the gun. I'll go and get the bitch. Right now." He reached over and snapped his fingers. The driver shrugged and unholstered the 9mm pistol under his jacket. The fair-haired guy grabbed it from him and started getting out of the car.

The woman stopped him. "Low profile, remember? We keep this clean."

"To hell with that. I say—"

"We wait," she repeated, and flashed him a warning look that silenced him.

That was when they heard the motorcycle.

It was exactly midnight.

2.

NEAR GALWAY BAY,
WEST COAST OF IRELAND
TWO MINUTES LATER, 10:02 P.M.
BRITISH TIME

Ben Hope had been standing there a long time in the darkening room, long enough for the ice in his whisky to melt away to nothing as he stared out of the window. The sun was dipping behind the Atlantic horizon, the sky streaked with crimson and gold, clouds rolling in from the west as night fell.

He stared at the waves as they crashed against the black rocks, lashing spray. His face was still, but his mind was racing and filled with a pain that the whisky couldn't ease. Visions and memories that he couldn't shut out of his mind, and didn't truly want to. He thought about his life. The things he was sorry he'd done in the past. The things he was sorrier he'd never be able to do again. The emptiness of the only future he could imagine lay ahead. The way the lonely days kept turning into lonely nights.

Perhaps it didn't have to be that way.

The bottle stood behind him on a low table. The whisky was a fine malt Scotch, ten years old. It had been a full bottle that afternoon. There were just a couple of fingers left in the bottom now.

Beside the bottle lay a Bible. It was old, leather-bound, worn with use. It was a book he knew well.

Next to that lay a pistol. A Browning Hi Power 9mm, well used, clean and oiled, thirteen shiny rounds in the magazine and one in the breech. It had been lying there for hours, cocked and locked, the sleek copper nose of that first round lined up with the barrel and its tail exposed to the striker, ready and waiting for him to make his decision.

That one bullet was all it would take.

From somewhere in the shadowy room, the phone

rang. Ben didn't move. He let it ring until whoever was calling him gave up.

Time passed. The sun slipped down into the sea. The waves darkened as night crept across the sky and he could see only his reflection standing there in the window staring back at him.

The phone rang again.

Still, he didn't move. After half a minute the ringing stopped, and the only sound in the room was the distant roar of the Atlantic.

He turned from the window and walked across to the low table. He put down his empty glass and reached out for the pistol. He picked it up and weighed the heavy steel in his hand. Stared at the weapon a long moment as the moonlight glimmered down its length. He clicked off the safety.

Very slowly, he turned the pistol towards himself until he was looking down the barrel, holding it backwards in his hands, thumb on the trigger. He brought it closer. Felt the cold kiss of the muzzle touch against his brow. He closed his eyes. In his mind he could see her face, the way he liked to remember her, smiling, full of life and beauty and happiness, full of love.

I miss you so much.

Then he sighed.

Not today, he thought. *Today's not the day.*

He lowered the pistol to his side and stood there for a while, letting the weapon dangle loosely in his hand. Then he clicked the safety catch back on. He laid the pistol down on the table and walked out of the room.